CHASING STONE

8

CHASING STONE

PHILL INGHAM

Matador
5 Weir Road
Kibworth Beauchamp
Leicester LE8 0LQ, UK
Tel: (+44) 116 279 2299
Fax: 0116 279 2277
Email: books@troubador.co.uk
Web: www.troubador.co.uk/matador

ISBN 978 1848762 251

British Library Cataloguing in Publication Data
A catal [illegible] rary.

Typeset in 11pt Garamond by Troubador Publishing Ltd, Leicester, UK
Printed and bound in Great Britain by TJ International Ltd, Padstow, Cornwall

Matador is an imprint of Troubador Publishing Ltd

A special thank you to
Sheila for standing by me and Margaret Hall for all her help

CHAPTER 1

I dropped to one knee trying to make myself a smaller target and fired two more shots then another two hoping to drop at least one of them. The first guy grabbed at his stomach yelling out loud from the deep burning sensation that had exploded inside him. At the same time his mate flew backwards dropping his gun having taken two shots directly to the heart. I couldn't help thinking what a fluke that had been as I ran forward grabbing the guns then headed for the cabin door just as two more men entered through the rear of the aircraft.

If I went out through the doorway of the plane and down the steps now there was a good chance I would be cut down in my stride before I reached the tarmac, so my only option was to stay in the aircraft for the time being. That and I didn't want to lose sight of the cases. The sound of people shouting at each other came from the far cabin. They were getting ready to make their move. I knew from the layout of the aircraft that they wouldn't have 'line of sight' on me until they had passed through the rear cabin area so I ran back through the main cabin heading towards the doorway with the MP5K in one hand and my silenced gun in the other.

I made my way around the end of the bar keeping out of line of sight from the front entrance as I didn't want anyone sneaking up from behind me. The bar unit was shaped in a U section meaning the only way someone would know I was in there would be if they actually went out of their way to look into the bar. Placing the MP5K on the soft deep cream carpet, I checked my guns again making sure each one had a round in the chamber. From what I could hear, a woman seemed to be giving all the orders, and she sounded like she knew what she was doing.

The other guys I had heard hadn't entered the plane. For some reason, they had stopped just short of actually entering the rear cabin. They knew something I didn't.

'*Meanwhile outside...*'

"Start at the rear of the plane and search every compartment on the main cabin and the storage area at the same time and make sure the wiring ducts are searched as well. He knows we're looking for him, so be alert; unit 2 hold your position at the front. Shoot to kill." She paused and added, "If he gets off this plane, I will hold you responsible."

"Hold who responsible" I said to myself.

I wanted to know who she was talking too, because if I managed to get a hold of his com's set I could pull the plug on their organisational tactics. They sounded ex-military which got me wondering just what that bastard Weister had dropped me in. Either way I made a mental note to kick the crap out of him next time we met. I had dealt with outfits like this before and there's always a unit leader who will lay out the tactical assault. Mercenaries are all the same, they just use their military skills and adapt them to civilian situations.

My mind raced. 'Shit', why did this always seem to happen to me? It wasn't that I had the advantage anymore, but being trapped like this wasn't my idea of a good flight home or easy money. My element of surprise had gone, and this lot seemed pretty switched on.

I didn't catch the last bit of her orders, but I got the gist of it. I still had no idea of how many men were looking for me, and hiding wasn't going to get me out of here, so the only option was to have a quick look to see if the coast was clear. Ideally a small mirror would have come in handy right now for looking around the end of the bar. I picked up the MP5K and switched it to full auto along with my hand gun. I tried to imagine every detail of the plane's layout in my head, places to hide, obstacles and the emergency exits. "Time to go" I said to myself. But I didn't get a chance. The reflection off one of the up turned bottles above me reflected the bright red dot of the laser as it scanned the wall only four feet above me. I sank myself into the rear of the hard wood bar unit leaving the MP5K on the carpet as the front of a dull black boot slowly appeared around the side of the bar. I had my gun aimed roughly where his knee would be as the front end of some kind of automatic gun slid through the air only a couple of feet from my head. The forearm and right hand gripping the body of the gun came into view. The black material didn't look like Kevlar to me; in fact it looked more like a jacket top. I knew from that position he would be able to see the MP5K lying on the carpet; raising my gun a little higher towards his balls I decided his time was up. His eyes were on the optics up above me. In a split second, I thrust the gun forward. His body tensed the second he became aware of the movement in the corner of his eye, but it was too late for him. I fired a short burst of rounds into his body from point blank range. There was no sound. The silencer pushed deep into the loose material of his trousers absorbing all the noise. Nothing happened at first, then his whole body went limp, and he fell to the floor almost on top of me. I grabbed the MP5K and made my way round to the edge of the bar section ready to head for the door when a hail of bullets exploded into the woodwork just above my head, showering me with razor sharp pieces of glass as the bullets tore through the bottles above me. The storm of bullets seemed to go into slow-motion as each individual shard of glass zipped through the air like tiny arrow heads shattering and exploding, creating a lethal rain of finely honed glittering pieces of glass all around me. I winced with pain as the alcohol ran into the tiny cuts all over my face and shoulders, grabbing the MP5K after dropping it when the hundreds of impacting bullets had ripped through the wood only inches above my head. I let loose at the bar in front of me hoping like hell I'd hit something or at least make them dive for cover while I grabbed a quick look. What was left of the bar unit hung in mid air suspended by long splinters of dark wood showing elongated lighter shades where the veneer had split. My eyes searched the cabin through the now gaping holes in the wood trying to see where they were. This was no longer a hiding place; I was a target just waiting to be shot at. I could see the five silver briefcases sat on the small coffee table that seemed to have avoided every bullet fired in the last few seconds. I wanted them and the others knew it.

A quick look around and I went forward. A shoe was poking out from behind a cupboard section that was opposite the rear exit door. I fired a few more rounds off at the seat in front of where the leg was – nothing happened. For every three steps I went forward I was checking my back making sure I was alone in here. I reached the rear door where three men lay sprawled across the carpet in different positions, their guns still in their hands. A deep red stain was growing across the carpet from beneath the dark blue suit of the biggest guy. I took his head earpiece and throat mike and listened. Nothing was been said over the coms. I wasn't about to stick my head out for a look so I made my way back along the rear cabin and into the main section of the plane.

So far they were three down and two more up ahead of me somewhere. As I moved I had my gun trained on the aperture of the front exit door. This area was open-plan not like a standard airliner full of seats; in here there were only a couple of high backed leather chairs and a fancy glass coffee table.

The two remaining men stood at the bottom of the steps that led into the aircraft waiting for orders they didn't want to follow, the coms plugged into their ears had become very quiet which wasn't good news. They both knew it was more than their lives were worth to do anything without their boss's instructions. The two men dressed in dark suits both carrying AK47s watched while she came down the steps that led up to the aircraft in her black trouser suit with her long blond hair pulled back into a pony tail. Her athletic figure and high cheek bones only added to her beauty. Both men had heard the gun fight above them in the aircraft and watched in amazement as she stood just back from the doorway not even flinching as the bullets impacted on the panelling only inches from where she was standing. She neared the bottom of the steps, then the tallest of the men set off towards the waiting BMW to open the door for her. She stopped when she reached the bottom saying to the armed man standing by her, "Bring the cases to me once you've made sure all the witnesses are dead. I don't want any loose ends."

"Right away," he replied. She looked at him then walked off. Once she had turned away, he went up the steps that lead towards the aircraft's doorway. "Come on you can do this" he kept saying to himself the closer he got to the oval shaped door.

Something moved in the corner of my eye, it's at times like this when everything goes into slow motion. I spun around to see both high backed chairs turning in unison to reveal two men dressed in dark suits brandishing AK47s. My eyes zoomed in on their trigger fingers as they pulled back to release the explosion of automatic fire towards me.

I dived sideways whilst spraying my targets in a hail of bullets. In my head I was trying to calculate how many shots I had left before the 'Click' happened. With my guns I knew just by their weight how many shots I had left, but this was an MP5K and I didn't know how many rounds it had in it when I picked it up. For all I knew it could have been used before without being reloaded. My other gun was down the back of my jeans. I could see it in my minds eye as I went into a roll, my right hand behind my back grabbing at the hand grip in one smooth movement. The carpet was exploding into fluff bombs all around me as I came up onto my knees, firing at the one remaining gunman. It's so easy just to empty your gun off in these situations and end up dead by not picking your target. Break it down 'Role Point Shoot' ignore everything going on around you. The spray of bullets cut a peppered pattern up the cabin wall as my bullet smacked into his cheek bone; my second one entered just to the left of the first exiting through the back of his head taking his life with it.

I looked out through one of the small windows to see a woman heading towards one of the BMW's. She must have been the one giving out the orders earlier on. The guys who had been firing at me now lay in awkward positions on the floor. Making my way past them, I noticed each of the men's eyes stared blankly into space. Every time you see that look on a person's face, it buries deep into the back of your brain. You just have to learn to live with it. I went back heading for the rear and reached the doorway only seconds before a guy in a dark suit came through it. He obviously wasn't expecting me, because he didn't even have his gun up. Anyone with an ounce of sense in that situation would either use a mirror to check the door or fire a couple of rounds off to clear the way.

"Don't fucking move," I said, pressing the gun against his temple. "Stay perfectly still, and only do exactly what I tell you. Do you understand?" I added making sure he was at arm's length in case he wanted to play at being the hero. His head slowly moved up and down in response to my orders.

"Good, now place the gun on the floor then put your hands in your pockets and kneel down," I said, standing back from him. I noticed the throat mike he had on. "Well organised and well armed," I thought.

"You won't get away with this," he said in a calm voice. "You're dead. You just don't know it yet," he added.

"You're very sure of yourself for someone on their knees, aren't you," I said, now standing in front of him. Looking past him, I saw the other BMW standing twenty yards from the bottom of the steps.

"That's my way out of here," I thought. I checked him over, taking his gun out from its chest holster and kicking the AK out of reach. I never had liked the AK47, its okay if you want to make loads of noise and kill about half of what you're aiming at. It's like choosing the right kind of car, you either like a 4x4 or a sporty job; I liked the sporty job. No ID, no cards, nothing. He was what I call a grey man. If they get killed, it's almost impossible to trace their identity. "Get up," I said.

Once on his feet, I noticed just how big the guy was. He looked like a bouncer but without the bow tie.

"Over there," I said, pointing at the briefcases. Slowly, he walked towards them still with his hands in his pockets.

I grabbed the case with the trigger mechanism then told him

to pick the other four up. He did as he was told, one under each arm and one in each hand.

Everything had fallen silent, this meant either they were regrouping or they were all dead.

I had a good idea we were the only ones remaining, this was more down to instinct then guess work.

"Good. Now head for the car," I said, poking him in the back with the gun. We made our way out the door and down the steps slowly, me checking in all directions for any onlookers, but the place seemed deserted. We approached the BMW slowly and I went wide trying to see if anyone was inside, but the windows were blacked out.

Now standing at the rear of the car big bloke said, "So now what?"

I looked at him then at the car. "Put the cases down, turn around, and walk in that direction." I said, pointing towards the huge hangar's far wall.

He followed the instructions. There's no easy way to gain access to a car with blacked out windows, either you blow one out using the gun or try to smash it with the butt, in both cases when dealing with highly organised people like this bunch, the car is going to have armoured, bullet-proof windows.

I started to open the front passenger door. Something moved inside, but it was too late to react because the door was kicked hard from the inside throwing me backwards to the ground. The door hit me hard. My gun flew out of my hand and went sliding across the tarmac surface. I took the impact well and tried to go into a roll, my eyes tried to make sense of this upside down world as I went head over heels.

I saw a pair of shoes and in that micro second knew I had fucked up. 'SMACK' as the guy who had been in the car kicked me in the ribs.

"Fu" was all I got chance to say before the second one landed in my lower back. I tried to roll away to buy a couple of seconds, but he dived on top of me, pressing down hard on my chest with his knee, forcing the wind out of my lungs. Smack! His fist connected with my cheekbone and another from the other side. I punched his lower ribs hard trying to break a few for good measure, but he carried on. I had to get control before his mate joined him, which would only be a matter of seconds away. I grabbed at his balls and squeezed with all the strength I could muster.

"ARGH!" His eyes bulged, his voice dwindled then the colour sank from his face. His limp body fell sideways onto the tarmac. I pulled the gun from my jeans firing a single shot to his head knowing his mate wouldn't be far behind him. I rolled over trying to work out where he had gone when his foot came thundering into my right thigh, and then a second later another kick landed in the same place, but time with all the force of a jack hammer. The pain exploded in my head as my forefinger pulled repeatedly at the small trigger.

I nearly passed out from the pain, my mouth dried up. I felt sick, dizzy and lost all at the same time. I had no idea where I was, as I lay there on the ground. My leg felt like crap along with my face and ribs. Shooting from that position and actually hitting him had been pure luck. He lay beside me quietly groaning to himself holding his belly trying to stem the blood that wept out between his fingers. It must have taken me at least twenty minutes to get to my feet and make my way over to the car, which only stood ten feet away. Eventually, I managed to get all four briefcases into the boot. I kept mine with me knowing the rest were useless without it. I made another mental note to sort Tony Weister out at the first opportunity, all the bullshit he had told me about diamonds and how easy this job was. The last thing I wanted right now was to get mixed up in something like this. "SHIT" I shouted sitting in the driver's seat smacking my fist hard against the wheel. "A bloody nuclear device" I moaned. "A nuclear bomb" I said to myself thinking of all those innocent lives that would be lost if this had gone ahead. And what was now lying in the boot of the car? My concern now was to get out of the immediate area. I did a slow 360 degree turn just checking the hangar for exits. I saw what looked like a standard garage door at the opposite end to the main hangar doors, slowly driving towards it then bringing the car to a standstill about ten feet from the sheet metal door. Something just didn't seem right. I looked at it again and then noticed the small black plates built into the tarmac. Leaving the car running, I opened my door. Taking the weight with my good leg, I gently pulled myself out of the car, using the door like a rest so I could get a better look without all the reflections off the overhead lighting on the windscreen. A section of tarmac had definitely been resurfaced about the width of a car leading up to the metal door. I couldn't see any harm in moving the car a bit closer, so I slid back into the seat, selected drive, and slowly moved forward over the plate. The car's front tire passed over the plate, a small red light started to flash on the wall as the door gently rose up into a track fastened to the wall. Flicking the car's lights on again, I drove out into the early November morning mist. It seemed that this exit was some sort of bypass from going through customs, there were no lights on the small dirt track I was driving along and definitely no security. Then something caught my eye in the rear view mirror. There it was again, a car some thirty feet behind me driving with no lights on, I didn't break or accelerate, I just continued following the old lane. Everything went into fight or flee mode, as the adrenaline surged through my veins. I watched the car close the distance between us; it could be customs or undercover – either way I was in the shit. Trying to explain a nuclear device sitting in your boot could be a bit tricky.

The two men in the Saab checked their guns in readiness to take the target. Sara had called them to prepare for trouble because the rest of the team wasn't responding to their call signs. I smacked the interior lights out using the butt of my hand gun then gently opened the door, whilst sliding the car into neutral. I opened the door watching the rough track pass by at a steady 15mph, 'this could go one of to ways' I thought and rolled out letting the car carry on. I hit the freezing cold grass verge with a 'thud' after smacking my knee on the hardcore that made up the single track. I knew from their prospective they would be concentrating on my tail lights.

After a couple of rolls I stopped about two feet off the lane in some dead grass, took aim and fired a single shot. 'PHFT', the silencer sounded quite loud even with the sound of jets moving around in the distance. A neat hole appeared right in front of where the drivers head would be; straight after the car lunged forwards then off the track ending with the sound of a headlight breaking, there was no sound at first then I heard the door opening and the familiar double-click sound of a gun being cocked. "Where are you my friend?" I said to myself. I wouldn't move a muscle until I saw him; my car had come to a gentle stop about twenty feet away. The temperature was just above freezing. Each breath as soft as a whisper, nothing else mattered now. Even the cold didn't bother me. I was aware of my leg but just ignored it, laying flat on the ground with the gun pointing out in front of me. The grass moved off to my right about ten feet forwards of where the car had ditched. Again, the tops of the long grass twitched.

He was well within my angle of firing without having to move my upper body; the silhouette of a head slowly emerged through the grass. 'Phwat', my bullet smacked straight into his forehead, sending him flailing backwards, his arms flying up from the impact throwing his gun off to one side in the process.

I didn't move for a good five minutes, then the grass over to my right flexed forwards then back upright, "Shit" I moaned to myself. Watching the second trace, knowing he would now have an idea of my location if he had anything about him.

He used the verge to move down to my right and closer to the other car. I wondered if he was going to make a run for it when suddenly up he popped firing a couple of shots back down the track, then he repeated the action. This is when the difference between a seasoned professional and a new boy comes into play. I just turned towards him totally ignoring the shots; I waited until he turned to fire again then fired a single shot. The bullet smacked into his left eye knocking him backwards in a spin, this caused him to lift his right leg as the inertia took him over and down onto the hard ground. I got to my feet and walked back to my car. I didn't need to check him, he was dead.

I climbed in closing the door behind me and placed my gun on the passenger seat, selected drive and turned the radio on switching it to 'Radio 2'. I flicked the lights to main beam as I drove along the frost covered track whilst trying to punch in the details of my postcode into the Sat Nav so I could get home as soon as possible.

"Keep a good distance, the client doesn't want this to be too public and if he sees us then we don't get paid," Echo 1 said into the com's set, as he watched the BMW drive past, "We take him once he stops for the night or gets to wherever he is going" Echo 1 added, seeing his men pull out and start tailing the target.

Meanwhile in the other BMW...

Sara Sasco looked at the laptop screen wondering why her men were not following her to the hotel. The screen showed the other car heading towards the motorway in a northerly direction. She flicked her phone open and tried to call the men she had left back at the hangar, but none of her calls were answered. She leant forward saying softly, "Head back to the hangar. It seems we have a problem."

'Back into Puerto Rico...

Tony Weister couldn't believe his luck. The way he had recruited the people to deliver the device had even surprised him. His boss had given him a budget of twenty million dollars to buy their loyalty and to make sure the money was only transferred once a successful detonation had been achieved, but at the sight of all that money, Weister had made alternate plans for the majority of it. He had only offered each man a maximum of one million with a threat that their families would suffer if they refused to collaborate with him; knowing that with the Sasco name behind him, they would just follow like sheep.

Weister was sick of been Karl Sasco's puppet. Karl Sasco was head of Sascorp International and the worlds most feared drug/arms-dealer. The Sasco family owned casinos, racecourses, and small airfreight companies all over the world. If Karl Sasco wanted you dead, the only safe place to hide would be deep space. His reputation preceded him wherever he went, and Tony Weister had seen his boss deal with people who crossed him at first hand, so he was taking no chances. The money had already been transferred to an overseas account, and his wife and daughter would be leaving for New Zealand in five days time, where he was having a new house built on the coast. He'd even arranged brand new identities for all of them. Nothing could possibly stop him now. The smile on his face turned to laughter. It was like a huge weight had been lifted from his shoulders at last. After ten years of bullying and abuse he would be rid of that bastard once and for all.

The air conditioning kept the white marble clad room cool from the intense midday sun outside as Karl looked at his computer screen studying the money transfer Tony Weister had made only that morning to a Swiss bank account, and the house he'd purchased in New Zealand. He gently typed away at the key board bringing all of Tony Weister's details on screen, his savings accounts, investments, and all transactions over the last six months. He studied them slowly, made a print out of all the details, and then pressed delete. After a short phone call to the managing director of the Swiss bank Tony had used, all the money had been transferred back into one of Karl's offshore accounts. Opposite him sat a smartly dressed man. His deep blue suit, shirt, and tie all looked and were very expensive. His blue tinted rectangular glasses only added to the coldness he projected. Baldman was his name. He dealt with people in a severe way, and never had he let anyone down. He disposed of people. That was his specialty. Nobody knew his background or anything about him and many had tried, even Karl's contacts in the FBI, DEA, and MI6 had no details on him, nobody even knew where he lived, he spent most of his time living on board his converted Boeing 747, it never landed at any of the main airports and with his three super yachts many wondered why he did the kind of work he did. Yet here he was; some Government agencies had even used him when their politicians had ruled against using such harsh methods to remove a rogue leader.

"We have an agreement then," Baldman said, getting to his feet.

Karl smiled. He liked Baldman, because with him, there was no hidden agenda, no lies or deceit. He came when called and carried out the necessary work to make sure everything was clean and deniable. Karl also knew it was a foolish and a dead man who didn't pay the Baldman.

"The money will be transferred into your account today," Karl said, spinning the ice cube around in his glass.

"We will talk later, Karl," Baldman said. He turned and walked towards the large oak doors that led back out into the large white marble reception area. Karl knew how honoured he was to have him actually come to his office in person, he didn't know of any other crime syndicate who Baldman met in person. This special relationship he had with him gave Karl Sasco an edge over all his rivals.

The screen sank back slowly into the black marble of his desk leaving only a trace outline as to its existence. He took a cigar from the small red leather box sitting on his desk; the bodyguard standing just behind him flicked open the gold lighter in response. He warmed the end of the cigar gently letting his boss enjoy the freshness and taste before fully lighting the hand rolled Cuban cigar.

BACK IN ENGLAND

The mist had gone and the clear November sky was on its way out as dusk started to form, ensuring a frosty night. It had taken me just over 6 hours to get to my cottage on the outskirts of Gargrave, a small village in the middle of the Yorkshire Dales not far from Skipton. I just needed somewhere I could relax away from everyone. Its location was perfect. There was only one-way in and one-way out, down a half-mile long dirt track that ran down the side of the local farmers' fields. I could see most of the track from my front window, but the last 100 yards was hidden because of the lie of the land. The gentle slope of the field took the track down a steady decline until it met up with the main road at the far end.

The cottage was old, and in need of quiet a lot of T.L.C., but it was home, and it was the only place I knew I could be safe. I also knew just how bloody cold it would be until the boiler had warmed through. I had spent the last six weeks in South America working (the last two weeks had been in Columbia) ending a five year dispute between a couple of drug barons. Now there was only one. I had received a phone call shortly after the hit asking for a meeting in Puerto Rico. I agreed and the rest is history as they say.

It made me think about the device in the boot of the car again, best not to, then again if it did go off I wouldn't know about it anyway.

Driving down the lane, my thoughts turned to getting a plan together. I couldn't just chuck them off a bridge or bury them in a wood somewhere. I had to find a place where they would never be found or damaged. The tyres crunched over the gravel drive that the previous owners had laid. From a distance, it looked quite good, but close up, you could see the patches where oil had leaked out staining the gravel and large sections where just the bare earth was starting to creep back through to the surface. It didn't bother me though. I wasn't any good at D.I.Y., and I had no plans to start chucking bags of gravel around just to make the place look pretty.

The area immediately in front of the cottage had just enough room to turn a decent sized car around in it, which made life a lot easier. I reversed down the side of the gable end and under the carport. Grabbing the brief case next to me, I slowly made my way round the back of the cottage trying my best not to put too much weight on my bad leg. It felt a bit better, but it was far from perfect. The back door was solid oak and didn't fit too well, it had the biggest lock and key I'd ever seen. I pulled the key out from under a stone opposite the back door. It was a good six inches long, covered in rust and dull black paint, but it did the job.

I decided to give John a ring once I was inside. He was a good friend, and although he knew what I did as a living, he never asked too many questions. I'd known him for ten years now, and I could trust him. We'd met in the gym squash courts. His mate hadn't turned up, so he'd suggested having a game, and that was that. His job took him all over the world buying and selling contracts for freight companies. I just said I was in construction. I didn't tell him what I really did for a living for another three years and that was only because I had to. I had been out of the country working, and the whole thing had gone tits up. Police were everywhere and someone had ID'd me. Back then, I had long hair and a beard, but nowadays, a short trim did the job and a clean shave. Things had changed a lot over the years, and having a friend like John made my life a lot easier. I needed an alibi as to my whereabouts at the time of the hit. He really put his neck on the block by giving me one. Since then, we had been best of mates.

As time had progressed, my ability to hit a long distance target grew. I practiced every day, by taking long walks right up into the middle of nowhere which isn't to hard in the Dales.

Then at the grand old age of 31 I did my first 1.1 kilometre shot and blew the target to bits. Everything comes into account when taking such a shot, wind, the spin of the bullet through the air, humidity and even the curvature and rotation of the planet. Many people think a bullet travels in a straight line when fired; it doesn't. In fact the second it leaves the end of the barrel it starts to drop. A shot fired from just under a kilometre will follow a long ark and literally drop onto the target, like a small high powered bomb, anything above that distance is a science, and it takes a shed load of working out to get it right, and in a lot of cases it just cannot be done due to turbulence or terrain. The shot I had fired, had taken over a month of legwork to figure out the precise angle, location the target was going to be in and that alone defined where I could take the shot from. Because my target lived on an island in the middle of a huge inland lake he thought he was safe. I had made sure the people I was working for knew exactly what to expect, but like all these types they thought they knew best and the guy in question was standing less than three feet from my target. I am just thankful I took payment in advance because bloodstains like that don't wash out. It still made me smile now seeing this guy explode like a bursting balloon full of ketchup. Don't get me wrong, it wasn't the guy exploding it was the guy standing a couple of feet away that did it.

Flicking the kitchen light on as I went through the door, it flickered a couple times before finally staying on. There was a smell of damp in the air coming from the large stain on the ceiling reminding me too mend the shower before using it again. Placing the brief case on the small wooden table in the centre of the room I gently pressed the small silver flap on the brief case lid. With a soft hiss, it flipped opened. The tiny screen read, "PLEASE ENTER LOCKOUT CODE."

That got me thinking. Was the code already intact, or was it asking me to enter one? I decided to make a cuppa while I thought about it. Most of the cupboards were empty, but I found some dried milk and tea bags so I was sorted.

While the kettle boiled, I eventually got the boiler going after three attempts then my phone rang, which was odd, but what the hell, I answered it.

"Hello." I said.

"It's John" he said.

"Whatcha, dickhead," I replied.

"My god," he said. "You're not dead yet then?"

"Are you in the country?" he asked.

"Yes, just got in a few hours ago. Why? " I said.

"Do you fancy a meet up sometime soon? No pressure," he said.

The phone went quiet for a second while I thought about what had been going on and if he could help. "Ok, meet me in Harrogate tomorrow. There's a small café just opposite the bus station on the corner of the shopping centre. I'll meet you inside." I said. "What time?"

"Three o'clock, and don't be late, Tom," he said, before ending the call.

He'd sounded a bit off with me, but then again trying to get a smile out of John could be classed as hard labour sometimes.

He listened to the other phone he was holding to his ear, "Did you get a lock? John said.

The voice on the other end said, "Yes, we can track him now, and John, keep him at the bar until we get there."

"You're coming over?" John said surprised.

"Yes, we're coming over. Sara's looking forward to meeting you." The call ended. John sat down not believing what he'd just heard,

"What have I done?" he said to himself. "What have I done?"

I poured the hot water over the tea bag, stirring the white milky powder in as I did.

Just then, a pinging sound came from the brief case. I looked at the tiny screen. The display had changed. It now read, "GPS

SOURCED AND LOCKED," with a load of numbers and letters following it. "What the hell did sourced and locked mean?" I thought; as I sat down to rest my leg. My eyes were tired after the long drive. They seemed to ache from the inside, making me frown. I scratched my head and yawned. The idea was to have a shower and get to bed, but six hours later, I awoke with a start still sitting at the kitchen table with the empty cup in my hand. My body was trembling from the cold. I stumbled through the door that led to the bottom of the stairs. Climbing them half asleep, I wandered into the front bedroom and crawled under the covers not bothering to get undressed.

The black M5 pulled up in front of the hotel foyer, but its occupant didn't get out. She was talking to her father on the phone and her bodyguards knew better than to interrupt her at any time especially if Karl Sasco was on the other end. She placed the phone back in her small Gucci bag. The car door opened. A young man in a porter's outfit came towards her. He was about to ask if she had any luggage when without any warning a large hand grabbed his neck yanking him sideways throwing him to the ground. The young man cowered on the ground not wanting to get involved while the three men in black suits walked past him. Sara stopped and looked down at the young man. Her face showed no emotions whatsoever.

"Wha, what's wrong?" he said, looking up at the slim attractive woman staring down at him.

She said nothing then carried on towards the hotel entrance, leaving the young man lying on the stone steps.

"Malk, bring the laptop to my room. It's time we found out what Mr. Lee has done with our package," Sara said, as they waited for the lift.

He'd worked for the family Sasco for over twenty years now, and in all those years, he'd never let his boss down. Karl Sasco had personally asked him to be his eldest daughter's bodyguard. She had only been twelve at the time, but Sara was still a target for Karl's competitors. Over the next 15 years, Malk had put his life on the line twice for her. He'd been stabbed and shot, but his loyalty to the family always came first. Now in his late forties, Malk ran all the security for the Sasco Corporation with Sara, but his first duty would always be to protect her.

"Any news from 'Product' Sara asked. Malk wanted to tell her everything was going to plan, but he hadn't heard any news yet. 'Product' was a very exclusive mercenary company who dealt with anything from corporate crime to hunting murderers down from the Special Forces if a politically sensitive situation had occurred.

Based in New York, they had offices in many countries, most of the men working for 'Product' were ex- Delta Force and on the payroll of Sascorp Securities International.

The back door creaked open as the first two men entered the old cottage looking for their target. They were both wearing body amour, having heard who they were dealing with.

"Echo 2, that's the kitchen clear" the voice said over the com's.

"Echo 4, that's the front room clear, repeat front room" the second man replied as they went from room to room in a standard search pattern.

They both stood at the bottom of the stairs, it was a bottleneck and an easy place to be picked off.

Using hand signals to keep everything quiet the lead man threw a flash-bang up onto the small landing. Both counted down from 4, 3, 2, something moved.

I sat listening to the sound of footsteps moving around below me. Both my guns were fitted with silencers and contained a full clip. In my mind I was moving around with them tracing their every move. I could have slotted one of them through the kitchen ceiling, because the bathroom sat directly above it, the exposed beams and timber ceiling below had quite a few holes in it making it quite easy to spot anyone moving around down below.

I had my head to the floor following the guy dressed in black beneath me whilst listening to the other guy making an entry through the front door.

I moved to the landing but out of view from the stairwell and flicked both guns to full auto. Then the small tin-can object landed right next to me, I recognised it immediately as a 'flash-bang' used by the Special Forces to scare the crap out of anyone in a room they were about to enter. I grabbed it and slung it straight back down, knowing what they were capable of.

'Echo 4' saw it first "MOVE" he shouted, diving through into the kitchen, but 'Echo 2' took it as the command to head up the stairs, the 'flash-bang' bounced off his head exploding within a second of doing so. The detonator may be small but when it goes off right next to your head you're going to go down. I had a quick look through my hole in the bathroom floor. I saw one guy standing by the table with his gun up pointing directly at the door. I took aim making slight adjustments just in case I was wrong, my eyes darting from the gun back to my target, I pulled the trigger. 'PHHPHPHTTDDT', the gun fired twenty shots of which at least thirteen drilled into his head. He wobbled around a bit then dropped to the floor just as the smoke drifted into the room from the hall and stairs after the explosion.

"Your dead mate" I said to myself, the smoke was creeping around the corner of the landing and into the tiny bathroom. I went forward; releasing the clip letting it drop into my hand then slid another one in. I couldn't hear any sounds of movement. That didn't mean they were 'static' though, one of them could be making their way up the stairs. I sat and waited. Echo 2 shook his head after the flash-bang going off just behind him; he waited a few seconds for the smoke to clear then went forwards up the stairs.

'Creek' 'I bet he hated that', because he would know I would know exactly where he was; third step down from the top. My guess was he would either rush me or freeze and think it out.

Echo 2 flew up onto the landing then around the corner into the bedroom spraying it with bullets in a long low swoop, hoping to blow me to bits if I was hidden behind the bed or door. I watched the large figure silhouetted in the doorway as he scanned the room for his target, I took aim and fired a single shot at the rear of his knee; from that distance it would blow his kneecap off. "AARRGH," he screamed dropping to the floor whilst letting a few rounds off as his muscles contracted. I went forward kicking the gun away. I pushed him down from his part kneeling position.

He fell forward as I grabbed his wrist pushing the thumb inwards to inflict a pressure hold. He went very quiet for a guy with his knee blown off. "Who are you?" I asked in a calm voice… pausing then slowly applying more pressure.

He was good; I had to give him credit he didn't say a thing.

I knelt down on the wound, knowing the kind of pain it releases to the victim, still no words, "You can actually come out of this alive my friend, all I ask is you have any kids and want to see them again I suggest you start giving me a little co-operation" I said, pressing his thumb in by the nail. If he didn't speak soon the second joint in his thumb would pop.

He didn't even whisper, it was then I heard a soft sound from somewhere behind me. Instantly I grabbed my gun and 'PHFT' he joined his mate.

Knowing how much the floor creaked in the bedroom I chose my next movements cautiously. The sun was streaming in through the bedroom window casting a shadow against the wall opposite me.

Outside, 'Echo 3' placed the ladder against the wall just below the window-sill, while 'Echo 1' moved up the smoke filled staircase that had cleared just enough to make it passable. He had seen 'Echo 4' lying in a heap on the kitchen floor and had no intentions of ending up the same way. "Keep this channel open and give me a running commentary of what you see" Echo 2 said. Making his way up the stairs whilst keeping his gun trained on the right-hand side of the aperture at the top of the stairs. The view through his scope gave everything a red tinge but he knew the approximate location of the target from the last communication from Echo 1.

Meanwhile Echo 3 made his way up the short ladder towards the window, noticing the dark blue flaking paintwork reminded him he needed to sort out his own when he eventually got home. Using a small telescope about 300 millimetres long he extended it up and over the frame to see into the room on the other side.

Placing my head against the wall I could just about hear the wood taking the pressure of each step the guy on the other side took. I guessed he was two thirds up making his head and shoulders at floor level. 'The old plaster walls made from thin laths of wood and horse hair plaster would need some tidying after this I thought.

Taking a step back I pulled both triggers releasing a barrage of bullets that thundered through the thin wall, sending an explosion of plaster and bullets into the narrow stair well. Echo 1 heard a sound then took another step, it was to be his last; a second later his body and the opposite wall were peppered with bullet holes. He stood for a second having taken twenty shots in his upper body. "Get... out" he rasped then fell backwards down the stairs taking the banister with him as he fell.

Outside, Echo 3 heard "Out..." then nothing. He tapped away at his headset trying to make it work. "Echo 1, come in" he said, pulling the small mouth-piece off and blowing into it.

I made my way around the door surround of the bedroom trying to use the picture of the cottage hanging on the wall opposite the top step of the stairs to get a view down the stairs; the glass had about two years of dust covering it. It seemed the last owners felt the same way about cleaning as I did. I squinted my eyes trying to build a picture up, 'there he was'. I moved with more confidence now, reloading the guns as I went. Taking the com's set off the guy in the bedroom I made my way downstairs. Then "Echo 1, 2, 4 come in, I think he is upstairs repeat, I think he is upstairs" a voice said. I froze one up, one in the kitchen, one in front. "Where are you my friend" I mouthed, I pressed the small button on the headset, "What's your location Echo 3" I said.

Outside Echo 3 suddenly heard a voice in his ear, "I am about to make entry through the bedroom window, the room looks clear where are you?" he said knowing Echo 1 should be on the landing by now.

I looked up at the guy slowly opening my window, raised my gun and smiled – then fired. He took it straight up the arse, then waved his arms around like he was trying to fly whilst grabbing at his backside – he fell sideways to the ground, a fall of about three metres. It may sound funny shooting someone like that but it's a slow and painful death for the victim.

Standing next to him I looked around trying to see any

vehicles, nothing they must have walked in leaving their transport by the main road. He looked up at me, then towards his gun that lay a couple of feet from his hand. "You can try and die or leave it and we can talk" I said, slipping a new clip into my gun. Having left my other gun tucked behind the front door. "You can't win Stone" he said looking up at me.

"Two questions then you can go back to your mates" I said, he looked at me in a quizzical way, "Go on" he said. I squatted down next to him. "Who are you working for and how do you know my name?" I said.

"I don't know the money behind the operation, all work is on a need to know basis..." he said then paused and added "The lead 'Echo 1' has all the information on the contract, I know your name because Echo 1 told the team your name" he said, as a sudden bolt of burning pain shot through his guts and lower intestine.

Mercenaries are bad news, they don't usually care who gets killed just as long as they get their target. 'What the hell was Weister playing at? Unless it was the blond who had sent them. My real concern was how they had found this location unless they had followed me all the way from London? That wasn't impossible but highly unlikely.

After dumping the bodies outback I decided to deal with them later, dragging a full-grown man takes some doing when you have a dodgy leg.

I started to go through in mind how I was going to explain to John about the device and what it was capable of. I was sure he'd know someone somewhere who could do something with it. I sat on the bottom step while I pulled my trainers on, my brain still going at six hundred miles an hour trying to work out the ifs, buts, and maybes.

I definitely wasn't going to tell him about what had just happened. He understood what I did but it didn't mean he liked it.

It was no good. I needed a cup of tea and something to eat. While the kettle boiled, I searched the kitchen cupboards for something to eat, but I was out of luck. That had always been my problem, never having enough food in. It just never occurred to me to go shopping or call in to a shop and pick some food up.

My leg seemed to be working better now, because a bad limp beats a hop any day in my book and dragging it around the kitchen like a dead weight was just hard bloody work.

Behind the cottage and running along its entire length was an old dry stonewall. It was a good six feet tall and connected up with the outhouse that in turn was attached to the cottage. Behind the wall the field was a good three feet higher than on this side, the only down side being my back courtyard always seemed to be damp and the wall was covered in a thick layer of dark green moss. I'd fallen a couple of times on the stone flags since the sun never reached round here, so it never dried out. The cold freezing air seeped into my bones again, standing in the open the doorway. My breath made plumes of white clouds in front of me. I walked gingerly across the ice covered flagstones towards the frost covered BMW. The boot popped open when I pressed the key fob. Inside lay the other four silver coloured briefcases. They were identical to mine in most ways apart from the built in key pad on "Case 5." Reaching into the boot, I pulled two of them out and placed them on the flagstones. I leant in to pull the other two out and nearly went head first into the boot space since my feet lost their grip. I grabbed hold of the car's rear wing to stop myself from falling over. "For fuck's sake," I growled, steadying myself. I yanked them out and made my way back across the yard placing them down just next to the outhouse and then returned for the other two. I rubbed my hands together trying to keep them warm, but the frost-covered stone just crept deeper and deeper into my bones while I worked away at the stonewall.

After ten minutes I had all four bodies piled up by the back wall. Using a sheet of tarpaulin, I covered them up placing some stones around the edges to stop the wind from blowing it off.

Just after moving in here, I had dug out a section of wall to create a secret store for my guns and other equipment. It was only a metre square, but it was dry, and if you didn't know it was there, you wouldn't have a chance of finding it. I removed each stone slowly until I revealed a metal door about two feet square painted dull black with a sliding bolt to the left hand side. Gently sliding it back, I opened the door just enough to slip my hand in and release the trigger mechanism. If I hadn't done this, the wire would have pulled six pins out of the grenades hidden just out of sight above the door and that would not be a good day out. I took a pair of 9mm handguns out, six mags, and a pair of knives.

CHAPTER 2

I checked and cleaned the guns and a few mags for later, ran a bit of oil over the knife blades and gave them a rub on my polishing stone to sharpen the blade. The handguns and silencers all looked okay, but a good clean check over never did any harm. I ensured all the working parts were free of any contamination from being stored away for so long, I slid one knife into my belt and one in to the sheath I had strapped to my left calf. This one was fixed with the handle pointing down making it easier to draw. My leg was still smarting, but that would pass. Getting everything working in my favour was now my main objective. I went through to the small lounge at the front of the cottage looking for my bike helmet. The smoke from earlier still hung in the air making it look like a haunted house from the 'Hammer films'; knowing it would probably be kicking around on the floor somewhere in there.

I found it down the side of the sofa covered in a fine layer of dust. It looked a bit scratched from one of my earlier encounters with a road I had bounced along and fence I had crashed through one Tuesday afternoon a couple of years back. I wiped it clean with a towel from the kitchen making it look even more scratched than before, then set it down on the table while I decided what to do with the case. My mind kept on drifting back to the airport, I wanted to know who was pulling the strings, because it all looked too 'clinical' compared with the way Weister had treated me.

I tried the helmet on, it felt odd, tighter then usual, instead of feeling like my head was stuck inside a giant tea cosy it felt more like being born again – way to tight and a bit wet and smelly. So after a lot of tugging I got the thing off. My head felt sticky for some reason so I went into the lounge and over to the mirror hanging on the wall. Right down the side of my head was the remains of a mouse; its guts had burst open leaving a surprisingly large gooey patch from just above my left ear all the way down to my jaw bone. "Oh for fuck's sake" I moaned, peeling the furry red and purple mess away, but there was still an eyeball and nose hanging from my chin. I nearly threw up on the spot. A quick look round and I grabbed a cushion, wiping it all over my face to get rid of all the remains; another look in the mirror, and all I'd achieved was to smear the mouse all over my face. "Argh fuck" I groaned doing double time up the stairs to get a face cloth, five minutes later and thankfully mousey mouse was well and truly down the sink.

I retrieved my black leather jacket from the hook where I'd left it and went to get the bike out of the shabby timber and stone-built shed that stood on the other side of the cottage. The frost seemed to have frozen all the gravel together turning it into a strange uneven surface. I'd had this bike for four years, and it had never let me down. I'd always liked the Triumph Daytona. It was a personal favourite, excellent for meetings because it's easy to park, has a quick getaway, and nobody can recognize you in a helmet.

After several attempts, and a bit of shouting, I eventually got the thing started. I suppose the lack of use and services had something to do with that. I left it running whilst I made everything secure around the cottage and placed the briefcase inside my rucksack hiding it in the shed behind some old boxes. Using a fine wire and one of the grenades from my stash, I set up a booby trap just in case anyone tried lifting it while I was away. My stomach rumbled telling me it wanted feeding because I hadn't eaten for over twenty-four hours. I knew a truck stop on the way to Harrogate that did a good all day breakfast sandwich. Trouble was it tended to get filled up with long distance lorry drivers, and when they start blowing off the air can get a bit, 'stale'. I wasn't too happy about leaving the briefcase, but the odds on someone finding the cottage were scarce, let alone finding the case.

I went through different scenarios in my head as to how John would react to what I had to say. None of them seemed too promising as I played around sorting out the MP3 player, these were handy little things and the guy who'd shown me how it worked in the shop seemed to know what he was doing. I used one of their terminals to login then downloaded all kinds of stuff.

This ride was going to be a 'Billy Idol' one, which meant plenty of speed usually.

It's never the meeting that's the problem with this job, it's the not knowing. There are so many things that can go wrong. I pushed the thought of a setup out of my head, owing to the trust I had built up with John over the years.

The sky was blue. It looked like the perfect day for a good ride, when I pulled the clutch in and put the bike into first. Letting the clutch out, I went slowly down the drive towards the lane leaving the cottage behind me. On either side of the track, the hedges had lost all their leaves into the ditches that ran along either side. Each one had a good 12 inches of freezing cold water running slowly through it, only stopping where the leaves had piled up creating a small dam. A small rabbit ran across in front of me startled by the noise of the bike sending tiny bits of gravel spitting out from under its tyres. The rabbit zigzagged a couple of times in front of me and then disappeared down the ditch and through the hedge. The sun was still low in the sky casting long shadows across the fields giving me a real good feeling about things. I suppose the sun brings out the best in most people. It did a world of good for me anyway. The sun reflected off the small puddles that had formed in the small dips on the track from where the local farmer had bounced his way down here in one of his tractors on a wet day. I came to the end of the track.

I noticed that there seemed to have been some car movement around the entrance. You could see where a car had gone up onto the verge and then skidded off.

The mud on the tyres stopped about eight metres up the lane.

Bringing the bike to a standstill, I climbed off and wandered over to have a look. I pulled the helmet off and squatted down. They were definitely car tracks though.

I wandered across the road with my gun inside the helmet; it was then I saw the nose of a black van just back from the hedge, reversed into a field entrance. After a quick check over it was as I expected, it was totally clean and void of any incriminating evidence. It didn't stop me from making a mental note of the license plate though.

I got back on the bike and set off again. I opened her up a bit to blow the cobwebs out relishing the fantastic feeling you get when you pull the throttle back and the G force grabs you.

I remember the first time I went on a plane. The force of the acceleration was a real thrill. It's the same on a bike, but you're the one in control.

Skipton came and went like a passing thought. Cars and trucks passed on their way to work with their windscreens and body panels covered in a dusting of frost. The people inside peering through the only part of clear glass they'd managed to scrape in the rush to get to work on time.

Just past Bolton Bridge, is a long steep hill that seems to go on forever, and nine times out of ten, you will meet a caravan or an "HGV" dragging itself up at ten miles an hour overloaded or underpowered. The overall effect is still the same – a screaming engine, the driver leaning forward trying his or her best to get that last bit of power out of the probably already knackered engine.

I flew past the big old blue quarry truck which looked like the driver had been doing some sort of serious off-roading cruising at a steady eighty and thinking, "Rather you than me, mate."

Sara looked up to see Malk enter the hotel room. He had the laptop in one hand and the power leads in the other.

"How long will it take you to set it up?" she said in a soft voice.

"About twenty minutes give or take. Don't worry, Sara. Once this program is running, we should be able to track him within a couple of metres of his exact location," he said, placing it on the small table in front of him.

"What do you mean 'should'?" she replied.

"It will," Malk added. Flipping the lid open the laptop screen came on automatically with the logo SASCORP Int. across the screen like a metallic flag blowing in a breeze. He entered his ID code and placed his thumb on the scan pad next the key pad. A light scanned his print from underneath, and then the screen changed from pale blue to dark blue with the words "ACCESS GRANTED" in large bold type.

He typed away entering his location and the numbers of Mr. Lee's phone and hit enter.

"SEARCHING"

"Found location."

Malk typed away ordering the computer to scan every twenty seconds for the phone connection and to search for the signal coming from the device.

A map of Britain appeared in full colour, and then it zoomed in on Yorkshire. The word "tracking" appeared again, and then it started to target North Yorkshire showing an area of twenty square miles with a red dot flashing in the centre of it.

"Target acquired."

"My god," Malk said out loud.

Sara walked over saying, "What's wrong?"

"Nothing, nothing's wrong, Sara," he replied. "The bloody things found him already," he added.

"Let me see," she said, looking down at the screen showing the target moving across the map. The display showed the road number A69 and the speed of the target (75mph).

"Well done, Malk," she said. "It looks like we're going to Yorkshire. Tell the others to meet us downstairs while I ring Karl, will you."

"Wait," Malk said, typing away. "Let me just try something."

Sara watched him enter numbers and numerals and pressed enter again.

The screen went blank for a split second, and then a new map appeared in one corner. The original map showed up opposite. The words "AQUIRING TARGETS," appeared, flashed once, and then several dots on the new screen started to flash.

"What exactly am I looking at?" Sara said, leaning in a closer.

"You know, the screen shows the target," Malk said, "Well, the second screen shows our men, and that," he said, pointing at the orange dots, "That's us."

"That's all well and good, Malk, but where are the cases?" she said, now sounding frustrated.

"The device has a separate signal, Sara. I have to program that signal into the new program before we can track it at the same time," he looked up at his boss in a bid to show he was doing his best.

"Just do it, Malk," she said, walking towards the bar area of the penthouse.

It was only 1:00 pm when I got to Harrogate, so I decided to have a scout around to familiarise myself with the unfamiliar area, and going off the events of the previous evening, I wanted to be able to make a clean getaway if needed. Even though I was sure no one had followed me, you never can be too careful.

After half an hour, I'd got my bearings and some short cuts sorted out. I parked the bike just down from Betty's tearoom. It looked quite posh in there with locals all sitting down sipping tea and eating fresh cream buns. "Very nice," I thought. As I strolled up the hill to the pedestrian crossing, the light went green, and everyone walked across. Most of the people crossing the road at the same time as me looked quite well off in their thick winter coats, carrying their designer carrier bags.

Businessmen always stand out at this time of year, because they never seem to get it right as to what to wear. Some have thick coats, and others just have shirt and ties on with woolly hats and gloves, all looking very smart in a winter wonderland kind of way. The local round table had a choir singing "Oh Come All Ye Faithful" as a couple of Santa's went around with collection buckets giving it the old "Ho ho". People dropped money in but they would shake the bucket making the change jingle to create a guilt trip for those who didn't. Eventually, I could see the little bistro on the other side of the walking precinct and went over to have a look at the menu on the wall. I couldn't see anyone that I would call dodgy hanging around the area, so I headed for the door.

Just then, my phone started to vibrate. I didn't recognise the number on the screen, which meant it could be a new customer wanting someone somewhere dealt with. I answered the call.

"Hello, please wait," I said.

I headed for a vacant shop doorway. I never give my name, because if anyone dials this number, it must have been through previous work.

"Mr. Lee," the voice said in a soft Spanish accent.

The name that the caller had used was directly connected to this job since I give each contract its own name and ID so if things go tits up, I can totally cover my tracks.

"This is Lee. What do you want?" I said.

"Mr. Lee, why have you broken our agreement? All we asked you to do was take one of our suitcases to England and deliver it to our associate in London. I can only presume that you have taken it upon yourself to try to negotiate a higher price for the said contract, Mr. Lee."

It was Tony Weister, the shit who'd talked me into this job. What had seemed to be a nice little earner had turned into a total gang fuck.

"I think you know full well why I have taken your briefcases, Weister," I said.

"Mr. Lee, YOU WILL bring the cases to..."

I didn't let him finish.

"Look, you fat little shit, you broke the contract by lying through your teeth from the moment we met. That's why we're in the situation we're in now" I said.

"Mr. Lee it was a simple mistake that anyone could have made" he said.

"Bollocks," I said. "You call transporting one of the world's most lethal nuclear chemical/biological weapons a simple mistake?

Weister paused and then said," Mr. Lee, don't be a fool. We are happy to renegotiate a more favourable deal with you, one that we will both be satisfied with."

"Listen up, Weister," I said, "I don't make threats. I only carry them out, and the clocks ticking, my friend."

"What do you mean?" he said.

"It's amazing how cooperative your friends on the jet were. It must have been the thought of sudden death that made them so chatty."

"I don't know what you're talking about!" Weister replied, sounding agitated.

"Why all the bullshit about diamonds?" I asked.

"If you think that you'll get away with this, Lee, you're wrong. I'll have you hunted down like a dog and...."

I turned the phone off, knowing he would call again. After all, he wanted his cases back, and I wanted the rest of my money.

'*Meanwhile in Puerto Rico*'

Karl sat back in his chair after listening to what Weister had said to Stone, he still couldn't believe Weister was so stupid as to think his boss wouldn't find out what he was up to. Karl cast a glance over to the picture of him sitting next to his son on the deck of 'The Storm'; his super yacht. His son was only ten years old when the shot had being taken.

He pressed a small button that was hidden from view under the desk. It alerted his personal body guard just outside the main office who, less than two seconds later, was standing by the large desk in front of Karl. His slight almost feminine physique made him seem weak and feeble, this was far from the truth. 'Dang' was an incredible martial artist, who Karl had met in his childhood and they had remained good friends ever since. Dang had never asked for any great rewards from Karl – his job was to protect his best friend, and for that Karl had a small house built in the grounds of the huge villa where Dang lived with his wife and son.

"Find any and all of Tony Weister's living family and bring them here. We will deal with his wife and daughter later" Karl said, knowing Weister's father and mother only lived a matter of twenty minutes away. Dang gave a slight nod and was gone.

Thirty minutes later in the cool darkness of Karl's huge garage that was sat neatly just off to the right of the main house an old couple set bound and gagged facing each other. Karl walked in removing his sunglasses placing them neatly into the pocket of his white Egyptian cotton shirt.

"You know who I am, and you know that by my being here you're going to die eventually don't you?" Karl said, in a soft calm voice. They both nodded slowly.

He walked over to the old table that sat neatly against the back wall of the garage; on top of which sat a small dark oak box. He flicked the gold bracket open and lifted the lid looking down at a set of ten small G clamps with a single spike to one side of the screw that had been set into a blue velvet inner lining. Each clamp had a soft gold sheen to it.

Karl glanced over at the two old people, they had a look of tiredness to them. Their clothes were cheap and dull. This he found difficult to understand knowing how much he paid Weister. He decided not to inflict a slow painful death on these hard done by people. Karl walked over to them and removed the old mans gag, "Does your son give you any money to live on?" he asked, looking down at the old man.

"No, sir we haven't seen Anthony for over five years now" the old man replied. Karl raised his gun and fired, the force of the bullet impacting into the silver-haired man blew him backwards and onto the grey concrete floor of the garage, the same was done to the old woman.

Karl turned and walked away, he didn't need to say anything as his men would clean the mess up and dispose of the bodies.

CHAPTER 3

I checked my watch again. It was 1:53 p.m. John would be along any minute now. I put my phone away and went over to the bistro. A young couple came out looking all loved up, letting the smell of fresh ground coffee fill my nostrils. The young lad held the door open for me, which I thought was very polite.

The place had been done out in an oldie-worldie kind of way with six round tables next to the windows surrounded by a variety of old chairs with the odd one dotted around the central floor area with old leather chairs. Down either side, some fancy booths with dark green crushed velvet bench seats were tucked away in the corners, giving the place a lived in look.

A long bar ran the full length of the back of the place with hundreds of types of coffee beans in large glass jars. The smell of fresh roast coffee combined with the warmth just added to the effect.

The guy behind the bar looked a bit out of place though. He'd put way too much gel on his hair. The sheen was like a black pinball, and his uniform hung on him like a badly made bed, but he seemed to know what he was doing when it came to making a good cup of coffee.

The waitress came up to me. "Bloody hell," I thought, "They didn't make 'em like that when I was that age."

She looked about nineteen, had short red/black spi
the reddest lipstick known to mankind.

Her white blouse was trying its best to just not
and her way too short black way too tight skirt, if y
it that – absolutely fine in my eyes!

"Can I show you to a seat, sir?" she asked.

I stood there trying to look intelligent like you do.

"Err yes" I said

"Would you prefer smoking or non smoking, sir." she asked.

"What? Oh err sorry, over there by the window please?" I said, and I sat down.

"What a dickhead," I thought, getting all daft over a young lass like that.

I ordered a large cappuccino and looked out of the window thinking about what I was going to say to John when he arrived. I knew he would say, "You chose this kind of job, and how many times have I said you'll end up in big trouble one day."

Just then, I saw him walking towards the bistro. He had an expensive looking winter coat on. It was dark blue, nearly black, but the royal blue lining seemed to shimmer when the light caught it. John was one of only two people who knew my real name. It had taken me over three years to actually tell him, because I don't naturally trust people. But seeing that we played squash together most weeks all those years ago, we had developed a good friendship.

He stood in the doorway looking to see if I had arrived. He had a strange vacant look on his face, the kind people get when they sit in front of the television for too long.

His eyes scanned the tables slowly until he saw me. A big grin swept across his face, and he walked straight towards me unbuttoning his coat.

"Sorry, I am a bit late, mate. I couldn't find a bloody place to park."

"It's all these bloody parking metres. I swear, if they could charge you for taking a shit, they would." He paused to take a breath and then carried on. "Anyway what's been going on with u? You look like six bags of shite," he added in his dry deep orkshire voice.

"It's nice to see you as well," I said.

Just then, the waitress came over. "Would you like to order a drink, sir?" she said to John. He looked around to see who had asked the question. He came face to face with the very ample firm looking pair of breasts still trying their best to escape the bra and blouse that were doing their damnedest to stop them from falling out. He glanced back at me with an even bigger grin on his face. He mouthed the words "Bloody hell," and then turned back to the waitress and ordered a large black coffee and a refill for me.

She smiled and headed off in the direction of the bar. "I wouldn't mind some of that," John said.

"You're way too old," I replied.

"You know they shouldn't be allowed to wear that kind of stuff in public," John said, still grinning from ear to ear.

"Oh, I don't know. I think they should wear whatever makes me feel happy," I replied.

The drinks arrived, and we got down to business.

"So Tom, what's wrong now? Because you know I will help you, if I can, but it seems to me that every time we meet something's gone wrong or about to and to be honest it's getting a bit tiresome."

I decided to tell him some of the details but decided to leave out the death and destruction parts, and seeing that I was still open to options, he might be able to offer a way out; John had contacts all over the world.

"Ok," I said, "But for Christ's sake, this must not go any further. I mean it, John. If you so much as mention this to anyone, it will cause us to fall out big time. You understand?"

"Yeh, yeh, no worries," he said, glancing out the window.

I stared at him across the table for a couple of seconds, until he locked eyes with me and said, "Look, Tom, I've known you for near on 15 years now. So don't start with this no trust thing" he said.

He was well pissed off with me. I didn't blame him. It was quite an insult I suppose to even think that John would do that to me.

"Sorry, mate," I said, "But the last couple of days have been fucking mad even by my standards."

"In what way do mean mad?" he said, now looking a bit more interested in what I had to say.

I leant back in my chair not sure of what to do next. He was one of only two people I could trust, the other one was Ian Walker, but I had no idea where he lived now so that put him out of the picture at least for now.

"Ok, John, this is the situation," I said, leaning in even closer. "A couple of days ago, I was in Puerto Rico on my way back from a job when I get this phone call." I said. John sat there all ears listening to my story.

"Anyway, to cut to the chase, this guy asked me to deliver something to England for him," I said.

"So what's the problem with that?" he said.

"Nothing, just listen will you," I replied. "The case he gave me had diamonds in it."

"So what" he said.

How could I tell him the truth? Saying that, how could I tell anyone about the bomb? "Look. What if it was something dangerous like a bomb? Would you still be as bloody calm about it?" I said.

He looked at his watch and said, "You said diamonds. You never mentioned a bomb," he said.

"I know what I said, John. It's just, well, you don't seem to be taking this too seriously, so how else am I supposed to get your fucking attention?" I said.

"So where have you hidden the case, Tom?" he asked.

"Well, at the moment, I've got it back at my cottage" I said.

"You know this is probably Mafia or Columbian don't you" he said.

"All right then. If you can think of another bloody…" I spat back at him.

He was about to speak when his phone started to ring. He pulled it out, looked at the screen, and mouthed to me, "it's the wife."

"Hi, darling, how are you? Have you had a good day shopping?" he said.

"Have you got the location yet?" Malk said.

"Yes, I have, darling. It's been wonderful." John said.

"Get him to tell you the exact location." Malk said.

I got up from the table and mouthed, "See you outside." He put his thumb up and carried on talking.

I paid at the counter, telling the waitress to forget the coffees, but I would still have a muffin. She gave me my change and my muffin in a carry out bag and went back over to the young lad who was busy serving a couple of young girls. I stepped outside into the cold fresh air.

John looked over his shoulder to make sure Tom was outside and then said, "I told you not to ring me. He was sitting straight opposite. He could have heard you." He said.

"That is not my problem," Malk said.

"If I push too hard, he's bound to suspect something," John replied.

"We are impatient. The merchandise must be returned as soon as possible." Malk said.

"I know," John said, adding, "Look Tom has already told me where the case is stashed, so we are more than half way to getting the delivery completed." John said.

The voice on the other end of the phone changed from a soft tone too harsh. "This isn't the fucking post office, you know. We need the location of Case 5 by Monday a.m., or he dies telling us. Ok?" Malk said.

"There will be no need to kill him. I'm sure of it," John said, trying to sound calm.

The phone went dead.

John thought about what they had said. What had he meant by Case 5? Had Tom lied about how many cases of diamonds he had? He called him back.

Malk looked down at his phone that was fastened to the car dashboard. He pressed one of the buttons on the steering wheel so the call went through the car's speakers and answered it with a simple, "Where and when?"

John just sat there for a couple of seconds and then said, "My car in ten minutes,"

"Good work, John. I'm sure Sara will be pleased with you." Malk said.

At that the call ended. John felt sick. He didn't know if he was doing the right thing or not. He got up and left heading for the door leaving a five pound note on the table.

Malk sat thinking about what John had just said; when he'd told him about the return of the merchandise John had said "Tom." Who the hell was Tom? He sent a text to Sara about the conversation and the name Tom and then carried on driving.

Malk had been heading for the target within ten minutes of locating it with the laptop. He was being followed by two other cars. Both had two men in each. The plan was simple: locate the target, lift him, and use whatever means necessary to retrieve all information regarding the device. Sara would follow later and give a running commentary as to the target's location.

John stood in the doorway watching me chomping my way through the muffin.

"I gather that was your wife, "I said, finishing off the muffin and rubbing my hands together to keep them warm.

"Yeh, she's just checking up on me. She likes to know what time I'll be back for tea, but really, I think she just misses me. At least, I like to think so," he said. With a puzzled look on his face.

"Let's take a walk, Tom, down to my car, and we can talk in private where no one can eaves drop on our conversation," he said, resting his arm on my shoulder as we turned to walk along the busy precinct.

"That sounds alright by me. It's bloody freezing out here, and it's starting to draw in a bit." I said.

We walked along slowly, both of us deep in thought. I really needed to talk to Ian about the matter because he had had some dealings with the IRA back in the seventies, and he knew some pretty shady characters. He had sorted me out with one of my first custom made sniper rifles all those years ago, but for now, I would just have to see how things went. John had dealt with buyers from all walks of life, so there was actually a very good chance he could off-load the diamonds for me and take a cut for his part. I glanced sideways at him. He had his collar pulled up to protect him from the sleet that was starting to fall, so I couldn't see his face, but I had a good idea of what he was thinking about. The freezing wind started to blow the sleet around pushing it into my eyes and mouth.

"Not far now," John said, through his teeth.

Something was bothering me but I couldn't put my finger on it, I turned to look back the way we had come. About thirty paces back I saw two men in suits, no jackets and judging by the amount of sleet on their shoulders they hadn't long been out of a car. It had only been a quick glance. I started checking everyone around us, people in doorways, couples, single men and women, everything and anything.

I trusted my instincts, in one smooth move I flicked my jacket and pulled my gun out bringing it to my front without John even realizing what had happened.

We rounded a corner, and at the far end of the precinct, John brought his left hand up and said, "That's my car just over there." As he pressed the key fob, I saw the indicators flash on the red Honda.

"Nice motor," I said, as we approached it.

"It's a company car," he said, making his way over to the driver's door. I was looking at the glass, it had taken many years of practice, but seeing things in detail through a reflection had saved my life more than once. I watched the huge black five stubby fingers reach-out then twist as the curve of the windscreen caught up with my motion.

I looked over at him as he spoke, 'drawing the gun' but he wasn't looking at me. His eyes seemed to be looking over my shoulder.

I spun around fast, catching the guy off guard who was about to grab me. I pushed the gun deep between the open jacket and into his belly then fired a single shot. His jacket and flesh muffled the shot. His eyes bulged as I spun him around throwing him onto the bonnet, "WHO SENT YOU" I shouted into his face knowing he probably had less than a minute to live. A micro second later; a pair of hands grabbed my shoulders yanking me backwards. "What the fuck!" I shouted. Whoever was doing the dragging knew exactly what they were doing, kicking the back of my knee first, making me drop uncontrollably and an easy target.

I was dragged backwards hard and fast dropping to the ground. I tried to spin around to control the fall, but whoever had me just kept on pulling. "Sod this for a lark," I grunted, pulling the knife from my belt, but his best mate saw it and lunged at it shouting, "He's got a blade! Watch it!" I had already started to spin myself round. All I needed was a second of advantage to bring the long blade up towards him. Everything went into slow motion. He stared down at me, he saw the glint of the blade, but it was too late for him to react. The people walking by us seemed to freeze in midstride like someone had pressed the pause button; even the tiny flakes of snow froze in midair while we fought. Everything was thrown into so much detail, my adrenalin rushed through my veins like a bobsleigh hurtling down a track. I could see the whites of my opponent's eyes, and the skin ripple when the muscles contracted beneath the surface of the skin. The speed and adrenalin caused the effect of a moment captured in time. The second my body caught up with me, everything rushed back to real time.

I could feel his grip intensify because he realised what was about to happen. With all my might, I rammed the blade a full five inches into his left thigh muscle. Twisting the blade a full 90 degrees with both hands, I pulled hard down with all my weight, flexing my wrist side to side. He screamed, "Aarrgh!" You fucker!" dropping me on the ground, just in time for his partner to launch a volley of kicks to my body. I tried to get to my feet, but he caught me on the side of my face which spun me round like a rag doll. I lost my senses for a second while the world drifted in and out of focus. I started to roll over but a massive punch hit me on the other side of my face sending bolts of pain bouncing around my head. My teeth cut deep into my cheek. The warm metallic taste of blood in my mouth ran between my lips. The big lump on my tongue where I had bitten a great chunk out of it throbbed painfully each time his fist collided with my face. Somehow I dragged myself to my feet only to take another punch to the stomach.

The few moments of attack seemed to last forever. I

plummeted down towards the flagstones, landing fast and hard. Smack! My face and shoulder impacted onto the freezing cold surface.

In my mind, I knew if I didn't get control of this fight I was a dead man. I rolled over three or four times to try to buy a couple of seconds. It worked. The one still standing said, "Come back 'ere, ya twat. We've only just started with you," and grabbed one of my legs. I could hear people screaming and others shouting but no one wanted to get involved. No one ever does. Better to be safe than sorry. All the sounds were slow, distant and muffled as if underwater. They could see the blood pouring out of the guy near the car, and my face couldn't have looked all that pretty.

I knew, and so did they that it was only a matter of time before the police would arrive. They came at me like a pair of dogs after a rabbit.

Dragging me towards the car, I rammed my hand inside my jacket getting a good grip of the 9mm. I drew it out and released the safety catch.

He saw what I was doing and dropped my leg reaching inside his coat for his gun, but his hand didn't even get part way in when I unloaded three rounds into his lower belly. He jerked backwards and forwards and then stumbled back towards the other car. When his hand started to fall from his front, I picked my aim.

"Time to go, fucker," I whispered. One shot straight through his left eye. The back of his head exploded like a watermelon over the car, and the people standing behind it. Everything went silent for a couple of seconds while it dawned on everyone what had just happened. Then all hell broke loose. People started screaming and running in all directions.

I had to get out of here. I glanced round whilst getting to my feet looking for the guy I had knifed when a fist caught my ear so hard I thought it was going to burst. The pain was unimaginable. It took me off balance, and I went over. Instinctively, I went into a roll and then onto one knee bringing the gun up ready to fire. I saw the bastard standing there half bent over with blood pouring down his leg.

We made eye contact and he saw the gun in my hand. I raised

it, noticing all the people standing behind him. I couldn't fire. It was bound to go straight through him at this distant and kill an innocent person. He could see what I was thinking. He turned, and pushed his way through the on looking crowd, dragging his bleeding leg. I could hear John shouting, "Get in the car for Christ's sake, Tom! Hurry! The police are on their way!" I got to my feet and literally fell into the back seat of his car. Just then the sound of siren filled the air.

I pulled the door closed, saying, "Drive."

He didn't pull away like a man possessed with screeching tyres and revving engine. He did quite the opposite in fact. He just pulled out like anyone else and drove off down the hill. I couldn't help but think if John had actually seen what had just happen because he didn't seem fazed at all. All I was bothered about now were my injuries and getting them sorted out. Punches always look worse than they really are. Bruising is all part of the healing process. John flicked the radio on as he slowed down to let an old couple cross the road ahead of him.

'BANG' "What the f" I groaned, as the car behind us rammed straight into our left hand side. I slid across the rear seat so fast I didn't have time to react, thankfully the soft leather was the first thing my head found.

John steered the car into the impact in a bid to stop us from smacking into the on coming traffic.

I popped my head up to see what was going on just when the rear window exploded all over me as the hail of bullets thundered through it, showering me with thousands of tiny shards of glass then exiting through the side window in another crashing sound. Some of the bullets smacked into the roof lining ripping long claw like gashes through it. "Bloody hell" I shouted ducking away instinctively. John accelerated hard down the hill and round the roundabout while screeching tyres filled the air. The quiet pleasant surroundings of Valley Gardens in Harrogate had turned into a scene from Miami Vice as the two cars smashed their way through the traffic, oblivious to what was going on. People ran for their lives having heard the tyres screeching as the realisation exploded into their heads that it wasn't just a young idiot trying to show off to his mates. Seconds later shots rang out from the two cars as bullets flew in every direction.

I took the chance to have another look and got 'eye to eye' with the guy from the fight. "Bastard" I mouthed, checking I had a round in the chamber of my gun, "Try and keep it straight for a couple of seconds will you" I shouted.

"I'll do what ever the fucking road makes me do..." he paused while we went around another bend adding, "Your gonna owe me for this Tom" he shouted.

I made myself comfortable by getting into a kneeling position then took aim using the rear seat as a rest.

The black Saab came tearing around the bend; I took aim and fired a couple of rounds off at his engine.

"You seem very calm about all this," I rasped, spitting blood out onto John's seat.

"Calm, my arse," he said. "If you think for one bloody moment I'm calm, you must have really banged your head this time, and why is it that every time you come near me, all hell breaks loose! I'm telling you, Tom, you're fucking cursed." I saw the guy hold something up then "Shit" he fired on full automatic.

Blowing their windscreen to bits along with most of the rear of our car the sound of impacting bullets smashing our tail-lights filled the air with more breaking glass off to my right.

The two cars flew down the narrow road that lead towards the entrance of Valley Gardens. Hundreds of people dressed in smart winter clothing were suddenly thrown into a world of violence and noise as the two cars came thundering towards them. A smart fashion boutique with a stunning winter scene set inside had caught the eye of the passers by. Suddenly the whole front of the shop exploded as a wave of stray bullets smashed into it sending the manikin flying backward into the busy shop. Huge chunks of plate glass exploded all over the innocent bystanders. A women screamed as a long shard sliced her face in a micro second before gashing her husbands legs on its way to smashing into the natural stone flags of the pavement. At least eight of the people had taken severe cuts from just being in the wrong place at the wrong time.

A young girl lay dead having taken four bullets to her upper body, her dog lay by her side with its tongue hanging from the side of its mouth, a large section of glass jutting out from its side.

Then like someone turning the sound off, everything went quiet and still like calm had fallen over the entire area until screaming began followed by shouting and dogs barking as reality caught up with what had just happened.

"Look," I said, pulling myself upright. "Take me back to the cottage. I know it's well out of your way, but I'm in no fit state to make my own way home."

"Have you seen the fucking state of my car lately" he shouted, smoke started to flow from the front of the Saabs grill, "Slow down" I said trying to keep him calm.

"Are you stupid" John shouted,

"Look, his car is dying just let me finished the bastard off" I said.

"Yeh, whatever," John replied. I had no choice now, I sat up again and took aim, letting a couple of shots off then another two using the previous impact zones to help track my aim as the car swerved from side to side. I calmed myself down ignoring everything that was going on around me, slowed my breathing right down took aim and fired.

Nothing happened at first then the car just ran off the road crashing straight into a parked white van which in turn smacked into the blue Mini parked in front of it. The sound of a car horn filled the air as we made our exit through the lights and away into the countryside beyond.

3 MINUTES EARLIER

Hearing all the commotion from down the hill an old man and his wife had decided to head back home. As the red Honda sped past them the sound of gun fire filled the air again, it made the old man stop and watch the car as it raced past him in-between the cars parked on either side of the road encompassing the park. He knew the sound from when he had served in the Second World War and never wanted to hear it again. His wife was scared and put her arms around him.

At 87 he was a proud man and hated the fact he was now old and no longer the strong person used to be, "Don't worry my love everything will be alright" he said holding her tightly.

He could hear her weeping. She didn't get out much because of her arthritis but they liked to take a walk in the park whenever they could. He looked defiantly at the black car as it swerved then smashed into the van parked ahead of them, he thanked God for the near miss just as the van smashed into the Mini. The small car leapt forwards and onto the wide pavement where the two old people were standing.

George Walker lay on the ground, with a bad cut on his forehead, and a broken leg, his wife Anne lay still having taken the full force of the impact. George looked at the lifeless body beside him his eyes full of hatred to those who had caused this tragedy. He wanted revenge but his old weak heart had taken to much stress with the loss of his wife, he reached out, taking her by the hand. He so wanted to say his goodbyes to his loving wife but time had run out. He passed away by her side.

I sat there thinking about the attack as the cold air rushed in around us trying to work out in my head when they had clocked me. John was lucky to have been on the driver's side of the car when they jumped us, or he could have easily ended up getting a good kicking or worse. Images of all the damage caused by the chase flickered through my head like a slide show; high detailed pictures of carnage and destruction and the face of the driver of the Saab were burnt into my head. Its not uncommon for this to happen because of the amount of concentration that goes into hitting a target under such volatile conditions. I wiped a drip of blood off the back of my right hand where a piece of glass had caught me then looked through the rear window as we headed towards the A69 en route to Skipton and on to Gargrave. These bastards who were after me didn't give a shit about anyone. I had to find out who was pulling the strings and come to some arrangement. Basically I wanted to kill the twat. All I needed was one of their men, and some time.

They must have spotted me in the bistro and waited

somewhere out of sight ready to make their move and then followed us to the car. Even then the odds of them finding me were outrageous. I sat there looking at the gun in my hand, turning it from side to side. It was covered in blood from the fight. I brushed more bits of glass from my clothing, and pulled a couple of chunks out of the cut on my forehead. My head felt crap, but it didn't stop me from thinking what the odds were of them actually knowing which way I had gone after leaving the airport, let alone which county or city. My only conclusion was the case had a tracking device inside. That still didn't give me an answer as to getting jumped in Harrogate.

"Fuck it," I moaned. My head was too messed up with trying to sort out which part of my body wanted to scream with pain first. My ear was really starting to smart from the cold draft blasting into my head. My mouth was full of bits of tooth that had broken off when dead boy had used my head as a football. I glanced out of the broken window. The lights in peoples' houses were starting to come on in the distance. It was fairly dark now.

John asked which way my cottage was. I told him the way and lay out on the back seat. My bruised ribs felt stiff and sore, making it almost impossible to get comfy, but I must have dozed off for half an hour, because the next thing I knew John was saying, "So where's this turning off you mentioned?"

Malk picked his phone up saying a simple, "Sara."

It was just something she liked, "Malk, find out the last name of this Tom person, will you? It could be important." She hung up.

Karl Sasco sat listening to the dialogue that Sara and Malk had just had, he pressed replay to listen again, "Find out the last name of this Tom person. Find out the last..." he pressed stop. Could it be that after all these years? Just then Dang came in carrying a small wooden box in his left hand. Karl knew straight away what it was. He had sent Dang to impress on a business client that to sell up and retire would be in his best interest. Karl had offered $40,000,000 for a large freight company, a third of its real-estate value, and told Dang that if he rejected the offer to take his hand in friendship, literally.

I looked up from the back seat feeling half asleep and realised that we were just outside of Gargrave. "Next right, mate," I said, yawning my face off.

He flicked the indicator on, "You've been snoring like a warthog, and you should see a vet about that arse of yours because it's gone wild. I mean, that's one nasty little bastard, keeps growling and belching like some mad beast." he said.

I had to laugh, but it hurt like hell.

We drove on for about ten minutes until we came to my track. "It's just in here, mate. Go right to the end, and you'll see the cottage. Just pull up in front of it," I said. As John turned into my lane I noticed the nose of the van was still parked in the entrance to the field, it gave me a little bit of comfort because if it had gone I just knew more of them would be waiting for my return.

John drove slowly up the drive, the car bouncing around when it hit the potholes that the tractor had made over the years.

"You sure this is it Tom? Looks a bit naff to me," he said, as the cottage came into view.

The cottage wasn't the sort of place I would have normally have used in a work situation. This was the place I wanted to retire to; a place to call my own and maybe one day actually have a normal life of some kind. When working, I like any digs I use to have multiple exits and if possible good views of all roads that lead to and from it, but this had just gone to shit now. I could only hope that John being my friend would keep this location to himself. This was my place and nothing to do with my work. I hated the fact that by having to get a lift back here from John, even though he was my best friend, it still compromised my only private place. My only hope was he would keep this to himself, because it only had one real entry and exit road which was a big no no in my line of work.

"Thanks. That's my house you're taking the piss out of," I said.

"Don't you ever leave any lights on? You know, to make the place feel a bit more welcoming?" he replied, bringing the car to a stop just in front of the front door.

I put the gun back into its holster inside my jacket and eased myself out of the car. I must have looked like an old man half bent over and groaning away to myself. John came round to my door and helped me to walk by taking some of my weight. We staggered around to the back door.

"So where are the bloody lights then?" John said.

"I don't have any round here. The bulbs gone," I answered.

"So how the hell are we supposed to see where we are walking then?" said John tripping on the old Yorkshire stone flags nearly taking us both crashing down onto the cold wet surface?

"Look. The doors by that old stone trough," I said.

"Where" John said, scanning the area.

"There, are you blind or something." I said.

"No," he said, "but it helps if you know where you're going." he added. The back door was solid oak and nearly two inches thick, but I had to duck to go through it, because it was less than six feet tall but quite wide. I suppose whoever built the place was short and fat, but that must have been way back in the 18th century judging by the state of the vinyl when I'd moved in.

"Put a brew on, will you," I asked John. "I'm dying of thirst here." I said, pulling a chair out from the table. Bit by bit, I manoeuvred myself into the wooden chair and sat down with a groan.

"Have you seen the state of your face, Tom?" said John with a slight look of disapproval. "You look like Quasimodo."

"Flattery will get you nowhere," I said, trying to cross my legs but failing miserably.

"Look. I'm going to ring the wife and let her know what's happened," John said, stirring the spoon in one of the cups.

"NO, you can't. No one must know about this, not even your wife. You understand? No one," I said. I had to make sure he knew I was serious, so I stressed the point for absolute discretion. "It's for your own good, John. If these guys find out where you live, god knows what they would do to your wife."

"Fair point," he said, resting my cup on the table.

"Ok then, what if I tell her I'm staying with an old friend in Skipton then?"

"Ok," I said.

He went into the front room and closed the door behind him. I tasted the tea. "Bloody hell, coffee," I muttered to myself.

John took his mobile out and dialled. It only rang twice, and then Malk answered.

"Do you have any information for us, John?" Malk said.

"Have you got a pen?" John replied.

"You know all calls are recorded so don't ask dumb questions. Now tell us what you know." Malk said.

"The safe-house he has is near a village called Gargrave. It's about ten minutes past Skipton. You'll see the sign posts for it. Just take the first right turning before you go into Gargrave. It's the only one, so you won't miss it. Go up there for about ten minutes and look for a track on the right. It's up there." John said.

"Listen to me very carefully now, John, because this next question is very important." Malk said. "Earlier today you said your contact was called Tom. All I want to know now is his last name?"

"That was a mistake. Forget about it," John said, realizing what he had done.

"TELL ME NOW!" Malk shouted down the phone.

"I can't. I just can't," said John as his heart stepped up a few paces.

"TELL ME or you die so slowly you will be begging me to shoot you," Malk said, gripping his phone so tight he actually broke its casing.

John knew what Malk was capable of. He had seen him use his finger vices and pressure spikes. "It's Stone. His name is Tom Stone," said John now sweating profusely.

"We will see you tomorrow, John, and John, make sure he sleeps in," said Malk.

"He's totally knackered after the beating your men gave him. You didn't need to do that, Malk. It's only bloody diamonds, after all," John said.

"Diamonds! Who fucking mentioned anything about diamonds? We want our fucking bomb back," Malk shouted down the phone.

"What? You can't..." John said.

"Who do you think you are to tell me what I can and cannot do," Malk fired back at him, finishing the call. John could feel a sense of guilt growing in his stomach. He didn't want his mate to get killed because of his own greed, but he knew if he led Malk and Sara to Tom, his gambling debt would be wiped clean and he could get the deeds to his house back. John had no idea what he was getting involved in now. He just wanted his slate wiped clean at the casino. He didn't want anything to do with people getting killed or bombs. But Tom could be his ticket out of all this. And the one thing Tom had only ever asked of him was never to reveal his true name. Now it was out, he knew nothing would ever be the same again.

"Do you want any of this bloody awful coffee or what?" I shouted from the kitchen.

"Yeh, I'm coming," he answered.

"Everything ok at home then?" I asked.

"She's a bit pissed off with me, but she'll live. I'll get some flowers on the way home. That'll sort it," he said, taking a sup from his cup. His face said it all and his nose crunched up as the bitter taste hit his taste buds.

"You got any whiskey to put in this coffee," John said with a glint in his eye. "You know, just to give it a bit of a lift." he said.

"A lift! It needs a bloody fork truck not a lift!" I said, trying to smile. He looked at me and added, "It'll probably help you sleep as well."

I could see his point and said, "If there is any, it's in the front room. There's a small cupboard just as you go in on the left hand side. You can't miss it." I said.

"You help yourself to whatever you want to drink, mate. I'm going to get a shower and a change of clothes," I said. Slowly pulling myself up from the chair, the pain from my ribs burnt through my side like a hot iron. My lower back was as stiff as a board. "Bloody hell," I thought, "I feel like ten bags of shit, never mind one." Slowly, I hobbled upstairs using the old wooden handrail to steady myself. It wasn't so much the pain from the beating that was stressing me out, it was trying to figure out how they had found me so quickly. I looked around for a towel. I must have sounded like some old git chuntering away going from room to room trying to find where I'd hidden them. It's not like it's a big stately home with dozens of bedrooms and loads of bathrooms. It's a two bedroomed little cottage with one very small bathroom with a shower that leaks. Whoever had lived here before must have liked a bright bathroom because there were more lights in this small room than in the rest of the house put together.

I stripped off and was just about to get into the shower when my mobile started to vibrate its way out of my jeans pocket. I looked at the number and recognised it as Weister again. I wondered what he wanted this time. I let it ring for a few seconds and then answered it.

Tony Weister wasn't up to speed on things on a good day, but he felt a sort of duty to Karl to see this one through, so he decided to chase Mr. Lee up. He knew things had gone wrong on the plane and the pick up at Harrogate had also been a cock-up, but what could he do over here in his large beautiful office that had views out over the palm trees while that idiot Malk chased after the target.

"What do you want, Weister?" I said.

"How are you, Mr. Lee?" he said in a slow, patronising voice. "I do hope that my associates didn't cause too much damage, Mr. Lee, I would not like for us to fall out over such a small misunderstanding, Mr. Lee."

The guy was obviously taking the piss big style. It would have been too easy to have just turned the phone off and let him keep pestering away at me until I gave him what he wanted, but he had picked on the wrong person this time, if he thought I was just going to let him have the cases, especially now I knew what the device was.

"Look," I said, "we need to sort this out so we can both get on with our lives."

"I couldn't agree more, Mr. Lee," said Weister.

I stood there stark bollock naked wanting to get in my shower, thinking, "Who the fuck does this twat think he is, ringing me when I'm about to get in the shower? It's just not bloody cricket. Bastard," I thought, looking down at myself and noticing all the bruising starting to show.

"Here's the deal," I said. "It's not negotiable, so listen up. You send one of your men to meet me at Leeds Bradford Airport at nine a.m. in the departures lounge this Tuesday."

"Why in the departure lounge, Mr. Lee? Why not in the arrivals," he said.

"Simple," I said, "Because your man will have gone through security, and I will know that he isn't armed."

"But where will you be flying to, Mr. Lee?"

"That is of no concern to you, Weister. All you have to do is follow my instructions, and you will get your cases, and I will get my money plus another £50,000 for all the trouble you've caused me."

There was no way he was getting his cases back, but I wanted to see if I could at least get more money out of him.

"So be it, Mr. Lee. We have a deal, but you must understand that if you do not turn up or you decide to take my property, the repercussions will be most terrible, Mr. Lee. Do you understand?"

"Understand this, Weister, if you do not comply, I will find your family and then you. You know I will. It's what I do for a living."

He didn't know I wouldn't go near his family, but I bet he wouldn't try me on it.

"It seems we are at an agreement then, Mr. Lee."

"It seems we are," I said, turning the phone off.

Meanwhile in Puerto Rico, Karl Sasco stood in his office looking out over the ocean below. He had just heard the recording of what had occurred during the flight over to England. Karl's private jet had recently been fitted with a full digital recording system, for when he held meetings with members of governments and other high ranking members of the world's judicial systems. He found it most convenient if they happened to let any secrets slip or use of his girls. Using the recordings for extortion had proved very profitable. When it came down to it, he trusted no one except his son and daughters. He had seen his rivals fall from grace through placing too much trust in the wrong person.

On the digital recording, he'd heard a man talking. Moments later, a shot rang out and then:

"You've killed Dean Sasco."

Then he had had a phone call from Sara, his beloved daughter. She had taken the news of her brother's death in her stride. She hadn't cried for him or broken down. He was a Sasco and so was she. Death was part of life, and she knew how to deal it out and how to accept it. She had told her father of the new information, regarding the device, but it had been the name she had spoken that had sent a chill down the neck of a man so cold hearted his stare could make a man literally wet himself, a name she had no knowledge of until today. Karl had told her to use every means possible to find him, use every means possible and as much money as it takes. "Today everything changes until we find and kill Tom Stone," Karl said, ending the call. He didn't need to know the name of the person on his jet, he had spent many years researching Stone. He knew the way he worked, making out he was an everyday Joe, made him less threatening, yet an assassin with over thirty kills to his name, still lived when he should be dead. Karl had unfinished business with Stone and he intended to catch him alive.

Karl knew death was part of life. He knew his son played a high risk game. He was so proud of him, but it wasn't the loss of his son that had caused him to throw the full glass of Southern Comfort smashing into and through the huge window that stood in front of him. It was that name, that name from many years ago. The bastard who'd murdered his wife and newborn child, the bastard who he thought up until now was long since dead, TOM STONE.

Two guards came running in from next door at the sound of the window being smashed. They stood in silence, looking at their boss. He turned to face them, saying in a soft voice as calm as a still ocean but as cold as sheet ice.

"Bring me Weister."

CHAPTER 4

After a couple of thumps and a bang, the shower started. I waited for a couple of minutes until it was hot enough then stepped in. It felt good, but my cuts stung as the soap washed over them. Resting my arms on the top of the shower I let the hot water run over my skin relaxing my muscles beneath. I was knackered and ready for a good sleep, but I knew I had a few things to take care of before I got my head down for the night. The little soap I had left disintegrated through my fingers into nothing, so I turned the water off and got dried knowing below me a steady dripping of water would be seeping through the cracks in the wood floor and down onto the kitchen floor.

John watched as the dripping water seeped around the light fitting wondering how the place hadn't gone up in flames. His eyes scanned the exposed floor joists following the electric cable until it disappeared somewhere out of sight into the wall, leaving a tell-tale blister crack that snaked along under the joists then suddenly stopped.

The cold air inside the bathroom was full of steam covering the spotlights and small mirror that hung next to the window. Tiredness was creeping over me, I was so knackered even the cold didn't bother me.

Most of my clothes were packed away in poly bags in desperate need of sorting from when I had moved into the cottage, but I had a couple of pairs of jeans and half a dozen T-shirts in the drawers. I finished towelling myself dry then flipped it over the top of the shower.

Blue jeans, white T-shirt, and all terrain boots, they were comfy and that's all that mattered. I looked around for a sweat shirt, but after emptying a couple of bags out, I gave up.

"John!" I shouted, down the stairs.

No answer.

"John, you fat git! Where are you?"

"Why hadn't he heard me," I thought. This is a small cottage, there's no way he couldn't have heard me, unless he was outside or on his phone again. Something wasn't right here. It was just a feeling I had, a bit like when someone walks over your grave. I don't know why, but something had spooked me. Trusting my instincts had saved my life on many occasions and I wasn't about to change things. I found myself with a head full of why's which is never a good thing in my line of business. Pulling a small section of plasterboard off I grabbed the two hand guns inside and checked they both had a round in the chamber.

Suddenly my little cottage didn't feel very safe, I felt vulnerable. "Shit" I cursed to myself, "This cannot be happening." Motionless, I recalled the events of the last couple of days trying to piece it all together, letting each scenario drop into place. Leaning back against the wall I let a long slow breath out, and cleared my mind.

Then it started to fit together. It had been John who'd contacted me just when I had got back into the country. He was the one to suggest the meeting in the bistro, and all he wanted to know was the location of the cases. He also took a call on his phone whilst I was there, and I had left him to it. "This is madness," I thought. It must be!

I had no real reason to suspect John apart from my own paranoia. Too many coincidences can make you see things that just aren't there. I leant up against the wall, running everything through my head again and again, but each time I got the same answer. I remember someone saying, "When all the facts have been eliminated even the impossible becomes possible."

Somehow in all the shit that was going on, John was mixed up in the middle of it. I looked at the peeling paint on the door surround where the gloss paint had gone off over years of neglect. I sighed again now trying to figure a way of John not being connected with what had gone on, but I just kept on getting the wrong answers every time. Wiping a drip of watery snot from the end of my nose I walked into the front bedroom.

Why hadn't I seen this coming? All the signs were there to see, but it wasn't the fact that I had missed them, it was simply because I thought that I could trust him. As much as I didn't want to believe it, I knew he must be involved at some level. But how?

I went back into the bathroom which is directly over the kitchen. The floor in there was varnished pine. It looks good, but it's a bit cold and slippery under foot. The other down side is that you can hear any noises in the kitchen and vice-versa. I could hear someone talking, so I knelt down and put my ear to the floor.

John was definitely talking on his phone, but I could only hear half of the conversation.

"Yes," he said. "I know, but you don't understand. If he suspects, he'll just take off." John listened whilst the other person talked.

Then he said, "I'll put it in his drink. That'll knock him out until you get here."

"The two faced fucker" I hissed under my breath! I'd heard enough. I went quietly into the front room and got both my guns sliding a new clip in each one. If John's friends were coming to tea, they'd better be well armed. I decided it was too risky to go down the stairs, just in case someone was down there with him waiting for me, why take the risk when I had the advantage. I screwed the silencer on while heading for the rear of the cottage.

The back-bedroom window looks out over the outside shed. It's connected to the house like a lean to. The roof was made of old Yorkshire stone tiles lapped over each other to create a waterproof covering, this would be handy because the thick stone would hide any sound I made whilst moving across it.

I tried the sash on the window, but it was glued up with paint. "Shit," I thought while I looked around for something to pry it open with, then I remembered the knife in my jeans. A few seconds later I had slid it down between the frames and worked it along gently easing the two apart. I had another go at pulling it up. "Come on, you twat," I hissed, as the window slowly slid open. Raising my leg up and out, I winced when the pain shot up my side, scrunching my top half down to climb out. Taking care not to let the sash slide back down, I wedged a book that was on the windowsill into the runners. "The Lord of the Rings." I'd seen the first film but never had the time to read the book. My foot just slid away from me the second I put any weight on it. "Jesus Christ," I thought. The entire roof had a thick layer of frost covering it and the moss beneath. I gingerly made my way across the tiles on all fours, trying to be quiet. Experience at seeking a target and sitting in wait had made me almost impervious to the cold. The second the adrenaline starts to flow your internal thermostat will keep you warm for a good time, which is usually until the immediate threat has been dealt with. Thankfully, the full moon cast a grey light over the roof giving ample illumination to enable me to make my way across to the edge so I could have a nosy into the backyard to see if anyone was lying in wait for me. Slowly I peered over. There wasn't any movement or unfamiliar sounds that I could detect. I was about to jump down and go through the back door to catch John out, when it opened.

I froze hardly daring to breathe. My heart was going like a steam hammer.

The light shone out through the kitchen doorway partially illuminating the back yard. A figure was standing there silhouetted by the light from behind. He took a long drag on a cigarette and blew the smoke out and up towards my face. I was only three feet above him with both guns aimed at his head.

"What the fuck are you doing up there? You scared the shit out of me, you silly twat," said John nearly falling over backwards. Dropping his cigarette in the process.

I flicked the safeties off. "Why didn't you answer me, John?" I said calmly.

"What? What? When, I never heard you shout?" he said, edging back slightly.

"John, why didn't you answer me?" keeping my aim true I tilted my head to get a better view of him.

"I swear, Tom. I never heard you. Now put the bloody guns away, will you." When he spoke his hands gripped the door frame, he was about to react, his body telling him to get the fuck out of there.

"I shouted twice John, and it don't take a genius to work out if you're in the house or not, because it's too fucking small. So I ask you again, John. Why didn't you answer me?" lowering the guns to aim at his stomach, just in case he got lucky when he legged it, I wanted an easy shot.

"Alright, Tom, I'll tell you why I couldn't hear you, but first please put the guns down."

"Empty your pockets, John." I said.

"Look. We're friends, Tom. What the hell has gotten into you? Don't you remember me saving your arse earlier on or what?" he said.

"I know exactly what happened. I was the one getting filled in. Strange though, isn't it, how they didn't even go near you. A bit odd don't you think, John?" I said in a calm but firm tone.

His face was starting to change from fear to anger now, the sort of change that can give a person away.

"Ok, let's hear your reason and make it convincing, because as you can probably tell, I'm not in the best of moods," I said, trying to ignore the cold penetrating deep into my skin.

"Will you put those bloody guns away, Tom? I mean it. You're pissing me off now. You always overreact by pointing those things at anything that spooks you. Don't you see that's why you're in the shit again?" he said. His voice changed from anger to almost pleading in a split second. "Tom, come on. Let's go inside and sort this out once and for all." He said, I saw his arm muscles flinch, he was going to react in some way, but he must have known he couldn't draw a gun and fire it before I fired.

I didn't move or blink. I just lay there watching his every move, the veins on his neck swelled from his frustration, and then the pulse on his temple started to gently throb. He was about to blow.

"You're not ordering me around, not now, not ever. Do you understand?" he shouted with rage up at me.

He turned to go back inside. I didn't want him dead, just wounded so I lowered my aim and fired a single shot 'PHFFT' straight at the rear of his knee joint, from that angle, the bullet would blow his knee cap clean off, it's a horrific wound. Many people have suffered such horrors when captured by the likes of the IRA back in the seventies.

Down he went, the force of the impact spinning him around as he fell, his eyes filled with rage, pulling himself backwards into the kitchen he slammed the door shut behind him.

"Here we go," I said to myself, making my way back across the tiles and through the window. I let the sash close behind me. Heading downstairs quietly but fast, I made sure not to step on the first step because it always creaked. To my right was the kitchen door, it was closed. The front room looked clear from this angle. The door was open, and the lights were on. I went forward with my gun out in front of me, 'nothing' I backed out pulling the door closed behind me, I didn't want anything sneaking up behind me. All this happened in less than 20 seconds, I just wanted to make sure the house was clear, because 'John the bastard' wasn't going anywhere.

The door to the kitchen however was closed. I could hear him moving around talking to someone on the other side. None of the doors in the cottage fitted to well so if it was a bit of privacy you were after this was the wrong place to be. I waited until I thought he was on the far side of the kitchen. I built a mental picture up in my mind of the layout of the room, and where I thought he was standing, the tone of his voice sounded like he was facing away from me. I knew the door squeaked once it was a third open, so very gently I pushed it open using the barrel of the gun in my right hand.

The view of the kitchen was partly obscured because of the way that the units had been fitted. I could see John – he was still near the back door sitting with his back to me. He was holding something in front of him in his left hand, but I couldn't see what it was from this angle. I had both my guns aimed at his head, he still had the phone to his head when he turned towards me. I stepped out into the room doing a sweep with one gun while keeping my right handed one aiming at John glancing back and forth just in case anyone fancied taking a pop at me. For all I knew his mates might be in the kitchen waiting for me to make my entrance. It appeared to be clear apart from John who was now facing me but off to my left. The whole world seems to come to a dead stop just for a split second, and then back to reality again.

His face said it all. The tears running down his face, while he pressed a towel against his knee.

He knew I was pissed at him.

In a situation like this, you can't afford to think of all the good times and friendship you've built up over the years. It's kill or be killed. It's that simple.

I had seen something in his hand but it was still obscured by the kitchen chair, and the towel covered in blood, my subconscious mind shouting 'GUN' it had been covered in blood and partly obscured by the towel.

"Gun," a voice inside my head screamed again.

I heard a shot.

All I could think about was dropping this two faced bastard each time I pulled the triggers. All I could see were the bullets slamming into his body. He seemed to jump up when the first bullets found their target, hitting him in the neck just under his right jaw. The rest went straight into his upper chest creating a streak of small explosions that ripped across his chest sending blood flying in all directions, this was a whole new version of the pink mist effect. He went over backwards onto the kitchen units, letting several shots off in the process while his hands flailed about. He managed to get another shot off, but it wasn't aimed at anything, it was just a reflex action. Trouble was it went clean through my side making a neat hole in the front but a messy exit wound on its way out, ending in the door frame behind me. A strange gurgling sound was coming from his mouth. While he swayed about, the gun dropped from his hand, hitting the work top, and then to the floor. His mouth kept trying to form words when he fell in a heap, sliding sideways across the work surface and down onto the floor. The blood was pouring out of the wound in his neck.

I stood there a moment, just getting my breath. Although only a couple of seconds had passed, it seemed I had been there for hours just staring at him. The whole thing was just totally surreal. I had known John for near on fifteen years, and yet I hadn't known him at all.

Looking down, I saw a dark red blood stain seeping through my T-shirt. Gently lifting the material up, I saw the hole where the bullet had entered my body and the exit wound just four inches to the side of it. "Oh for fuck's sake," I thought. He must have got a lucky shot off; the bullet had entered and exited my flesh. I considered myself to be one lucky son of a bitch, a second later and it would have been me on the floor. That's not to say that I wasn't a bit worried about having a couple of holes in me, but I had seen worse.

I pulled the T-shirt off and tended to the wounds with what little medical knowledge I possessed, which is next to none. I cleaned the wounds and placed a couple of medi-pads over them to try and stem the bleeding. I had bought this medi-kit from an army surplus shop. It had all kinds of things in it including information leaflets on how to treat just about every kind of wound anyone in a fire zone would need.

I wrapped the bandage round as tight as I could until it ran out, hoping it would do the job holding it in place with a large section of sticky plaster.

I went over to John who looked a bit worse for wear. I thought, "It's bad enough having a dead body on your kitchen floor, but this dead body had seen fit to empty half its fluids out all over my kitchen units as well, ungrateful bastard." And he hadn't made that cuppa I wanted. I pulled a chair out and sat down opposite John's body.

"Trouble is," I thought, who had he been talking to, because I had just got off the phone with Weister, so it couldn't have been him, unless he had a guy in this country overseeing the job, which would make sense from his point of view. I thought about the woman I'd seen. She must have been the contact Weister was using.

Even so, that still left me with the meeting I had arranged with one of Weister's goons on Tuesday. He must be the one who John had been dealing with, but it still didn't add up. But given enough time, I was sure everything would become clear as to how John had got mixed up in all this.

I decided to put the kettle on. It was still warm from when John had used it, so thankfully it didn't take long to boil. Patience at this point were not high on my agenda!

"At least he hadn't used all the powdered milk," I thought. Now that would have really pissed me off.

I noticed John's mobile on the floor near the bin. I went over and picked it up trying not to bend too much because of the pain from my wounds. It was still turned on, and the lock was off.

"Well, well, this looks interesting," I thought, scrolling through the list of numbers on the screen. I got my phone out and checked if any of the numbers corresponded with mine. After a couple of minutes, "Bingo!"

He had been in touch with Weister. I checked the time and duration of the calls. It looked like John had been a very busy little bee. There must have been ten calls in the last couple of days alone.

I wandered through to the front room whilst looking at the other numbers on the phone. Turning the lounge lights off, I glanced across at the window which looks directly down the drive. The deep grey shadows cast by the moon made everything look so cold and still, which wasn't far from the truth at this time of year. The frost slowly creeping across the front window pane seemed to have a life of its own. I stood there for at least ten minutes just staring out through the window, almost mesmerized by moonlight, wondering what the next 24 hours would bring.

The conversation that John was having with his pals had mentioned them coming to get me, and to make sure that I slept in, but having not heard what time they were due, I had to presume that they could arrive at any time.

"Time to leave, me thinks."

I went upstairs to get my ID set. It comprised of five full false identities and various amounts of money in several different currencies.

All I needed clothes-wise was what I had on for the moment. My main priority was to get as far away from here as possible with the case and a good supply of ammunition.

02:04 a.m. It won't be light for a good few hours yet, so hopefully, his mates won't be along for a while. Who knows, they might be waiting for John to give them the all clear, but I very much doubted it. All I could think of was that if they were coming for me, my chances of seeing Christmas were going to be dramatically reduced.

With the briefcase in my rucksack, it didn't leave much room for anything else. I laid it on the table and went through what I could comfortably carry without it looking too outrageous.

My crossbow, unfortunately, was out of the question as it was simply too big, but my sniper rifle was a must as its one of the main tools of my trade. I had rifles in over ten different countries which made it easier to carry my work out. The less time a precision weapon spends in transit the better, so to get around the problem of getting my tools of the trade through customs, I placed them in safe lock ups around the globe. The one posted back to myself wouldn't be back in the UK for a couple of days yet so that would just have to sit in its box until I had a chance to retrieve it. The one laid on the table in front of me, I had custom built two years ago; it had never let me down yet, made from plastic, aluminium and a blend of super light high tensile materials, it really was a work of art. I placed it on the table along with my pistols and silencers. I put the spare clips for the guns in the rucksack down the side of the case and a couple more in my jacket pockets.

You just don't know what's coming at you until it arrives.

I didn't want to have to leave this place, so in order to keep it I would have to tie up all the loose ends, which in this case meant no witnesses. Anyone involved with trying to get me sorted out was in for a bad day out unless they got me first.

I remembered how many men Weister had with him before, so

more than likely, the ridiculous odds clause would come into effect, but I had the advantage of surprise as I knew they were coming, but they didn't know I knew.

Trying to find a bunch of guys is always easier than finding one. I can just disappear if needed, but that would mean losing my cottage, and that was not going to happen.

Glancing over at the body on the floor, I thought, "Did I ever know you, or were you just playing me all this time?" I went over and checked his pockets to see if I could gather any more information off him, but there wasn't a thing. I got to my feet, and looked at his left hand, no ring, not even a mark. I checked his other hand, nothing. I pulled his sleeve up to see if he had a watch on, again nothing, the guy had no ID at all apart from his phone. His keys were on the worktop, so I grabbed them and went outside to check his car for anything I could find.

The frost had taken a good hold now. I looked up at the night sky. The stars were out. Even the ground was rock hard. The bits of gravel had frozen together, making a strange hard surface that made no sound when I walked across it. The car glistened with frost, and all the windows were iced up. My breath rose in gentle clouds above me as I tried to push the key into the lock, but it was no good. The frost had done a fine job of seizing it up solid.

I was concentrating so hard on what I was doing that I almost missed the beams of light sweeping across the trees on the other side of the field.

You can't see the road from the cottage because of the slight rise in the field half way down the track. It creates a mound in the middle obscuring the view of the lane on the far side, but at night, you can see if a car pulls onto the track by the way the lights strike across the field hitting the trees opposite. I stood and watched as another then another pair swept the trees like a lighthouse beam sweeping across the ocean. "Oh shit," I thought.

I ran inside ignoring the pain in my leg and stomach, grabbing the rucksack, then slinging the rifle over my shoulder.

Running back outside to see if they had started to come over the brow of the hill yet, but there was no sign of any movement. "They must be walking up the track, which I knew would take them at least ten minutes," I thought just when the first car came into view with its lights off driving dead slow. "Very clever," I thought.

I made my way over to the field on the right hand side of the track trying to keep to the shadows . The gravel had frozen solid making a strange uneven surface, the metal gate had been left open as usual by the farmer. I stumbled on the hard ground that the tractor had churned up and now frozen solid cursing when I hit the hard ground, the pain exploding from my wounds soon made me get to my feet.

Fifty yards into the field stood an old barn with a tin roof that backs onto the hedge row and trees behind. The hay loft looks out across the front of my cottage and up the lane, the perfect spot to take a shot from.

I glanced back up the track, while I made my way towards the barn to see three large black cars creeping down the slight hill towards my cottage. They were still a good two hundred yards from where I thought they would stop, which would put them 70 yards from my shooting. This was okay for now.

Malk checked his gun as Stiff drove the car slowly towards the target's house. In the back, Sara Sasco was giving instructions to the others in the two other cars. She didn't want a bloodbath as her father had asked her to bring the target back to him alive. He hadn't said why, but he had been very insistent about it. She leant forward, saying, "I want him alive, gentlemen, so let's not get carried away."

Malk looked back at her, gave a wink, and said, "Whatever you say."

"Might as well just ask him to come with us then," the Stiff said sarcastically.

"It's not just about killing," Malk said.

"And what if he comes out shooting? You know, like the way he wiped out everyone on the plane, then what? Do we just say, 'Listen here, old boy. Let's not get upset.'"

Malk looked across at him and said to Sara, "He has got a point, you know. This guy isn't to be messed with, Sara. He has a track record that tends to leave a trail of bodies in its wake."

"Shoot to wound then," Sara said.

I made my way into the pitch-black interior of the barn. I stumbled over something laid on the floor. I cursed when the pain came back with a vengeance, struggling to my feet checking to see if I had lost anything. From memory, I knew that the steps that lead up to the hayloft were somewhere off to my right, but my night vision hadn't kicked in yet, so I had to stand still to get my bearings because it was totally ink-black in the barn.

Slowly, I started to see objects in the darkness, odd shapes and strange shadows, and then my eyes caught sight of the steps. I made my way over to see if they would support my weight. They looked a bit iffy from what I could see, which was next to nothing, so I took the rucksack off placing it behind the steps, out of sight. A long creaking sound came from the first tread as I put my weight on it.

The second one just broke away and fell onto the ground below. "Brilliant," I thought and gingerly carried on trying to get to the top as quickly as I dared but every other step just crumbled into dust.

My head came level with the loft floor which in some ways was a good thing, but in another, it meant that if the wood was as bad as the steps, I was in for a fun time.

I crawled on all fours across to the loft window. It was perfect. The view from here looked straight out towards my lane and the front of the cottage, but I knew that from the lane, the barn was literally invisible because of the trees behind it and the angle that you look across towards it. The whole barn just blends in with the background.

I got my night sights out and fixed them to the rifle and then screwed the silencer on. I wanted to have a good look at how many people were in the cars before they got too close.

I got the front car in my sights. I counted four shapes inside, two in the front, and two the back.

The next car had four or five it was hard to tell as the windows in that vehicle were well misted up. All I could see were shapes inside, but the back car only had a driver, and for some reason, he was going slower than the other two.

"You're dead, boy'o," I thought.

I trained the cross in the sights on his head, following the movement of the car as it bounced up and down the pot holes with an almost hypnotic rhythm. My breathing became slower and slower, and then I pulled the trigger. "Phwt" A split second later the car windscreen had a tiny neat hole in it just in front of the drivers head. I half expected the car to go tearing off down the road and slam into the one in front of it, but the car just came to a stop. I looked through the sights to see if the others had heard what had happened, but they were still moving down the lane. If I could reach that car before they got to the cottage, then I could make a run for it, or use it as a road block and give them the good news from up there. Trouble was though, if they got around behind me I'd be stuffed.

"Bollocks to it," I thought. Time I wasn't here.

I shuffled across the timbers until I reached the steps. Looking over the edge, I noticed just how many treads had gone sailing down to the ground. "Shit," I thought, "This is going to be fun."

I turned round and went backwards over the edge feeling with my feet as to where the treads were. My foot connected with the third tread down as the ones above that had gone. I breathed a sigh of relief and let my weight go down onto the next one. Just as I thought that this wasn't too bad after all, with no warning, the whole lot collapsed with a splintering and cracking of old timbers. Anything I grabbed hold of seemed to fall to bits. As the bottom of the steps gave way, the top section swung under the loft, opening with me hanging on to whatever I could. It must have looked like some kind of circus act by the way I was swinging around with my legs flying in all directions.

The timber I was holding gave way, and off I went through the air with the greatest of ease like a stupid prat with no trapeze and with no net!

By the way that I landed, I must have done a complete summersault, because my arse was the first thing that made contact with stone cobbles that made up the floor. The only thing that softened the blow was a thin covering of straw.

It felt like being kicked up the backside by an elephant. God, it hurt. I rolled over onto my side and lay there in the dark whilst the pain in my arse eased off a bit. After a couple of minutes, I got up and wandered over to the barn door to see what was going on, still rubbing my arse.

The first car pulled up in front of the cottage.

No one got out. They just sat there as if waiting for some instructions, and then the second car stopped. Again, no one got out. It just stayed in the lane about twenty yards from the cottage. The third car was well back. It was a good fifty yards from the first car, which was a good job seeing that the driver had a neat hole in his head.

"What's that silly twat stopped for?" Stiff said, looking in the door mirror. "You know he's a liability that one."

"What you asking me for?" Malk said.

"Would you two give it a rest. Call him on the radio and ask him why he's stopped," said Sara's soft voice from the back seat.

"Oki doki," said Stiff.

"Stiff to Johnny, come in."

"I tell you he's gone for a piss. He's always pissing that one is. Wherever you go got to have a piss," Malk said, looking out towards the cottage.

"Enough," Sara said from behind. "Try him again, and don't stop until he answers. Malk, give John a call on his mobile to see if everything is ready for us to go in," Sara said, whilst typing away on her laptop.

He punched in John's number, it started to ring.

I nearly jumped out of my skin when the phone started to ring as I lay there on the ground in the pitch blackness of the barn. I pulled it out of my jacket pocket, looking down at the tiny screen it read withheld number. I had to think fast. If I didn't answer it, they would suspect something was up, but if I did answer, would I be able to do a convincing impression of John.

I pressed the answer button.

"What do you want," I said, in a harsh low whispering voice, making out that I was in the other room so I had to keep it quick and quiet.

"We're on the drive. Is he asleep?" Malk said.

"No; give it 10 minutes," I said in the harsh whisper, pushing the end button on the phone.

"Well, are we on?" asked Sara from the back seat of the car.

"10 minutes, and then we go in," Malk replied.

"Alright," she said in a soft voice. "Stiff, go tell the others to get ready, and keep it quiet as our friend is still awake," Sara said in a soft firm voice.

"Right," Stiff said, getting out into the cold night air gently closing the car door behind him. Stiff had made a good name for himself in the Sasco family by being fast and ruthless. His driving skills were second to none. The only thing he loved more than driving was himself. He was so vain it was embarrassing which Malk took full advantage of whenever he had the chance.

I got to my feet, brushing any straw that had stuck to me off my clothes, pulling the rucksack on as I made my way over to the barn door. I took the night sight off the rifle so I could use it like a telescope to see what was going on. They seemed to be getting themselves ready to go in, so I took a chance and made my way over to the hedge near the gate. I could hear them moving around, but no one was talking. These guys were good. They were organized and seemed to be pretty switched on. From what I had seen, there were six of them. This didn't particularly bother me as I had surprise on my side, and I knew the ground.

I thought I could probably slot at least four of them before they had a chance to react.

Sliding the rucksack off, I got the spare mags out and then slid it back on again fastening the buckle this time in case I had to make a run for it. A quick look over the hedge told me that this could work. Most of them had their backs to me, and the others were busy with something in the car boot, which could only be guns I reckoned. Taking the fight to them was now my only real option. I tried to work out my best escape route if it all went tits up and decided that to run like hell up the side of the field would not only be slow because of the terrain, but I could end up with a busted ankle to boot.

I checked my guns were ready to go, and the spares were secure in my jacket pockets, and then I slowly stood up from my crouched position. Because of all the adrenalin rushing through my veins, I'd forgotten how cold it was. I looked up noticing my breath was making clouds in front of my eyes. Oh shit!

All I could hope was that they hadn't been looking in my direction, because I might as well have lit a fire for all the clouds coming from me. I stepped back from the hedge to get a better view of the targets, but as they came into view, I noticed straightaway that there were only two of them left standing next to the car. I thought they must have gone inside.

Just as I was thinking what to do next, I heard something off to my left. Down I went into the shadow of the hedge, bringing both guns to the aim in the general direction of the sound.

Slowly, a figure came round the corner of the gate, stopping every couple of steps to take in the surroundings. He was carrying some kind of gun with both hands. From this angle, I guessed it was something like an AK 47, but I wasn't going to give him chance to show me.

I took aim as he hadn't seen me. This was an easy shot as he was silhouetted by the moonlight. My first bullet hit him in the centre of his face flicking his head backwards in an instance. The gun dropped from his hands as his body went limp and fell to the hard frozen ground, but even with the silencer on, there was no way his mates wouldn't have heard what was going on. I didn't move at first. I just held my ground for a couple of seconds, waiting for the next one to appear. Everything seemed to close in around me as my senses tuned into every little sound and smell around me. In real time, maybe two or three seconds had passed, but it always seems a lot longer than that when you're in the shit.

I leapt forward grabbing his gun, checking the safety was off. The sounds of voices came from the other side of the hedge, and then without warning, a hail of bullets came thundering through it, blowing small impact craters out of the hard frozen ground all around me. I dived to the ground crawling as fast as I could along the side of the hedge hoping like hell that one of those bullets wasn't going to smack me in the arse. "Shit, shit ,shit," I cursed as my elbows smacked against the frozen soil. I rolled over spraying the hedge with bullets in a hope of cutting them down, but these guys weren't born yesterday, as their return fire soon let me know.

"Holy shit," I gasped, as the hedge just above my head seemed to fall apart from the amount of bullets exploding through it. Twigs and branches were hitting my face and body as I wanted to respond, but my automatic reflex was to protect myself. I rolled over and went like hell up the ploughed edge of the field, my ears ringing from the deafening sound of the guns only a few feet from where I had been lying. "Don't you dare kill him. I want him alive," Sara shouted from the car, adding, "Aim to wound him." She hated the madness of a gun fight. Clean shot only was the way she did her business.

The shooting stopped as quickly as it had started, leaving a ringing in my ears. I carried on, part scrabbling, part crawling for all I was worth. More voices. I turned round just in time to see three figures coming round the corner of the field cautiously with guns at the ready. I got a proper hold of the gun I had taken from their mate and let rip with it knowing the flashes from the end of the barrel would give my position away instantly. The sound from the AK47 was deafening after the stillness, but it certainly did the job. Two of them dropped like rag dolls instantly as the third dived to the ground, but I wasn't done yet. I carried on firing until I knew he was well ventilated.

I couldn't see over the hedge now, because of the depth of the field on this side, so I had to presume that the others could be running up the road to try and cut me off.

I squatted down and tried to listen, but it was no good. My hearing was totally fucked for now. My heart was pounding like a steam hammer. I opened my mouth slightly to increase my hearing slightly. "This was creepy," I thought. "Why aren't they doing anything? Is it me? Have I gone deaf?" I snapped my fingers just to make sure. "Nope, I heard that."

"Sod it," I thought. "It's time to go." No point in hanging around waiting for them to get organised. I made my way up the hedge side taking care not to go over on the ploughed hard surface of the field. I kept thinking to myself, "There has to be a better way of making a living," as I went over again on the hard rough surface.

CHAPTER 5

The tall slim figure of Sara Sasco got out from the back of the car. She strolled over to the second car as if she were walking along a beach in the middle of summer, not even aware of the freezing cold night air around her. She looked at the cottage and then back up the way they had come.

"Call Steve. Tell him—" she said. She paused looking about her like a large cat searching for its prey, "—tell him to expect company, and that we've taken some casualties." She went around to the passenger door, opened it, but she didn't get in. Sara had always been good at second guessing people. She knew how to play the game, and she didn't like to lose.

I thought about the guy I had slotted earlier on at the barn and reckoned there was a good chance I could use the car to get away, if his mates hadn't already got there first, but that didn't seem too likely as I would have heard them come past me.

I carried on, trying to stay low. These guys were switched on, they knew I was supposed to be in the cottage and that I might have the briefcase with me.

I moved fast along the hedge bottom, but the frost had turned the once soft earth into rock hard mounds of sharp jagged trenches, some had small pools of ice that cracked under my body weight making me freeze until I knew no one had heard me. The hedge seemed to loom over me like some strange black living creature trying its best to trip me up or catch me out. Its roots stuck out at awkward angles into the field, even the frost had found a way of creeping into my flesh, through any part of my exposed skin, freezing the tiny droplets of sweat on contact.

The base of my spine felt numbed from cold, and every time I took a tumble and fell onto the hard ploughed field my hands lost a bit more skin. I tried so hard to breathe slowly and keep calm, reducing the warm air that bellowed up giving away my position. Scrambling along on all fours like some kind of animal I eventually covered the long distance from the gate up to where I thought the car had stopped.

My eyes had adjusted to the dim light of the night. I could make out most of the ground where I was scurrying along, but it didn't stop me from going down a few more times. I started to look for a way through the hedge. Being winter, all the leaves were off the branches. I spotted a gap, and reckoned if I took the rucksack off I might be able to squeeze through without too much trouble. I slid it off slowly trying not to stretch too much because of my wound. With a bit of tearing of material I pushed my head through the hole half expecting to get a good smack when my face appeared on the other side. I looked around. Below me was the water drainage ditch, it was half full of iced over water. The car was only four metres away but I had actually over-shot it. It looked safe enough to me, so I slid back and then pushed the rucksack through the hedge and pulled myself through. Breaching the water, I really didn't want to get sodden with freezing cold water if I could help it.

Once on the other side, I stayed on the verge for a couple of seconds just taking in any sounds and movements. Treading carefully, I grabbed the nearest lump of root sticking from the hedge. It had the look of an old mans arm, only a lot thinner. It was ice cold and slippery; I let my hand slide down until it lodge on a broken joint, then I chose my footing and leapt across the small creek. Once across, I slung the rifle over my shoulder and drew one of the pistols. It looked safe, so I made my way down to the rear of the car. The engine was still running. Holding the gun out in front of me, I moved forward taking care not to make any sound as my eyes darted around looking for any sign of trouble. I was nearly level with the back of the car. The only sound was from the car engine gently ticking over. I looked at the car, then at the road and back to the car. Why had the car just stopped? The track is slightly sloped all the way down to the cottage. That means that the brakes must have been applied and to do that you usually need to have a pulse, which in turn means whoever was driving could still be alive.

DOWN AT THE HOUSE

"The house looks to be empty apart from John's body" Malk said into his throat mike.

"Stiff, you head up the field until you reach the main road. We don't want him doubling back on us" Sara said, speaking into the laptop's mike. Pressing the enter key, she said, "He's on his way. Make sure you stop him, and don't forget we want him alive." Her eyes watched the tiny red dot barely moving on the screen. She knew he was on the track about one hundred yards behind her. She also knew he would probably kill Johnny and try to use his car for a getaway vehicle, but he wouldn't get far.

I looked around. The only place for someone to hide up here would be in the ditch, and the moonlight was shinning straight down into it. I moved across to the other side of the car keeping a good distance all the time, still checking behind me as I went. Everything looked so still. I pulled the night sight out to get a better look. There was some movement down at the cottage when one by one the lights came on. It looked like they were checking the place out. They must have thought I'd gone back into the cottage.

I lowered the night sight, flicked the covers back over the lenses whilst holding the gun under my arm pit. Bringing the gun back into the firing position, I tried the back door handle. It was unlocked. I yanked it open fast firing a couple of rounds in for good measure. Even with the silencer on, the dull thud from the gun seemed so loud inside the car.

Sara typed away, bringing up the details of Johnny's car. She scrolled down until she found the security system. She typed "test alarm system" and hit enter.

Without any warning, the bloody car alarm went off, lights flashing, the works. "Oh for fuck's sake," I cursed, slamming the car door in frustration. It was fair to say they knew I wasn't having a kip upstairs in bed now. Sara knew if Johnny was in the car he would type in the security code and turn the alarm off. She waited.

The body in the front seat didn't move when I ran around to the driver's door keeping the gun trained on him as I moved.

"Come on, you twat," I said, grabbing a hold of the dead bloke, pulling him out of his seat and onto the road in a heap. I pulled the rucksack and rifle off, placing them on the passenger seat and then climbed in, closing the door behind me. "Very nice," I thought, full leather interior and air con. It was all very nice in here, but the bloody alarm wouldn't cut off, so it wasn't going to be a sneaky get away. It was only a matter of time before this guys mates would be heading my way. I had to get out of here, and the only way to do that would be to reverse back up the track because there was no way I could turn a car like this around in the width of the track. I looked down at the cottage just in time to see both cars turning around, and this time they weren't hanging around. I could hear the tyres spinning on the gravel surface. I started reversing like a man possessed up the narrow lane doing my utmost to miss the pot holes, all the time that bloody alarm was making my brain spin from the violent ear-splitting siren.

It was no good, the car leapt from side to side fishtailing all over the place as I tried to steer with one hand on the wheel and the other hooked behind the passenger seat to keep me steady. Everything in front of me illuminated red, I had to keep my foot partly on the brake whilst I drove, just to create some kind of light to see by. Then I would hit another pot hole and everything was thrown into blackness again.

I came to the crest of the hill and could see down to the main road about two hundred yards away. Everything was in shadow down there and because of the trees it was totally pitch-black, even the moon couldn't cast any light into the shadows of the tree lined entrance. At first, I couldn't make out the junction too well due to the reflections in the glass, but slowly, I started to make sense of the shapes and shadows in the distance. I had no choice. I had to stop and take a look to see if they had left a road block. Slamming the brakes on, the car slid to a stop. I knew I only had a matter of seconds before the other cars came over the top of the hill. From where I was, the junction looked blocked by a couple of vehicles. One was a people carrier of some kind. The other was some sort of car. Two figures moved around, probably waiting for me to make an appearance and to stop me from leaving. Either way, my way out of here was most certainly going to be a bit challenging to say the least. No sooner had I got back in the car, a couple of bullets whizzed past my head from somewhere. I dived back inside, jamming the car into reverse and hit the accelerator just when the hedge and gravel started to glow from the headlights coming up the track. I must have looked like a rabbit caught in the main beam of a car's headlights. They were only forty odd metres away, and they weren't too bothered about how much noise they were making. I flicked the headlights to full beam, just to try and making things a bit more difficult for them

"Don't kill him, you idiots. Wound him!" Sara shouted down the phone at the others waiting at the entrance to the lane. She knew Karl would go mad if Stone was killed before he had a chance to get to him.

The car bounced up and down as it hit the potholes, throwing me around inside the car. My foot kept slipping off the accelerator making the car jolt even more. The rucksack flew through the air along with my rifle. "This is bloody madness," I thought. I could see the guys at the junction bringing their guns up to the aim. I had a quick look back up the track just to see the pair of headlights coming straight at me. "Oh for fuck's sake," I thought, trying to make the car go faster, but the engine was already screaming frantically when the car started to fishtail again. I held my foot in place hoping I could keep the bloody thing on the road. Things were flying all over now; the tyres spun each time the car heaved out from one pothole into another.

The car was bottoming out every few seconds, and I could hardly see where I was going for all the crap that was airborne. While all this was going on my mind figured out what the men down at the junction had in their hands. My interior illuminated as the other car gained ground on me. What could I do – reverse isn't built for speed!

The guys watching me from the junction must have thought the car was out of control by the way it was coming at them, but it didn't stop them from opening up on me once I was within range.

The back window suddenly exploded inwards filling the back seat with tiny shards of glass, with the rain of bullets ripping through the cars interior each one thundering into the seats and dashboard. Then in the same instant, the front windscreen exploded into a thousand pieces all around me. "Fucking hell!" I shouted at the top of my voice, pulling myself down below the level of the seat, trying to keep my foot on the pedal. I didn't have a clue if the car was going to roll or hit them square on. All I knew was that it was going to happen and in the next couple of seconds. The bullets rained in on me from every angle sending bits of sound proofing and glass in all directions.

The dashboard took hit after hit. I had to let go of the wheel and try to get my guns out ready for action. I knew the moment the car stopped or hit them they would open up on me like a shooting range. I had to swing this situation in my favour. The bullets slammed into the car again, this time the dashboard and steering wheel took the brunt. Bits of hard plastic exploded into thousands of pieces with shredded leather floating all around me.

Suddenly, the car heaved then "Oh shit!" I tried to hang onto the seat as the car started to swing in an erratic manner. The g-force did the rest, throwing me from side to side and then back and forth. My head slammed into the passenger door then I smacked into the seat and back down into the foot well. I sprang up to try and get my bearings with my guns ready to start firing, but the car heaved again. This time the whole vehicle lurched, up ending with the nose pointing at a 45 degree angle. I plunged forwards over the front seats and through what was left of the rear windscreen. I slid head over heels down the boot thinking, "Maybe I should have put my seat belt on." Into the ditch, I hit the icy cold water on my back next to the exhaust which was still belting fumes out. There might only have been three or four inches of water in that ditch but it felt like pins being pushed through my skin. When the ice cold water engulfed my back and neck, I realised that the car must have spun right round because I was now looking back up the track towards the oncoming lights.

I popped my head up to see what the other two were doing and got a blast of their guns as a response. I had to turn this situation around somehow. I flicked both guns to automatic and rolled over getting into a squat position. The other two had stopped firing so I could only hope they were reloading or heading towards me. I scrambled up the bank and into the middle of the road whilst firing on automatic. My eyes zoomed in on theirs. The look of surprise said it all. That's all it ever takes in this business. A split second advantage is the difference between life or death. I must have caught them unaware because one of them dropped like a stone. Being hit by several bullets in the stomach has that affect. And the other took a few rounds to his leg by the way he went down. "Pity it didn't kill him," I thought, because then the threat was gone, but as he was he could still pull a trigger.

I reloaded both guns in a matter of seconds. It always seemed to take forever, thankfully it doesn't. The driver in the approaching car had obviously seen what had gone down and was now speeding along the track like a maniac. I took my time. It seemed like minutes were passing, but in real time, it was less then a second. I fired two shots at a time so the recoil of the gun didn't take my aim off target. The driver stamped on the brakes and then started to come forward again. The windscreen had a neat set of holes in it, which wasn't bad considering the light and the movement of the car.

They were only twenty metres away. "Time to go," I thought. I fired again.

"Jesus! Is he just going to let us run him down?" Malk shouted, readying his gun. "He won't move! What's with this guy?" Malk continued shouting.

Stiff was running down the track behind them, not wanting to miss any of the action. As he came to the crest of the hill, he could see Malk's car being fired on but couldn't do anything about it from where he was.

I just stood my ground and kept on firing, hoping to hit the bastard driving at me.

Through the windscreen, the headlights bounced around highlighting the target and then making him disappear in an instant. At that moment the target fired again, but he still didn't move from his position in the middle of the track. Malk looked across at his driver who was now slumped forward having taken two shots in the upper chest. He tried to grab the wheel, but the car had already started to slide out of control. Seven metres away from me the car skewed sideways, then down it went into the ditch.

Sara watched the figure suddenly vanish from view. "He has no fear," she said to herself.

"Hold on, Sara!" Malk shouted, as he fought with the steering wheel.

I dived in through the back window of my car, landing on the rear seats, grabbing the rucksack and rifle. Kicking the rear door open, I rolled out into the ditch again, letting off a few rounds at the other car when I got to my feet. I ran towards the people carrier with my gun trained on the guy on the floor who wasn't dead but not very happy.

He looked up at me shouting, "Do you know who I am?"

"Nope," I said. With my foot on his throat, I shouted, "Who are you working for?"

"Fuck you," he replied.

"Fine," I said. Levelling the gun at his eye, I pulled the trigger.

I looked back at the other car. It had stopped at an odd angle with its front end well and truly wedged down the ditch.

Sara slid across the seat so she could see what the target was doing.

Malk looked at her, asking, "Are you alright, Sara."

"I'm fine," she replied, still watching the man firing a shot into the head of one of her men.

"We should get him to work for us," she said under her breath.

Malk was about to get out and start shooting when Sara said, "He'll kill you from this range, Malk. Let's wait until the odds are more in our favour, shall we." She flipped her phone open, saying, "Steel." The phone dialled the number automatically.

The voice on the other end answered with a simple, "Sara."

She spoke fast and to the point and then finished the call.

"How long until they get here?" Malk asked.

"Twenty minutes," she replied. "He won't get far in that time," she added.

The people carrier was sitting with its engine running. I approached it aiming my gun at the open side door just in case someone was waiting inside to give me a couple of taps to the head. Everything was going at a thousand miles an hour. I had to concentrate, or I could end up dead. I count my way through situations like this: "1: Approach door. 2: Check opening. 3: Visible area clear. 4: Back check (behind me). 5. Enter." It breaks the confusion of a situation down when all hell is going off in multiple directions. I threw the rucksack in and then the rifle. I let off a couple of rounds at the other car just for good measure. It may have been a waste of time, but it made me feel better. I jumped in the driving seat. "Where's the fucking gear knob?" I shouted, flapping, and then realised it was a column shift. I'd never driven a column shift before and made a bit of an arse of it at first, but soon got used to it. I hit the accelerator and went screaming down the lane in a hope of putting some distance between me and the gun club boys. I knew this road well but didn't fancy it, because like all Yorkshire Dales roads, they're narrow and twist and turn with blind bends every few hundred yards. It has its good points though. It keeps whoever is chasing you right where you want them, 'behind'. There are no street lights up here and no cats eyes to guide you, up here it is dark, dangerous and very icy.

Sara approached the dead body in the middle of the track.

"Stop here," she said to Malk. She looked down at the face she had known for so long. His cheek bone had shattered as the bullet had passed through the lower part of his eye socket. She tilted her head slightly to line her eyes up with his and mouthed, "Goodbye, dear brother."

She looked around at the wrecked car and the dead bodies and then walked back to Malk just as Stiff arrived next to him out of breath.

"Get Weister on the phone, will you, Malk, and fetch the laptop from the car. We will follow him in this one," she said, walking towards the Saab that her other man had been driving.

He did as he was told, knowing only too well that when Sara was in this kind of mood it didn't matter who you were. If you didn't do what she asked, it could mean a bullet in the head.

Stiff looked at him, saying, "Do you know anything about this guy we're chasing?"

Malk just looked at him, saying, "I don't know who he is, but I've only ever seen one person shoot like that in all my years."

"Go on," Stiff said, "Who?"

"It doesn't really matter. Karl had him dealt with over ten years ago," Malk said as they walked towards the car.

"Tell me." Stiff went on.

"Enough," Malk said, when they approached the car.

'*Meanwhile back in Puerto Rico*'

Tony Weister had been on his way to Karl Sasco's house when he'd taken the call to see him. "Probably wants to thank me for a job well done," he thought, driving up the long private drive towards the huge multi-million dollar villa that overlooked the surrounding countryside down to the ocean below. He smiled to himself, "One day, my day will come," he said to himself out loud and laughed, slowly pulling the gleaming black Mercedes 500 SL with its tinted black windows into the carport. He made his way across the natural sandstone driveway and up through the beautifully manicured gardens to the entrance of the huge white villa. Karl had made sure the architect designed the building with all the main rooms facing the magnificent views over the 1000 acre grounds that gently sloped down towards the Atlantic Ocean beyond.

The afternoon sun was making him sweat profusely. Tony wasn't one for keeping fit, he loved his food and was quite partial to a drink. Topping the scales at 20 stone and being only 5 foot 4 he was a walking heart attack. Even using the best tailors available he still looked a bit odd in his pale blue suit and white hat. Fashion never became a friend of Tony and his long suffering wife had just given up trying to pull him out of the seventies. He liked the power his job gave him and many times he had found himself with the odds well stacked against him, and if it hadn't being for the fact he worked for Karl Sasco, Tony Weister would have probably being long since dead and buried. He walked up to the big oak doors with the thumb print entry system to the left hand side. He paused to wipe his brow and then pressed his thumb against the small panel next to the doors. Seconds later, a gentle hiss and one of the doors swung open, they were hinged on pivot style hinges, this added to security and design. The cool air inside was refreshing from the 40 degrees outside. A cool waft of air rushed over him from above. Karl had seen the cool wall system in a magazine and insisted that every entrance to the villa had one fitted, they acted like a curtain of cool refreshing air that kept the warm air from penetrating the interior.

Tony walked passed the two guards sitting behind a low line black marble desk. Giving them a slight nod when he walked past, they returned the gesture, but still had their fingers held next to the triggers of their guns under the polished marble top. Two colour LCD monitors sat neatly to one side of the guards showing the entrance from an outside view. The main security centre was deep down in the centre of the villa, where every view of the entire complex could be viewed in any light spectrum required. Karl Sasco slept well at night, knowing nothing could get within 300 metres of his villa from land, sea or air.

Tony sat down behind the large white marble desk that matched the floors and walls of the no expense spared office. Expensive works of art hung from fine wires just millimetres from the pure white walls. The whole room looked like an art gallery. He sat at his desk thinking of the week ahead of him. Karl had asked him to come to his villa for some reason unbeknown to him, but that wasn't out of the ordinary because Karl ran most of his business dealings from here, and Weister knew not to question his boss ever.

He slowly spun the high backed leather chair around to face the full height glass wall behind him. His mind raced, when he thought about the new life he was going to have with his wife and daughter in New Zealand. A smile crept across his face. He'd actually done it at last. In less than six days time, he would be rid of Karl Sasco for good. The gentle whir of the air conditioning was the only sound in the room, until the large oak door that lead into Karl's office opened with a soft hiss. Somewhere in his boss's office, Tony could now hear the familiar sound of ice spinning in a glass. The one thing he liked about his boss, was his ability to enter a room without making any sound. Karl Sasco always spun the ice after finishing his drink. Seconds later:

"Have you got nothing to do, Tony?" said the soft voice from behind him. Tony could see his boss's reflection in the wall of glass, the white suit just seemed to appear, like an illusion.

A bead of sweat ran down Tony Weister's forehead, but he didn't move. Even after all these years, he still felt awkward in his presence.

"I've plenty to do, Karl. I'm just having a rest," Tony replied, adding "I'm going to get my heart checked out, I need to get in shape" he said, trying to be calm.

"Rest," Karl said, slowly placing his hand on Weister's shoulder.

Karl leant forward so his lips were just inches away from Tony Weister's ears and said, "Tell me, Tony what was the name of that man you hired to deliver my briefcases, and tell me why he killed everyone on board my plane including my son?" Sasco's voice never went above a whisper as he spoke, not even when he mentioned the death of his son.

Weister tried to turn the chair round to face his boss, but Karl held him still in the chair. Both his hands gripped Tony Weister's shoulders now, then he whispered again, two words that went through Tony Weister like a bolt of lightning, two words that crushed him, broke him, made his guts twist into knots: "Tom Stone."

"What? No! That's not possible. He's dead. We saw him die. I SAW HIM DIE!" Weister shouted, getting to his feet.

Karl held a small silver disk in his left hand. He placed it on Weister's desk, saying, "This is the recording of what went on during the flight you arranged. One of the men claims his name is 'Tom Stone.' The same man killed everyone on board and most of my men in the hangar on his way out the other end. So you can imagine, Tony, just how frustrating it will be if you've lost the only known photo of this assassin."

Weister was flapping now. Fifteen years ago, a contract had been taken out against the Sasco family. Only, it went wrong, very wrong. Instead of Karl Sasco, the assassin had taken out his wife and newborn son by mistake in the explosion, and it had taken Karl all of three days to find the name of who had arranged the hit. He'd gone over to London, England, in person to kill the assassin responsible.

He found out where he lived and had the whole building destroyed with him in it, killing at least thirty innocent people in the process. Then Karl with only two other men walked straight into the casino in the centre of London knowing Johnny Meakes was inside, and shot him in the legs while his two guards obliterated anyone in their way. The reputation of Karl Sasco had now well and truly landed in England. Johnny Meakes was the head of the largest organised crime family in England. He was a ruthless man with three sons and two daughters. His wife ran the massage parlours while he ran the casinos. His sons took care of the bookies and drug distribution. Johnny was in his mid fifties, and enjoying his life, he had heard of a young man call Karl Sasco trying to make a name for himself by extortion and gun running. Johnny had tried to find out where this vicious little bastard had come from, but all his contacts just kept on coming up with blanks. Sasco was undercutting his prices and had murdered four of his men in the process. So not wanting to be under cut Johnny sent a warning to this young trouble maker, by finding out who he was supplying and making sure they understood just who was pulling the strings.

But Sasco just kept on pushing and pushing, killing anyone

who tried to stop him. Johnny had tried to be reasonable, now he was pissed off. A meeting was set.

Johnny sat in his dimly lit office that overlooked the bright lights of London's West End. This was his stomping ground where he had grown up. A knock at the door and a young man walked in, his short brown leather jacket and shoulder length hair silhouetted from behind. He walked in closing the door behind him. Johnny stood up and gave his young friend a warm hug, "My boys not feeding you" he said in his deep gravely voice, "Your boys eat too much" the young man said. He was 21 years old and reminded Johnny of himself at that age. "I have a job for you Tom, it's a difficult one, and you're going to need your wits about you." Johnny said. The young man just listened to the old man talking. "I want you to kill Karl Sasco, he is becoming a liability to the organisation" Johnny said, passing Tom all the details on the man. "You've been like a son to me Tom, this card has enough money in its account to see you well for plenty of time if things go wrong. I want you to blow this fucker off the planet, never mind shooting him," Johnny said, sitting back down behind his desk after shaking Tom's hand. Two weeks later an explosion had killed Karl Sasco's wife and new born child.

Tony Weister remembered it all like it was yesterday, the way Karl had gone insane with rage, lashing out at everything, until he found out who had ordered the hit. Karl had his wife and children brought to the casino and burnt them alive. He stood there watching until they were dead, and then sent a message out to all the other crime families in London, "The family Sasco" now owned all the assets that the Meakes family used to own. The rest was history by the time he was in his late twenties. Karl had most of the local government in his pocket along with the chief of police. He looked after all his contacts well, showering them with money and expensive gifts. They all knew a time would come when he would call on them for something, but the way they saw it was what harm was he doing. The Sasco family employed thousands of local people and his donation of six million dollars towards a new hospital only added to his reputation of being a kind and wealthy businessman, so a blind eye was turned when anything happened that concerned his name. The legitimate side of his empire employed over two thousand local people in and around Puerto Rico. He felt safe here even though both the FBI and the DEA kept close tabs on his movements. Every murder and drug deal that they just knew he was involved in could never be actually connected to him. Even Interpol wanted him but didn't have enough evidence to take him to court. Karl Sasco was literally a genius, albeit a bad one. He had high court judges and senators in his pocket, and until any of the government agencies had enough evidence to put him away, he wasn't going anywhere. The only contact anyone ever had with him was by phone or bullet. Apart from the Baldman. He was like the grim reaper, whenever he was about it was for one reason – to sort someone out.

"So tell me, Tony," Karl said, walking back towards the now trembling man standing in front of him. "What was the name of the man you hired to work for me?" Karl had a soft smile on his face, when he talked, he knew the answers, he just wanted to make Tony squirm.

Weister pulled a pure white handkerchief from his pocket and wiped his brow. "His name was," he corrected himself, "is Mr. Lee. That's all he told me. He came very highly recommended, Karl, so I felt no reason to question it." The name had come directly from Baldman, and Tony Weister feared him a dammed sight more than Karl. Baldman's reputation for torture was global, rumour had it that Baldman could keep you alive using all kinds of medical fluids while he tortured you. He would kill you and then bring you back for more.

Karl Sasco looked deep into Tony Weister's eyes, saying, "Who recommended him to you, and where's the photograph I hear you have of him?"

"What photograph?" Weister said, now really starting to panic because he remembered his meeting with the so called Mr. Lee and the fact that he'd let him have the photo back.

Just then, the phone started to ring on his desk. His eyes flicked towards it and then back at Sasco.

"Answer it," Karl said softly.

Tony pressed the answer button saying, "Weister speaking. What do you want?" he said in a harsh voice.

The voice on the other end of the line didn't make his day any better, he looked over at where his boss had been standing just in time to see him disappearing into his office closing the solid oak door behind him as he went.

It was Sara. A cold sweat came over him when he sat in his chair terrified at the way he had spoken to her and at the repercussions that would come his way. He tried to be really polite if that was possible without sounding like a complete wimp.

"Oh, hello, Sara. I hope your visit to Europe is going well," he tried to sound cheerful, but his gut was tying him in knots.

"Who do you think you're talking to, Tony, demanding of me what I have to say?" She was winding him up, but he didn't know that and would spend at least six months worrying when his time was up. What did she care? It kept him on his toes.

"I am so sorry. Please forgive me. I, I didn't know it was you. You know that I would never ask, let alone demand, anything of you, Sara."

"Tony, be a darling. Would you tell Karl that I need to speak to him, and Tony, tell him it's urgent," she said in a soft calm voice.

"Yes, yes, of course. I'll tell him right away."

What could he do? She would have him killed just for not doing what she said, but Karl would probably get medieval on him.

He took a deep breath and pressed the intercom button on his desk knowing his boss was already in a bad mood. He waited for the reply nervously. Nothing happened, so he tried again, but this time he held the button down.

No answer.

He pressed it again. This time he kept pressing and releasing the small black button until a voice answered.

"Yes, Tony, what do you want?"

"Your daughter needs to talk to you urgently, Mr. Sasco. She's on line one now," Weister said, trying to sound calm.

"Thank you, Tony," he said. The com went dead.

He knew by experience that just because his boss had been polite over the intercom didn't mean he wasn't boiling over with rage. Karl Sasco was a master at hiding his emotions.

"Hello, darling, how's your little venture going over there? I trust you've caught that little fish you were after," Karl said in his strong soft voice.

"He's killed Simon," she said.

"Do you want me to come over there?" he replied with a concerned tone to his voice. Sara would always be his little girl, no matter what her age.

"No, but can you ring your friends to give me a hand in sorting this out, Dad?"

"Yes, of course, my dear. I will speak to them as soon as we are done, and would you like me to contact your sister? She's in France. She could be of some help."

"Thanks, Dad. I'll call you later," she said, turning her phone off. She knew how to wrap him around her finger, and she knew he would always help her no matter what she wanted.

Once he'd finished talking to his daughter, he pulled a small red leather diary from his inside pocket. Flipping through the pages, he found the name he was looking for: Robinson, Martin. He worked for MI5 and unbeknownst to his superiors had a big gambling problem. He owed one of Sasco's casinos in excess of a hundred thousand pounds. He also liked the young men and women who worked there. His wife didn't know about either, and if he wanted it to stay that way, he had to keep Karl Sasco happy. Robinson knew if he didn't do as he was asked, Sasco would send the photos of him and all the details of his gambling habits to his wife and employers.

Robinson picked up his phone, answering it with a simple, "Robinson."

The moment he heard the voice on the other end of the line, the hairs on the back of his neck started to creep up making him shudder.

"Listen carefully, my friend. I want three men to help Sara track down a problem I have. You will ring her with the details once we have finished talking. Do you understand, Robinson?" Sasco said in a slow deliberate voice.

"What do mean by problem, Mr. Sasco," Robinson asked.

"All you need to know is whoever you send must be able to take orders without question and must not have a problem with killing." Sasco then repeated, "Do you understand. Robinson?" He paused and added, "I expect your full cooperation on this matter, Robinson, or you know what will happen." At that, Karl Sasco finished the call and walked to the door of his office. His hand ran down the solid oak door feeling the grain. He stood there thinking about the loss of his sons. He glanced at the picture of the two of them on the back of the *Enterprise*, his son's super yacht. He thought about the time his sons had asked to join the family business and how proud he was of them. He caught his reflection in the large mirror and paused. Never again will he see his sons standing by his side. Karl Sasco was a dead ringer for Robert De Niro from a distance, but the closer you got to him, the more menacing he looked from the four inch scar running across his left eye or the chiselled hard features of his face.

He went out into the open plan area where Weister sat behind his large marble desk. He was on the phone with his back to Karl chatting and laughing to a friend of his. He had no idea that Karl was just behind him.

Weister felt his presence and ended the call. He spun the chair round slowly until he was facing his boss. Karl Sasco was a big man, and none of it was fat. His hair was the purest of black's, it had stayed the same since his youth, and if it wasn't for the wrinkles on his face, he could easily pass for a man in his thirties. He stared at Weister with those ice blue eyes then asked, "Who was that on the phone, Tony?"

"Oh, just a friend, you, you wouldn't know him. He ....."

Sasco cut him short. "Why is it that you presume I would not know the person who you were talking to, Tony."

Weister was flapping now. He knew by the way Sasco was talking that it was only a matter of time before he blew his top.

Sasco looked over at the large windows that ran the full length of his villa. They in turn looked out over the hills and forests leading down to the small bay where his yacht the *Storm* was moored next to the *Enterprise*. He walked over to the glass wall just standing there looking out to the horizon.

"Get me a drink, Tony," he said in a quiet voice.

Tony walked over to the bar and poured a large Southern Comfort and then dropped two pieces of ice into it. He took it over to Karl on a small silver tray.

He took the drink down in one, leaving the ice spinning in the bottom of the glass and then, without any warning, spun round hitting Weister square in the face with his huge clenched fist.

Weister flew backwards with his arms out in front of him. He literally came off the floor as his legs lifted from the sheer force of the impact. The first part of him to hit the white marble floor was the back of this head which instantly started to bleed along with what was left of his nose and top lip. He lay there groaning. His arms flayed about out of control. He was totally out of it.

Karl walked over to where Weister was splayed out on the floor, squatting down next to him, in his white Arabian cotton suit checking his reflection in the highly polished marble floor saying:

"Do I really need to tell you why that happened, Tony?"

Weister didn't respond. He just made a strange gurgling sound and tried to move his legs.

Sasco gave a deep sigh and tilted his head so their eyes met. Then he leaned closer to Weister's face, and whispered:

"I hope for your sake that the answer that you're grasping at is yes, Tony, because if you make me correct you again, we will have to renegotiate your position in my employment. Do we understand each other, Tony?"

A slight movement of his head gave Sasco the answer he wanted. "Good," he said. "Now when you've finished fucking around on the floor, come into my office. We need to talk about what progress you've made with finding that photo." He stood up, straightened his jacket, and strolled back into his office, closing the door behind him.

CHAPTER 6

Weister lay there thinking about why he had ever agreed to work for this bastard, and then he remembered that card game all those years ago. He was so sure his hand would beat the young flash looking stranger that he upped his bet to ten thousand dollars. The stranger looked nervous but looks can be deceiving as he pulled a pile of notes out of each pocket saying, "There's ten thousand dollars, and I'll raise you $100,000."

You could have heard a pin drop in the dimly lit, smoke filled room as the young man pulled a huge wedge of money from inside his white suit jacket pocket.

Now this put Weister in a real predicament. He knew that his must be the better hand. He asked the house if he could lend the money, but they knew better. They had all seen this before. Time and time again this man had cleaned the house out to the point he owned a 50% stake in the joint.

He looked up at Weister through the smoke saying, "I'll lend you the money, my friend." The bartender heard him, and just turned away shaking his head.

"What?" said Weister.

"I'll lend you the money, if you think you can beat my hand," said the stranger.

"But, I don't even know your name."

"It's Sasco, Karl Sasco, and I assure you I am good for the money, my friend, as any of these gentlemen will tell you," he said, as he sat there slowly spinning the ice in his empty glass with an almost hypnotic effect.

Weister sat there not quite believing what was unfolding in front of him. He looked at his hand. He had the five of hearts, six of spades, the seven of diamonds, and the eight of hearts. Then he looked at the young man sitting opposite him. He looked at his cards again and then back at his opponent.

"Get me another drink," he said out loud, holding his empty glass in the air. The old guy walked over, filled Weister's glass, and mumbled something about fools and money. Weister took the whisky down in one and said, "You're on."

"Ok, shake on it," said Sasco.

As Weister got up to shake Sasco's hand, he let his cards fall onto the table face up. Sasco grabbed his hand holding it tightly. With a slow deliberate up and down movement, he shook Weister's hand. As he did this, he let his cards fall to the table. Weister looked down at the royal flush. The colour that had been there started to drain from his face.

"No, no, no, this can't be. You ,you only…no, I don't…I don't understand," Weister said, backing away from the table. "I haven't got that kind of money."

Karl stood up, gently placing his glass on the table. "Let's talk, Tony. Let's talk about how we're going to sort this mess out."

"Yes, yes, that's a good idea," said Weister.

"My car's outside," said Sasco. "Let's take a ride while you tell me how you're going to repay me."

"Repay," said Weister. "I can't repay you. Where the hell am I going to get that kind of money?"

Karl Sasco took a deep breath and put his hand on Tony Weister's shoulder. "I think I know how we can resolve this situation, my friend."

And that was that. That was how Tony Weister ended up working for Karl Sasco.

He pulled himself to his feet and staggered over to the small marble wash basin next to the bar. He washed his face trying to get his head straight. He took a look at himself in the mirror. "Bloody hell," he thought. "Where's my nose gone?" He couldn't see too well because of his eyes swelling up, but he knew if he didn't hurry up and get into Sasco's office, he would end up on the end of another beating or worse. He straightened himself up and walked across to those big oak doors that seemed only to bring bad luck to his life. He knocked twice and went in.

Karl was sat on the edge of his desk with a big smile on his face and a cigar in his left hand. "Come in, Tony, and pull a chair up. Don't worry about what happened out there. That's all forgotten about now. You're still my man, aren't you, Tony," he said and then took a long drag on the cigar.

"Of course I am," Weister said, dabbing his nose gently with his handkerchief.

"Good. Then down to business," Sasco said, walking around to his leather chair. He looked over at Weister; "When Sara was on the phone earlier, she said things aren't going too well over in England. Would you know anything about that, Tony?" he asked, whilst sitting down.

Tony looked up, saying, "All I know is that the person who was carrying the formula and the final detonation device has taken it upon himself to try and get more money out of us before he hands it over."

"And that's all you have to tell me, is it," Karl said, adding, "Please correct me if I'm wrong, but I had been led to believe that the exchange would be taking place today at 3.30p.m. Do you realise what will happen if the exchange doesn't go ahead on time? Well, let me enlighten you, Tony. My clients will go elsewhere, and I will be $30 million out of pocket. You don't want me to be $30 million out of pocket, do you, Tony?" Sasco said, staring at him. Still in a calm voice, he added, "Get me all the information we have on this Tom Stone you hired for this job. I want to know what makes him tick."

"But I didn't know it was Stone," Weister blurted out, adding, "He's just using that name to bluff us."

"That is of no interest to me now," Sasco said calmly, adding, "If you want I can ask the Baldman to sort this out, I don't mind either way its up to you Tony" he said.

Weister may have looked like he was listening, but his brain was going in several different directions at the same time. He remembered when Karl Sasco had said to him, "When you find a carrier for this contract get all the background on him just in case things go to the wall because we don't want any fuck ups, do we?"

"WELL!" Sasco shouted at Tony.

He hadn't heard the question, because he was still trying to think of a way out of this. But he still said, "I don't know."

"You don't know?" said Sasco. "What do you mean you don't know? How can you not know the name of the person you hired? What bloody planet are you living on, Weister?"

"Look," said Weister in a raging voice, "My mind was elsewhere, okay? I'm finding it a bit hard to concentrate at the moment, because you found it in your infinite wisdom to smash my face in just ten minutes ago, so please forgive me," he said in a sarcastic voice, "If I seem a little side tracked." At that, Weister got up and walked out of the office slamming the door behind him. It was the first time he had ever dared raise his voice at Karl Sasco. Saying that, it was the first time he'd even answered him back. He sat in his chair with his head in his hands, tears pouring from his eyes at the thought of what Sasco would now do to his family for his outburst. He had to hold it together for his wife and daughter's sake.

Karl lit another cigar and sat back in the large leather chair. He knew Weister would be in a right state in the other room. He smiled and couldn't help thinking of the power he had over this pathetic individual. Pressing a small button on the arm of his chair to activate the mike built into the high backed seat, he told his crew to get the yacht ready for sea. It was time to use some misdirection on all the special ops watching his villa. Sasco had even gone to the trouble of having several body doubles due to the amount of times his rivals had tried to kill him. He knew all the roads were watched by the Feds. They liked to keep track of him, so if he wanted to go anywhere without the authorities knowing, he would send a decoy by sea and then by air under cover of darkness. It was a pain in the arse, but most of his customers didn't have a very good reputation with the authorities. It wasn't too hard for him because most of the local police and government were in his pocket much to the annoyance of the FBI and Interpol. Karl often used police cars to travel in. He had his security unit, that were all ex Delta Force and very loyal, he paid them well and expected total obedience. His head of security was a monster of a man who trained with Karl every morning, kick boxing running shooting, they had become good friends over the years, only Karl knew his real name, everyone else just called him Pitch. It wasn't an insult because of his colour, it was because he had told them to call him that, and unless you wanted a bust nose, you called him Pitch.

Weister looked at the gun lying in his desk drawer. He always kept it loaded just in case.

"What if I kill him?" he thought. "His family won't know until it's too late. The new identities will be ready at the end of the week anyway. Yes, that's what I'll do. I'll kill him." The thought of Karl Sasco out of his life brought a new wave of strength to Tony Weister's sad, downtrodden existence. He looked at the gun again in the deep drawer. Looking at it gave his confidence a boost. He stood up, a drop of blood dripped from his nose landing in the middle of the clean white marble desk top.

Wiping the tears from his eyes, he took a couple of deep breaths. The pain in his nose throbbed like a hammer, but he had only one thing on his mind, "Kill Sasco."

"This is it," Weister said to himself, walking towards the door that almost seemed to have a strength of its own, making him sweat the closer he drew towards them. This time he didn't bother to knock. This time he went straight in.

BACK IN ENGLAND

I didn't bother to check my rear view mirror whilst I headed along the narrow road that would take me deep into the Yorkshire dales. I wish I had, because I would have seen the headlights in the distance and done something about it. My eyes strained when the fog grew thicker by the mile, forcing me to slow down to almost a crawling pace. The speedometer read 15 mph, and all I could see out of the windscreen was a wall of light grey freezing fog. The bonnet looked like a furry white blanket, the frost wasn't shifting from the bare metal and I knew my headlights would be freezing over only adding to my predicament.

I flicked the headlights from main beam to dip and then to fog lights, but nothing seemed to improve the lack of visibility. Every hundred yards or so, my tyres rubbed against the grass verge, each time a sharp corner came upon me without any warning I ended up going over the snow covered grass and back down onto the road again, making me over steer onto the opposite bank. The only good thing about the situation was it would slow the others down. If they tried to follow me at the speed they were going, they would be in great need of a recovery truck. I flipped my mobile open which in turn turned the power on. After a couple of seconds, the screen said no signal, but I decided to leave it turned on until I got one.

Malk drove at a steady 30 mph, the hot air blowing around the interior made his eyes dry, but Sara wanted it nice and warm and who was he to argue. He had to slow down once the fog became too thick. "There's no way he's going anywhere fast in this weather," he said, peering into the freezing fog.

Sara looked up from the laptop for a second answering with a simple, "Keep going." 'Malk glanced back at her through the small rear mirror, 'Keep going, keep fucking going' he thought.

She didn't like asking her father for help, but this was getting out of control, and she knew that once he was involved her position in the task would be secondary, because Malk would then answer to Karl directly and not to her. She wasn't about to let Malk know who was running the show now, ordering him to call the rest of her team to meet up with them en route because the target was now transmitting again.

"He's about three miles up this road heading northeast. Looks like he's hit fog or something by the speed he's going," she said, looking at the laptop.

"Excellent," Malk said, whilst using his hands free set to contact the rest of the team.

"How long until the others catch up" she asked now peering out the side window into the fog.

"Should be with us in ten minutes, depending on how bad the fog gets on the Skipton road." Malk replied, with his eyes glued to the road, trying to catch a glimpse of the target's car taillights.

'*Back in Puerto Rico*'

Karl was sitting in his chair smoking a cigar when Tony Weister burst through the large office door holding a gun out in front of him.

Karl watched him like a cat watching a mouse and then said, "You seem a little upset, Tony."

"It's time someone sorted you out, Sasco!" he shouted, in a very nasal tone still wiping the blood from his face with one hand while the other waved the gun about while he spoke.

"Oh, I see," Karl answered, taking a long slow drag on the Cuban cigar.

"And how exactly do you intend to sort me out then?"

"Look at you. You're pathetic," he paused then added, "You really think it's that easy, do you." Karl didn't even flinch while he was talking to Weister. In fact, he was totally relaxed.

"Put the gun down, Tony," he said.

"Put it down, and let's talk about why you are so upset. Is it about the disagreement we had earlier, because I had put that behind us?" His voice was hypnotic like a snake drawing its prey in.

"Come on, Tony," he said with a smile on his face.

"Give me the gun, and let's sort this out."

Tony Weister was no fool. He knew if he backed down now he would end up dead.

"No," he said, "This time you won't talk your way out of trouble. You're a dead man, Sasco. You're history." Coughing a long drooling line of blood and snot up, that slid from his bust nose right down to the floor.

"Tony, Tony, Tony, I'm not a dead man. I am very much alive. Now put the gun away, my friend. You've had your little tantrum. Now let's get on with things. You need to see the doctor first and get that mess sorted out."

At that, Tony levelled the gun at Karl Sasco and pulled the trigger.

The sound went through his head like a hammer echoing around the room. He pulled the trigger again and again just to make sure that it was happening.

Three more times he pulled the trigger, and each time the sound echoed in his head. Karl sat there, looking perfect, his deep aqua green silk shirt didn't have any holes in it, and there wasn't blood running down that cotton jacket.

Click, click, and click every time he pulled the trigger. "Click." His face was contorted with frustration. Why wasn't he dead? He kept pulling the trigger, his eyes filling up with tears. His knees buckled and he fell to the floor sobbing.

"Why can't I kill you? Why? You bastard! I hate you!"

Karl walked around from his desk. He looked down at Weister placing his hand on top of Tony's head.

"You know," he said, "You should always check that the gun is loaded before you try shooting someone."

Weister turned his head to look up at Sasco, saying, "How did you know? I mean, you couldn't have known that I hadn't checked the gun before coming in here."

"Trust me, Tony. I always make sure the odds are stacked in my favour, just like they were all those years ago." At that, he started laughing out loud, "You're such a fool," he said, patting him on the shoulder. Then he walked off and out of the office.

Weister stayed where he was for a good ten minutes on his knees trying to figure out what he was going to do now. There was no way he could stay here. Sasco would have him killed without a doubt for trying to shoot him. He got to his feet and walked slowly into his office still with the gun in his hand. The other thing that was really bugging him was why Sasco hadn't shot him there and then. Maybe by standing up to his boss, he had gained some kind of respect from him. Weister looked at his watch. It was nearly time to pick his daughter up from school. He always picked her up because his wife worked for K.S. Imports, which was in turn owned by Sara Sasco. She liked to get her money's worth out of the people she employed. He hated the fact that they both worked for the Sasco family especially when his wife knew nothing of the corrupt side of the business.

Tony walked over to the concealed cupboards that were built into the wall, he pressed the panel, and it gently slid open to reveal a full set of white shirts and various colours of jackets. Karl insisted that all the rooms had this setup, for that 'just in case' situation that tended to occur. Tony washed his face in the perfect white basin, leaving blood on all the white towels, he stuffed tissue paper up his nose to stem the blood, while he changed his shirt for a clean one.

His wife ran the office over at K.S. Imports, and she was good at it. It had only taken her two years to become manager of the entire admin department, much to the annoyance of the other junior managers who had been there for a lot longer than she had; but she had a lot of respect amongst her colleagues and was proud of what she had achieved. She had no idea that her promotion only happened because of her husband working for Karl. She knew Tony worked for a large shipping company, but she had no idea that his boss owned both companies.

Weister got his keys out of the desk drawer and headed down to the carport at the bottom of the building where his Mercedes was parked. It was one of the benefits that came with being Karl Sasco's right hand man, his car, his house, his lifestyle was that of a well paid executive, but part of the cost was having to put up with the violence that Sasco was capable of. His reputation was known all over the world. He was not a person to cross or be in debt to. Sasco had killed at least ten people that he knew about. So the fact that he'd just tried to kill him had put Tony in a bit of a dilemma. He decided to call him on his mobile to arrange a meeting just so they could clear the air between the two of them.

Karl was expecting the call and answered it the second the phone rang.

"What do you want, Tony?" he said in his usual calm voice.

"I just wanted to apologise for what happened in your office," said Weister.

"Oh, and that's the matter closed in your eyes, is it, Tony?"

Weister didn't like the way this was going at all. "Well no," he said, trying to think of some way he could reap back some of the rapport they had.

"Well no," said Karl. "Is that all you can think of? You pulled a gun on me, Tony. You know I cannot let you get away with that, don't you?"

"But Karl, no one else saw what happened. We were the only ones there, and you know I won't tell anyone about it, don't you," said Weister, walking along the terrace towards the carport.

"Tony, Tony, Tony," came the soft voice over the phone. I tell you what. Seeing that you've been so loyal over the years, I'll give you a choice."

He could only guess at what his boss was going to say. He knew by the way Sasco had just talked to him that it was going to be bad, terrible, or worse. He pressed the key fob to unlock his Mercedes. Still holding the mobile to his ear, he sat down into the cream leather driving seat of the 500 SL.

"You can fly over to England and deal with our mutual friend, and when I say deal with him, I mean find out where his parents live or sisters, brothers, any living relative, then bring them to me, or you can stay here, and I will personally deal with your family. You do understand, don't you Tony," Karl said, finishing the call.

Tony sat there thinking for all of two seconds and then tried calling him back, but his phone was busy. He tried three more times, but he still couldn't get through. His nose started to bleed again, which only added to his frustration. Eventually his temper got the better of him as he slammed the phone into its cradle bending it in the process.

"Bastard!" he shouted out loud, hitting the steering wheel repeatedly. He knew Sasco was playing with him, making him sweat. He'd seen it so many times, but he never expected to be on the receiving end of Karl's mind games. He tried wiping the blood from his nose and chin but only managed to smear it across his face and along the sleeve of the new pale yellow jacket. Tears of frustration grew in his eyes when he imagined what his little girl would think when she saw her daddy covered in blood, but what could he do? He had to pick her up from school. He looked at his watch, 3.45p.m. He was already late. Hitting the accelerator, the big Merc literally leapt out of the carport, its tyres screeching when the big car tore down the private driveway, passing the perfect lawn, gardens, and palm trees on either side of the hand-laid cobbled driveway towards the heavy steel gates that kept the outside world away from Karl Sasco's huge villa and grounds. The two armed guards watched the car coming towards them at a ridiculous speed. Neither of them moved. Karl had given them instructions to only let Tony Weister leave the grounds when he contacted them. Weister couldn't understand why the guards hadn't opened the gates when they saw him coming. He waited right until the last second before slamming the brakes on. The anti-lock system brought the Mercedes to a silent standstill only feet from where the guards stood.

Weister lowered his window shouting, "Open the fucking gates now!" It came as a shock to him when neither guard moved, after fifteen years of people doing what he told them to do instantly.

He shouted again, "You know who I am, so open the fucking gates!"

The guard closest to him walked forwards while the other raised his gun pointing it directly at Tony Weister's head.

"We have instructions to hold you here until we are told otherwise."

"Who gave that order?" he barked back at the guard, already knowing the answer in his head.

"Mr. Sasco," said the other guard. "Oh and he asked me to give you this" the guard said, Tony looked up at the guard, wincing from the sun being directly behind him, 'SMACK' the guard belted him straight in the nose, looking back at his mate – they both burst out laughing. Tony didn't even see the punch coming. The impact squashed his nose right across his face, splitting the skin leaving bits of bone showing. Tony Weister was about to pass out when the guard lent in through the window, injecting him with something. 'Adrenalin' just enough to keep him alert.

Tony closed the car window so the air conditioning could do its thing. He felt terrible yet very awake at the same time. He knew there was no point in arguing with them. If he tried anything, they would just shoot him. He used his shirt to pad his nose, he looked a state, quietly thinking about what he'd done and the repercussions that would follow. He only needed to make it through this week, and he would be rid of all this forever. He had to buy some time for his family's sake. But the sound of sirens from the far side of the wall broke his train of thought. At the same time, one of the guards tapped on his window gesturing for him to move. It was only then that Weister realised the huge steel gates had been opened.

MEANWHILE IN THE YORKSHIRE DALES, ENGLAND

The gentle sound of my phone bleeping away was nearly lost in the background noise as all my concentration was on the road ahead. The heater was on full blast, but it didn't seem to be doing much to the overall temperature inside the car. My hopes of a quick getaway were long gone. Bit by bit I had to slow the vehicle down to an almost walking pace. I had no idea of how far I'd come or if I'd lost my pursuers, and the only thing in my favour was the freezing fog. My left hand scrambled around on the passenger seat trying to find the phone, but it seemed to have disappeared. Eventually, I gave up and pulled over to have a proper look only to find it laying face down in the foot well. "Five bars" on the signal strength. "That'll do," I said to myself, pressing the scroll button to find Ian's number. I d' known him since we were at school together, and over the years, we'd tried to keep in touch. But one thing had led to another, and like all friendships, our contact with each other had been lost from time to time, but we always seemed to catch up every now and then. He was a big bloke and strong with it. Not the kind of person you'd want to get on the wrong side of. He most definitely fitted into the "stand and get battered or run like hell category." I remember the last time we'd met up. He'd set himself up as a buyer and seller of anything he could make a profit on, from toilet rolls to houses. If he could find it cheap enough, you could guarantee he'd buy it, stick a couple of quid on the price, and flog it on to some poor unsuspecting punter.

When we'd met up, he had a grin like a Cheshire cat across his face. Before I had a chance to say "how you doing," he put his arm around my shoulders saying, "You won't believe what I've got in the lockup, Tom. We're goanna make a killing, I tell ya."

We headed for his lockup while he told me about the fortune we were about to make, and the flash cars we were going to be driving. He was so hyped up over his latest venture I just nodded away letting him do his sales pitch to me. Eventually we got to his lockup after what seemed like the world's longest five minute walk. He slid back the large grey rust covered doors to reveal the biggest pile of jeans I'd ever seen.

"Now that's one big pile of washing" I said, casting my eyes over the blue denim mountain.

"No, you don't understand," he spouted. "These jeans don't have any labels in them yet."

I looked at him with a vacant expression on my face then said, "So."

"Don't you see?" he said, walking around his big blue denim mountain. "Once we put the big brand labels in them, we'll make an absolute fortune."

"Ok," I said, looking at the pile of creased unpackaged jeans lying all over the cement floor, scratching my head. "How do you intend to fasten the labels on, and package them, presuming you have the labels anyway, and who's going to do it?" I said, still standing in the doorway to the lockup.

He walked over to me saying, "This is the opportunity of a lifetime, Tom, easy money, and we can share the profit 60/40."

"60/40," I said.

"Hey, I did all the negotiations, you know, and it was my contacts that found them," he said, trying to look the big business man.

"Ian," I said, looking at him, "My job isn't exactly mainstream stuff. You know that," I said.

He looked at me for a second. "Do you still use that rifle I had made for you?" he said.

What could I say? Yes, it plucks an eye out at a thousand yards and I'd like another please? "It did a fine job for many years Ian, but like all precision instruments it eventually needs replacing at some point," I said. The one thing I could never get my head around was how he had the skill and contacts to make a lot of money in my kind of business. Yet he had this thing about trying to make a couple of quid on all sorts of shitty little scams like some kind of market trader.

He looked at me for a second and then said, "You'll regret it, you know." I was about to say how I could mentally cut it off, when he added, "There's a good chance you could end up with a couple grand in your pocket once we've moved them on, you KNOW." He raised his voice trying to persuade me.

"I tell you what, Ian," I said, placing my arm around his shoulder this time, "You deserve to take all the profit on this one, so let me buy you a drink as a thank you for offering me such a great opportunity."

"But, but," he said, still trying to sell me the idea of sewing a thousand labels onto a thousand badly creased pairs of jeans.

"No, I insist," I said. Needless to say, the last time I saw him he was sitting next to a huge pile of jeans with a big smile on his face sewing away like a man possessed. His face said it all though. "More profit for me then" was written right across it.

That had been nearly three years ago now, and we'd only spoken twice over the phone, I had no idea how he would react to me phoning him at quarter to six on a cold November morning, but I was about to find out. I let the phone ring for a couple of minutes until a voice on the other end answered.

"Thanks for calling. I'm not in so leave a message." It pissed me off a bit because I never liked talking to answer machines, so I left a brief message.

"Ian its Tom It is of the utmost urgency that you call me as soon as possible." I repeated the message adding my number each time, hoping he would check his calls whenever he returned.

The fog hadn't lifted in the slightest since I'd pulled in to make the call. In fact, it seemed to be getting thicker. It's not so bad driving in these conditions, if you know the road, but I really didn't have a clue where I was now. For all I knew, I could have missed several turnings on the passenger side of the vehicle because I simply couldn't see that side of the road. I set off again hoping the fog would clear. It did from time to time raising my hopes for maybe a quarter of a mile. A thick white frost covered everything the headlights lit up. Even the road surface had a glistening grey white appearance. Then patches of fog appeared again, and back into another wall of light grey freezing fog. A red light on the dashboard started to flash catching my eye, and then I noticed the temperature gauge. "Oh, that's just fucking spot on," I moaned, I watched the tiny pale green illuminated needle creep past the red line on the dash. Then as if by magic, the oil light joined the temp gauge, flashing away. It wasn't just fog now in front of me. There was steam coming from under the bonnet.

"The target's only one or two miles ahead," Sara said, looking down at the laptop. When she spoke, Malk looked in the rear-view mirror. Sara's face looked so pale from the illumination of the screen.

"Just how long until Stiff, and the others catch us up?" she said, still watching the screen.

"Type his ID code in then press enter," Malk replied.

She typed away for a couple of seconds, and then a small blue dot appeared on the screen with a set of tiny letters next to it: *stf*. The small icon seemed to be almost on top of their signal. She looked up from the screen saying, "He's just behind us. That is, if this data is correct."

"Trust me, Sara," Malk said and then added, "Stiff's one of the best drivers I know. You can bet he didn't drop much below a hundred getting here no matter what the conditions were. It's like he knows what's coming before he gets there. He paused and added, "That and the fact he's a complete nutter," he said, looking in the mirror.

I pulled onto the grass verge and turned the engine and lights off. It wasn't like I had a choice in the matter. I had to let the engine cool down, or I would be walking from now on, and by the looks of the weather, that was most definitely out of the question. Flicking the interior light on, I checked how many rounds I had left in each gun, reloading where necessary. I stuck a couple of clips down my jean pockets, which is bloody uncomfortable but handy. Once I'd done that, I turned the light off. I didn't want a flat battery as well. While I sat there in the darkness trying to make some kind of plan, something got my nerves going, and it wasn't sitting in the middle of the Yorkshire moors on a cold winter's night. I opened my door letting the freezing cold air rush in. "Fuck's sake," I moaned, the difference in temperature took my breath away. I just sat there dead still, listening. Everything seemed to close in when my concentration was trying to focus in on something that my mind just couldn't place. It wasn't the hissing of boiling water forcing its way through whatever hole had blown out from under the bonnet. It was a car's engine. "A car engine, oh shit," I cursed.

"He must be within a hundred yards," Sara said, closing the laptop and leaning forward. She was about ask Malk to pass her the charge cable for it, when without any warning the tail lights of the targets car appeared from nowhere out of the dark grey fog.

"Malk," she screamed into his ear, but he'd seen the lights at the same time as she had and was already aiming the car at the targets rear end in a bid to ram it off the road.

I slammed the door shut just when the fog behind me started to grow lighter from the headlights piercing through it. Seconds seemed to turn into minutes as I turned the key, but nothing happened. "Come on, you bastard!" I shouted. I turned it again, willing the bloody thing to start. The engine turned over and then stopped again.

"Start, you fucker! Just fucking well start!" I shouted again, just when the engine burst into life. My hand automatically reached to where the gear stick would normally have being, until I my mind caught up with the rest of my body. It felt like everything I was doing was in slow motion, but subconsciously, I knew only a fraction of a second had passed.

The wheels spun on the ice when I hammered the accelerator. I was literally leaning forward in the seat trying to get the bloody thing going just when the car rammed my rear end, throwing my arms involuntary into the air making me bounce back and forth in my seat. The impact pulled my foot clean off the accelerator, making the people carrier's engine nearly stall again, but thankfully it didn't. The impact had pushed me back into the centre of the road. I hit the accelerator again. This time, the vehicle lurched forward, the tyres found some grip on the icy surface.

Malk was about to set off after the target when "Crunch!" The force of the impact smacked Sara straight into the back of the front seats, smashing the laptop in the process. The car that hit them pulled up alongside lowering its window. Malk lowered his and was about to give the other driver a mouthful, when a familiar voice said, "Silly fucking place for a picnic, don't you think."

Malk looked over at Stiff's grinning face through the car's window and said, "I think Sara wants a word."

The smile quickly disappeared from his face when he mouthed, "She with you?"

Malk nodded slowly, Stiff's mobile started to ring.

He flipped it open saying, "Sorry about that Sara."

"Just get after him now," she finished the call seeing Stiff's car speed off into the fog, disappearing almost instantly.

"He better not lose him," she said, looking down at the broken laptop.

"He won't," Malk replied, setting off after him.

This was total madness. I couldn't see a bloody thing before, and nothing had improved in the last few minutes. The people carrier bounced from side to side as I fought with the wheel trying my best not to hit the dry stone walls that lined both sides of the steep grass verges, nor did I need to check my mirror to see where my pursuers were when their headlights illuminated the walls on either side of me. I'd been in car chases before but nothing like this. These were not the conditions to be driving at break neck speeds down deserted country lanes. Blinding fog hid every corner giving me no room for any mistakes. Without warning, the fog would just vanish letting the full moon give me a glimpse of the surrounding country side and then straight back into the freezing fog.

It's not like in the films where the chase goes on for hours as miles pass by and the hero always gets away. In the real world, there's only one plan, and it's not complicated: Drive like your life depends on it or stop and get shot, and I knew from experience that once an engine overheats, it's only a matter of time before it seizes up. First, the water evaporates into high pressurised stream putting extreme pressure on all the gaskets, and then the oil will start to lose its ability to lubricate the high speed movements of the engine parts. After that, it's only a matter of time before the oil alters its density and becomes too thin to be of any use. After that, your clock's ticking towards a bang and a shit load of steam.

The long straight section of road and clear night sky gave me a chance to build up some speed, but the car behind me just had the edge and was closing the gap between us all too quickly. Both vehicles being pushed to their limits as the road followed the steep contours of the hillside. The guy chasing me seemed to have no fear of speed or crashing. He was literally pushing me along. My heart sank when I saw the fog bank up ahead. I glanced down at the dash board: 97 mph, and it was lit up like a Christmas tree with warning lights. My grip on the steering wheel tightened with the imminent impact of what ever lay beyond the dull white wall of freezing fog, I could feel the engine starting to stiffen up from over-heating, and all the time my mind raced 'head down and just go for it or the second I hit the fog slam all on, dive clear and wait for the crash.

The grey wall of freezing fog grew closer and closer. He must have being doing well over a hundred down the straight because he hit my rear bumper with so much force I nearly lost control.

Stiff dropped a gear in the BMW M5 and floored it, he didn't give a shit if he knocked the target clean off the road, just so long as he wouldn't have to get any dirt on his new Armani suit. "Fuck off!" I shouted. Casting a glance in the mirror that seemed to last for an hour, his face illuminated in red by my rear tail lights, that image buried its self deep inside my head. I knew he couldn't possibly hear me, but it made me feel better. Seconds later, he rammed me again. Two seconds and the road plunged back into the almost solid wall of freezing fog.

"Oh no," I said quietly to myself. My mind raced as to what I could do. Grabbing my gun, I part turned in my seat and fired several shots over my shoulder through the rear window. His reaction was immediate, the car's headlights dipped, showing me he had his foot firmly on the brakes. "Fuck, fuck ,fuck" I jabbered away looking at the frosted glass windscreen I had to try and see through, I couldn't see a bloody thing, then a metallic banging came from somewhere ahead of me, the engine had decided enough was enough black smoke belched out from under the bonnet. I was still doing 80mph though, and now a strange smell of burning rubber filled the cars interior underlining the shit I was about to be in.

Malk drove hard and fast through the gloom until it lifted to reveal a long straight. In the distance, they saw a pair of tail lights for a couple of seconds before they vanished back into the fog.

"That must be Stiff," Malk said, accelerating down the long steep hill. Sara sat back in the seat not speaking. She knew it was only a matter of time before the target made a mistake and crashed. She flipped her phone open, but it showed no signal. This didn't bother her. The call could wait.

MEANWHILE IN PUERTO RICO

Weister's phone chimed away in its holder, until he pressed speaker on the steering wheel.

"Tony, have you got an answer for me?" said Karl Sasco in his usual calm voice.

"Yes, I have," said Weister.

"And," said Sasco.

"I will go and sort out our problem in England," he said, doing his best to sound relaxed.

"No, you won't," came the harsh reply.

"But you said..."

"What I said was you go and sort the problem out, your problem, not ours. Now was there anything else you want to waste my time with, or are you done?" Sasco's voice was so full of rage that Weister nearly lost control of the car out of fear. He ended the call before Weister could reply, knowing this would get Weister's nerves going. Karl had a slight smile on his face as he looked out through the tinted windows of the black Bentley as it glided along the road that lead down to the private marina where his super yacht the *Storm* was moored. He'd bought it at the same time as the *Enterprise* for his son. Both yacht's were identical in looks apart from Karl's was fifteen metres longer than the *Enterprise*. This had been a matter of respect for his father. Both yachts had helipads and a full crew.

The gleaming black Bentley approached the entrance to the marina, and the wrought iron gates opened automatically, operated by the guard behind the bullet proof glass window of the offices that sat alongside the entrance. Karl typed a code into the armrest then pressed send. The man behind the window looked down at his screen beneath the window when his car passed by, the code simply confirmed who was in the car so the guards and sniper could stand down, to Joe public nothing had occurred.

The guard wrote in his day book that Mr. Sasco had arrived and the registration number of his car "S1." The beautiful Bentley pulled to a gentle stop. One of the marina's staff ran forward to open the door for Mr. Sasco in a hope of getting a tip when a large man in a dark blue suit and sun glasses stepped in front of him.

"Step back please," he said.

The porter didn't argue. He knew Karl Sasco had his men everywhere in the area. He tilted his head down and walked away quickly not wanting to cause a fuss.

The man in the suit opened the door for his boss passing him a small piece of paper. Karl read it while his driver pulled the car into its parking place. Without even looking at the man he said, "Bring her to me alive," he paused and added, "I want her here as soon as possible." Looking across at the yachts, his ice blue eyes glistening in the bright mid day sun, he pulled out a large cigar from his inside pocket and a silver trimmer. Snipping the end off, he ran the cigar slowly under his nose taking in the fresh smell of tobacco and then placed the hand rolled Cuban cigar in his mouth. The bodyguard standing next to him held a gold lighter up letting his boss gently waft it over the flame. After a couple of seconds, both men walked slowly towards the jetty. The bodyguard walking a couple of steps behind his boss looking from side to side, knowing his back was covered by the rest of the team spread around the grounds of the marina.

'*Meanwhile up at the head quarters of Sascorp Int*'

The three men walked into the reception of Sascorp Int. One stopped just inside the large glass doors letting the other two head towards the receptionist's desk. The young girl looked up with a smile on her face saying, "Good morning, gentlemen. How can I help?"

The youngest man in his late twenties said, "Can you tell Mary Weister that Mr. Sasco would like her to join him on the *Storm* immediately?"

The young girl's face said it all. She'd never have guessed that her manager actually knew the Sasco family personally.

"Yes of course," she said, fumbling with the phone. The two men didn't move from their positions until they saw Tony Weister's wife coming down the stairs. She was an attractive woman in her mid-thirties with long dark brown hair, but she always wore it up for work. The pale blue trouser suit she had on fitted her well, complementing her figure. When she approached the two men, she asked, "Why does Mr. Sasco need to see me on his yacht and not in his office?"

"Please come with us Mrs. Weister," the older man said, stepping forward, placing his hand behind her to guide her out of the building.

She looked over at the receptionist, saying, "Hold all my meetings until I return."

She walked outside with the three men, again she asked what was going on, but the men just replied, "All we've been told is to take you to the *Storm,* Mrs Weister" the eldest man said. He was in his late fifties with a well trimmed beard and greased back grey hair. The black Mercedes was parked just out of sight of the main entrance to the massive new green glass-fronted building of Sascorp. When they approached it, one of the three men pressed the key fob opening the boot. Before she could say anything, a hood was placed over her head, then a pair of hands grabbed her legs. She felt the drawstring on the hood pull tight around her throat making it nearly impossible to breathe through. Seconds later, her ankles and wrists were bound together then all went quiet as the boot lid closed above her. Seconds later the large car pulled out from the entrance gates and accelerated down the long full width drive that lead down to the main road with its extra passenger safely concealed in the boot.

Weister pulled over and stopped, his mind going at a thousand miles an hour. How could he tell little Carrie that he wouldn't be home for her birthday? Mary, his wife, would want to know why he just couldn't say no when his boss asked him to do some stupid job. He set off again down towards the school, but he wasn't concentrating on what he was doing. His mind was miles away in England trying to sort out the mess he had gotten himself into.

Karl pulled the custom made gold plated gun out of its shoulder harness and looked at the engraving round the grip:

TO STEAL A SOUL AND KILL A MEMORY

This gun had been a present from his son and would be the bringer of justice to Karl Sasco's enemies and his friends if need be.

CHAPTER 7

Tony Weister looked a mess. He had blood all down his shirt, and he was panicking about what the hell he was going to tell his wife. "More lies," he thought. He seemed to spend all his life lying to his wife about where he was or what he was doing, and it all boiled down to Karl Sasco .

The school buildings dominated the immediate view out of his driver's side window. The former monastery buildings had been totally restored some twenty years ago into a luxury private school. The whole thing had been financed by Sasco, just so he could send his daughters there and gain an even tighter grip on the local government who's children just happened to end up enrolling free of charge.

As Weister approached the beautifully manicured gardens that preceded the entrance to the school, two men stepped out from behind the large stone pillars that marked the boundary of the grounds. He recognised one of the men instantly to be one of the security team from the villa. Bringing the car to a gentle stop just short of the two men, he climbed out saying, "What's the problem, gentleman?"

The man standing off to Weister's right said, "There's no problem here. Just so long as you come with us, everything will be just fine," he said, pulling the gun out from his chest holster.

Weister's head was still in slow mode from earlier on as he stood there looking at the man pointing the gun at him. He didn't even hear the man walking up behind him until it was too late. Everything went black as the hood was slipped over his head. Seconds later, a fist crashed hard into his stomach dropping him to the ground instantly. Pulling the draw string tight around his neck, he tried to grab at it to loosen it off, but someone had a strong hold on both his arms, he shouted for all he was worth in a hope that anyone would hear him, until something was rammed into his open mouth pushing the hood in with it. The last thing he heard was the sound of tape being wound around his head holding the gag in place. He tried to kick out, but his legs had been bound as well. He knew it was no good. As he struggled to breathe through the heavy material, his strength had all but gone as he felt himself being lifted into what he knew to be the boot of a car. Someone said something to him, but he couldn't make it out as his hands were pulled behind his back and tied to his ankles in a hogtie, and then everything went quiet as the car boot slammed shut above his head.

CHAPTER 8

I had no real idea of where I was or how far I'd come. That's the trouble with fog; it totally alters your perception of time and distance. Unless you knew the mileage before the journey began, it would be down to guess work.

I'd passed a sign for Grassington half covered by a thick layer of frost making it impossible to make out the distance to the village but that had been well before all the dash lights had come on.

I tried to picture it on a map, but it was no good. All my concentration was focused just keeping the people carrier on the road. Again, the fog behind me grew lighter in colour. I knew the other car would appear any second now, so I hit the accelerator in a bid to get away from this madman who was chasing me. It's not like me to be scared, but this was totally insane. The speedometer dropped to sixty and just at that very second my eyes zoomed in on the grass curb straight in front of me. I couldn't do a thing about it as I hit the grass curb and literally took off, the steering wheel smacking me in the face from hitting the grassy snow covered curb; then a stone wall seemed to drop out of the air and straight under the front of the vehicle.

"Where the fuck is he going?" Stiff mouthed to himself watching the people carrier leap into the night air and then disappear from view. He slammed his brakes on bringing the car to a slued skid across the lane ending where the other vehicle had literally taken off. Climbing out, he drew his gun ready to give the target the good news if need be. Slowly, he approached the gap in the dry stone wall checking around him as he went just in case the target had jumped out before sending the vehicle crashing into the abyss of the freezing fog. After a couple of minutes of trying to work out just where the other car had gone, he heard a car coming from the same direction he had come. He slid his gun back inside his jacket holster and walked back over to the car trying to think of a reasonable answer to what Sara would ask him the minute she arrived with Malk. He knew she wouldn't accept his version of events.

"He flew off into the night" wouldn't really cut it with her. He sat on his bonnet in the freezing night air knowing he was in for a right bollocking as soon as they arrived, which was seconds later.

"Oh my god," I mouthed as the road vanished from right in front of me. The only thing I could see through the windscreen was fog. The steering went feather-light, the engine screamed from lack of traction on the road then slowed and seized up tight. My stomach heaved when the whole car nosedived towards whatever lay beneath. My mind raced over what to do right up to moment the headlights found the grass wall that came from nowhere.

I only got chance to say, "shit," before the car went end over end, smashing hard into the frozen solid ground. With each impact I was slammed into the dashboard then back again floating in mid air with no sound then BANG; another impact slowly turning the people carrier into a giant metallic football. Stiff could hear all the banging and smashing of glass, he winced at the sound of smashing glass knowing what it felt like to be in a bad one himself.

It seemed to take forever, each rotation spun the people carrier in a slightly different direction, scattering the contents of the car. My mind tried to process which way was up. The next landing seemed to take longer to arrive than the others, which only meant one thing: it was going to be bad. I saw the grass in great detail, then in a slow, precise detail it rushed up and smacked me in the face. The people carrier landed on its roof, this time sliding, rolling, and then spinning. My head hit the steering wheel, and then something flew into my mouth when I shouted out in frustration and anger. Suddenly, everything went silent. It was weird. The only sound I could hear was wind and my heart pounding inside me. Then a strange feeling of weightlessness and a deep fear came over me as I realised the car was in free fall. It seemed to last for hours, my eyes scanned the smashed interior of the people carrier in a strange detached way—no sound or feeling of any kind—but in real time it was only a matter of seconds. I found out afterwards, the car had only fallen twenty feet or so, thankfully landing on the three wheels it still had, though the impact still felt like a bomb going off under my arse.

Sara's car slid to a stop at the bend in the road just behind Stiff's car.

"What's he doing?" she asked, looking at Stiff sitting on the bonnet of his car. Malk knew by the way he was acting that something was very wrong. For all he knew, the target could be just out of sight ready to ambush them the minute they got out of the car.

"Stay here, Sara, while I check this out," he said, slowly opening the car door, holding his gun close to his side out of view.

"Is everything ok?" he shouted from his position behind the car door,

"Everything isn't ok," Stiff replied, glancing back to where his boss was standing.

"Where's the other car?" Malk said, as he walked over to where Stiff was now standing. He knew it was safe to do so because of the answer Stiff had given him. If the reply had been all clear, that would have told him to back off and take cover.

Malk put his hand on Stiff's shoulder, saying, "So what happened then?"

"He went straight on instead of taking the corner. That's what happened," Stiff said, pointing at the gaping hole in the stone wall.

"Fucking great," Malk said, raising his hand to let Sara know the coast was clear.

She walked with purpose to where both men stood looking through the gap into the fog. The ground just seemed to vanish on the far side of the wall.

"What the fuck," Stiff said, straining his eyes in a bid to see where the other car had gone.

"Don't just stand there," she hissed, "get the torches and find him."

Malk squatted down to examine the tyre tracks that just disappeared over the steep grassy curb.

"Go," she said, "Bring him to me." She turned to Malk, adding, "Don't let me down, not again." She leant close to his face. Her lips were so close to his he could feel the warmth of her breath, as she whispered, "I will have your balls if you don't please me, Malk." At that, she ran her hand down the front of his jacket to his trousers and gently squeezed his manhood twice, stopping each time he winced.

"Off you go now," she said, turning away walking back to her car.

"Oh, and Malk, take that with you," she said, looking over at Stiff who was lighting a cigarette up as she spoke.

He looked at her but said nothing as he took in a long drag and then blew a huge plume of smoke out into the freezing night air. He watched her walk away and leant towards Malk, saying, "Man, what I'd do for a piece of that."

"Whatever," Malk said, as both men made their way up the frost covered grass banking to where the vehicle had crashed through. Stiff lost his footing and went down onto his hands and knees cursing as he did. "Oh fucking hell, man. This is a new suit," he said, doing his best to brush the snow and mud off.

It made Malk smile knowing how much Stiff spent on his clothes. After a couple of minutes of sliding around, they reached the top.

The two men stood there thinking until Malk said, "You first then."

"You can't be serious about going down there," Stiff said, looking into the foggy black emptiness in front of them, not wanting to get his new Gucci shoes covered in crap.

"Just go, will you," Malk said, pulling his gun out. He didn't want go down there either, but he knew if they didn't, Sara would probably shoot them for disobeying her.

I sat there not knowing what to do. My head was bleeding and blood had started to seep through my t-shirt where I had been shot earlier. I tried the internal light which was more of a dangling light now. Thankfully, it still worked. My head felt top heavy from hitting the steering wheel. Gently, I ran my hand over the large bump that was slowly growing on my forehead to see if it was bleeding. My finger touched the open wound making me wince with pain. My whole face felt sticky. I looked at my hand. It was covered in blood from the wound. I pulled the door mirror inside as it was half hanging off anyway to get a proper look at the gash.

"Oh, that's just fucking great," I thought, looking at the four inch scar that went from just below my right eyebrow to halfway across my forehead. Most of the blood seemed to be from the end nearest my eye making its way down my cheek and away under my chin. It wasn't gushing blood. It was more of a dribble, but it would need seeing to at some point. I couldn't see any other damage, so I took a deep breath and had a go at getting out of the driving seat. There was no immediate pain, so I slowly made my way out of the car through the smashed windscreen because the door was bent in at an awkward angle. I rolled slowly onto my side for a couple minutes while I got my breath. Eventually, I got to my feet and took a look inside what was left of the people carrier. The passenger seat was empty, which was not good, that was the last place I'd seen the rucksack.

"Oh, for fuck's sake," I moaned. It was like the night had closed in around me, sinking its wet cold clammy throngs of freezing cold air right into the very fabric of my skin. The mist clung to everything, covering the ground with a white frost. It all looked totally surreal. The only light was a dim yellow glow from inside the people carrier.

I scrabbled around inside the car looking for the rucksack, but it had gone. My rifle was still in the front foot well with the night sight on, but in this freezing fog, I doubted if it would be of any good. The cold was so intense my fingers were numb, and my feet felt like blocks of ice.

"Shit, shit, shit!" I shouted, more through frustration than anything else, as I started to feel my way around to the back of the people carrier to see if I could find the rucksack. I found a big rock with my knee then a thorny bush with my face, but no rucksack. "Shit, bollocks, bugger, and damn the bloody thing!" as I caught my ankle on another rock.

"What was that?" Stiff said, standing motionless in the night.

"What was what?" Malk replied, gingerly making his way over the stones and down into the frost covered long grass of the field that seemed to fall away at a severe angle.

"Thought I heard a voice"

"Really," Malk said, looking up at Stiff, who was now a good six feet above him shining the torch directly into his face.

"If you don't mind," he said, gesturing to him to point it somewhere else. "Thanks, mate."

"Don't mention it."

Stiff made his way down to where his boss was standing. They swept the torches from side to side before heading down the steep snow covered field, the beams illuminating the snow as it fell making it even harder for them to penetrate the freezing fog.

As the two men went forward, they'd only gone twenty feet before Malk shouted, "Over here!" He was squatting down next to a large scuff in the grass where the people carrier had first hit the ground.

Stiff made his way over to where he was and then said, looking at the six feet wide gash in the ground, "Jesus, that must be a good fifty feet from the road."

"Closer to twenty," Malk replied, looking back up the way they'd come then down into the darkness, making an airborne route with the torch beam from the verge to where they were now standing.

"Thing is though," Stiff said, squatting next to him, "where's the rest of the tracks? I mean, we know he landed here, but there's no more tracks."

"So that can only mean he bounced here and took off again," Malk said, pointing the torch down the field trying to see where the next scuff would be.

"Yep, and me thinks if we follow the line of that there impact, we'll find our friend at the bottom of this field," Stiff replied, putting a Cornish accent on.

"Stop the stupid voice and follow me." He brought his gun up, holding it level with the torch ready to shoot anything the beam lit up. Stiff went off to the left slightly so they could cover a wider area of the ground. It was slow going now as the field fell away at quite a steep angle and neither man had the right footwear for the conditions.

I fell over and landed on something soft.

"Thank fuck for that," I said out loud, as I realised it was the rucksack. After a couple of minutes of searching, I found the torch. "Bingo!" It wasn't anything flash, but it made my life a whole lot easier.

I scanned it around but couldn't see anything much past two or three metres. "Ok," I thought, pulling the small metal compass out. "Let's see which way we're going to go then." It wasn't a very hard decision really, as there was a cliff straight behind me that I had just come down and bugger all else in all the other directions. Suddenly, I remembered the other car that had been chasing me. What had happened to them?

Since I didn't know, I reckoned I had better make a move. It's always fascinated me how, as soon as you get busy, the cold or the pain just goes to the back of your head. Good thing really, because I was bloody cold and not short of a bump or two.

I checked the rucksack was secure, pulling it on and fastening the straps good and tight just in case I had to leg it. I didn't want anything falling out. My rifle looked okay in the dim light of the torch, but even a slight knock can put the sights out of line, so I decided I would check them out later.

The ground was hard going with large clumps of grass and half frozen bog between them. With each step I took the moss crunched under my feet, and then the freezing water would seep into my boots. I couldn't see a thing and was making very little progress. The sound of people shouting came from somewhere behind me. I froze like a rabbit caught in a car's headlights, my heart pounding in my chest. I looked back in the direction I thought the sound had come from, straining my eyes to try and figure out where my pursuers were, but it was no good. It could have come from any direction as sound travels much faster through mist and fog. I tried to quicken my pace, but it didn't seem to make much difference.

"Here's another one," shouted Malk, "but this one's a slide. Looks to me like the car's gone arse over tits and then off down there somewhere."

Both men were making better progress now the people carrier had left a clear track through the field.

Stiff shone his torch out in front of him and said, "Is it me, or is that a big hole?" Malk wandered over to where he was standing, looking into the inky blackness. "Bloody hell. Where's he gone?" Malk said, standing three feet back from the edge of the abyss.

"That's a cliff edge," Stiff said, "and I think it's fair to say that our friend went over it along with our package."

Just then, Malk's phone sprang into life. He flipped it open saying a simple, "Sara."

She didn't mince her words. "What's the situation, Malk?"

"We've found some tracks that the target's car made when it landed in the field. They seem to go over a cliff edge, and at this moment in time, we cannot see a way down," he said blankly.

Her reply was short and sweet: "Find a way." At that, she finished the call.

He put his phone away, saying, "Shine the beams down there. Let's see how far down it goes."

The beams of light swept across the top of the cliff like something from another planet searching for its prey. It was only then I realised I had only travelled 20 or so metres. I heard a voice from somewhere up above me.

"How deep is it?" It was a man's voice.

"Hard to say," replied another voice. That made two of them, but there could be more.

The torch beams scanned around in the fog searching until they found the people carrier. It scanned the area for a couple of seconds before slowly making its way towards where I was crouching.

"Look, I can see something down there," Stiff said, in a raised voice.

It was only then I noticed the trail I had left on the frost-covered ground.

"Ok," I thought, "let's see how good you are." Bringing the rifle up, I aimed directly at the light. My first shot blew the torch to pieces in a split second.

"Holy shit" Malk shouted, as he dived to the ground, dropping what was left of his torch as he did.

Stiff instinctively swung the light in his direction to see what had happened only to have his torch blown clean out of his hand seconds later.

My second shot found its target, but unfortunately, whoever was holding the torches must have been okay judging by the shouting that was going on above me.

"Get down!" shouted Stiff, as he dived to the ground along with Malk.

"Shoot the bastard!" Malk shouted.

"I CAN'T SEE A FUCKING THING!" Stiff shouted back at him, adding, "It's pitch fucking black if you hadn't noticed."

Malk grabbed hold of Stiff, pulling him so close he could smell his expensive aftershave. "Listen to me, you idiot. He's close, very close, and he doesn't know how many of us are up here, so play along with me, and all being well, he will stay put while we close in on him."

Malk shouted, "Dave, John, Steve, go left! You lot go right and get behind.

I could hear them shouting as the sound of gunfire rang through the fog. I crept along over the wet uneven freezing cold ground trying my best to keep the torch pointing straight down in front of me, knowing it was only a matter of time before they caught up with me.

Malk stood in the dark freezing fog trying to see any movement, but it was almost impossible in these conditions. Stiff held his gun out in front of him, and then something caught his eye just as Malk said, "Down there. Something's moving."

Stiff followed his pointing hand. "I see you," Stiff said, as he fired a couple of shots.

Thwack! Thwack! Smack! As the bullets hit the ground not

two feet to my side, I leapt in the opposite direction landing on a large lump of half frozen grass. Rolling off it into the icy damp moss, bullets were flying all over the place which in one way was a good thing, I tried telling myself, because that means they're just hoping to hit me and don't actually know where I am.

"Get up and run, you silly twat," I said to myself.

I was sodden and covered in snow. I had only taken three steps when down I went. The ground just disappeared from under me. "Oh shit," I mouthed and braced myself for the landing, expecting frozen hard ground or rocks, but it wasn't what I expected.

"Hold your fire, will ya!" shouted Malk, but Stiff carried on for a couple blasts. "Stop bloody shooting, for god's sake," Malk said again.

"Ok, ok," he replied. "At least we know where he is now," Stiff said sarcastically. "Are we off down there then?" he added.

Malk's phone rang again. He didn't bother with the usual bollocks. He simply said, "He's gone over another cliff edge, and no, we haven't got down the first one yet, and yes, that was gunfire you heard, and yes, the target is still alive," he paused, waiting for the screaming voice on the other end of the phone, but it didn't come.

Malk frowned and said, "Is that you Sara?"

"Yes, it is, and do you think he survived the second fall or not?"

"To be honest, Sara, we don't know. He's shot out both our torches and left us totally blind, so our only real choice is to return to the car," he said flatly.

There was a moment of silence. Then she answered, "Ok, come back," was all she said.

"Well?" Stiff's voice said in the pitch blackness of the field.

"We go back," Malk replied.

"And which bloody way is back then?" Stiff said, clearly pissed off.

"Just head uphill," Malk replied, already making his way back up the steep snow covered field.

Sara climbed out from the warmth of the car's interior and walked over to the gap in the dry stone wall. She stood there just starring out into the darkness of the field. Her eyes glistened. She wanted this bastard Tom Stone. She wanted to look into the eyes of the man who had killed her brothers.

I hit the surface of the river face first. It was so cold it took my breath away. I thought my heart was going to burst along with every blood vessel in my body. The icy cold water rushed into my open mouth and up my nose throwing me into a world of confusion and panic. I couldn't see a thing; inky blackness filled my head pounding inside my very soul. My skin seemed to tighten around my face as the muscles contracted. There was no way of knowing just how deep the water was, swept along over stones and broken branches I just kept that thought in my mind 'keep calm' but I wasn't going to wait and find out. I kicked hard with my feet whilst reaching out with my hands. I could feel the tension of the water against me, but which way was up? The strange muffled sound in my ears seemed to be pressing on the inside of my skull as the water swirled around me dragging my dead weight along in the fast flowing current. Lack of air in my lungs made me lash out in all directions just trying to grab a hold of anything I could, knowing it was only a matter of seconds before my reflex would force me to take a breath even if I was under water. Suddenly, my hands broke the surface, but the rucksack dragged me back under before I had a chance to take a breath.

Again, everything was muffled under the water. Strange gurgling sounds swept around me. I could hear myself shouting out, but nothing came of it as the water rushed back into my mouth again.

I reached as hard as I could, kicking my feet to try and break through the surface of the water once more. In a last desperate bid to survive the freezing cold water, coughing and gasping for air, my lungs burning under the strain, I broke the surface gulping down a mixture of air and water in a bid to tread water. Bit by bit, my strength came back, I managed to get more air into my lungs. Treading water fully clothed is hard enough, but with a rifle in one hand and a rucksack on your back makes a recipe for disaster. I couldn't work out which way to swim because I couldn't see the bank on either side of the swollen river. I swam across the current until my feet started to catch the river bottom, and then without any warning, a huge log burst out from under the surface pushing me away from the shallows and back towards the centre of the river. I grabbed at it in a bid to swing it around me using its weight and motion to sling shot it past me. The strength of the current pulling me away from the banking was outrageous. My legs kicked away into the night. I had to push myself harder than I'd ever done before just to keep afloat. My shoulders burnt from over use but it worked, and what seemed like hours later, my feet hit the rocky bottom again. My free hand touched a large rock that protruded well out of the river. I managed to wrap my arm around it, holding on, getting my breath and strength back before I carried on. For those few seconds while the water rushed around me, I felt no pain or cold. Just a strange sense of peacefulness seemed to pass over me. I had to move, or the cold would just take me.

The bank was steep and rocky, but I was able to scramble my way out of the freezing cold water and get my breath back. I lay there for a moment my chest heaving, coughing up water. Slowly, I rolled onto my side resting my head on my arm just trying to get my breath back. The torch had had it, but that was the very least of my problems. If I didn't get out of these wet cold clothes, I could be heading for the morgue.

I released the straps on the rucksack and slowly pulled it off. This was slow going because of the sodden clothes and freezing conditions. Each movement sapped my body of what little strength I had left.

It was like working blindfolded, but I knew what I was looking for, and I knew where it was. Item by item, I took out the contents placing each object by my side making sure that it wouldn't fall into the river or roll away. You just can't rush things in these conditions. You have to picture it all in your mind as each item is removed then replaced. Eventually, there it was. "Gotchya," I said, as my hand closed around the plastic bag which held my other clothes. I pulled the plastic bag out and held it between my knees while I put the other things back, placing the briefcase back on top. I fastened the rucksack back up and placed it carefully next to me. Once I was satisfied it was safe, I stripped off my soaking wet clothes.

I must have looked a right pillock, half stooping, stark naked, and soaking wet in the middle of the Yorkshire Dales taking a piss by moonlight, although it felt more like life was taking the piss out of me. I pulled the dry clothes on, which takes some doing when your skin's wet, its pitch black, and one wrong move would see you back in the swollen river. I sat down on some large stones to pull my trainers on, but my jacket was sodden and of no use to me whatsoever, so I decide to bin it.

I couldn't carry the rifle as well as the rucksack, using both hands, so there was only one thing for it; I'd have to pull the rucksack back on. It only took a couple of seconds for the damp to creep through to my back again, but I could deal with that for now. I had no time to check my pistols, but I knew that I would have to sort them out as soon as the opportunity came to hand.

I made my way up the steep banking, double checking each foothold as I went. Once I reached the top, I noticed the moon pushing its way through the fog, which must have thrown a dark shadow over the riverbank. The fog was definitely lifting as my eyes started to make shapes out in the darkness, trees and the odd bush but not a lot else. The scene looked like a negative shot, with shades of grey blending into the blackness. As my night vision started to kick in, I headed into the wood hoping it would give me some cover from the freezing night air.

By the time, Malk and Stiff had got back to the road, Sara had got out the tracking device and two more torches and was studying a map that she had laid out on the bonnet of the BMW. She glanced over at the men making their way down the snow covered banking towards her. They looked a mess, covered in mud and snow, but she wasn't concerned about that. Malk was about to suggest going back to the hotel and getting a change of clothes when she said, "At the bottom of this field, there's a river and beyond that a small wood. It's my guess that he will attempt to cross this river and make for cover of the trees."

The two men just stood there listening to what Sara was saying and trying to nod at the right time.

"If he doesn't cross the river and heads north, then we can corner him in what looks to be a steep valley where the river looks to source from a cave, but if he heads southeast downstream, he will eventually come to this bridge," she said, pointing at the map.

"That looks to be about four miles, give or take," Stiff said, looking down at the map.

"This guy is no fool, Sara. He ain't just goanna walk straight into your hands. He's smart and he's a bloody good shot," Stiff added.

Sara looked up saying, "Hasn't it ever occurred to you that walking around with a big torch in the dead of night looking for someone who you know is armed and doesn't want to be caught is asking to be shot at?"

"Look," Malk said, "Let's get back down there and split up. Start checking along the riverbank in either direction, because if you hadn't noticed, the signal has stopped."

"What?" Sara said. "But it was there not two minutes ago."

"It's possible that he tried to swim the river and got the phone wet, which means that it won't work until its dried out," Stiff said.

"So why don't we go by car down to the bridge and cut him off?" Malk said.

"If I were in his position" Stiff, started saying.

"But you aren't, are you," Sara interrupted. "Now get back down there and find which way he's heading. Once we know where he isn't, we will know where he is, won't we."

Stiff looked blankly at her and then at Malk and then back to Sara, as he pulled out his cigarettes. "Fine," he said, lighting it. "Just one thing, Sara," he added.

"Go on," she said.

"Just how good is this, guy? I mean, what does he do for a living? You know, is he a fetch and carry guy or something else?"

Sara looked at him and then at Malk, who folded his arms, knowing Stiff would blow his top once he found out just what sort of a person they were chasing.

"His name is Tom Stone," she said, "and it's fair to say that he's probably one of the most lethal assassins working today. He's a very resourceful killer with or without weapons. If you give him a chance, he will kill you. We know he has at least several identities that we are aware of, and he has our property that we would very much like back. Oh, and did I mention that he killed both my brothers only a couple of hours ago." Stiff just stood there with his cigarette hanging from his mouth not quite believing what he was hearing.

He looked at Malk and said, "And you knew all this and didn't think to mention it to me?"

"It wasn't my place to say anything," he replied.

"What"

"It's your job to do as you're told and not question my orders," he looked directly at Stiff and then added, "Just because you're on the search squad doesn't mean you need to know why you're looking for something. Understand?"

Stiff grabbed a torch and set off back down the hill, moaning away to himself as he went.

It didn't take them long to reach the riverbank now they knew which way they were heading.

"Where the fuck is he?" the first voice shouted from somewhere behind me. I couldn't help thinking what a couple planks these guys were who were tracking me. Every so often, someone would shout, "Where is he?" or "I can't see a bloody thing." It made me smile, and under the circumstances, that was quite something.

"He must be in the bloody river," another voice.

I squatted down, ducking behind the nearest tree.

"You go downstream, and I'll go up this way. He must be hiding on the bank somewhere," said the first voice again.

One of them shouted, "He must be on the far bank." And then, "There's no way anyone could cross a river moving that fast."

I couldn't see them from here because of the thickness of the fog, but I might be able to hit one aiming at the direction the voice was coming from. The trouble with that idea was sound does travel through fog faster than air because of the increased moisture content, but the movement of the water would have a travelling affect on the sound waves, and give my position away.

Two beams of light swung back and forth scanning the riverbank. Now and again, one of them would stop and shine across onto my side and then carry on searching the opposite bank. At least it gave me an idea as to how wide the river actually was and how fast it was. "Oh, you guys are making this too easy," I said to myself getting my gun out. I aimed just above and to the side of the torch beam that was moving from side to side and up and down. In my mind, I tried to picture the actual person holding the torch as it moved behind trees and shrubs. Trying to ignore the freezing cold and stop my body from shaking, I took a couple shots at the nearest torch. It dropped to the ground, but that didn't mean I'd hit the person holding it. The other torch went off the second I fired at the first one. I sat and waited for twenty minutes and then moved off.

I had no idea which way I was going, so I made the decision to hold up in the wood until day break and then make my escape. The gun club boys wouldn't cross the river, so as far as I was concerned, I was safe for the moment.

I sat there in silence just going over the past couple of days, so many questions but without the answers. I was stumped. "How can something so simple go so wrong," I thought. John had been such a good friend over the years, yet did I ever actually know who he was? I don't know why but a tear came to my eye for some reason unbeknown to me. I felt like I had lost a close friend and that what had passed over the last few days hadn't happened. How could it have? My world had turned to shit, and I was at ground zero. I felt so lonely sitting in this cold dark place. Slowly, I sank to the ground, holding my head in my hands and resting my elbows on my knees. The bark was digging into my back, but I couldn't be arsed to move. A numbness crept over me taking all the aches and pains away as it did. My mind felt like slush, as part of me screamed, "Wake up or die, you idiot!" I watched my hand moving slowly towards the rucksack, but I felt separate from it, like it belonged to someone else. I rummaged around for what seemed like hours, and then slowly pulled a small box out the size of a large packet of matches from somewhere inside the rucksack. My eyes tried to focus on it, but it was no good. It was like watching a silent film of the "creeping hand" as I started to shake the small box, a strange warmth started to grow in the hand. It was my hand I was looking at. The box. Suddenly, my thoughts started to clarify like a window demisting. "The heat box," I muttered to myself.

When you shake the box, it causes a chemical reaction which generates heat. It's not enough to start a fire, but it would burn your skin if held tightly. Thankfully, it was enough to get my mind back on focus. Bit by bit, the energy crept back into my freezing cold limbs. I had to get more heat into me somehow. I knew it wouldn't be long before the cold would win the battle, if I didn't find shelter and get a fire going.

Stiff lay in the wet and filth not daring to move. Stone had somehow managed to blow a hole clean through his new Armani suit just next to his shoulder without actually breaking the skin. He would actually have rather taken a shot in the neck than totally ruin his new suit. Malk had dived to the ground the moment he heard the shots. He hit the ground hard, landing on an exposed tree root, smacking his shin hard, but all he could do was bite his lip. Any sound and a bullet would be on its way.

Malk wandered along the riverbank looking for Stiff, but without the torches and only the sound of the swollen river to give him any idea of his location, he felt pissed off. He didn't want to call Sara, because she'd only say, "You must keep searching."

Stiff sat up playing with the headset, trying to get some kind of sound from it. But it was pitch black down here, and his suit was knackered. Then Malk buzzed him over the headset they were now both using, as the phone signal down by the river was totally useless.

"You had enough?" Malk said.

"No," came a very sarcastic answer.

Stiff had had enough now. His best shoes were totally caked up in all kinds of shite, and his suit didn't look any better. He called Sara on the headset.

"He must have swam the river, although I don't see how, because it's in flood and going at a right old pace he took a couple of shots at us but missed. What do you want to do?"

Sara was sitting in the car looking at the map. It had been over an hour now since Malk and Stiff had last called in.

"Back to the car," was all she said.

"Thank fuck for that," Malk said after hearing Stiff over the headset.

They both made their way slowly back up the steep field again to the car. They were cold, wet, and after being up for over twenty-four hours they were both feeling petty pissed off. Sara was standing by the driver's door, when Malk and Stiff came over the edge of the field. "Get in. We're going," was all she said.

"Where," Malk asked.

"You're no good to me in that state, so I've arranged some food and rest," Sara said.

Before Malk went over to his car where Sara was waiting, he told Stiff to just follow his lead as he had no idea what Sara had planned.

"Head for Skipton, Malk. We're booked into Herriot's Hotel," she said from the rear seat.

He didn't have room to turn the big BMW around in the narrow lane, so he decided it would be best to carry on until he found a spot to do so. As he pulled off, Stiff followed him, and both cars disappeared into the freezing night fog.

I closed my eyes trying to relax, but it was too cold, and the ground was hard as hell. I shifted round a bit until I felt more comfortable. "Comfortable," I said to myself. "Yeah right," I thought, shaking the little box for the umpteenth time. I must have dozed off, because when I looked up, it was starting to get a bit lighter. I had a go at standing up, but I had totally seized up and just rolled over half laughing, part cursing. "Holy shit. What happened there," I moaned, slowly stretching my legs, rubbing my calf muscles. I rolled onto all fours then got up a bit at a time using the tree to steady myself. I stood there, one hand on the tree trunk, the other on my lower back. "Shit, shit, shit," I muttered.

"Right," I thought. "Time to get my act together and make a move"

The early morning mist had started to clear, and I could hear the odd bird starting to sing. As I walked along, I noticed the lay of the land was quite varied. Small clusters of trees were spread about what looked like a paddock with the river running round the edge of it. There was a small stable off to my left so I headed in that direction.

The sun was still very low in the sky casting long shadows down the valley. It was bitterly cold, but the low sun seemed to be cutting through the early winter morning bringing that much needed warmth to the bottom of the valley. The ground was covered in a soft layer of new snow that looked to be melting in front of me as I made my way across the open ground thinking, "Those clouds look a bit dodgy. It would be typical if it started to snow now." The barn wasn't much to speak of with straw spread around the floor and the odd rotting bail over in the corner, but it was dry. I looked around for a couple of minutes, but it was a waste of time. The place was empty. I wandered back outside and noticed a track leading off towards a gate over at the far side of the paddock. "Now that's what I'm looking for," I mouthed, hoping that it would lead to a farmhouse which meant food. The thought of food gave my legs a new strength and helped to raise my spirits a bit. After ten minutes at a good pace, the wonderful smell of bacon being grilled drifted down the country lane towards me. My mouth literally started to drool, the lane must have been cut into the hillside many years ago as the smoke coming from a chimney down to my right, through the trees. The muddy track obviously led down to the farm house. I slowed my pace as I drew closer. For all I knew the blokes who'd been chasing me could be down there having breakfast. As I came around the long curve of the track, the house came into view. It looked to be a good two hundred years old with a chimney stack at both ends of the main house with stone flags on the roof. The windows were old box sash with eight small panels in each section. They had seen better days by the looks of them.

I squatted down while I sussed things out. Everything looked as it should. The track hadn't been used today, because it still had ice covering the pot holes, and the frost on the main gate hadn't been disturbed from what I could see.

My stomach growled away telling me to get a move on. I sighed and then got to my feet.

I slung the rifle over my shoulder and walked slowly towards what I thought to be the front of the house. I could see a light through one of the downstairs windows and as I got closer the room gave itself away as what looked like the kitchen. I was about to knock on the door when I noticed that the actual farmyard went around the side of the house. I stood still for a moment listening. The sound of some kind of machinery seemed to be coming from the other side of the farm house. I had a look round the corner. There was a large building on the far side of the yard, and judging by the size of the cobbled area, you could easily turn an articulated truck around in it. A pile of pallets and forklift truck had been tucked away under the sheltered area. It was obvious that at some point I would come across whoever worked here. I just wanted it to be on my terms and not someone shouting.

Looking back towards the kitchen area and back again made me wonder if it would be worth the hassle getting spotted. No one knew I was here, so if the others came knocking, they'd just draw a blank, but it didn't solve the problem of getting some food inside me.

Parked up next to the house wall and in front of me was a trailer stacked high with potato bins, making a kind of walkway down the side of the building. I went between the trailer and the gable end of the house then turning a corner and walking along the side of an old barn until I came to another gate. It was aluminium, sprung at one end with a huge leaver to lock it in place. I slid the bar back and went through closing it behind me, trying not to disturb the frost covering the framework. This must be the front of the house as I could see six cars parked next to each other in front of a small white picket fence. "Too easy to be seen from the house," I thought. The gravelled drive which looked well looked after had two barbed wire fences that ran along either side of it and off over the hill which I reckoned would lead to the main road.

Twenty metres past the house I could see three white and red tractor units parked nose in to the back of another barn. They all looked less than a year old by the lack of dirt and rust and would make a good getaway vehicle if I couldn't get a car. The whole place looked very organised. Just then the front door of the house opened, and a young girl came out. She looked in her mid twenties with long dark hair. She was wearing jeans and a long shaggy sheep skin coat. I stepped back behind the corner of the house watching to see where she went. I looked over at the cars as the indicators flashed on the silver Mini Cooper. She put something in the boot and then got into the driver's side. I was about to poke my head round to have another look when she got out again with a scraper in her hand. She cleaned the screen and side windows of ice and got back in. The reverse lights came on as she backed out and went like a nutter down the gravelled driveway. I couldn't see how I could possibly get to the tractor units going this way, but saying that it was the most direct route, and if I ducked down in front of the house windows, I reckoned I might just make it. Studying the house from such a slight angle made it difficult to work out the length of the building. My only real concern was if someone came out of the house whilst I was nearing the door, or if anyone came down the drive. I decided to go for it and set off at a slow jog towards the first window. When I came closer to it, I could hear music coming from inside the room. Jerry Lewis was on the radio, but whoever was singing along couldn't. There was also a faint sound of typing and a woman's voice, but I couldn't work out what she was on about.

I crouched down onto all fours and carried on, the next window was a bit higher than the first with no light coming from inside. Might have been empty, but I wasn't going to risk taking a look though and carried on. The door was two metres in front of me when it opened. I froze. I heard voices.

"When are they due?" came the first voice.

"Sometime around nine, but don't hold your breath to it," said the voice at the doorway.

First voice, "Bollocks to em. You can give me a hand loading."

"Well, if you think we'll have time later," said the voice at the door.

The door closed again.

I crept towards the opening; it was solid wood with a large brass knocker in the centre of it, so I couldn't see if anyone was about to come through it. I could still hear the people talking on the other side of it. I ran forward keeping as low as I could past the next two windows. I had a quick look round the corner of the house to make sure it was clear and jogged across the open area to where the tractor units were. It was getting towards full daylight now, but in the covered area, the shadows gave me plenty of cover.

I reached up and checked to see if the cab was locked. It opened. I took the rucksack off and threw it up on to the driver's seat followed by the rifle. I climbed up into the cab gently closing the door behind me.

"Bloody hell, it's big," I said under my breath. It was the first time I had been in a truck cab, and this one looked to be eight feet wide. The word "Scandia" was written in chrome across the centre of the steering wheel. Everything looked pretty clean and straightforward. Although I had never driven a truck before, I reckoned it couldn't be too hard.

The keys hung on a little black plastic stick on a hook next to the CB radio which was fastened to the cab roof lining. I took them off and read the tab, "Rocky boy." That must be the nickname of the driver I guessed. Putting the key in, I turned it once and lights lit up all over the place, and then the CB hissed into action and some voices started chatting away. One of the lights went off after a couple of seconds and then another. I checked the fuel. "Full up," I mouthed as I pushed the clutch in, checking to see if it was in gear and started her up. The whole thing shuddered as the engine ticked over.

"No point in hanging around," I said, putting the gear lever it into reverse. "It's like driving a bloody house," I thought. I edged my way out onto the gravelled area gently turning the wheel as I went, to get it pointing in the right direction. I was surprised at how light the steering was. It didn't feel any different to a large car. I glanced down at the gear lever and pushed it into second and set off giving it some revs as I went. The massive tyres spun at first then got a grip.

"Woe boy," I said to myself easing off the power.

As I drove off down the drive, I kept checking the mirrors to see if anyone was running after me, but no one came out of the house. I took it steady as I wasn't used to the width of this thing yet. Parts of the driveway had places that were obviously meant for passing vehicles. I just wanted to get to the end of this lane now and onto the main road. Suddenly, the CB burst into life through some speakers just above my head that I hadn't noticed.

"Base to Rocky Boy. Base to Rocky. Come in. Over."

"Oh shit. They must have seen me drive off," I thought.

"Rocky Boy, you fat twat, bring us some fags and a paper, will you, on your way back. Over."

I didn't answer at first I just carried on and then, "Base to Rocky fat boy. Pick up," came the voice again.

I picked up the mike and pressed the button on the side and said, "Fat boy," and released the button. Next thing I heard was lots of laughing through the speakers.

"Call by the baker's in Grassington and pick up the sandwich order, will you. It'll be ready by the time you get there, over."

I pressed the button again and said, "Rocky Boy to base. Will do, fat head." I put the mike back on the side of the CB and drove down to the end of the lane. I had the heater on full blast now and was starting to enjoy the ride.

As I came to the road, I noticed that there was no sign. "Great," I thought. "Which way do I go? Right/left? Sod it." I went right. It was only when I turned onto the main road that I realised just how wide this thing was. "Bloody hell. What do I do if something comes the other way?" I muttered, scratching my head. The road looked so narrow from up here.

The sun was very low in the sky which made it difficult to see the road ahead. I pulled the visor down and got a lap full of maps, the clock on the dash said 8.35 a.m. I reckoned it could be right and had it confirmed when the travel news came on the radio.

I passed small houses and farms on either side of the road but thankfully no traffic. After twenty minutes, I saw the sign for Grassington, saying, "Please drive carefully." "At last," I muttered and started to look for this bakers shop the people on the CB had mentioned, because as far as I was concerned that meant free butties for me this morning. The roads were ridiculously narrow, and I had to go onto the pavement a couple of times much to the annoyance of the locals. One old guy started waving his stick and shouted something about being sick of us always coming through here, adding that it shouldn't be allowed.

I smiled and waved back at him, but for some reason, he took offense. I can't think why. I found an open area which looked like the sort of place I could park up. All the leaves had fallen from the trees that had been placed randomly in the large cobbled area. There was the odd car parked about and a delivery van unloading in front of what looked like an outdoor centre.

"Now that's what I'm looking for," I mouthed. Next to it was a gift shop, and next to that was the baker's.

"Free butties for breakfast this morning, mi old mate," I said to myself with a grin on my face. I turned the engine off and climbed out of the cab and made for the outdoor centre. It looked closed, but the front door was open where the delivery driver was walking in and out. I wandered over, saying to the bloke in the back of the van, "Morning, do you know if the owners about?"

Without looking up he said, "Yeah, you'll find her inside. She's called Helen. Just go in," he said. He gave me a glance then carried on with his work.

"Cheers," I said and walked towards the front door. As I poked my head inside the doorway, I said in a loud voice, "Is Helen in?"

From behind a rack of red and blue Gortex coats, or at least that's where the voice seemed to come from, "Won't be a minute." I stood there for a couple of seconds just looking around.

"Can I help you?" she said. I turned round as she was walking towards me with a box of shoes in front of her. She had what I would call a happy look to her complexion, long dark hair tied back into a pony tail, and I thought she must do a fair bit of outdoor pursuits as her general build looked fit. Her sweat shirt had "Grassington outdoor activities supplies" across the front of it.

"I know you're not open, but is it possible I could buy some things as I've got to meet some friends in twenty minutes," I said in my best unorganised bloke kind of voice. She looked at me in my wet trainers, dirty jeans, and white t-shirt. She frowned, saying, "Aren't you cold in just a t-shirt?"

"Well, now you mention it, yes, that's why I would like to buy some stuff, if it's okay" I said.

"Go on then. What do you need?" she replied.

One pair of good waterproof walking boots and a pair of trainers, all weather light weight trousers, one of those camouflage jackets, a couple of sweat shirts, and socks. She stood there not quite believing what she was hearing as I went on.

After a good half hour and me spending upwards of a grand on clothing, high power binoculars, and a couple of good multipurpose tools similar to Swiss army knives, a water proof torch, and a new rucksack, I said, "That'll do me for now. Do you mind if I get changed into this new gear as most of what I am wearing is wet?"

She smiled and said "There's a changing room through the back."

"Thanks," I said and went to get out of my old stuff.

It felt good to be in clean new dry clothes. I checked all my pockets for my cards, etc. The new shoes fitted like gloves.

"You look a bit more respectable now," she said with a smile on her face.

"Thanks and I am sorry for keeping you from your sorting out."

"Don't be sorry," she said. "Not after the amount you've just spent."

I put the new gear into the new rucksack and paid using one of my credit cards.

As she swiped it, she asked, "If you don't mind me asking, what happened to your head? Because you've got some terrible cuts and a right lump on your forehead" She was looking concerned.

"I had a car accident a couple of days ago. That's all. It's nothing to worry about," I said as I picked the bags up and slung the rucksack over my shoulder. "Anyway I've got to get off now, and thanks again for your help," I said and headed out the door. I decided to dump all the new gear in the truck and then get the butties. I strolled over towards the tractor unit feeling a whole lot better about things. The sun was shining, and apart from all the cuts and bruises I felt that all things considered, I was in pretty good shape.

I opened the door to the cab pushing the new rucksack up onto the driver's seat, when a voice came from behind me. "What's your name?"

I turned around. A man in his mid thirties was walking fast towards me. He had that look of "I'm going to smack you" about him.

"Why?" I said.

He kept on coming, but now he was starting to roll his sleeves up. "Because that's not your truck. Now, who the hell are you?" he said in a loud voice.

I could see that the way this was going there was a good chance I wouldn't be getting my free butties from the baker's.

I rolled my neck to loosen the muscles and readied myself to sort him out. I stood at an angle to him, saying, "Calm down, fella, and I'll tell you." but he wasn't having any of it. He knew it wasn't my truck, and as far as he was concerned, this guy was up for a good kicking.

He got within a metre of me and went to grab a hold of my jacket whilst raising his other hand in a clenched fist.

I waited until he was just in the right position and gave him a powerful jab to the kidneys followed by one to the throat. His eyes glazed over in an instant as he went down moaning. I squatted down next him, saying, "Look, I don't want to fight you, because you'll lose. I do this for a living. Now, what is it you think I've done?"

"That's Rocky's truck," he said, still half curled up in a ball on the cobbles holding his side.

"I know, so what's the problem?" I said.

"You must have nicked it, because no one drives his truck." He looked up at me gritting his teeth and repeated, "No one."

I leaned in towards him gripping his shirt and pulled his face close to me whispering into his ear, "That may have been the way it was, but things change, my friend. This is mine now, end of story." I let him slip back to the ground. As I stood up, I cast an eye around the immediate area to see if anyone was watching.

The old guy who had waved his stick at me earlier on was making his way over. He wasn't a problem. I climbed into the truck, moving the new gear over to the passenger seat and started it up. Looking over towards my only real exit, I noticed the delivery van blocking most of the small lane that led down to the main road. It looked a bit tight, so I took it steady. The huge tractor made a soft rumbling sound as it went over the old stone cobbles as I got closer to the van I could see there was no way it was going to fit through the gap. I hit the horn without a second thought and nearly leapt out of my skin as a massive air horns blasted out colonel bogey at eight hundred decibels almost sending a sonic boom down the sleepy village streets.

"Oh bloody hell," I cursed, as people started to stick their heads out of shop doorways and windows trying to see what was causing all the commotion. I just wanted to sink out of sight behind the dashboard, but I couldn't because of the driving position in the cab. I looked in the mirror and saw two or three people walking towards me, one of them being the bloke I had had the scuffle with. "Shit," I said out loud. "This looks like a bloody lynch mob to me." I slammed my foot on the accelerator which threw me backwards as the huge truck lurched forward with a thunderous roar from the engine easily pushing the van onto the pavement and through the doorway that led into the supplies shop. I rammed the gear lever into second keeping my foot firmly on the accelerator. People dived back into the shops, as bins, bikes, and hanging baskets all got the same treatment which was either flattened or smashed to bits. It was like riding some kind of insane roller coaster or playing a computer game. None of it seemed to be really happening, but it was. The trail of destruction I left behind was outrageous. Thankfully, no one had been hurt from what I could see. As my hand grappled with the seat belt, I saw a car coming up the narrow street towards me. I flashed the main beams at him. He just flashed his back and started pointing to me and mouthed some words like, "You just go back the way you came," and something like "Arsehole." It was hard to say with the sun on my screen.

"You better move, dick face, 'cause I'm coming through," I said, bracing myself for the impact. Just then I saw something to my left, but it was too late. I hit the lamp post with a huge round metal hanging basket suspended from it. The windscreen of the cab smashed like a huge spider's web along with the passenger door and part of the cab framework. "For fuck's sake!" I shouted as the whole cab lurched up in the air at a precarious angle then smashed back to the ground. At the same time, the airbag exploded in my face. I was holding onto the steering wheel for grim death. I couldn't see a bloody thing, and then BANG! out of nowhere, the sound went straight through me as I hit the car that had been coming towards me. I heard someone screaming. Then I heard the sound of metal being scrapped along stone. With all the confusion, I had totally forgotten I had my foot firmly planted down on the accelerator. I didn't dare take it off though, in case I got caught or the truck stalled. I flattened the airbag down with one of my hands to try and see where I was going. What I saw wasn't pretty. The car that had been coming at me was now been pushed backwards by the truck, but the driver mustn't have been wearing his seat belt because he had gone head first through the windscreen. He must have somehow got stuck half way and was now flopping around on the car bonnet. He looked dead. "Oh no," I said, "This was the last thing I wanted to happen." This was getting way out of hand. It was obvious to me that the moment anything out of the ordinary happened up here, the plod would be on the case. Most small villages in the dales share one police car between every six or seven villages. The nearest large town to Grassington was Patley Bridge, and I was heading that way, so no matter what happened in the next ten minutes, I needed a change of vehicle.

There was no time to be sorry now though. I had to get out of here. The car slowed the truck down a bit, but even I was surprised at how easily it pushed it along the ground. After a good fifty yards and several wheelie bins later, we came to where the road widened out to a T-junction. I pushed the car into the middle of the main road to try and block it off, and reversed back just enough to get a look at the road sign that stood opposite the junction. It wasn't a hard decision really, seeing that the way I'd come was nothing short of a warzone, and the idea of pushing the car with a dead body hanging out the front windscreen further down the road didn't really do it for me. I looked down at the man's body. It was the first time I'd actually killed someone by accident and it felt bad. It felt awful, but thinking about it wouldn't bring him back. I blamed that bastard Weister for this. I set off down the road heading for Patley Bridge knowing the Police would be coming from that direction. It may sound daft to head in their direction, but the odds were in my favour of changing this truck on a busy route than a road that led up into the dales.

CHAPTER 9

Tony Weister had all but given up as he drifted in and out of consciousness when he'd heard a terrible sound.

"Daddy, Daddy."

Had he imagined it, or was it his daughter's voice he'd just heard? Again, he heard the muffled sound of his daughter's voice through the canvas hood that covered his head. He tried to struggle free, but it was no good. Tears formed in his eyes at the thought of what was to come.

His daughter was pushed into the car and told to be quiet or else. She sat there sobbing, not wanting to get into trouble.

Weister awoke to the sound of water lapping against the side of the *Storm*. He was lying on a large beige leather seat in the bright midday sun. There was a gentle breeze blowing over him. Slowly, his eyes started to come into focus. He tried to sit up, but his stomach muscles ached from the kicking he had taken.

He looked around and recognised the *Storm's* open aft deck, and there sitting opposite him was Karl Sasco talking on his phone. He looked over at Weister and nodded but carried on the conversation.

Weister managed to sit up after a few attempts and took a couple minutes taking in his surroundings. He ran his fingers through his hair looking out across the bay towards the open ocean.

"Drink?" asked Sasco, still sitting in his leather chair with what looked to be a Southern Comfort and ice in his hand. With a gentle movement of his wrist, he made the ice spin inside the glass.

Weister looked across at Sasco sitting there in his white trousers and deep turquoise silk shirt, his eyes shaded from the bright sun light by a pair of Versace slim line sun glasses. He uncrossed his legs and stood up still looking at Weister. He strolled over to the side of the super yacht and rested his elbows on the highly polished handrail still spinning the ice in his drink. As he looked out across the marina he spoke, "Do you know why I had you brought here, Tony?"

Weister turned to look at Sasco and said, "Why did you have to bring my daughter into this?"

"I didn't," replied Sasco. "You see, that's what I'm talking about, Tony. Always passing the blame to someone else or trying to cover up yet more cock ups. Do you have any idea the amount of money you've cost me, Tony, have you? Well have you?"

Sasco looked down at the crystal blue water that lapped against the hull of his yacht. He gave a sigh and turned to face Weister, taking his sunglasses off, placing them in a small gold case.

The large tinted glass doors slid open that led into saloon area of the yacht. A man came out. Weister recognised him as one of the crew. He was carrying a polished silver tray in one hand with two drinks on it. Both glasses had been chilled as per Karl Sasco's instructions. You could see the condensation on the glass. When the crewmember came closer to Weister, he could hear the ice knocking against the sides of the glasses.

"Have a drink with me," Sasco said, now leaning against the hand rail.

"Your drink, sir," the young man said, holding the tray in front of Weister.

He took the drink, not bothering to acknowledge the waiter in any way. He could see the swirling golden liquid as it mixed with the ice in his glass. As he brought the glass to his lips, he took a good swig of the icy cold drink and then another, leaving only a couple of ice cubes in the bottom of the glass.

"Another," said Weister, holding the empty glass up towards the crewman. "And this time make it a decent size drink."

The crewman went over to Karl who took the other glass. "Get our guest his drink," he said, staring at Weister.

"Yes, sir."

Weister stood up and started to walk towards Sasco, his eyes full of hate. The drink had given him confidence, but in the back of his mind, he knew it would take more than a drink to beat this bastard.

"I wouldn't do that if I were you, Tony." Karl Sasco's voice was loud this time, strong and purposeful.

"You see, we both know you're a bit unbalanced at the moment. You're not yourself, Tony."

As he talked he put the sunglasses back on and turned to look out over the bay again.

"You're upset about your daughter, Tony. Anyone would be. I don't hold it against you. You have a right to be upset, but what you don't have a right to do is pull a gun on me."

He turned back to face Weister,

"Tony, that is why you're here. That is why you will go over to England and find Tom Stone. You see, he's laying waste to all my associates. He killed my sons for Christ's sake, Tony."

At that moment, the crewman came out with the drinks again. Weister took his first and then Sasco.

Weister was standing in the centre of the deck, glass in hand, looking very awkward.

"Look up there, Tony," Sasco said, pointing towards the flight deck.

Weister turned to where his boss was pointing. Resting on the back of the beige leather pilot seat was a gun barrel. Behind that was a tanned face with dark sunglasses and short blond spiky hair. Weister recognised him instantly from before at the school.

"I believe you two have met previously," Karl said.

"Yes," said Weister, adding, "but we haven't been properly introduced, as I was a bit tied up at the time."

"Really," Karl said, sounding almost surprised. "Where are my manners."

"Tony, this is Vladimir. Vladimir, this is Tony Weister. Now we're all properly introduced we can carry on, if that's okay with you, Tony," he said in a very dry tone.

Weister took a sip of his drink. He looked at the man pointing the gun at him and then back to Karl Sasco. He had no choice as usual. His boss had covered all the angles. He went back to where he'd been sitting and sat down again, scratching his head as he took another big gulp of the Southern Comfort and said, "I can see what you're saying, Karl. I am upset, but please, tell me why you had my daughter brought here. She's only a child. She's innocent in all this."

Karl leant back in the soft leather chair, crossing his legs as he took a small sip from the glass and then placed it down on the small table next to him. His hand reached for a small gold box next to the glass. He opened it and took out a cigar.

"You're booked on a flight tomorrow, Tony. You're going to England. When you get there, you will get in touch with Sara who you now work for. If you think I am being unreasonable in any way, please tell me, Tony. Under normal circumstances, I would have had your entire family killed for what you have done."

He paused to light his cigar and carried on, "I know what you're thinking, Tony. You're thinking that he's taken my daughter so what have I got lose by not going. Well, that's a good question, Tony. One that I feel I can answer for you."

He got to his feet, saying, "Follow me."

The two men went inside into the air conditioned cabin, and through two sets of doors and along a corridor with dark wood panelling with cream-colored carpets and soft lighting. Karl opened a door to his right and asked Weister to go first. It lead down some steps to a large room with a slightly raised section in the centre. Over in the corner was another one of Sasco's men pointing a gun directly at him, and sitting next to him was Tony's little girl, her hands and feet tied together with a black hood over her head.

"What's all this about, Karl? What you gonna do? Shoot me here?" said Tony, looking at Sasco.

"No, I just want to show you something, Tony," he said. At

that, he gave a nod to the man in the corner of the room, who pushed a button next to him. The raised section of the floor in front of Sasco and Weister began to open up like a book, eventually sliding back to reveal a huge glass section of the boat, through which Tony Weister could see his wife under water with a scuba mask on with an air pipe leading somewhere out of sight. Her hands had been tied tight, stretching her across the underside of the boat, pressing her breasts hard against the glass bottomed section of the super yacht. They had done the same with her legs pulling them wide apart. The ropes were so tight that her hands and feet had gone purple. Through the mask, her face had a look of absolute terror on it. Weister knew she couldn't swim. Her hair was moving gently with the water, but he could see the panic in her eyes.

"This is why you will go my friend. She will have air as long as you do as you're told. It's that simple," Sasco said.

"And you won't hurt them, if I do this job for you?" Weister's voice was trembling now.

Karl Sasco looked at him taking a long slow drag on the cigar then said, "Deal, my friend. We will be even again, and I will let you leave my employment if you wish it."

Sasco put his hand out to shake on it. Weister looked down at the hand then at his wife and daughter.

"You swear on it, you bastard? You swear you won't hurt them?"

"I swear, Tony. I won't touch her."

The two men shook hands.

"After you, Tony," Sasco said. As they left the room, Sasco looked back at the man and gave a slight nod and then walked out.

The man walked over to the glass panel and looked at Weister's wife spread eagled across the bottom of the boat. He picked up a small box with a cable attached to it, the box had two buttons on it, one green, one red. He showed it to Weister's wife on the other side of the glass. Under water, she watched his finger touch the green button. Slowly, the ropes started to pull tighter, pulling her body taught. She shook her head, franticly letting air bubbles run across the bottom of the boat.

He stopped the pulleys by pushing the red button.

He smiled at her and pointed towards the handset and waved a finger at her as if to say naughty, naughty. She understood and nodded. Her breasts were pressing hard against the glass because of the tension of the ropes pulling her arms in opposite directions.

He waved again and smiled at her, pushing the green button and walked away laughing as he did. Pulling a large knife out, he approached his victim. He stood in front of the small child for a moment and then slowly pulled the knife across her throat.

CHAPTER 10

I'd only been going for less than five minutes when the truck started to vibrate as the smell of burning rubber started to fill the cab from down below. It worried me how far I was going to get in this once gleaming tractor unit. I hadn't exactly treated it well but saying that, the thing still had plenty of power left in it. Just then, the off side tyre blew.

"Fucking twat!" I shouted. "What else can go bloody wrong with this thing?"

I punched the dashboard out of frustration, bringing the truck to a standstill in the middle of the road which wasn't much wider than it was.

I sat there sorting my stuff out swapping everything from one rucksack to the other, putting my double holsters back on. I had a quick look at my hand guns to see if all the working parts were in order. They seemed okay, but time would tell. The new jacket fitted well over the weapons. I was about to have a look at my phone to try and sort it out after the episode in the river when a blue car came around the corner with what looked like a young couple inside it. I pushed the power button on the phone just in case it had some life left in it.

"Come on," I mouthed, looking at the tiny screen and looking back up at the approaching car. The young girl driving slammed on the brakes, but there was no way she wasn't going to hit me. I could see her through the windscreen, arms locked, eyes wide shut, waiting for the impact. Her passenger was doing the same. It was quite odd to see this car sliding towards me, knowing that there was no way I would be hurt up here.

I sat there and just watched it coming towards me, and then it hit the truck with what I thought was very little impact. The truck gave a slight jolt, but that was it.

The phone lit up, which I thought to be quite something. After what it had been through in the past twenty-four hours, I decided to check it out later and slid it into one of the inside pockets.

The young guy in the car looked pretty pissed off. It could have been at me for parking in the middle of the road, but I reckoned he was more pissed at the way his girlfriend had run into me. I got some plasti-cuffs out of the side pocket of my new rucksack and jumped down out of the cab. Taking a look at the front of the car as I went past it, it looked a bit dented, but that was all. I carried on to the passenger door and knocked on the glass, saying, "You alright in there?"

I could hear the girl screaming as the young man tried to calm her down. I heard, "Shut it, will ya. He's standing next to the door. It was an accident."

This I didn't have time for, so I did the only thing I could do in the situation—I removed the problem.

She carried on crying and was starting to get hysterical. I tried the handle and opened the door.

"Out you come," I said, dragging him backwards out onto the road.

"What the fuck," was all he got chance to say, as I whacked him as hard as I could. He wasn't a big bloke, just tall and skinny. Down he went. I spun him over and bound his hands together. I checked for a pulse on his neck. He'd live.

The girl was going for it big style now, screaming and waving her hands all over the place. I leapt over the car bonnet and yanked the door open.

"No time to fuck about now, girl. Out you come," I said, grabbing hold of her wrists. "Bloody hell," I thought. "She's like some kind of mad bitch. Her legs were kicking everywhere as her body rived up and down. She had a go at biting me, but I managed to get my hand out of the way. I let go with one hand and slapped her hard across the face. She stopped instantly and looked at me with a strange puzzled look on her face. She felt her cheek and then smacked me straight in the face with her clenched fist.

"Blodfrrr," was all that came out of my mouth, along with a splat of blood. I still had a hold of her other wrist when a saw the foot coming at me at a great rate of knots. I twisted my body to try and move out of the way, but her foot made good contact with my shin.

"Argh fucking hell!" I shouted and swung around with my fist closed. I found my target and hit her square in the face. I felt bad about hitting a woman, but it's fair to say she could hold her own in a fight.

She lay there totally sparked out, blood running from her upper lip. I gently lifted her head to check that she was still breathing.

She was okay. I picked her up and carried her round to her boyfriend laying her down next to him. He was moaning away to himself, so I squatted down and said, "You know what, mate, your girlfriend there has more balls than you have. I dragged them one at a time through the open field gate just down the road laying them side by side. Take care now." I got my stuff out of the cab as fast as I could and threw it in the car. It was a manual five speed Vauxhall Vectra, quite a nice a car in my books. I backed away from the tractor unit. I jumped out leaving the engine running and ran back up to the tractor unit. It started after a couple of turns, and then I gently took it into the field and left it there. A minute later, I was driving down the road in my nice new car

Looking at the fuel gauge, I sighed. "It just gets better, this does," I said to myself "Below a quarter full." At a guess, I reckoned I would get a good fifty miles if I didn't get pulled over first. I set off trying to work out where I could head for, knowing I could reach Patley Bridge, which meant I would be able to refuel or even change cars, but it still meant I was running not planning, and I needed a plan, if I was to sort this whole shit state of affairs out. Twenty minutes passed before I saw the police car coming towards me with its lights flashing. I gave him a nod as he passed me like you do to the nice police officer. I knew they would see the truck abandoned in the field and stop. This meant they would find the couple as well so they wouldn't die of exposure. The police would know which way I was travelling, but that wouldn't be for at least thirty minutes, because their duty would be to take care of the injured first. That gave me at between 30 and 45 minutes to change cars, and seeing that Patley was only at the most ten minutes away, I figured everything should be okay.

Sara watched the laptop screen as the signal started again. She typed away, and then the screen showed their position. The map pulled out to show both the target and the car she was in. She typed away again. A small box appeared in the corner of the screen showing the distance between the two flashing icons, 45 miles, 46miles, 47miles, she smiled knowing the target could run for as long as he wanted, hide anywhere. It didn't matter. She could have him when she was ready now.

After half an hour of driving and racking my brain, I came to the conclusion that the only person who could hide me was probably Ian Walker. I checked the clock on the dash board – 9:15 a.m. As I passed a road sign that showed six miles to Patley Bridge. I'd been to Patley once many years ago and hadn't thought much of the place, but I remembered it had a small garage, the type that sells your average family saloon, nothing too flash.

I opened the glove compartment as I was driving and pulled out all the paperwork. "This looks interesting," I said to myself, pulling into the side of the road, flicking the hazard warning lights on as the car came to a stop partly on the grass verge.

The hotel that Sara had booked had a look of grandeur about it. The old stonework added to the impressive frontage of the Victorian building.

She walked through the hotel entrance with all the confidence of a professional businesswoman in her black Versace trouser suit. She wore her long blond hair in a ponytail and a small black briefcase in her right hand. When she approached the reception, the young man behind the counter looked up and gave her a welcoming smile saying, "Good morning, Miss Sasco. The parcel you asked about will be here at 10:30 this morning."

"Thank you. Call me on this number the moment it arrives," she said, handing the receptionist her card. Picking the brief case up as she turned to head for the lift, she overheard something about a stolen truck and a fatal crash in Grassington this morning. Coming from the radio behind the reception desk, she paused just for a split second and then carried on towards the lift. When the doors slid open, her mind was putting the pieces of the puzzle together, where they had lost him and the distance from there to this Grassington place. She stepped into the lift and pressed the button for the sixth floor. As it glided upwards, she got out her mobile phone, pressed one button, and waited. It didn't even ring twice when Malk answered it. He knew who was calling, "I'm just parking the car now. Stiff's just entered the car park, so we will be up ASAP!"

She stepped out into the luxurious hall that leads to the penthouse suites. A young man in a butler style uniform came over to her and asked if he could carry her case for her. She looked him up and down and then handed the case to him.

"Please follow me," he said in a light tone, as he set off towards the suites he'd been told to have ready for her. At the large wooden door, he pulled a credit card from his pocket. He gently slid it across the panel on the door frame. A small red LED light turned green as the door unlocked. He was about to enter when Sara said, "You were doing so well."

The young man looked at her and asked, "What do you mean, miss?"

"Ladies before gentlemen," she said, as she walked into the room ahead of him.

He looked at her for a second and then followed in behind her.

"Put the case on the table and leave," she said, now looking out the large window that overlooked the main road at the front of the hotel.

He placed the laptop on the table and stood there waiting for his tip.

Sara looked over at him and then back out the window.

"I asked you to leave. Now go, or I will have you removed," she said, not even looking at him.

He took the hint and left the room but didn't bother closing the door behind him in a show of protest at not getting his tip.

She heard Malk and Stiff well before they reached the door to the penthouse. They were arguing about something. Seconds later the two of them appeared in the doorway. Both looked a bit puzzled as to why the door was wide open. It just wasn't like Sara to be in a room with the door open. They looked at each other and Stiff said, "Why's the door open then?"

Malk looked at him then said, "What makes you think I would know?"

"Well, you're the one with all the answers, aren't you."

Malk was about to let rip into him when Sara just sat there listening to them arguing and said calmly, "Please be quiet while I phone Karl." It was like someone had turned the volume off. Both men stopped instantly.

"Thank you" she said, flipping her phone open.

She paused before pressing the dial button and then looked up, "What are you waiting for, gentlemen?" she said.

"Oh, sorry," Malk said and headed back out the door pushing Stiff out in front of him, closing it behind him.

Karl Sasco was standing next to the Captain of the *Storm* when his mobile started to ring. He looked at the tiny screen, which read Sara calling. He answered, "Hello, my darling. How are you?" The smartly dressed Captain left the moment his boss's phone started to ring to give him privacy.

"Fine, Dad, but this contract is getting out of hand. Tom Stone seems to be able to slip through the tightest of snares," she said in a little girl lost voice.

"Don't worry. My friend in London will help you out. I will deal with it as soon as we have finished talking," he said in his calm soft voice. "You know you only had to ask. Use Malk as the contact. He's done it before, so he knows what to do," Karl said.

"I'll call you in a couple of days to give you a progress report, Dad. Bye."

"Take care, angel," Karl said, closing his phone and then reopening it he pressed the memory button, found the number, and pressed call. The phone rang for a couple of seconds before Martin Robinson answered it.

"Robinson speaking," he said in a dead tone.

"Good afternoon, Mr. Robinson. I trust you know who I am."

Robinson knew this voice. He'd hated this voice for over ten years now, ever since that day in the casino.

Robinson's gambling addiction had got him deep in debt. He would have lost his house, his car, and almost certainly his wife and daughter, and holding a high position in MI5, he would probably have lost his job, too.

He was up to his limit at the casino when he was called into the manager's office to discuss settling the outstanding debt. He knew he couldn't repay the outstanding debt unless he won it all back by playing on. It was the classic circle that so many gamblers fall into. The more you lose the more you want to win. It was then Karl Sasco, the owner, had come in and offered to settle the debt at the casino and the bookies by offering him a deal he couldn't refuse.

"You owe me £123,545,00, Mr. Robinson, plus interest, and my girls say your strange ways aren't cheap either, so here's the deal: the slate is clean as far as your family is concerned. I will let you play the house. If you win, that amount will be deducted off your debt. If you lose, you owe me favours, which I will call in when I need your services. Do we have a deal, Mr. Robinson?" Karl Sasco said, holding his hand out to shake.

"You know we have, Sasco. I've got no choice, have I," said Robinson. He shook Karl Sasco's hand and went home. That's how fast it all happened—one moment he was about to lose everything he owned, the next all his debts had gone. He also knew if word of this ever got out, he would end up in prison.

"What do you want this time, Sasco," Robinson said.

"Three good men to hunt down the man who killed my sons. "You know the meeting place, and you know what I expect, and Robinson, they will be dealing directly with my daughter, so make sure they understand that." Karl Sasco had always considered himself to be a fair man. He only ever expected a debt to be paid in full and on time, without exception. He ended the call to Robinson and then placed the phone down on the glass table in front of him. He wondered if he should head for England or let his daughter deal with the contract. She was good, very good, but this was different. Stone had never been caught out, even after all these years in the business. This killer had murdered his wife and children and even when Karl had put a contract on his head, he still managed to stay alive. Now his eldest daughter was tracking this killer, but this time Karl knew he had the edge on his old enemy. He was being tracked by satellite, and he didn't even know it.

Sara called to Malk to come back in after a couple of minutes.

"Looks like you're in the shit, mate," Stiff said with a smile on his face.

"Thanks," replied Malk as he turned to go back in.

"Close the door will you, Malk," she said, getting up out of the chair.

"What's the problem, Sara," he said, trying his best to look relaxed. He'd heard rumours of Sara killing people for not following her instructions, and he didn't want to become a rumour just yet, even after all the years they'd worked together.

She walked over stopping so close to him he could smell her expensive perfume. She looked into his eyes.

"Do you find me attractive, Malk?" she whispered.

Tiny beads of sweat started to form across his forehead. What was the right answer? Of course he did. You'd have to be blind not to, but if he said yes, what then? It could be the wrong answer or could it?

Her lips were nearly touching his. He could feel the warmth of her breath on his face. He wanted to kiss her, to hold her slim toned body close to his.

"You know I do, Sara. I always have," he said, leaning forward to kiss her.

She pulled back instantly, saying, "That's so sweet of you. Now listen, time is not on our side. I need you to go to this address," she said, handing him a piece of paper. "There you will be met by three men. They are aware of the situation and will follow you back here. Call me when you're on your way back. Oh, there's one more thing," she said, "before you go. That boy out in the corridor with the stewards uniform on, teach him some manners as to how to treat a lady, will you."

"How many manners would you like me to teach him," Malk replied knowing full well what she meant.

Sara didn't bother to answer him. She just went to sit in the plush leather chair next to the coffee table.

"Off you go then, and don't forget to call me when you're on your way back."

Stiff shrugged his shoulders saying, "I'm off downstairs to have a look around and check the place out." Malk just followed him out the door closing it behind him.

"You want a hand with that," Stiff said, before heading in the opposite direction, not wanting to let Malk have all the fun.

"No, you just do whatever it is you do until I return."

The lift door opened, and Stiff disappeared inside lighting up a cigarette.

Malk walked down to where the young lad was standing. He gave no warning or hint of what was about to happen. He just smacked the young lad in the face so hard it took him off his feet sending him backwards over the glass cabinet he was standing next to. Before he had a chance to say anything, Malk pulled him to his feet, and holding him upright with one hand, he hit him repeatedly in the face with the other, whilst saying, "If you ever disrespect Miss Sasco again, I will personally put you through that fucking window." As he finished what he was saying, he threw the young man's nearly unconscious body across the corridor knocking a tall oriental vase from its stand. Malk looked down at the heap on the floor, straightened his collar, and waited for the lift to come.

As I flipped through the papers I'd found in the glove compartment, it looked like everything that I could need was here, insurance certificate, vehicle registration document, MoT, even the odd old bill. I checked the mirror and set off again. The road seemed to go on forever round tight bends and long straights, until

I came to the long steep hill that led down to Pateley Bridge. I'd forgotten just how steep it was until I'd gone half way down the bloody thing. Parts of it had a sheen of black ice covering it making me flap big time as every now and again the car would skid sideways then back the other way. "Gently does it. Gently does it." I'd be saying, hoping like hell I wouldn't end up in the hedge or worse over the very steep banking that kept appearing on my left each time the dry stone wall showed a gap.

After five minutes, the odd house started to appear then the road levelled out a bit and some shops came into view as well as the first garage, but it didn't sell cars. It just did repairs. The old sign looked like it could do with a coat of paint, as did most of the tired looking cars that had been squeezed onto the forecourt.

The narrow road had cars parked on either side as most of the houses here had no drives to speak of. Thankfully, most of the traffic seemed to be turning right at the junction up ahead, giving me a straight run down to the same junction without having to stop. The garage I was looking for from memory was on the left just round the next bend. I decided it would be best to just ditch the car and walk round to the garage. I drove down a bit further to the entrance of the old industrial park. I turned in and went about two hundred yards down one of the tracks that led to some closed down units where kids come to muck about. I grabbed all my stuff, wrapping the rifle up inside my new coat. I knew it wouldn't fool anyone, but in these parts, most farmers had guns anyway. I only had a couple of hundred yards to walk so I had no real worries about being seen. Leaving the keys in the ignition, I set off at a casual pace not drawing any attention to myself. People will always notice someone running or walking fast, because it's not normal behaviour. Most people walk, so that's what I did. I glanced back at the car and smiled.

It looked like it had been punched in the face a few times. The air seemed a lot colder here in the bottom of the valley. It must be the river bringing the mist with it, I thought. People were out scraping ice off the windscreens while their cars warmed up, belching clouds of exhaust fumes up into the cold morning air. A couple walked past me with two golden retrievers taking their owners for walkies. The woman kept saying, "Stop pulling, Brannie," but the dog had that look of "its munchin' time" on its face, as she half slid and half walked past me. The other dog looked like its nose had been welded to the pavement. I smiled, thinking how nice it would be to live a normal life where you come home to someone you love in your own home.

"One day," I said to myself. "One day."

The garage forecourt came into view as I rounded the bend. It wasn't much to speak of, but he seemed to have a good selection for a place this size. From where I was standing, I could see someone moving around inside the showroom. He kept looking through the floor to ceiling glass windows in a hope of catching some unsuspecting customer to give them the best deal for miles.

Most of the cars were totally iced over, apart from the ones under the carport. Only their bonnets had a slight coating of frost. I knew the minute I stepped onto the forecourt he'd be out, so I put my interested face on and wandered over between a couple of Ford Mondeos.

An old guy came out wearing a bright red ski style jacket, rubbing his hands together. He had a good tan with silver grey hair, and obviously liked his food, but he looked healthy on it. His trousers had a crease in them that you could cut fog with.

"Morning," he said, still making his way past some of the cars.

"Anything take your fancy, because we have more stock inside if you can't see what you want out here," he added as he approached me. Raising his hand to shake mine and he said, "The name's Derek, Derek Thompson."

I took my hand out of my pocket and just said, "John, morning," that was the name on the car document, and luckily for me, it was also the first name of one of my other ID's. I picked common names because it's just easier to source them when setting up a ghost identity. So that was who I was now.

"Okay John, what is it you're after today? Something sporty or a family saloon or could I interest you in a four wheel drive?" he said, still rubbing his hands together, trying to smile and look like my best mate.

"I need a fast reliable car with plenty of space inside and

preferably four wheel drive. Oh, and I want take it straightaway," I said.

"What kind of budget are we working with, John," he replied. I could see the cogwheels turning in his head as spoke.

"Well, I would like some change out of…let's say…£20,000," I said casually. He nearly hugged me and started rabbiting on about how he had just the car I was looking for and that it had only just come in and how much interest he had had in it with its full dealer service history and because it was me, he would throw in six months tax and six months warranty. I tried to nod and shake my head in the right places and mutter things like "Oh, that's good," and "really." As we walked into the showroom, I could see why he was so excited with himself.

Standing by itself, looking rather nice, I might add, was a Subaru Impretza turbo estate in a deep metallic green with gold wheels. On the car's windscreen in big white sticky back numbers was the price: £19,999. I had to smile. This must be the most expensive car by ten grand in the whole place. I walked round to the driver's side and got in. It was very nice, black leather and loads of toys to play with when you're bored. I got out, went round to the back, and opened the hatch—plenty of space for my stuff. Derek was about to start his selling spiel again, when I said, "Do you take cards?"

"Yes, we take cards, sir," he said, his smile now even wider than before.

"Good," I said, "give me a full tank of petrol with it and some of those floor mats, and we have a deal."

Derek looked at me and then at the car and then back at me again rubbing his chin and said, "Come and have a seat, John. Do you want a coffee?"

"Never mind the coffee, Derek. Do we have a deal or not?" I said.

Derek looked at me and said, "That's a hell of a car for under £20,000, you know. It's a really good buy, and I'm hardly making a thing on it as it is."

I looked at him, frowning. "Do you want this sale or what?" I said, "because I can go elsewhere."

He looked at the car and said, "You drive a hard deal, John, and I just know that other couple will be disappointed, but seeing it's you, go on then," he replied, and we shook hands.

"Deal," I said.

We did the paperwork, and he gave me a coffee while he moved a couple of cars that were blocking the showroom doors, and then he drove the car out onto the forecourt, giving me a voucher to fill it up at the petrol station next to the corner shop. I think it's fair to say I made his day, but I knew that would change in time when the credit card company eventually caught up with Mr. John Anderson's account, seeing that he didn't actually exist. I slung my stuff onto the rear seat and shook his hand again, and we said our goodbyes and off I went in my nice new car. I filled it up and bought some meat pies, crisps, and a cup of hot chocolate from the vending machine. I took the B6165 out of Pateley for a couple of miles and turned off onto the 6265 and pulled into a small lay-by to have some scoff and a hot drink.

While I was munching on a pie, I got my mobile out and had a look at it, a steady drip of water seeped from the bottom. "Well, that'll explain why it's not working," I said to myself. I put the car heater on full and held it in front of the air vent for a couple of minutes, wafting it about in an effort to dry it out faster. I fiddled around with the circuit board in a bid to dry it out as well and then put it all back together. Nothing happened. I gave it a shake and then tapped it on the steering wheel, like you do. After a couple of minutes, it dawned on me to turn the bloody thing on. The tiny screen glowed pale blue as the Nokia logo appeared.

Stiff returned to the hotel room, chomping his way through a bag of chips, and sat down in front of the laptop while Sara poured a glass of wine for herself. He'd been looking at the screen for a couple of minutes when a small pinging sound started as a red dot flashed on the map on screen. He looked over at Sara, asking, "Is this flashing red dot the target we're looking for?"

She smiled and walked over to where he was sitting. "Show me," she said. He spun the laptop around to show her.

She looked at the screen then flipped her phone open, saying, "Malk" into it.

In the car on his way to Leeds, Malk's phone started to play a little tune. He pressed the answer button knowing it was who it was.

"What's wrong, Sara," he said.

"Nothing. Which laptop do you have with you, Malk?" she said.

"The tracking unit. Why," Malk replied.

"Well, it should be here, shouldn't it." She put the phone down and looked at Stiff. "Can you track him with this one?"

"To a degree, yes."

"What do you call a degree?" she said, sitting down opposite him.

"Well, I could track his direction and his location within a square mile, but we need the other laptop to narrow the field down to within a metre," he said, starting to feel a bit uneasy.

She got up and went over to her bag that was sitting on the bar top. She pulled out a handheld tracking device.

"Use the GPS system out of the laptop and download it into this," she said, powering the unit up.

Stiff walked over to her not having seen the handheld unit before. She moved in front of him so close their bodies were touching. He could feel her breasts under her blouse touching his chest. She gently kissed his lips and then with one hand felt for his balls.

"Do you find me attractive, Stiff," she whispered. "Do you want me?"

He looked down at her and replied, "Yes, Sara, I want you."

She closed her hand around his balls and squeezed hard. He groaned, falling to the floor in agonising pain. All the colour from his face drained away. His breath came in small rasps as he tried to stop himself from passing out.

"I told you, but you didn't listen," she said, standing over him. "I told you if you let me down, I would have your balls." She squatted down next to him, lining her eyes up with his. "Don't make me correct you again." At that, she stood up straightening the creases in her trousers as she did.

Stiff had no idea what he'd done wrong, and he wasn't about to ask.

"In twenty minutes, a car will be delivered outside the front of the hotel. Use it to find our friend. Use this phone to contact me," she said, throwing a small mobile phone at him. He lay there moaning trying to sort himself out.

Sara looked down at him as her mobile started to chime like a set of tiny bells. She flipped it open, and a smile instantly came to her face. On the small screen was the name Roxy $$ with her signature two dollar signs after it.

Roxy was Sara's younger sister. She spent most of her time in Europe working for the family business. At 23 years old, she was one of the most respected women in Karl Sasco's empire. Her dark complexion and stunning looks had taken her places where her rivals could only dream of. Like her sister Sara, she was just under six feet tall and built like an athlete. She always had her hair deep red nearly black in a bob cut. She was a mixture of beauty and the beast with eight kills to her name in less than three years working for her father.

"Hi, baby," Sara said, smiling. "Where are you? Dad said you might be coming to England. Say you will. I haven't seen you for nearly two years now."

"I've been here for a couple of days. I had some business to take care of in London," said Roxy, sounding nearly as excited as Sara did.

"Where are you now, babe," Sara replied.

"Well, at this particular moment, I'm just heading out of York in your direction. Dad told me what happened, Sara. Don't worry. Together we'll get him. I promise," Roxy said, adding, "Do you know where he is?" Now sounding more like her sister.

"We have a good idea but he seems to slip away every time we get close to him. Our last signal put him somewhere near a place called Glasshouses. It's in the middle of nowhere by the look of it," Sara said, whilst looking at a map of the area.

"How many roads lead out of Glasshouses?" Roxy said.

"Looking at this map I'd say he has three possible escape roots," said Sara. "I'm sending one of our men to try to locate him, but we're short of a laptop to get his precise location," said Sara into the phone.

"That's not a problem. Can use mi. It'll only take me a couple ours at the ost to get to your tel..."

"Roxy, you're breaking up," Sara said, pressing the phone against her ear. "Roxy, can you hear me? Roxy?" Sara looked at the phone. The tiny screen read: call ended. She tried the number again, but the signal had gone.

Stiff limped out through the lift door into the hotel lobby where a young couple stood just in front of him laughing and joking until they saw him very pale and covered in sweat.

The young girl asked, "Are you alright? Do you need a doctor?"

Stiff held a hand up saying, "No, no, don't worry yourself, love. I will be just fine in a minute. Thanks." Making his way across the lobby towards the large glass doors, once outside, the fresh air was a real tonic. He couldn't stand totally straight yet, but at least, his balls seemed to be getting back to their normal shape. He was about to sit down on the stone steps when a very smart looking young man came over and said, "Excuse me, sir, are you Mr. Stiff by any chance?"

Stiff looked up at the fresh-faced man, saying, "Why? Who wants to know?"

"I've been asked to give this envelope to a man matching your description," he said.

"And what description is that?" Stiff replied, getting up off the stone steps.

"I was told to give this envelope to a man holding his balls with a painful expression on his face at the front of this hotel, sir."

"Well, you got me there" Stiff said, taking the envelope. At that moment, the phone Sara had given him started to buzz like a demented bumble bee. He answered it, saying, "I've got the envelope, Sara."

"Good," she said, "now listen. I want you to head for a place called Glasshouses. Just type it into the keypad and press enter. Once you get there, call me. Don't go after this guy by yourself. Do you understand?" she said slowly. "Just try to find him." She ended the call.

Stiff put his hand on the young man's shoulder, saying,

"You'd better show me where this car is then, fella." The two men walked round to the back of the hotel to the car park. The winter sun was bright, reflecting off the wet tarmac, making it difficult to see without squinting. There was a large pile of leaves half blocking the path making Stiff walk through the slush that had built up in small rifts along the road. He was walking better but still wasn't too happy with the state his balls were in.

"Where's this car then?" he said, lighting a cigarette blowing the smoke at the man standing next to him.

"It's over there, the Ford Focus," he said, pointing.

"Which one, dick head," Stiff said, looking at four or five of them.

"As requested, sir, it's the black Cosworth."

A smile came to Stiff's face. "Well, bugger me," he said. Walking over to the car, he pressed the key fob, and the doors opened. He got in, closing the door behind him. The man got in the passenger side. Stiff looked over at him saying.

"What the fuck are you doing?"

"I need a ride back to the garage. The lady said it would be okay."

Stiff put his seat belt on and started the engine. "Look. It's nothing personal." Stiff's tone went from calm to shouting in a split second. "Get the fuck out, you piece of puke! Right fucking now!"

The car salesman opened the door. Without saying a word, he got out, gently closing the door behind him. Stiff looked at the small G.P.S. screen with the colour monitor in the centre of the dashboard. He typed in the word Glasshouses, and a female voice said, "Please wait." Then she started to give directions on how to get to his destination. He synchronised his handheld unit with the cars. He slid his sunglasses on. "Coming. Ready or not, arsehole," he said to himself as he left the car park.

CHAPTER 11

Once I had finished chomping my way through the pies and crisps, I set off again. The road twisted and turned up the long steep hill. Most of the trees had lost their leaves, and the sun was behind me for once. I was beginning to get used to this car and the way it handled, but I wasn't particularly impressed with the sound it made when I accelerated, but that's just my opinion. "Must be getting old," I thought.

I'd only been going ten minutes when a sign for a bed and breakfast and good food served all day caught my eye. "That'll do," I said to myself. It had been ten minutes since the sign. I was about to turn the car around to see if I had missed the turning when the road started to go down hill. Standing in its own grounds was this big old pub painted white with a stone roof a bit like my cottage. The car park out front had a few cars dotted around, but in all, the place looked quiet. I flashed my indicators and pulled into the car park. As I did, I noticed some old black metal steps leading down to the side road from the fire exit on the side of the building. I brought the car to a stop and then reversed back down the side of the pubs gable end. The tyres crunched over the gavel and I brought the car to a stop in front of one of the side windows displaying dark wooden shutters on either side.

A large silver pipe was belching what looked like steam out of the kitchen. At least, I presumed it was the kitchen by the smell of roast beef in the air. I grabbed the rucksack and went in through the front door. It led into a small dark hallway with a large notice board on one side with bits of paper stuck all over it: "Book now for Christmas" and "This Friday 70's disco." I read on about car boot sales and sheep fairs, nothing of any interest to me though. As I opened the second door, the smell of roast dinners and pipe smoke filled the air. I wandered over to the bar where a middle aged woman with blond hair, bright red nail varnish, and a bit too much make up was pulling a pint. She looked up and gave me a big smile, saying, "Hello, dear, what can I get you?"

"Are you still serving food, luv," I said.

"I should think so, darling. It's only twenty past twelve. Here's a menu, and the specials are on the board. It's leek soup today where it says soup of the day," she said, passing the pint to a bloke who looked like he'd been here all week by the redness of his cheeks.

"'Av one yerself, Viv," he said in a very broad accent and went off to join his mates next to the large roaring fire. They all looked settled in for the day.

She came over and asked, "Have you decided what you fancy, love," picking a small order pad up with pen at the ready.

I hadn't even seen the menu yet, so I just said, "Yep, I'll have roast beef please, and a pint of Landlords, and do you have any vacancies in the bed 'n breakfast?"

She stopped scribbling on the pad. Looking down the bar at a young girl in her late teens, she shouted in a loud voice so everyone in the pub could here, "Do we have any rooms available, Sonya, for tonight?"

"What makes you think I would know, mother. Anyway when was the last time anyone ever stayed here?" came the reply. I didn't know where to look. I felt that awkward as the mother flew at her daughter with a volley of verbal assaults. There was "You never let me go anywhere," and "After everything I've done for you," and then "I hate you," as the daughter walked off slamming a door behind her.

"Is that a no then?" I asked, taking a sip of beer.

"No," she said, "it's a yes." She gave a smile and apologised for the upset, saying, "Teenagers. Who'd 'ave 'em?"

I smiled back at her, saying, "How much per night?"

She looked at me and said, "Excuse me?"

"The room. How much for the night?" I repeated.

"Oh, the room. Sorry, I was miles away then," she said with a smile.

"I bet you were," I thought.

"£30.00 for a single or £50.00 for the double," she said, now holding a large diary. "How long were you thinking of staying" she said without looking up.

"I don't know yet. Maybe a couple of nights. I'll just pay as I go, if that's okay with you," I said.

"That's fine," she replied. "All the rooms are non-smoking, and breakfast is served at half past eight. Payment is in advance please."

"Do you take cards?" I asked. "Because I'll pay for two nights now and this lot as well."

"Yes, we do, but there's a small surcharge on cards," she said, hoping to get cash.

"That's fine by me," I said, passing her the gold card with the name John Lawson on it. Like all my false ID's, this card had a decent credit limit. I made some bullshit up about liking the view at the front of the pub, and would it be possible to have a room there.

She said, "The stairs are at the far end of the bar. Go straight to the top and then turn right. Your room is the last one on the left overlooking the car park." She gave me a Yale key with a yellow disk on it with the number 6 etched into the disk. "The room's ready when you are, and your food will be five minutes, through there in the dining area," and then she went off to serve someone else.

The food was as good as the beer, and I soon found myself ready for a kip, so I made my way up the creaky old stairs to my room. I opened the door turning the light on not expecting too much, and I wasn't let down. It had definitely seen better days. The red carpet was fraying, as were the matching curtains, but the wallpaper looked okay from a distance; a good distance. On second thoughts, it was crap, too. I put my rucksack on the bed and had a look out the window. At least, I had a good view of the car park, and the fire exit I had seen from outside was literally next to my bedroom door. Looking out the window, the sky looked full of snow, and I noticed the hills around here had already had a good dusting.

I went to see if they kept the fire door locked or if it was the standard push bar type. It looked okay, but I noticed two small holes in the door about an inch from the leading edge. On closer inspection, I found they were rotating slide bolts, the type most people fit to windows. "That's a bit naughty," I said to myself, easily dealt with though. I went back into the room to get my small tool kit out that I'd bought from the outdoor centre. Two minutes later I had the door how it should be—unlocked.

I decided to get some shut eye before I made any phone calls, as I was in great need of some decent sleep having not had any for 48 hours. Taking my shoes off, I lay back on the lump of dough they called a bed and rested my head on the breeze block filled pillows. I couldn't be bothered to get undressed, and before I knew it, I was out for the count.

Roxy looked at her mobile, "Call ended,"

"Great," she said, dropping a gear to pass the truck she was behind. She loved to drive fast and had a bit of a reputation. Her latest purchase was a black BMW Z4 which she was in now. Breaking the speed limit was an occupational hazard for Roxy. Everywhere she went, she went at speed. One hand on the steering wheel, the other trying to get through to Sara on her phone, she passed two more cars whilst checking her server. The more she tried and failed, the faster she went. She saw the roundabout ahead and dropped the car down to fifth gear. Then straight into third. The engine screamed as the revs hit 6000 rpm. She laughed out loud, taking the car to its limits and then floored the accelerator as the car went sideways round the roundabout, tyres smoking. Someone blew their horn, but she took no notice. The back end of the BMW slid out in the opposite direction as she came out of the skid, but she was ready for it and compensated by steering into it. "What was that place Sara had said?" she thought to herself. Grassington, Glassinton, Glasshouses! That's it. She typed it into the Sat Nav on the dashboard. The soft male voice she had had specially requested said, "Please wait," and then he started to give the directions for the most direct route. The small screen also showed the optimum route, through a place called Knaresborough on to Ripley then on to the B6165 which goes straight to Glasshouses. "Easy peasey," she said to herself. As she came to the outskirts of Knaresborough, a speed camera flashed as she went past it at twice the legal limit, and then through a set of lights that had just turned red. But she had to slow down when she came to the next set, as the traffic was so heavy. Roxy tried her phone again, still no signal. Up ahead a bus was trying to negotiate through the cars and into what looked like a bus station. Just to make things awkward, a delivery van had parked up on some double yellow's, partially blocking the road creating a bottleneck.

Roxy just sat there feeling very pissed off, checking her nails, and putting some more lipstick on. As she was looking in the rear view mirror, she saw a police bike trying to squeeze through the traffic four cars back. Its blue light was flashing, but no one could move out the way as all the cars were nose to tail.

She leaned over and got the briefcase out from the passenger foot well. Pushing the tabs in opposite directions, the lid sprung open. She took out a small black box with a digital timer on the front of it. She set it to 55 seconds, and then placing it under the driver's seat, she checked her makeup once more and got out taking the briefcase with her, leaving the car in the middle of the road. She was in no hurry. As she walked between the traffic and then out of sight, she followed the footpath round the end of the building.

She looked at her slim gold watch, the shock wave followed by a huge fireball shattered all the windows in the immediate area of the explosion, people started screaming as bits of debris and car parts flew through the air on fire. Car horns and shop alarms were going off everywhere and a huge dust cloud swept up the street. Roxy looked at her watch and frowned. "That timer was fast," she said quietly to herself and then carried on walking like nothing had happened. Almost immediately, Roxy heard sirens ahead and a fire engine pulled out just in front of her. "That's very efficient, I must say," she thought to herself, watching them trying to make their way through the traffic. Pulling the phone from her leather jacket pocket, she checked the signal again. "Four bars. I suppose that'll have to do," she thought. Scanning the memory, the word "car" lit up. She pressed dial, and it only rang twice.

The voice on the other end of the line knew what would be asked, "A top class fast car delivered within twenty minutes to one of the Sasco family."

"Its Roxy," she said, "I'm in a place called Knaresborough. Do you have it?"

The man on the phone said, "I have it on screen now. What car do you want, Roxy?"

"A black BMW Z4 M power soon as possible." She could hear him typing in the background.

"Twenty minutes, if it's red. 45 minutes for a black one," came the reply.

"Fine, get me the red one," she said. "My location is," she looked around but couldn't see a road sign so just said, "fire station. I'll be waiting. Oh, and don't go thinking you've got away with this. You know what I'm talking about, don't you." She hung up. She scrolled down to her text and messaging section pressing the "scramble on" button, and she quickly sent a text to her father. "I HAVE THE LIST AND THE BONDS, ROXY." She then slid a small data compression card into the bottom of the phone and pressed send. Less than ten seconds later the tiny screen read "complete." She smiled, sliding the phone back in her pocket.

A phone started to ring in the manager's office at the BMW garage in Harrogate, which happened to be only ten minutes from Knarsborough.

"You have a BMW Z4 M power in stock?"

The manager said he did, but it was sold yesterday and that the customer was about to collect the car. The voice on the other end of the phone explained what would happen if his instructions weren't complied with. He was then told in no uncertain words what would happen to his son who was attending Edinburgh University. He was also told he would be paid £5,000 for the inconvenience. At that, the manager agreed. His phone went dead, and he relayed the delivery details and time of delivery to his head salesman, telling him to deal with it immediately.

"But the customer's sitting in the bloody car now," he said exasperated. "I can't just say 'oy, fuck off. We've sold it to someone else.'" The manager told him to do it or find another job. "Fine then," he said and went back to the customer in her new BMW looking very pleased with herself.

"Would you mind just stepping out of the car please, Mrs. Walker? I just need to do something," he said in his best salesman voice.

"There's not a problem. Is there?" she said, getting out of the car.

"No, no problem," he replied. "Excuse me," he said, as he slid past her and sat in the driver's seat, closed the door, started the engine, and drove off at speed, leaving the customer looking very puzzled, standing on the garage forecourt, wondering what to do next.

It was dark outside when I woke up face down on the bed, my face like a lump of play dough, very stiff and misshapen. I lay there for a couple of minutes yawning and then decided to get up and make a brew. Pushing myself up and turning over, I sat on the edge of the bed just taking in my surroundings. Stretching my back straight and having a good scratch, I made my way over to the little wooden sideboard where the white plastic kettle sat with matching cup and saucer. It felt like the kettle was about half full, so I flicked the switch and went to have a quick wash in the smallest basin I'd ever seen. "No bloody hot water, face cloth, or towel," I chuntered to myself, checking the bandages were clean and not weeping anymore.

After a quick wash, I dried my face on one of the pillowcases, as rubbing my face along the carpet didn't really appeal. I looked at my watch. "Shit. Twenty past four." That meant I'd only been asleep for a couple of hours, which is probably why I felt like a bag of shit. I opened the door and listened. I could hear the juke box and that familiar smell of roasts cooking in the kitchen confirmed it was mid to late afternoon. I had another stretch and went back into my room.

My cup of tea was a bit weak, but it did the job. Placing it down on the bedside table, I opened the rucksack pulling the brief case out and sitting it on my lap. I laid it flat with the handle facing me. On the top side of the case was the small silver flap. I pressed it once, and it gently flipped open to reveal a set of numbers from 1 to 60 followed by eight letters on a touch screen system. I sat there just looking at it, I had to open it to make sure no water had penetrated the inside. I took a deep breath and touched the screen gently.

P.3.6.0.3. I paused before pressing the enter button. I rubbed my hands together like a safe cracker would. Nothing happened at first, and then a low hiss as the seal released its grip, the suit case slowly opened by itself to reveal its contents.

In Karl Sasco's office a red light started to flash on the front of a small black case on his desk, but Karl was on the *Storm* dealing with Tony Weister.

Black preformed foam held six glass tubes, each one the size of a large syringe with a pale cream liquid in two of them. The others varied from red to totally clear. They were all connected by small chrome tubes and various wires. Along the bottom was a long piece of metal that looked like aluminium with a small black and yellow radiation sign on it. On the lid section that was now at a right angle to the base set into more foam were more glass tubes and two larger packs similar in shape to the one with the radiation sticker on. The finish on these looked like lead, but I wasn't sure. It all looked dry and intact, which was surprising considering what it had been through in the last 48 hours. I closed the case gently and pushed the dials on the front edge towards each other. Again the case gave a low hiss and the LCD screen on the top confirmed that the case was air tight. I pushed the small silver lid back down into place, taking a deep breath saying, "Thank fuck for that." Turning sideways, placing the briefcase next to me on the bed, I took a large swig of tea and went to put the kettle on again.

I pulled some clean stuff out of the rucksack and got changed, taking some time to check the state of my wounds again. They were starting to scab over now, so I left the bandages off, hoping the air would help the healing process. Large purple bruises were forming all over my body. The odd one had started to turn a yellowish green. It had been a long time since my body had taken so much hammering, and it's fair to say it felt like it, too. I was very stiff and badly bruised, but all things considered, I reckon I had come out of the last 48 hours on the winning team. The gun club boys had taken losses, and I had lost them to boot. The kettle started to boil, so I made myself another cuppa and set about cleaning my guns, stripping each one down at a time, making sure all the working parts were clear of any obstructions as I went. I screwed the silencer onto one of them, leaving the other without. I tried them in the holster, but the one with the silencer was just too big and awkward, so I unscrewed it putting it back into the side pocket of the rucksack. "Time to give Ian a ring," I thought, getting my mobile out, pressing the green logo shaped like an old phone. After a couple of seconds, the buttons lit up, and a message said, "Loading from SIM card." Scrolling through my list of numbers, I eventually found his and pressed the dial button. I let it ring for a good two minutes before ending the call. "Sod it. I'll try later," I thought.

Putting the briefcase back into the rucksack, I noticed a tiny red light no larger than a pin head flashing next to one of the click switches near the handle. I couldn't remember if it was there before or not. All I knew was the seal was secure and everything looked hunky-dory inside. Looking at it, I suppose it must have been there before. I'd probably just forgotten about it.

As I slid the case back into the rucksack, I heard someone coming up the hall towards my door. I pushed it home pulling a gun out ready to deal with whatever was coming. Someone knocked a couple of times, and then a female voice came from the other side of the door.

"Mr. Lawson, are you in, love."

"I bloody hate being called love. It's always love this or love that with some people. It gets right on my tits," I muttered away to myself.

Sliding the gun into my jeans behind my back, I replied, "Coming." I opened the door. It was Viv, the landlady, looking all tarted up with a big smile on her face. She wasn't bad looking, but she needed to buy a mirror. Most of the clothes she had on were at least two sizes too small, and how the hell she managed to walk in those heels I didn't know. If her faded jeans could talk, I swear they'd be screaming.

"How can I help?" I said, leaning against the doorframe folding my arms in front of me.

"I've come to apologise for the shouting earlier on, love. It's not like that all the time. It's my daughter, you see, love. She gets very frustrated working out here." As she spoke, she was looking in a downward direction.

"Forget it," I said. "It's not a problem."

She looked up at me stepping closer, saying, "I could make it up to you."

I looked down at her. This close she resembled Yoda out of *Star Wars* but in drag. I smiled, saying, "Really, that's nice, but as I said, it's not a problem," giving a nervous laugh as I spoke.

She placed a hand on my chest saying in a soft voice, "Well, if that's your final answer. If you need anything, my room's at the end of the hall, or I might be in the bar."

"End of the hall then, if I need anything," I said, not wanting to sound too forthright.

She turned and walked slowly away down the hall. I stood there watching her. She turned around, saying, "Are looking at my bottom, Mr. Lawson?"

"No, nope, absolutely not, bye!" I stepped back in the room, closing the door behind me.

"Fucking hell! That was scary," I said to myself. "Now I do need a drink. Oh no, what if she's down there all tits and slap. If I got drunk, then what?" I shuddered. Go for a drive. That's what I'll do. Yep, go for a drive. I got my gear together not rushing exactly but not hanging around either. I put the bedside light on and pulled the curtains closed, and then locked the door putting the key in my jacket pocket. I pushed the bar on the fire door down. I heard the click letting me know the door was now unlocked. Very slowly, I eased it open, checking to see if there were any magnetic strips to set the alarm off. A rush of cold air came through the small gap, still no sign of any trigger system. I wondered if that was why the owners had put a couple of locks on it to stop guests from leaving without paying. I pushed the door all the way open. It was then that the alarm went off. What a fucking racket it was, too, totally ear piercing.

"Oops," I said, half laughing going down the steps like a man possessed. I slipped a couple of times nearly losing my footing on the thin layer of snow that had come down. Seconds later, I was at the car. I threw the rucksack over onto the back seat placing the pistol on the passenger seat next to me. I set off, gravel flying all over the place as the tyres took a grip on the loose surface. I headed back along the road I had come from earlier on, as I knew it lead down to the B6165, which would eventually take me to Harrogate. My thoughts were that if I could get the rest of the cases together I could take them up to Ian's place in the lakes. It was a piece of mind decision more than anything. I didn't want my new best mates to get their paws on them and try to detonate what part of the device I had left back at my place. That's if they hadn't found them when they came for me before. It's strange how thinking about what could happen if this device was ever actually detonated made me drive faster. I suppose it's the adrenalin that gets you going.

It was starting to snow again. I glanced at the small gauge that gave the outside temperature: -1. I'd have to slow down if it got much colder. I didn't want to write off my nice new car, did I.

4.30 p.m. it read on the dashboard as I came to the T-junction: right for Patley Bridge or left for Harrogate. I turned left accelerating through the gears and then having to break hard as I came to a corner that was tighter than I realised. It seemed to pull in the further you went round it like a hairpin bend. The black and white arrows reflecting my headlights back at me as the sky seemed to be getting darker by the second. I felt the back end of the Subaru twitching on the wet slippery road surface, but it held. I carried on taking it a bit steadier. Stiff pulled in to the side of the road in front of a small shop. He was pissed off with just about everything at the moment. He just sat there thinking about maybe changing jobs or going freelance. Outside, people were rushing around with their hoods up all wrapped up from the cold. "Silly fucker," he thought.

The road turning almost back on itself as the arrows started to point in the opposite direction. "Oh shit! Too fast!" I shouted out, as the car started to slide on the black ice. I tried to steer into it and accelerate out of the bend, but it wasn't looking too promising. "Come on! Come on!" I shouted, my heart pounding away like a steam hammer. I yanked the handbrake up for a split second to try to get the car pointing in the right direction. It did the trick. As the back end slid out, I floored the accelerator spinning all four wheels. Water spray spewed out from the sides of the car. "Shit! Oh fuck! No! Bloody hell!" I shouted, trying to regain control of the car. As the road straightened out, I managed to ease off a bit. My heart was still pounding and sweat poured off my brow. I took a deep breath and tried to calm down. Up ahead, I saw a small shop that looked like a newsagents. It was glowing in the dark like a small lighthouse for cars. People were coming out pulling their collars up to protect them from the snow and sleet. I pulled up behind a black Ford Focus that was parked in front of the shop with its engine running. I put my headlights to dim and got the phone out to try calling Ian again.

CHAPTER 12

Stiff wouldn't have minded if he knew what this guy he was looking for actually looked like, as he had only caught a glimpse of him back at that bloody cottage. He rubbed his eyes and stretched, letting out a tremendous fart at the same time. The handheld tracking unit showed the target in the immediate area, but that didn't help his cause as the target could be anywhere. He sniffed screwing his face up.

"Bloody hell," he said, opening both front windows to let out the eggy stench, but it was no good. He pressed the small button again and got out, wafting his hand in front of his face, his other hand searching deep in his pocket looking for some money to get more cigarettes with as he went into the newsagents.

As I sat there waiting for Ian to answer his phone, I saw the driver's door of the car in front of me open. A man got out wafting his hand in front of his face, I smiled, thinking that must have been a good one. Still no answer from him. "Where the hell are you, mate, when I need you?" I muttered. "Might as well pick some more scoff and drink up from this place," I thought. I've got a long drive in front of me. I slid the gun into my chest holster locking the door behind me. The shop was a lot bigger on the inside than it looked. The owners must have knocked through the back wall and extended it a good twenty feet or so. Two old dears were discussing the state of the weather and that it's all down to that global warm up thing. The floor was wet with dirty foot prints coming in from outside. It looked like a busy little place judging by the queue at the counter. Most people were wearing winter coats with either the collars pulled up or scarves wrapped tightly round their necks half covering their faces. Some kids looked like they were up to no good over at the sweet counter, shouting and carrying on. "Why is it," I thought, "that young people just don't feel the cold?" None of them had a coat on, and one of the lads was only wearing a t-shirt. "God, I sound old," I thought.

Making my way over to a fridge where the supposedly fresh handmade sandwiches were on display, my eyes scanned across: chicken salad, chicken and mayo, chicken and tomato. "Bloody spoilt for choice, I am, "I said.

"Sara, it's Malk. We've just got back. Do you want me to bring them up to your suite or tell them to wait in the car?"

"Just bring that fucking laptop up here right now, Malk. He's just started to transmit again," Sara said impatiently, adding, "Tell them to wait in the hotel bar and that I will see them shortly."

Malk literally ran through the hotel entrance just getting to the lift before the doors slid shut, leaving the three men heading for the bar.

Pushing the top floor button not giving the people in the lift a chance to do anything, a man tapped Malk on the shoulder saying.

"Excuse me, but we were first." Malk looked at him then turned back, not wanting to be bothered with him, but the man started to reach past him to press the button for his floor deliberately knocking into Malk. Just when the out stretched finger went past Malk towards the panel, he frowned, got a good hold of it, and in one smooth motion pushed the end of the finger back over on itself breaking it at the base. The man screamed with pain holding his hand close to his chest shouting, "You fucker! You've broken my fucking finger! Jesus that hurts, you twat," he said, looking in disbelief at the bloke in front of him.

Malk looked back at the guy, saying, "Don't be such a cry

baby. It's a finger for fuck's sake. It's not like I shot you or something." He turned back to face the lift door when they opened he stepped out saying, "Next time, you won't be so cocky."

"What was all that about?" she asked "Oh nothing," Malk replied, handing her the laptop.

They went into her suite and plugged the tracking device into the side of it.

"Why isn't it working?" Sara asked impatiently.

"Give it a minute," Malk replied, typing away at the keyboard. The screen went black and then back to colour again. In the top left corner, the word tracking was flashing. "Found subject." Then a new window opened showing a street map of Glasshouses.

"My God," said Malk, "There's only twenty odd houses."

Above each house was a set of flashing numbers. "What are they?" asked Sara.

"Postcodes," Malk said, "They're bloody postcodes. Each house has one of these, Sara, and see that red dot there? Well, that is where our friend is at this precise moment." Malk typed away and then a second later the name of the property came up and the telephone number.

"It's a shop," Sara said, and then she asked, "Can you bring Stiff's location up on this thing?"

"Give me a second," he replied, as he carried on typing. "Sara, look at this," he said a moment later.

"What am I looking at?" she asked, looking at the screen, and then she noticed the red dot was now flashing blue and red.

"Does that mean what I think it means?" she said, looking at Malk.

He turned towards her smiling. "Yep. I think you should get Stiff on the phone, don't you," he replied.

I picked up a couple of sandwiches, a packet of cheese and onion crisp's and made my way over to the checkout counter. As I did, I noticed the guy in front of me stood out like a sore thumb. I mean most people in the queue had their winter stuff on all wrapped up like Eskimos, but this guy was in a top dollar suit, short hair, and a good tan. At a guess, I thought he was either ex army or police, but going by my past guesses, he'd probably be an accountant.

The queue was moving very slowly as the old guy liked to chat to his regulars. Didn't help my cause though.

The big guy in front of me turned round looking very impatient. He looked at me, saying, "Good 'ere, innit?"

"It's always like this," I said, sounding as if I was from around here.

He looked back at me again, "You live around 'ere then," he asked.

I couldn't help thinking I knew this guy from somewhere, but I wasn't going to ask. You never know who you could have upset in my business.

"Yeh, just up the road," I replied. "It's you."

"What?" he replied.

"It's you. Your turn," I said, "at the counter."

He looked round and asked for some cigarettes. I just wanted to get served and get on my way.

The old bloke was serving someone else while the bent-over-granny-looking old bird asked for my things. I passed them over to her, and she rang them through slowly, putting each item into the bag for me.

"That's £3.46." I gave her the right change and headed for the car. As I came out of the shop the big guy was still at the counter getting served. I pressed the key fob to unlock the car. The snow was really going for it now.

Looking down the road, I could see a thin covering on the surface. A layer of slush had built up in the centre which was bound to make driving a bit tricky. I got in kicking my boots on the sill to get rid of the excess snow. Starting the engine, I flicked the wipers on to clear the screen and then put the windows down to clear them as well. Turning the heater up to full, I indicated and pulled out just as the big guy was coming out of the shop lighting a cigarette as he walked. When I drove off I couldn't help looking in the mirror. I suppose it's just a natural reaction you pick up being a driver. As my eyes locked onto that small reflection, something inside was nagging away, but for the life of me I couldn't figure out what it was. The road went round a gentle bend with terraced houses on either side partially illuminated by the soft orange glow of the street lamps. Up ahead, I could see a spinning yellow light coming towards me on the opposite side of the road. As it drew nearer I recognised the familiar shape of the gritter with its plough down pushing a small mound of snow and slush into the side of the road. As it went past, my car got a good peppering of grit salt from the rear rotating disk. I instinctively ducked. Always have when that happens. I know it seems a bit daft, but there you go.

All the brake lights of the cars in front of me suddenly started to come on, and everyone ground to a halt. From where I was, I couldn't see what was going on, so I just sat there with the radio on watching the snow getting heavier.

Stiff stamped his feet trying to loosen the snow off his clean shoes, not wanting the salt to mark them. He took one more long drag of his cigarette and then flicked it into the gutter. His car was totally covered now by a good layer of snow. He looked at it and wiped the passenger window clear to reveal the dark interior of the car. It was then he noticed the small bright green screen of his phone flashing away. "Oh no," he said, as he automatically felt his jacket pocket and the absence of his phone. He fumbled about looking for the car keys in his trouser pockets, seeming to take forever, pulling out hotel keys, coins, and then, "Thank God." He found them. Pressing the fob, the doors unlocked. He lunged at the phone, knocking it off its holder and in to the foot well on the driver's side. He scrambled over the seats picking it up, but the caller had hung up.

"Fucking hell!" he shouted at himself. He knew it was Sara calling. He got out of the car pressing the call button.

It only rang once.

"Stiff." she said calmly. "You're parked outside a newsagents, aren't you?"

"Yes" he said, trying to figure out how she knew that.

"Tom Stone is in there right now. We've just had a transmission from his phone. Now listen, Stiff," she said calmly. "There's a good chance he won't recognise you, so try to locate him while I send some men over to back you up."

Stiff butted in saying, "And how the hell am I supposed to recognise him? I don't even know what he looks like."

"Think," Sara said. "Think back to when we were at the cottage. You were driving. You must have got a look at him. Come on, Stiff," she said. "I'm relying on you."

Sara knew not to start raising her voice as it would only make him lose his concentration. He thought back to that night. The man in his headlights, short brown hair, medium build, but he just couldn't make the face out. He went back into the shop. Standing in the doorway, he scanned the whole shop, but none of the people inside matched what he was looking for, and then it clicked: the guy in the queue, slight tan, short brown hair, with a cut on his forehead. It must have been Stone. He ran to the counter pushing people out of his way.

"Do you have a closed circuit system in here?" he asked the old man.

"Do you mind not pushing my..."

Stiff didn't let him finish. "Listen to me," he said. "Do you have a closed circuit system in this shop. A simple yes or no will do."

The old man looked back at Stiff, saying, "Yes, it's there. Why?"

"Ok, does it record this queue?" Stiff said now a bit calmer.

The old man wanted to get on with serving his customers, but Stiff was blocking the counter. "Will you move?" asked the old man, starting to get annoyed.

"Not until you give me the tape with the last twenty minutes on," Stiff said in a firm voice.

This didn't impress the old man one bit. Who the hell did this bloke think he was coming into his shop demanding this and that. He turned to his wife, saying, "Edith, call the police."

Stiff didn't miss a beat. He cracked the guy immediately behind him on the nose. As the guy went down, he leapt over the counter and head butted the old man before he could do a thing. His wife dropped the phone in terror. Stiff then punched the eject button to release the tape, grabbed it out of the video recorder, and was back over the counter in a split second. One of the customers was about to have a go when Stiff pulled his gun out. The young guy backed off immediately.

"Stay where you are and nobody gets hurt!" Stiff shouted, running out of the shop. He slipped on the icy surface but didn't go over, making his way round the front of his car through the snow. A car went past spraying slush all over him. Stiff looked down at his sodden trousers then at the car that had just gone past. "You fucker," he said. "Oh that's just fucking brilliant."

Another car went by, and the same thing happened again. Stiff opened the car door and got in totally wet through now. His phone started to buzz.

"He's on the move." It was Sara again. "He's heading out of the village towards a place called Summerbridge, but he must be stuck in traffic, because the signal has stopped moving," she said.

"I've got him on video tape," Stiff said into the phone.

"You've got what?" Sara replied sounding surprised.

Stiff repeated what he said, adding, "I know what the fucker looks like, Sara. I've seen him face to face."

"Well done, Stiff," she said. "Don't lose him. I'm sending some men over to help you."

"What about Malk?" Stiff replied. "Isn't he coming over?"

"That is of no concern to you now, Stiff. I have you on the screen. Why isn't your car moving when the target is only a hundred metres from you?" she asked in her usual tone.

"On my way now," he replied.

Sara finished the call and turned to Malk saying, "Give this information to the men downstairs along with these phones, and then come back here."

Roxy had to slow down at the roundabout as the weather was starting to get outrageous. Snow covered the entire width of the road. She didn't like snow, not one bit. Carefully, she eased the car into third gear, not wanting to get into a spin. The first sign said to Ripley Castle and Village. She went past heading north towards Ripon. Up ahead, she saw the next roundabout. "This must be mine," she said to herself, slowing down again, as the voice on the GPS system said, "Take the second turning on the right." Roxy followed the instruction and started to accelerate again along the snow covered road towards Summerbridge then onto Glasshouses. She had the idea of finding this Tom Stone and sorting him out in her own way for killing her brothers. She started to go faster from the anger growing inside her, her confidence growing stronger by the minute.

I'd been waiting for the car in front to move when in my mirror, I saw headlights coming straight down the middle of the road, other cars were doing their best to get out of the way. I had a bad feeling in my gut about this and eased the car into reverse giving me enough room to manoeuvre round the guy in front of me. I decided it was time to go and fastened my seatbelt. The gap between the car in front of me and the terraced house wasn't much to talk about, so I just went for it onto the curb then foot down. A small dog ran out from nowhere, but somehow I managed to miss it. I carried on along the pavement that was a good seven feet wide, obscured by small steps jutting out from doorsteps of the terraced houses. I continued for a good thirty yards, knocking wheelie bins all over the place. One flew off my bonnet and hit a small yellow sports car.

"Bollocks to em," I thought. My need is greater than theirs at this moment in time. I looked in my rear view mirror to see what had happened to the guy in the other car. Nothing yet. I was about to tell myself to stop being so paranoid when the pursuing headlights came bouncing over the curb negotiating the previously scattered bins.

I pressed on pushing the car to its extremes on the icy surface. Other drivers did their best to get out of my way, now that the traffic was starting to thin out which I thought was very decent of them. The engine screamed as the tyres did their best to get a grip on the snow, all four wheels spinning as I went sideways down the narrow street. Between cars and pedestrians, up and down the curb, I went making the car bottom out every time I breached the high curbing. My windscreen wipers worked overtime as I fought with the steering wheel. "With a bit of luck, I might just get away with this," I kept saying to myself. Then the back end of the Subaru clipped one of the cars parked on the side of the road. It wasn't much but it was enough to throw the back end out the other way, throwing the car into a spin. "Shit, shit, shit!" I shouted, but it was too late to stop it. I didn't have a clue which way was what, easing off the power to try and regain some control.

It was then I noticed the lamppost. The headlights illuminated the heavy snow as it fell all around me as everything went into slow motion. I saw people standing watching as I went sliding down the road again the lamppost came into view then raced off again to my left. A young lad pointed at me tugging at his mum's arms trying to show her the car spinning around and around. I could hear the engine revving, and my heart beating. Snowflakes seemed to be frozen in mid air, people standing like statues, their eyes fixed in my direction. I could see a young mother holding a mobile phone to her ear. More than likely she was talking to the police about the maniac driving down the pavements. Turning my head slowly, I looked at the lamppost as it came into view again. I could see all the detail: the grey black of the shadow partly obscured by the blowing snow. It all seemed so surreal until I actually made contact with it. BANG! I didn't have a chance to brace myself for the impact it happened so fast. Cold air rushed in as my head punched the side window. I don't know how hard I hit it, but the glass didn't break. It took me a couple of seconds to figure out where the cold air was coming from. The rear panel behind the door had taken the full impact of the crash shattering the lights and bending the boot up like a cardboard box. The back window and side window had shattered sending tiny shards of glass all over the interior of the car. My rucksack had snow and flecks of paint all over it. The car, having achieved a full 360, was pointing back up the road the way I had come. My engine was still running, but I didn't fancy my chances of being able to just pull away from my new closest friend – Mr. Lamppost. I turned round to see where the other car was wishing I hadn't. It was in the middle of the road just sitting there with its engine running, maybe 50 feet away, headlights on main beam.

From my position, I couldn't see a thing. My only hope was that he might think I could see him as well as he could see me. Turning the wheel as far as it would go using four wheel drive I engaged first gear while keeping an eye on the other car and gently pressed the accelerator. "Come on, my beauty," I kept saying. "Come on." To my surprise after a bit of wheel spinning and scrapping of paint, I managed to slowly pull away from the lamppost. Unfortunately, the rear bumper and lights decided to stay with its new best friend, which was a bit of a shit.

The second I started to move, the other car came forward. I couldn't understand why he wasn't on me all guns blazing, but I wasn't about to give him the opportunity. Pressing a button the passenger window slid down as I manoeuvred the car into a three point turn. Once I was sideways on to him, broadside across the road, I pretended to stall the engine. The other car kept coming. At the most, he was only twenty feet away now. "No time to spare." I brought the desert eagle up to the aim firing four shots at his windscreen then his headlights blowing them both to pieces. I dropped the gun on the seat as I accelerated away, snow spewing out behind me as the tyres tried to get a grip on the snow covered road.

"Yippy yi ya, mother fucker!" I shouted out the window. "Bet ya didn't see that one coming, did you?" I was starting to love this car. It was a dream to drive in these conditions. Apart from the gaping hole in the side of it, I couldn't fault it.

The village melted away into darkness replaced by open countryside. Everything was white, even the branches of the trees had a good covering. My lights pierced through falling snow flakes like the beam from a lighthouse. I must have hit my pursuer with a lucky shot as he was nowhere in sight. The road was fairly straight with the odd rise and fall, but nothing this car couldn't handle. Bends were very dodgy, with the snow on the ice underneath. It just meant taking it easy round them.

I had just started to accelerate out of a long steep bend when BANG! The force of the impact took my hands clean off the steering wheel yanking my head back onto the headrest. "What the f ..." Bang! Again, I could feel the car being pushed along. It started to skew to one side, skidding out of control.

"No, you don't," I said to myself, fighting to keep the Subaru under control.

I steered into the skid and accelerated hard breaking free from my pursuer. He tried passing me, but I managed to block his way through. My car twitched from side to side as I increased the power. I had to pull away from this bastard, if I was to stand any chance of taking him out, but he didn't seem to have a problem keeping up with me.

We tore along the snow bound road, each one trying to out drive the other, tyres sliding on the icy surface, wipers only just keeping the my view clear. Up ahead, I could see the familiar black and white arrows indicating a sharp bend to the right. Another sign came into view. "Oh shit," I said out loud. "One in fucking four." How the hell am I supposed to get round and down that?" I shouted out loud, trying to hear myself over the wind rushing in through the gap where my rear door had been. Looking at the speedometer, it read 85 mph. I checked my mirror. There he was right up my arse. Bloody fool was trying to pass me again. One minute he was behind me, the next he was level with my passenger door. I tried ramming him sideways, pushing his car onto the raised verges. Snow was going everywhere as we hit the deeper drifts, going from one side of the road to the other. My gun had fallen into the foot well. I tried steering with one hand while scrabbling around for it, but it was no use. Bit by bit he was creeping ahead of me slowly gaining the advantage. I steered into him again and again scrapping and denting his car, but he wouldn't budge. The bend was less than a hundred feet away. I didn't see how we could possibly make it. He must have seen it as well. He steered away for a split second and then rammed my front wing, trying to push me into the dry stone wall. I hit the brakes as hard as I could. The car nosedived trying to get a grip on the slippery surface. The Subaru slowed a little as he flew past me, his engine screaming. I dropped it into third gear and accelerated again hoping to ram him off the road for good this time, but it was too late. The sharp right hand bend was upon us. I had no choice now. I had to try to take this bend on the inside, using him as a buffer against the sign. I got part way alongside him when he turned into the bend. It was at that exact moment we got eye contact as he looked over his shoulder at me, eyes glairing, shouting something. For a split second, everything stood still in time. Sparks flew everywhere as I forced him into the sign using him to get round the bend. "Does this twat ever give up?" I screamed, trying to keep the Subaru on the road, sliding from side to side like a bobsleigh. The hill was long and steep but fairly straight. It could have been a ski jump if it wasn't for the trees, it was then my eyes zoomed in on the lights coming the other way. Reality came back with a vengeance as he rammed me again. He wasn't mucking around this time though. He just kept on pushing me faster and faster down the steep snow covered hill. "Shit, shit! Fucking stop, you mad bastard!" I was shouting at the top of my voice.

The car heading towards us looked like an idiot was driving it. As it slewed around on the slippery surface, I hit the accelerator managing to pull away from him for a split second yanking the hand brake up whilst turning the wheel as hard I could—not a good thing to do at 85 mph in the snow going downhill.

His reactions were faster than I guessed as he slammed all on trying to gain some manoeuvring space. As the Subaru slewed sideways, I reached for my gun in the foot well closing my hand around the grip as everything went from side to side as he rammed me again. I popped up from under the dashboard firing at his windscreen nonstop until I ran out of bullets. His car slid sideways spraying snow into the air like a huge wave. Throwing the empty gun into the foot well, I pulled my other one out and carried on shooting, blowing my screen out as I fired through the glass. I didn't care anymore. I kept on firing as the Subaru spun around I tried to keep my aim on the target blowing all the windows out from the inside. His car came out of the spin and accelerated hard towards me hitting my front wing sending him hurtling off into the dry stone wall that was buried beneath a thick layer of snow. The impact sent the Subaru spinning out of control, and I lost all sense of direction.

My eyes caught a glimpse of bright red paint work—the other car. BANG! The violent impact threw me around like a rag doll as the BMW hit me head on. My air bag did its best to attack me as all hell broke loose. I saw flames raging in front of me, and then something inside me told me to duck as the Ford Focus came sailing over the top of me hitting my bonnet and then the BMW's nose first. It seemed to pirouette for a second with its rear end high above me and then went spinning off at an odd angle sliding down the hill on its roof with flames pouring from its upturned engine bay.

I sat there in shock just watching the flames trying to clear my head. I wanted to jump out and dive for cover like they do in the films, but I couldn't. My legs weren't budging, and my neck felt loose and floppy. Watching the snow falling through the shattered windscreen reminded me of when I was a young boy on bonfire night. Suddenly, the explosion from the other car's petrol tank brought me back to reality, as the huge fireball mushroomed into the night sky.

"Bloody hell. That was impressive," I said out loud, part coughing and wincing at the same time as I undid my seatbelt. I checked my legs by shuffling them about. They seemed to work okay. I slowly and cautiously moved my neck aware that if it was fractured, it could be wheelchair time. Slowly, I stretched it one way then the other, I heard tiny cracking noises, but that's normal for me. My door seemed to be jammed, so I decided to wriggle out from the half crushed driving position and climbed over onto the back seat. I knew how lucky I'd been not to get jammed in my seat by the force of impact or have my feet wedged under the peddles. I squirmed around until my body was in a position where I could climb out over the seat and through the hole where the rear door had been. Looking around, I couldn't help thinking "What a bloody mess." There were bits of car all over the place. Small areas of snow glowed orange, reflecting the burning car parts that lay all around me as I walked around the other side of the wreckage that had been my car. The size of the crash site shocked me. I couldn't help but look up the long steep hill and then down to where I was standing. I scratched my head. "Jesus. Someone up there must be looking after me," I thought.

I looked down the hill at the other car and then back to the sign trying to work out how he had managed to become airborne, not that it mattered to me that much. Whoever he was, he wouldn't be bothering me again.

"Shit! The driver of the BMW." I tried running over to the

car, but the icy surface took my feet from under me. I went down banging my elbow hard against the road. "Argh! Shit!" I shouted. Slowly getting to my feet again covered in wet snow, I took it more steadily this time brushing the snow off as I went. Both cars were write off's, front ends smashed beyond repair, with smoke starting to rise from under my bonnet. I peered in through the door window of the BMW, but it was too dark too see anything, so I tried opening it but it seemed jammed. It was then I noticed a crease in the front panel,

"The force of the impact must have twisted the shell of the car," I thought.

Still trying the handle, but it wasn't shifting. I went back up to my car and tried the rear door. It opened easily. "Nice one," I said, reaching inside for the rucksack and rifle. "First things first," I thought, reloading both my hand guns and then checking the rifle. I squatted down next to the rucksack just taking in the scene, and I shook my head slowly. "What a mess!" All around me small fires made the snow glow, casting strange shadows across the empty road.

"This is madness, total bloody madness," I thought. The snow was a good six inches deep across the road apart from where the crash had happened. I stood upright looking around me thinking how far I would have to walk to find any shelter in this weather. I got my knife and went back to the BMW, jamming it hard into the seal at the top of the door glass and then twisting the blade through until only its handle remained. Using my body weight, I pressed down hard until the glass shattered. I slipped the knife back into its sheaf and pulled with all my strength on the door frame. "Oh, come on, you fucker!" I shouted.

BANG! The door mirror next to my face exploded.

"What the fuck!" I shouted, falling backwards into the snow, as another shot rang out. My eyes searched desperately to find where the shot had come from. Bang! again. "Whoever was firing at me must be blind," I thought, looking towards the other car I saw a figure staggering around. He fell over and then pulled himself to his feet again. Still holding his gun out in front of him, he fired again and then fell flat on his face sprawled out like a starfish. "Some people just don't know when to die," I said, getting to my feet. He looked out of it, but you never know. Might be playing with me.

I pulled my gun out and slowly walked towards him. It was then I noticed the trail of blood in the snow, a good trail at that. It was positively oozing out of him. "Boy, you're in a state," I said, as I neared him. He groaned and tried to stand, but he was too weak. I kicked his gun away and pulled him over onto his back. Squatting down, I asked, "What's your name, fella?" His eyes just stared back at me.

I checked him for weapons, but he only had a phone on him. I pocketed it. His hand reached up to take it from me but fell short landing on his chest. He tried again, but he was too weak.

I looked at him, saying, "You're going to die my, friend. Nothing can stop it, so why don't you tell me who you are?"

His head slowly turned towards me, but he had gone. I reached over closing his eyes with my fingertips and got to my feet.

"Oh well, another one bites the dust." I headed back to the wreckage to try to get the other driver out of the car.

After some heaving and pulling, I managed to get the door half open, which was enough to get a hold of her and gently pull her out. She must have smacked her head pretty hard, knocking herself out. I checked for a pulse and found one. It was faint, but it was there.

I took a guess at her age being mid twenties. Her clothes looked very expensive, long leather coat, short leather skirt and matching boots, all in black. Her top felt like cashmere. "Who the hell are you" I thought to myself. I checked her for ID, but found nothing. I noticed a gold chain around her neck and pulled it up over her head.

"Well, I presume this is your name," I said, looking at the diamond necklace, "Roxy. Well, Roxy, I'm Tom. Nice too meet you."

CHAPTER 13

Malk headed for the hotel bar where the others would be waiting. He didn't like using outsiders. Things always got out of control. As he went through reception, he asked if there were any messages for Miss Sasco. The woman had a quick look and replied, "Sorry, no. Were you expecting anything?"

"No, just asking," Malk said and went into the bar. The three men looked over at Malk as he approached. They were quietly chatting to each other. The one in the centre directly facing him stood up. Malk didn't like these guys and trying to get them to do exactly what he wanted would be a problem. 'He just knew it'.

"Get us some drinks, will ya?" the huge mountain of a man asked. His name was Conner, and standing at six foot six inches and built like a brick shithouse, his strong Glaswegian accent made it damned near impossible to understand a word he said, but Malk got the gist of it. He looked at the other two, remembering their names from the slip of paper he had stuffed in his inside pocket, Price and Jones, "I suppose you want one, too?" Malk said, they both nodded.

Once they had their drinks, he looked at them for a second. "All the details for this job are in this envelope, you will keep in contact with us on these phones" Malk said, placing them on the small glass topped table, then carried on… "The target is to be taken alive, and the briefcase returned to us unopened. A full description of your target is in the envelope along with all information we have on him at present."

The three men looked at each other then opened the envelope, passing bits of paper around. The one called Jones said, "When do we start then?"

Malk looked at him, this one looked very switched on, then said, "Well, we're not paying you to sit around drinking, are we now?" he said, turning away from the three men. When he did, one of the others said out loud, "There's no photo of this guy. How we supposed to find him?"

Malk turned back to face them, saying, "It's easy. Just follow the trail of destruction." He paused and added, "I'm serious, guys. This one's a real live one." At that, he left, heading for Sara's room.

Ten minutes passed by while the three men studied the documents in front of them. They were just about to leave when Conner's phone started to ring. Putting it to his ear, he asked, "Who is it?"

The soft female voice on the other end said, "This is Sara Sasco. When this phone rings, you will simply say, 'Sara,' and wait for my answer. Do you understand, Conner?" she said.

Conner replied in his usual manner, "Listen, lady. I'll do what I've been asked to do, and that's it. Your problem will be sorted out, and you will pay us in cash on time, or we will fall out. Do you get me?" he said.

Conner turned the phone off, the other two laughing away making fun about "Yes mi lady" and "No mi lady." A few minutes went by when Price noticed a stunning woman standing in the doorway that led into the bar area. He nudged his pals, telling them to get an eyeful of the bit of stuff near the bar. She was all in black, fancy high heels, tight black cords with a black cashmere top. Her long blond hair pulled back into a ponytail. She smiled at Conner and then slowly walked over to where the three of them were chatting.

Conner got up, kicking Prices feet out of the way so he could get around the small table to meet this stunner.

"Hello," she said softly, "and what do they call you?" She

kept coming forward until she was so close to him her lips were only inches from his.

Conner was actually lost for words for once in his life. She was stunning, and her perfume almost intoxicating. "It's Conner," he managed to get out eventually. The other two just sat there totally gob smacked at how this amazing woman found anything remotely attractive about the big ape.

"Put your hands on me," she whispered to him. He gently placed his hands on her waist holding her slim firm body close to him.

"Do you want me?" she whispered again.

"Too fucking right I want you," replied Conner in his best romantic voice, doing his best not to drool.

She ran her hand gently down towards his manhood. Unzipping his fly, she slid her hand inside to find his penis. Conner was sweating big time now as were his mates, their eyes out on stalks almost as if they were in a trance.

She moved even closer, their bodies now touching, kissing him softly on his lips. She took a good hold of his erect penis, gently rotating her hand from side to side.

She said softly to him, "If you ever call me lady again, I will pull your dick off and personally ram it down your throat." When she said this, her grip on his penis tightened like a vice digging her fingernails deep into its flesh.

He needed to scream with pain, but his body just wanted to curl up into a ball. His legs gave way, but Sara hung on. He pleaded with her until she let go, watching him fall to the ground.

She looked down at Conner smiling, then stepped over his body, saying to the other two who just sat there open mouthed not quite believing what she had done, "My name is Sara Sasco. You will call me Sara. You will do as I ask when I ask it. Do you understand, gentlemen?"

Price and Jones got up still looking at the blood dripping off her long polished fingernails.

"Well, are we clear on this matter, gentlemen?" she asked again.

"We are most definitely clear, Sara. We're about as clear as clear gets," Price replied with Jones nodding away next to him.

She stood looking at them then asked, "Why are you standing there? Get moving. I will call you in one hour. Oh, and don't turn your phones off, boys," she said, turning to leave the room.

Jones and Price watched her go. "You've got to admit it. That woman's got one tight little arse," he said, smiling at Price.

"That may be the case," his mate replied, "But look at the damage it caused." They both looked over the table at Conner and started to laugh.

"Come on, stud. We've got a fish too catch," Jones said. With one man on either side of him, they pulled Conner off the floor. He was groaning away to himself and looking very pale. They headed out the bar across the reception and out through the entrance doors heading for the Land Rover TD5 that was parked in front of the hotel. One of them held Conner up while the other opened the rear door. "One, two, three, up you go, fat head," Price said, pushing his large bulk onto the seat.

"Oh, that fucking bitch ," Conner moaned, while he lay there curled in a ball. Jones got into the driver's side, starting the engine up straightaway, while Price sorted some maps out tying them up with his GPS.

Five minutes later with the roads full, cars heading to and fro from the supermarket, the three men watched the heavy snow falling out through the partly misted up windows, headlights and heaters was the name of the game today. Skipton was a busy little town on a quiet day, and today was no exception, everyone wanted to get home before the snow really started to cover the roads. So at a steady pace of just over three miles an hour the men hired by Sara slowly headed towards their target.

"Ok," Price said, reading the map whilst Jones pushed his way through the traffic. "I reckon if we make good time, we should be on target within the next hour or so. The forecast is for more snow. This should keep Joe public out of our way once we clear the town."

"Good. Get Sara on the phone," Jones said. "Tell her we need the exact location of the target and where her man is in relation to that location."

"Oki doki," Price said, already getting his phone out, pressing the call button.

Sara stood gazing out the penthouse window just watching the snow falling. She'd spent most of her life in warmer climates, and even though she was an accomplished skier, she still liked to watch snow falling. It took her back to when she was a young girl. Her dad used to take them skiing in the Alps, but that was a long time ago. Her phone started to chime. She pressed the receive button and simply asked, "What do you need?"

Price told her what they wanted and how long it would be before they could be on target.

"Hold on," she said, while Malk checked the laptop.

"This can't be right," Malk said, looking at the screen. "If this is correct, Stiff must be standing within three feet of him,"

"Check it again," Sara said, walking over to him. She looked over his shoulder at the screen. Both coloured dots were flashing on top of each other.

Price put his hand over the phone, saying, "Sounds like they have a problem. She's on about being within three feet of him."

"We need you there ASAP. Something's come up," Sara said calmly, giving him the information he had asked for, then ended the call.

Malk looked at Sara, saying, "I think you better give Stiff a call, don't you?"

She went over to the bar and poured herself a glass of white wine, "Do you want one, Malk?" she asked.

This took him by surprise. He had only ever once been offered a drink by one of the Sasco family, and that was years ago. He looked over at the bar getting to his feet, saying, "Don't mind if I do. Thanks, Sara." She brought the large glass of chilled wine over to where he was standing. She placed it on the small table next to the laptop instead of handing it to him.

"Don't rush it," she said. "It's not cheap."

Malk had to ask, "What have I done to deserve this?"

She took a sip from her glass, saying, "You are now my official bodyguard, Malk. You've been promoted. Karl has agreed to it, so from now on, you're mine." He stood there not quite sure if this was a good thing or not. He picked his glass up saying, "To the future then." They clinked glasses, as Sara got on the phone to Stiff.

BACK AT THE CRASH SITE

I took my jacket off, rolled it up, and placed it under her head, I didn't have anything of any use to keep her warm, so I had a look inside the BMW to see if she had anything in there I could wrap round her to help keep her warm, but all I found was a black brief case and a mobile phone, which I put in my pocket for later use. The case must be something to do with her work I thought, so I threw it out onto the snow covered road. Just then the mobile I had taken off the other guy started to buzz.

I pulled it out and looked at the tiny screen. It read, "Sara calling." I pressed the receive button and said, "Hello Sara."

Sara didn't recognise the voice to be Stiff's, so she knew it could only be the target. She couldn't believe the nerve of this guy.

"Hello," I said again.

"Hello, Tom," came the reply.

I froze, not believing what I had just heard. I pressed the end call button. "Fucking hell," I thought. That was bloody surreal. I just stood there lost in a world of names and numbers trying to match faces to them, in real time it was probably a matter of a couple of seconds, looking at the small phone in my hand. I turned it off, putting it into my pocket. 'This just wasn't possible. No one knew my real name, and everyone on the plane was dead' but somehow these people had got my real name, which as far as I was concerned couldn't be worse. I didn't have time to start thinking of what the future might hold for me now my true ID was out in the open.

I watched the snow falling for a couple of seconds before I carried on. It had already covered most of the tyre tracks, and both cars now had a good covering making them blend in well. I went over to the Subaru, but I stopped half way. Judging by the flames pushing their way through the gaps in the bonnet, it was fair to say it was well and truly knackered.

The BMW might be a starter though, just because it looked like someone had smacked it in the face a few dozen times didn't mean it wouldn't start. I checked on Roxy again. She seemed okay. She was still out cold, but that's hardly surprising, all things considered. I got in the BMW and decided to have a go at trying to get it started. I turned the key. All the dash lights came on. "This looks promising," I thought. Turning the key all the way, something made a clicking sound from under the bonnet, but it didn't sound like a BMW engine to me.

"Oh, bollocks," I said to myself. Getting out of the car, I stood there scratching my head. "What the fuck do I do now?" I muttered out loud. I looked at my watch, but the face was smashed in.

The snow was getting on for eight inches deep now, so I knew any chance of a passing car was out of the question. I went over to the rucksack brushing the snow off it.

I had a spare set of waterproofs in the rucksack just as a backup. I got changed, the extra layer didn't do much for the temperature, but it would keep me dry.

What I was going to do with Roxy, I had no idea. My best bet was to try and wake her up I reckoned, pulling the rucksack on and fastening the waist belt, so it wouldn't slip about when I moved around. Kneeling down beside her, I started to ask her name gently slapping her face. Nothing happened for a good while, then slowly, she started to come around. Her eyes opened, and she looked at me saying, "Wha, what happened?"

"You've being in a car crash, Roxy," I said, trying to sound calm.

"Who are you?" she said quietly.

"My name's Tom, and I believe you are Roxy, if this gold chain means anything," she tried to sit up, but she was still a bit shaken from the crash.

"Steady now," I said, taking her weight. "Just take it easy for now."

"Where are we, Tom?" she asked.

"Well, that's a good question, Roxy, because unfortunately, I don't know. We're somewhere near a place called Summerbridge, but I'm not sure how far it is from here." I said keeping it simple for now. Her eyes seemed to brighten suddenly like she had some kind of power cell kicking in, then she said looking straight into my eyes.

"Well, Tom, we can't sit here in the snow all night, can we." I knew it was the adrenalin kicking in, I had seen this kind of reaction many times and knew it would only last a short time.

"Put your arms round my neck so I can lift you up," I said, gently. She locked her fingers behind my neck, then sliding my hand under her legs, I lifted her up. I was surprised at how light she was. She asked me how long she'd been unconscious. I took a guess and said, "Half an hour, something like that. To be honest, I'm not sure," I told her.

I asked her if she knew what caused the crash, gently letting her feet touch the ground. "I don't know. It all seems a bit vague," she replied.

"Are you married?" I asked, hoping to get some kind of background on her.

She looked at me and started to cry.

"Hey, come on, Roxy, don't cry," I said, putting my arms around her, trying my best to comfort her. "Why are you crying? What's wrong?" I was starting to feel out of my depth now. I didn't know how to do this caring thing that most people find so natural.

She looked up at me saying, "I don't know who I am, Tom. I can't remember anything." Her eyes said it all. She was totally lost.

"Don't worry," I said, trying to sound confident. "Somehow we'll sort this mess out. I promise you."

She smiled and kissed me on the cheek. "Thanks, Tom," she said. "What do you think we should do now?"

"Well, you see that light way over there?" I said, pointing up towards what looked like a farmhouse in the distance fields.

"Yes," she said.

"Well, that's where we're heading, because where there's light there's heat and most probably food," I said, not letting on that light travels a bloody long way at night. It could have been half a mile or five miles. I just didn't know. The only thing in my favour was the falling snow. You can't see too far when it's snowing which brings the distance considerably and it covers any foot prints we would be leaving.

"How do we get there, Tom?" she asked, not really thinking.

"We walk, Roxy. We walk, so if you don't mind, I need to break off those five inch heels of yours," I said smiling.

"I know you're going to tell me anyway," she said, "But why do you need to break my heels?"

"It's simple, my dear. Those spikes will sink into the snow, and heels aren't the best kind of footwear for going over fields," I said, smiling at her.

She smiled back at me saying, "You're the boss, Tom." I snapped her heels off one at a time, then she said, "I like you, Tom."

I looked up and paused. "Thanks, Rox. I like you, too."

"Are we boyfriend girlfriend, Tom, because I feel I should know you?"

I got to my feet and helped her to stand in her new sawn off boots. "I think you're a pretty amazing person, Roxy, and I would be a liar if I said I didn't find you very attractive."

She looked up at me, saying, "Well, I feel the same, Tom. I know I have feelings for you. I know I have." She reached up and kissed me softly on the lips, a long slow loving kiss. We held each other close, neither of us wanting to let go, but it had to end. I pushed her away gently, saying, "We have to make a move, Roxy. It's getting late, and this weather's only going to get worse." She smiled and agreed with me.

I had no answers to her questions yet, so the only thing I could do was to look after her. She seemed genuine, and I had no reason to doubt her, so like all things in my life, I would just have go with the flow.

We couldn't move fast, because of the snow, and Roxy's shoes weren't up to much. I lifted her over the dry stone wall taking care not to drop the rifle not that it mattered too much as the sights were probably way out of sync now. I just didn't want to clog it up with snow, that and it was like an old friend to me, we had done a lot of business over the years and if it was knackered, then I would find time later to try and sort it out.

"What's the gun for," she asked.

"Let's talk about that later. Trust me, Roxy. Everything will be fine," I said.

"Oh," she replied, still sounding a bit dazed.

The trouble with snow is that it levels everything out. What looked to be a nice flat field turned out to be heavily ploughed, making the going very hard and slow. Roxy held onto my arm, trying her best not to fall over in her new low profile boots. Credit to her though, she didn't whinge about the cold or dampness. She just trudged along beside me.

After what I thought to be a good half hour, we started to go over the crest of the field. I hadn't seen it from the road because of the angle, and the snow blending one field into another had totally hidden the lay of the land. This meant we could no longer see the headlights at the top of the hill, where the black and white arrows indicated the sharp bend in the road that led down to the crash site. I knew it was bad practice to lose sight of roads in this sort of weather, but what choice did I have? We just had to keep going.

Conner was talking to Sara on his phone, when he tapped Jones on the shoulder twice. Jones knew this meant stop. He brought the Land Rover to a slow stand still. At the crest of the hill, he killed the lights but left the engine running.

Conner put his phone away saying, "Sara's tracking device puts the target down there," he said, pointing at the crash site. He carried on, "From what we know, this guy is good with a gun. He's a professional assassin, and by what Sara told me, he shoots first asks questions later."

"So why do we have to bring him in alive?" Price asked.

"Because he has something in his head that our client needs. That's why," Conner replied.

"Anything else we should know?" said Jones.

"Actually yes," Conner said, "He should have a silver briefcase with him. Under no circumstances are we to damage it."

"What happens if it gets shot up by accident?" said Price butting in.

"It won't get shot up, kicked, or thrown under a bus," Conner said, sounding more like himself.

He got out and walked over to the crest of the hill. Jones and Price followed.

"Ok, this is how we will play it. The main impact is half way down the hill in the centre of the road. We can't be sure if the target is still down there, so I'll set the sniper rifle up here. You two use the walls on either side for cover.

Go all the way down on the far side of the wall until you're level with the crash site. Once you're there and I've scanned the sight from up here through the NVGs I'll give you the all clear?" Conner said. "Let's get suited up then," Jones said.

All three men went to the back of the Land Rover to get their kit out.

Each man had a set of white coveralls with matching gloves and covers for their boots. They put their belt kits on and got their weapons out.

"Which do you want?" Jones asked Conner, holding a G3 in one hand and a Heckler & Koch 9 mm MP5SD in the other.

"Neither," replied Conner, pulling out his 9 mm MP5K. "Price, you all set to go?"

"Yep," he answered, checking his MP5K. They all checked the coms, then Conner passed each one of them a 9 mm pistol with three spare mags each.

The two men set off down towards the crash site wading through the deep snow drifts that had built up behind the dry stone walls. Price and Jones had only been gone five minutes when Conner heard the sound of a car coming.

"Stand by," he said.

The other two crouched down where they were.

As the car came closer, Conner moved from his position in the centre of the road to behind the Land Rover, which was parked at an angle across the bend but on the verge, slowly the other car drew near, Conner screwed the silencer onto his pistol.

The car stopped just behind the Land Rover, and the driver

got out. The guy looked in his early twenties, thought Conner, not that it mattered, he fired one shot into his head. The young guy dropped down out of sight, then the passenger door opened as his girlfriend got out, trying to see where her boyfriend had gone. Conner simply aimed and fired again.

"All clear," he said.

The other two carried on.

Conner quickly put the bodies back inside the car. He started it up and reversed back to the small turning just a way back from where the Land Rover was. Taking the car just ten yards down the small lane, he parked it well off the road, thinking the snow would cover it in a matter of thirty minutes making it virtually invisible unless you knew it was there.

Then he went back to his position. Looking through the sites, he could see the burning Subaru, but he couldn't make out the other cars from his angle.

"Jones, how you doing?" Conner asked over the coms.

"I'm opposite the rear of the first burning vehicle now. It looks like a Subaru. It's had a head on with a small sports car. There's another car about twenty metres down from the main crash site. It's on its roof. Looks totally burnt out," Jones went on. "There's a body lying face down, halfway between the burnt out car and the sports."

"Price, what can you see?" asked Jones. There was a slight pause.

"I can see inside the Subaru from here. The rear passenger door is missing. There doesn't appear to be anyone in the front. My guess is whatever happened here we missed it."

"Price, stand by" Conner said,

Price held his position while Conner checked the site again from his position, then Conner started to move forward down the steep snow covered lane, "Keep coming We have you covered."

"On my way" Conner said, slowly making his way down the hill towards the wrecked cars, scanning his night sights from side to side as he went.

He approached the rear of the Subaru, and went down onto one knee holding his gun to his shoulder, saying, "Rear of target. Clear."

Jones slowly crept over the dry stone wall and went forward with his gun at shoulder height ready to shoot. He took the pin out of his stun grenade and tossed it in through the Subaru's windscreen. The second his hand let go of the grenade, he went down into a crouch position waiting for it to go off.

Two seconds later, there was a muffled bang from inside the car as smoke belched out through the shattered windows. At the same time, Price leapt over the wall to give cover from his side.

I looked back towards the car when I heard the dull bang, but the rise in the field blocked my view. Roxy asked if we could stop and rest. I put my arm round her saying, "It's not far now, Roxy. I know you're tired, but we have to get to that house, and you're in no fit state to spend all night outside in the snow."

She gave a long sigh and said, "I know you mean well, Tom, but I am so tired, and my head hurts."

"Roxy, I can't carry you, so let's just give it one last push, then we will stop for the night. I promise you," I said.

What she hadn't realised is that while we were talking we had carried on through the thick snow towards the second dry stone wall. What I hadn't counted on was just how deep the snow had drifted up the side of it.

"You take a sit down while I dig a way through that lot?" I said.

"Don't you want me to help you, Tom?" she asked in a very pitiful voice.

"You need the rest, Roxy," I said. Taking the rucksack off, I sat the rifle down next to her, saying, "It's loaded, so please don't point it at me."

"Ok" she said, watching me plough through the deep snow. It only took a few minutes to make a decent path, flattening it down then scrapping huge chunks out with both hands, then we were off again.

Conner went forward slowly looking in through the car's windows as he went. "Nothing" He met Jones and told him to check the body out, while Price gave him cover from behind the sports car.

Jones walked slowly towards the body keeping his gun aimed straight at it. He could hear Price giving details in his head set scanning the area on Jones's blind side.

"You're all clear, mate," he said.

Jones kicked the arm of the man lying in the snow. There was no movement. His body lay still. He knelt down, brushing the snow off to check his pulse. He was dead. Jones wiped the snow off the man's face, saying, "Give Sara a call, will you? This might be our man."

Price came round from the other side of the red sports car saying, "where're the other bodies?"

Jones turned around, looking up and down the crash site, saying, "It looks like we're two short then."

Conner told them to search the immediate area while he phoned Sara.

Malk was typing away at the laptop, when Sara's phone started chiming. He was about to answer it when she came into the room. He passed it to her, "Thanks, Malk," she said.

"Sara, its Conner. I think we have the target here, but he's dead. There's no sign of a silver briefcase, but we have a black one near his body." Sara asked Conner to describe the dead man to her, she listened. The second he mentioned the short blond hair, she knew it was Stiff.

"What cars were involved in the crash?" she asked.

Conner walked along with the phone to his ear studying the wreckage.

"Well," he started, "It looks like the Subaru hit the BMW head on. I'd be surprised if anyone survived that kind of impact without a lot of injuries. I can't work out how the Focus ended up on its roof though," he said calmly.

"What type and colour is the BMW?" she asked.

"Wait a minute." Came the reply. "It's a red Z4. Why?"

"It's okay," Sara said. "Call me again when you have more information." She ended the call, turning to Malk saying, "I thought Roxy had been in a crash for a minute there."

Malk hadn't seen her like this before. She looked almost loving. "Don't worry," he said, walking over to the bar. "Roxy's probably in a hotel somewhere out of the snow." Sara looked at Malk, but didn't say anything.

We eventually got to the house, I began to realise the scale of it. It was more like a mansion. There must have been thirty windows on this side alone. "Oh well," I thought to myself, "One house is as good as another. We made our way along a small hedge to a gate. I was virtually carrying Roxy now, she was doing her best to walk.

We went around the side of the huge house to what I thought to be the front. "Come on, Roxy. We're here. We've made it," I said, trying to keep her going.

We shuffled past two Range Rovers and across to the front door. I rang the bell hoping someone would answer. Seconds seemed to last for hours as we stood there in the freezing cold, waiting for someone to come and open this bloody door.

Then a voice came from the other side of the big old doors,

"Who are you? What do you want?" I saw a tiny pin prick of light in the centre of the big wooden door. I thought, "Good idea having a peep hole when you live out here."

I said in a loud voice so she could hear me, "My name's Tom and this is Roxy. We've been in a bad car crash down on the hill. Can we rest here please? Roxy's been hurt."

She asked me to stay where I was, and that she'd be back in a minute.

"Okay," I said, "But please hurry."

I don't know where she went, but she was back before I could think of doing anything like nicking one of the cars. The big old door opened to reveal a very plush entrance hall with deep red carpets and antique furniture dotted all around. The walls were covered in large oil paintings and huge rugs.

I looked down at the old lady standing in the doorway. She was wearing a tweed style jacket and skirt in different shades of green with creamy coloured scarf tied around her neck. I thought it was the Queen at first, she looked that posh.

She saw how ill Roxy looked and then said, "Oh, you poor child, come in quickly. Follow me," she said, closing the big door behind us. The old girl must have being in her late seventies, but she was very sprightly for her age. We went through into a huge living room area, while she told me how bad that stretch of road was at this time of year, and how many times she'd complained to the local council about it, but they never seemed to do anything about it.

"Here," she said, "sit her down here, while I get you two something warm to drink."

I lay Roxy down on the big soft sofa that had a velvety feel to it, supporting her head with one of the many cushions. Taking my rucksack off, I placed it on the floor next to me and slid the rifle behind it, not wanting to scare the old lady with it.

Pulling one leg off at a time I took my water proofs off and then the top. It felt good to be in from the cold. Roxy fell asleep almost straightaway, so I left her clothes as they were but pulled her boots off so her feet could get some warmth to them. I looked at her whilst I massaged them one at a time trying to get the blood circulating. "I've never felt this way about anybody before," I said quietly. "You make me feel good about myself. You make me want to be a better person, yet we've only just met."

High above us the two large crystal chandeliers filled the room with a soft light, it felt odd being in a stately home where someone actually lives, I wasn't looking at her face. I was just thinking out loud when a voice said, "You really love her, don't you?" I looked up to see the old lady smiling at me. She was holding a silver tray with two bowls of what smelled like tomato soup on it. She gently placed the tray on a low table next to the armchair, saying, "I'll get some warm water and a cloth so you can clean that cut on her head."

"You're very kind," I said, getting to my feet, stretching my back.

I sat on the edge of the sofa next to Roxy, gently saying her name, but she was fast asleep. I decided not to wake her because she obviously needed the rest.

Just then the old lady came back with the water and things, saying she would be in the other room if I needed her.

Dipping the face cloth in the warm water then ringing it out, I cleaned Roxy's cuts as best I could, and then left her to dream.

The soup looked and smelled too good to waste, so not wanting to seem rude, I finished both bowls off. I pulled the armchair up next to Roxy and tired to relax. Gazing around the room, it fascinated me how people managed to gather so much wealth. I'd always been told that money goes to money, which would probably explain my present situation. The only money I had at the moment that was readily available was the £20,000 I had got off Weister, that all seemed a thousand years ago, and most of that was still back at the cottage. The rest I think went down the river when I had my little winter swim.

Before I knew it, I was fast asleep.

CHAPTER 14

Conner put his phone away, looking at the wreckage, trying to work out what his target would have done after the crash. He wandered over to the edge of the road, checking for footprints as he went.

"Jones," Conner said into his mike, "Check the area above the crash site for footprints. Price, you check the area beyond the burnt out car. He must be close by, so let's move like we have a purpose."

Conner walked along what looked like the roads edge, disturbing the soft snow sending it out in small explosions with each step he took. He estimated its depth at seven inches.

"Deep snow," he thought. "No one can go through this stuff and not leave a trail. It's just a matter of time before we click onto him."

Jones had been wandering up and down the road for thirty minutes now, but all he'd seen were Conner's footprints.

"We're all clear up here," he said into his mike, making his way back down to where Conner was searching. Price had cleared the whole area beyond the wreckage and was now making his way back up towards the others, when he came closer he noticed a set of tracks going off at a right angle from the BMW. He called the other two over who were still searching along the opposite side of the road.

Conner and Jones walked over to where he was standing, Price pointed towards the snow covered dry stone wall, saying, "Squat down and look at the snow at the base of that wall, and then take a line straight up to the top. That's where they went over. You can see a slight delve in the snow." He made an outline in the air with his hand.

"Good work," Conner said, standing up.

Jones, still squatting down, was lining the indentation in the snow up with the cars. He looked back towards the BMW and stood up. Slowly, he retraced the steps back to the car and then squatted down again.

"What you seen, Jones?" came Price's voice.

"I'm not sure," he replied, "But I think one of the two people who survived this has an injury."

"Go on," Conner said, walking over to where Jones was now standing looking at a slight indentation in the snow.

Jones went over to the BMW and tried closing the driver's door, but it wouldn't. He pulled it open again looking at where the door made contact with the main body. It seemed to be a good quarter of an inch out of line, and then he noticed some bits of glass on the seat. It had him wondering while he ran his hand along the door frame, he noticed the mirror then moved closer to it. Conner asked what he'd seen.

"Just a sec," he replied.

Pulling his gloves off, he inspected the small hole in the back of it. It was an exit hole. Keeping his eyes in line with the door mirror, he looked back along the car body. He stood up, saying, "That dead boy down there took a shot at someone standing here. Now either he missed his target, or he wounded him," Jones said, pulling his gloves back on.

"That might explain why a body or something was laying here next to the door," said Price, now pushing the top layer of snow away from where the head would have being.

Conner looked over at the wall and back to Price as he cleared the snow, saying, "How long ago would you estimate this took place?" he said, looking at Jones.

"I have no fucking idea," Jones said in a pissed off voice. "All

I know is that it's been snowing nonstop now for at least three hours. We know he was here when Sara told us about the signal, and with the fact that he may be wounded, I would say he's within a three mile radius of here," he said, walking over to the wall.

"Right," Conner said. "Let's see where that trail leads."

The three men climbed over the wall, dropping down into the field. "Well, that's fucking blown that plan out the bloody water," Price said. Looking across the wide open snow covered field, there wasn't a trace of footprints anywhere. He squatted down, but it didn't help. It was obvious the ground was uneven under the snow. "Why don't you just give Sara a call," Price said, out of interest.

"Because I'm not giving that fucking ball crushing bitch the pleasures of making me look a bigger twat than she already had done. That's why." Conner shouted, still having nightmares about what his dick would still be capable of.

"Just asking," Price said.

"Well, don't," Conner said.

"We split up," Jones said. "Price, you head left. I'll go right. Conner straight on, if that's okay with you guys." They all agreed and set off through the thick snow.

"Sit reps every thirty minutes, chaps." Conner said, speaking into his mike.

Because of the strong wind that was now blowing into Conner's face, it had taken him just over a half an hour to cover the distance between the road and the other dry stone wall at the top of the field. Jones and Price hadn't had any luck yet either. They all seemed to be drawing blanks. He turned round looking back the way he'd come. He couldn't see a thing for snow blowing around. When Conner drew closer to the wall, the snow got deeper until it was nearly waist high. He hadn't worked in these sorts of conditions since selection all those years ago, he thought it was a bag of shit back then and his opinion hadn't changed in all that time. His one and only plus sign was he had found where the target had dug through the deep snow, creating a sort of funnel to walk into just ahead of the wall.

"This is bloody daft," thought Conner, holding his hand up

in front of his face, trying to keep the snow out of his eyes. "This must be the way they came," he thought to himself. Slowly, he climbed over the dry stone wall, the wild blinding snow was coming at him from all directions. He heard a faint voice in his headphones, but the noise from the howling gusts blocked it out.

Dropping down the other side, he tried to call Price. "Conner to Price. Come in," he shouted, covering his ear with one hand trying to hear something, anything. "Come in, Price. Where the fuck are you?" he shouted. It was no good though. "The weather must be messing up the signal," he thought.

Meanwhile, Price was making his way through a small wood at the bottom of the hill when he heard something in his headphones,

"Com, lker, fuck, you argh shi." He stood still trying to hear what was been said, but the message didn't repeat, so he carried on searching.

Jones had reached a small lane that he thought must lead onto the main road off to his left, but he wondered where it led to the other way. He decided to check it out.

"Jones, to Conner. Come in," he said in a raised voice, trying to outdo the wind. He knew the moment he broke cover from the trees the weather would close in around him, so he wanted to let Conner know which way he was heading.

He tried again, "Jones to Conner. Come in."

A tiny voice started to speak in his headset, "Jones, this is Price. I think Conner's out of contact. It must be the weather. I've reached the far end of the forest at the bottom of the hill. Over."

"Jones to Price, I'm heading east along a small lane away from your position, I will contact you again in thirty minutes over and out."

Jones walked into the centre of the small lane, he noticed some tyre tracks that looked recent. He squatted down for a closer look. "Off road tread," he thought, feeling the rough edge of the pattern. The depth of snow here was getting on for ten inches, and it was quite sheltered. Everything had that negative look to it, he thought, pure white roads and fields giving a sharp contrast to the blackness of the trees. He carried on. Jones knew that any sign the target had left would now be well and truly hidden.

He held his hand up in front of his face, when he cleared the tree line trying to protect himself from the howling wind and snow that was now blowing across the fields.

Price was battling against the blizzard now he was in open ground. His plan was to cut across the field he was in and head east up the valley side, meeting up with Conner and Jones. Doing this, they would cover any place their target might be sheltering in.

He ploughed through the nearly knee deep snow like it wasn't there. He'd worked in conditions far worse than this loads of times, he thought, biting into his Mars bar. "Piece of piss," he said out loud, seeing the far end of the field. He changed direction heading east, this would eventually lead him towards Conner's position, if all went well.

Near the top of the hill and totally exposed to the elements, Conner was making his way through the next field. Step by step, the snow seemed to be getting deeper and deeper. He couldn't see a bloody thing in this storm. "We're not getting paid enough for this shit," he muttered to himself, leaning forward into the wind. His next few steps brought the snow up to his waist, which meant either the ground was falling away from him, or there could be another wall up ahead that the snow had drifted over. Using his hands, he dug away at the snow, pushing it from side to side making a hollow for him to stand in. He repeated this action until he found the wall. At this point, it was nearly shoulder height. He packed the snow back, pushing at it with his hands, until he had made a small cave in the side of the hollow just big enough to sit in out of the blizzard. He sat down in his little shelter resting his forearms on his thighs. It was quiet in here out of the wind, so he tried raising Jones again.

"Conner to Jones. Come in." Static filled his earpiece. He repeated the message four more times, and still static filled his ears. Then he did the same to Price. "Conner to Price. Come in." "Price, do you read me, over." "Bollocks to it," he said, picking his gun up, walking out into the snowstorm. He looked northwards following the line of the wall and then south. There was "fuck all" in any direction. The snow had covered everything. He walked back fifty yards the way he'd come trying to get a better perspective on things.

Suddenly, his earpiece burst into life.

"Jones to Conner. Come in, over."

"Conner here, where've you been? Over," he shouted into his mike, pressing the earpiece hard against his head.

"I'm in a cow shed, sheltering from the storm. How you doing? Over," Jones said.

"Do you have anything to report? Over." Conner shouted, still trying to hear what was going on over the deafening noise around him.

"I'm going to follow this lane for another two miles and then I'm turning back. I will meet you back at the Land Rover. Over and out." Jones didn't intend spending all night out in this weather, not when the guy you're hunting kills people for a living. He opened the old cowshed door holding onto it before the wind caught it. He stepped out into the storm pushing the door closed behind him.

"Conner to Price, come in."

"Conner to Price, come in."

"Lker, t nnor in, ver," then static again.

"Shit," Conner cursed to himself, his mind kept wandering to the new million pound villa his brother had just bought in Turkey, "BASTARD" he shouted, kicking at the snow sending a plume of white crystals up that instantly got blown sideways and off into infinity. Then the thought of that briefcase the target was carrying popped into his head, "Bet that's worth a few quid" he said to himself, thinking he might just take that case for himself and sod the others.

He started heading north. That would keep him parallel with the wall and on a heading to meet up with Jones eventually.

Price came to the top of the field now on his third Mars bar, looking back the way he'd come, across to the forest, and along the half buried wall in front of him. He checked his watch, "Conner should be somewhere off to my left but forward of my position," he thought to himself, "so that'll put Jones on a northeast bearing from here. If I head up over that next field, I should meet up with them in approximately 45 minutes," he thought, making his way through the deep snow towards the wall. There was nothing smooth about the way he went through deep snow. He was like a human mole. He just went through it like a knife through butter. Eventually, he came to the wall, got a couple of good hand grips and was over in one swift movement, straight into a snow drift on the other side that came up to his shoulders. It slowed him down for a while, but it wasn't long before he was heading up the field again. As he came to the crest of the hill, he could see what looked like a set of head lights off to his left. Slowly making his way towards them, noticing the ground seemed a lot flatter under foot, he retrieved his night vision goggles. He squatted down to have a better look at what lay ahead.

The headlights turned out to be two glass lamps one on either side of a large front door. The house looked huge, more of a stately home than a private residence. Scanning across the front of the building, he saw two vehicles parked up to the left of the house. He scanned back in the other direction. There was a large fountain structure, and then some out buildings and a tractor and then open fields. He went forward on all fours until he was within fifty metres of the house.

"Price to Conner. Come in. Price to Conner. Come in." Nothing. He tried six times in all but only got static.

"Fine," he said to himself, "I'll check it out myself." He pulled his binoculars out looking for any sensors that may set an alarm off. It was no good though. The blowing snow obscured most of his view. He lay there just watching the house for twenty minutes, totally blending into the background in his white overalls. Then he went forward again. He was only ten feet from the Range Rover, and again he lay still, just watching, looking for any signs of movement. He had his gun to his shoulder now ready to fire with the safety off.

Slowly, he made his way around the car until he was level with the front of the house. He squatted down next to the rear bumper and tried calling Conner again.

"Price to Conner. Come in. Price to Jones. Come in. Any

fucker listening. Come in," he said in a quiet voice not wanting to draw attention to himself. He couldn't see any infrared systems or ark lights on the front of the house, so slowly, he went forward scanning the gun from side to side as he approached the nearest window. It was an old box sash style, four feet wide by at least seven feet high. Gently brushing the snow off the glass and frame, he checked for alarm wires. He saw a tiny yellow wire with two sensors on it inside one of the panes of glass, next to the main wooden frame. He pulled out his micro-torch checking the whole frame for trip wires. As he did this, he noticed the heavy curtains in the room. "That's good," he thought. "With some luck, the room will be clear," he thought. Even with the front of the large house giving some shelter from the blizzard, it was still blowing a gale.

Holding the tiny torch in his mouth, he set to work on the alarm system, making a bypass so the electric current wouldn't be broken when he entered the room.

Five minutes later Price started to slide the window up after removing one pane of glass, fixing the loop in and sliding a bolt round to release the bottom sash. Gently, he pushed it up enough for him to slide through, trying his best not to let the wind blow the curtains around.

His left foot touched the wooden floor, taking his weight, and then he swung his body through. Both his hands held the window frame supporting him as he slid into the room, closing the sash behind him.

I sat straight up listening. Something was wrong. Something was very wrong. Pulling my gun out, I quietly went towards the curtains to have a look out the window, holding it out in front of me with both hands ready to fire. There it was again. "Someone must be behind one of the curtains," I thought. I stood still, my eyes and ears trying to work out where the sound had come from. There were three sets of curtains in this room all down one side. From where I was standing, two of the three were a good fifteen feet away. The other one was directly in front of me. I cricked my neck to get the cramp out of it from sleeping in the chair. The room was very dark with only a faint orange glow from the open fire giving off what little light there was.

It was then I noticed the curtain in front of me move. Still in the aim position, I moved towards the right-hand side of the curtain, putting myself out of the line of sight. Whoever it was coming into the room wouldn't see me until it was too late.

Bending down in the small space behind the curtain, Price lifted the bottom off the floor to see if any light shone through, "Nothing- Excellent," he thought. Now he knew the room was in darkness, the target would more than likely be resting, Price slipped his night vision goggles on, he checked his gun again.

Then sliding his hand along the wall behind the curtain, he started to pull it back, giving him access to the room. He moved smoothly and stealth like not making a sound.

Scanning the room with the NVGs until the curtain revealed the grandeur of the interior of this grand old manor house, slowly Price stepped out from behind the curtain keeping his gun to his shoulder ready to give anyone the good news if he got jumped.

He started to take in his new surroundings tainted green by the night vision goggles. Over to his right, he could see an open door that probably went out into the hall and a big old sideboard with a couple of what he thought to be antique chairs stood next to it and a large mirror hanging on the wall. Price thought about the door again" Must lead into the hall then back towards the front door. Building a mental picture up in his mind of the house interior," he scanned around to the centre of the room.

He noticed some more furniture, an armchair, and a sofa. He paused and looked at the outline on the sofa again. It was definitely a person, and then he noticed the rucksack. "Bingo," he said softly, stepping forward. Just then something moved in the corner of his eye.

"DON'T FUCKING MOVE!" I said, in a calm firm voice. The big guy froze as he felt the gun push against his skull just behind his ear.

"Listen up, snowman," I said, "Place your gun on the floor real slow. That's it," I said as he bent down placing it next to his feet. All the time I had the barrel of the gun pressing firmly against his skull.

"Now kick it away," I said.

He kicked it a good distance into the middle of the room.

"On your knees, nice and slow...slowly now," I said, still holding the gun against his head.

Suddenly without any warning, he spun around smacking me hard in the face just below my right cheek bone with his forearm, I flew backwards from the force of the impact trying to keep my balance, but he was on me in a flash.

Somehow he managed to get my arm twisted round at a really bizarre angle, then "SMACK" as his fist ploughed its way into my stomach. The pain was tremendous bursting open one of my wounds from earlier on.

I tried kicking out at him, but he was too fast for me. "Arrgh!" I groaned when his knee made contact with my ribcage. I fell to the floor thinking, "For fuck's sake." Twisting around I managed to give a couple of good jabs in the face smashing the NVGs in the process, it must have wrecked one of his eyes from the amount of blood that burst out from the impact, he staggered backwards still keeping an iron like grip on my wrist dragging me back with him, I sent a powerful punch straight into his side only to find he was wearing some kind of body amour under the white body suit. Yanking the NGVs off he twisted my arm round forcing me to bend over backwards, I knew what was coming next because it was a move I used, the pain exploded through me when his clenched fist slammed into my diaphragm. I fell into a world of pain, my back arched up as he punched away until he bust my lower ribs then dropped me to the floor while he sorted himself out, this had all happened in a matter of seconds and with very little sound.

He picked me up again holding me by my neck in a huge hand, I tried to punch him repeatedly in the face and upper body, but he just didn't seem to feel anything. He pulled his other hand back launching his fist at my face. I don't remember what happened next, my body flew through the air from the force of the impact, for a couple of seconds everything was fine, I felt no pain and had a strange sense of calm, it didn't last long though, my barely conscious body smashed into the huge mirror in the centre of the antique dresser, upside down and head first I took out all the fancy ornaments that had spent so many years being looked after by the old woman who lived here, the sound of glass shattering and wood splintering filled my head, sudden burning sensations covered my head and face, when thousands of bits of razor sharp glass exploded all around me, I slid to the floor bruised and covered in cuts and splinters of wood that had buried themselves deep into my face and hands.

Snowman pulled his knife out and looked down at the man on the floor, saying, "You're Tom Stone, aren't you?"

My eyes were going all over the place. I felt drunk but in a bad way. I lashed out in a hope of hitting him, but my strength had gone. Never before had I taken such a beating in such a short period of time. It was as if he was just playing with me. I couldn't work out if I was falling or been lifted, but one thing I did know for sure, I was in the shit big time.

He walked over to me and picked me up like a child above his head, holding me there one hand gripping the throat, the other gripping me between the legs. He held me there for a couple of seconds then flung me into the large wall mirror. For no other reason than he could.

I was airborne for what seemed like an hour, then a searing pain shot through my head and shoulders when I hit the mirror.

I fell to the floor covered in cuts and those minute shards of glass that sting every time you move. I didn't know or care what was going on now. I was in my own little world of pain.

Price stood over the pitiful excuse for a human and smiled pulling his plasti-cuffs from his belt, slipping them round my wrists pulling my hands tight behind his back. "You're not going anywhere, mate," he said, fastening another set round my ankles pulling them tight as well, then linking the two together he pulled the target's hands and feet so tight they were touching.

I moaned as the pain of stretching muscles and tearing cuts ran through my body.

"Shut the fuck up," Price said, placing the drawstring canvas bag over the target's head. Yanking it tight, he stood up and kicked me hard in the stomach. Price had never lost a fight in his life, even when one of the instructors in the SAS had set about him, he'd put the guy in hospital. He heard a sound from behind him and reached for his pistol, but it was too late, a volley of gunfire went off. He didn't have time to react, because the bullets tore through his upper thigh knocking his legs from beneath him. The moment he went down, he grabbed his MP5K flicking the switch to automatic. Pulling the trigger back, he let loose a barrage of bullets that streaked across the wall at a thunderous pace. Blowing the old lady back out into the hall where she'd just come in from to see what all the noise was about. Her small weak body was shot to bits, but Price didn't care. He was too busy trying to kill the bastard who'd fired at him.

Roxy dived behind the sofa in one leap, still holding the gun she'd just fired. Tears filled her eyes when she saw Tom through the gap underneath the sofa. "She had to get to him."

Price was still firing, drawing a line of holes right round the room. The bullets impacting into the walls, sending bits of plaster off in all directions.

She lined her gun up with the man's body and pulled the trigger nonstop, screaming at the top of her voice, "Die, you bastard!"

Price jigged around like he was doing some kind of break dancing, with the bullets hammering away at his body.

His face took on a vacant look. In his ears, he could hear a woman screaming, he wanted to keep firing, but his hand went limp. The gun fell to the floor, and then the sound faded along with his life. The white coveralls now covered in blood where the bullets had torn through into his body.

Roxy lay on the thick Persian rug breathing heavily. Her body felt totally exhausted, as the adrenaline left her muscles. Slowly, she dragged herself to her feet, still holding the gun. Tears running down her cheeks she slowly walked over to where Tom was lying on the floor, she fell to her knees sobbing, pulling at the canvas bag covering his face to reveal a badly swollen and battered mess.

"Tom, speak to me," she kept saying. She tried snapping the

plasti-cuffs, but it was no good. Looking around, she grabbed a piece of glass, using it as a knife to cut through the cuffs that had been pulled so tight his hands had started to turn blue.

"Please, Tom, please, wake up," she cried, rocking backwards and forwards holding my head in her lap.

Conner kept trying to raise Price on his headset but to no avail, so he carried on along the top edge of the field with the snow blowing across his path forcing him to keep his head facing away from the large house that was now only100 yards off to his right. In the distance, he saw the shape of the small wood Jones had told him about. It lifted his spirits a bit knowing the trees would give him some shelter for a while.

Jones stood in the middle of the lane, looking around him. "This is bloody madness," he thought. The snow was blowing sideways across the lane, causing the snow to drift nearly halfway across where he was standing. Turning round, he looked at his tracks and then back the way he was heading. He decided to call Conner.

"Jones to Conner Come in, over."

Conner stood still when he heard the voice in his headset. "Conner here What's up? Over"

"I'm heading back to the Land Rover. The snow's way too deep up here to make any real progress. Over"

"Conner to Jones I read you. Sounds like a good idea. I'll let Price know what's happening. Over and out," Conner said into his mike.

"Conner to Price, Come in."

"Conner to Price, Come in."

He kept on trying, but there was no answer. After a while, he tried Jones again and got him straight away.

"Jones, can you have a go at calling Price. I can't reach him on my set for some reason," said Conner, as he entered the wood.

Jones tried six times in all, but Price wasn't answering. This didn't feel right. He knew Price should be well within transmitting distance. Jones pulled his battery pack out checking all the connections as he went. All he could think was either Price's battery was dead or he'd come across the target and he was dead.

He trashed that idea knowing how fast he was. He didn't know anyone who could beat him in a straight fight. Jones and Price had been to a Celtic Vs Newcastle football match, on their way back to the station they had being ambushed by a bunch of hooligans wanting to vent their anger on someone and take a few wallets in the process. Trouble was they didn't know the two were in the Regiment. Price didn't give a fuck about being out numbered four to one and Jones didn't even get a look in which made it eight to one. Each of them went down with one punch. They were hanging off him, laying the boot in and Price just grabbed them by the neck and SLAM BANG! Down they went. He was arrested and spent two weeks on Colchester military prison. On his return his Commanding Officer pulled a few strings to keep him from being thrown out of the SAS, only to get a smack in the mouth for demoting him, 'the rest was just history'. Back then he was greasy fast and a crack shot, but he drank a lot, and it ended with him and one of the Staff Sergeants rolling around in the mud and the rain one winter's morning – which only added to the long list of reasons for his rapid departure from the regiment. He called Conner again telling him to meet him at the edge of the wood.

Conner slowly made his way through the forest. It wasn't particularly hard going. He just felt a bit knackered after being out in the storm. At least in here, the trees kept most of the wind off his back. Up ahead, he saw Jones standing next to a farm gate that must lead out onto the lane he'd told him about.

"Have you been in contact with Price yet?" Jones asked Conner, watching him approach.

"I've tried several times, but he ain't answering," he said, as he came level with Jones resting his arms on the old wooden gate.

Jones looked at him then said, "Price never misses a trick. I think he's onto something."

"That might be," Conner replied, still leaning on the gate watching the snow. "None of us know what this guy is capable of. Anyway, he's probably out there looking for us as we speak. Just because his radio's out doesn't mean he's dead, does it?"

"Let's head back to the vehicle. It's where he'd go, if he couldn't contact us," Jones said, walking past Conner. The two of them started along the road, each step crunching through the deep snow. Both men leaned into the strong wind as snow lashed at their faces making it hard to see where they were going. It was just over a mile from their location to the vehicle, but it still took them over an hour to reach it.

Jones spotted a car covered in a thick layer of snow. Conner told him not to worry since he had dealt with it earlier on.

"What do you mean, 'dealt with it'?" Jones asked.

"When you two went to check the crash site out, they pulled up behind me, so I had to do something," Conner said, as he walked along.

"You shot them, didn't you?" Jones said in a raised voice.

"Yeah, I shot them, alright," Conner replied.

"No, it's not fucking alright," Jones came back at him. "What is it with you? You're not in the Army now, you know. You can't just go round killing innocent people."

Conner looked at him shaking his head. "You still don't get it, do you," he said. "Just because we're not in the regiment now doesn't mean we've stopped being soldiers," Conner said, staring at Jones. "Don't you see? This is what we do. If you wanted to play at happy families, you wouldn't have gotten in touch with Robinson, would you?"

Jones didn't say anything. In the back of his mind, he knew Conner was right, but it still didn't mean killing people for the sake of it was right.

While Jones pushed the snow off his door trying to find the handle, Conner did the same on his side.

"Start her up while I clear the screen, will you?" Conner said, pulling huge lumps of thick snow off.

Jones pumped the accelerator a couple of time and turned the key. It started first time. He took his kit belt off, placed his gun on the rear seat and, turning the heater to full, he unzipped his white snow suit. "Are you going to call Sara then?" Jones asked Conner, who was still pulling great lumps of snow from the windows.

"All in good time mate. Get a brew on first, then I'll call the bitch," he said in a loud voice through the side window, gesturing to Jones to get the brew going by cupping his hands together to simulate drinking hot tea.

Jones plugged the travel kettle into the cigarette lighter after part filling it with snow. He decided to try Price again.

"Jones to Price, come in."

"Jones to Price, come in." he listened to the static on his headset and then gave up just as Conner climbed in, kicking his boots on the side steps knocking the snow off them.

"Any luck with Price then?" he said, unzipping his whites.

"Not a bloody thing," Jones replied.

"Right then, once we have warmed up, we'll head off in the same direction he took down the field through the wood and then track across to where the original meet up point was. We'll keep calling him every 15 minutes. If we have no luck in finding him, then we call it into Robinson," Conner said. "After all, he's the one who hired us for the job."

Jones looked across at him and said, "Deal."

CHAPTER 15

I heard a voice saying my name, but I couldn't make any sense of what the words meant, the pain in my head taking precedence over anything that was going on in the outside world. I didn't know or care where I was. All I wanted was for the pain to go away.

Someone touched my hand, saying my name again, "Tom, please wake up."

Slowly, I started to remember what had happened. The guy behind the curtain, the fight that felt more like a bloody massacre to me, the sound of gunfire, "Roxy," her name jolted me back to reality. I tried to open my eyes but could only manage the left one. The other was too badly swollen. Everything looked blurred and hazy as the room slowly stopped spinning.

Roxy looked down at me smiling. She was holding my hand, her thumb softly stroking the back of mine.

"I thought that man had killed you, Tom. I didn't mean to shoot him." She started crying when she told me how she'd seen me drop my gun when the man attacked me.

"It's not a problem," I tried telling her. "He only got what he deserved," I said slowly sitting upright, small explosions of pain going off all over my body. "Come on, Roxy. Everything's going to be okay." I said, feeling the lump on my forehead under the bandage Roxy must have put on. It was then I noticed all the other plasters and bandages on my arms, hands, and legs. My clothes were ripped and covered in blood, "You've been busy," I said, putting my arm round her. She snuggled up to me, saying, "What do we do now, Tom. If the police come, they'll think we killed the old lady."

"Roxy," I said, "there's something I need to tell you. It's why we can't tell the police, and it's why we had that crash." I got to my feet with Roxy's help, and we both made our way over to the sofa. I noticed two empty syringes laying on the floor, "You found my emergency kit then" I said, noticing that just about everything that had been in the rucksack was now out and laying all over the carpet.

"I found all this stuff when I was looking for something to sort your wounds out with, and the writing on the side of each syringe saying one 'shot only' but you looked so ill I thought I'd better give you both shots" she said.

I looked at her, then gingerly I sat down, holding my side. She passed me a towel with something inside it. I looked at it.

"I've put some ice in it from the kitchen. It'll help the swelling to go down," she said trying to smile. She sat next to me, taking my hand saying, "You can tell me anything, Tom. If you're in trouble with the police, we can work something out, can't we?"

I pressed the icy cold towel against my head, more concerned about the amount of drugs she had pumped into me. I used them in case I got shot doing a job, a quick shot of adrenaline and you'd be surprised how far you can go even with a bullet in your leg, two doses could kill me, but looking at the state of me she had probably done the right thing.

What was I supposed to say? "Hey, guess what babe? I'm an assassin. Oh, and by the way, there's a nuclear bomb in that briefcase."

I held her hand and said, "You're right in a way, Roxy, but it's not that straight forward. You see, in my line of work, I need to stay out of the loop, as far as Joe public are concerned."

She looked at me worried, saying, "What do you mean out of the loop, Tom. What is it that you do?"

"Look," I said, "There's no easy way to put this, so I'm just going to say it. I kill bad people for other bad people." I waited for the reaction, but she didn't even blink. She just stared at me. "Well," I said.

"Well what?" she replied.

"Don't you want to know the why's, wherefore's, and, how wrong it is?" I said, now feeling a bit odd about her reaction.

Her hand was still holding mine, and she looked totally calm. "Is that man anything to do with your work, Tom?" she said, looking at the dead body lying on the floor.

"There's a very strong possibility," I said, "And I doubt he's alone."

"Is that why you had so many guns and knives on you, Tom?" she asked bending over picking one of them up.

"Roxy, there's a lot of bad people in this world. My job, is to reduce their numbers a bit. I'm not trying to justify what I do is right." She placed her hand on my lips before I could say any more.

"Tom, it's not a problem," she said, running her hand over the gun, feeling its weight and the coldness of the steel.

"How long was I out for Roxy?" I said.

"A good hour why" she answered, still inspecting the gun.

"Because we don't want to be here, when his mates show up. That's why," I said, getting up off the sofa and making my way towards the body to get a closer look.

I knelt down pulling the body onto its back. I cringed when my tongue caught the end of an exposed nerve on one of my smashed teeth. The pain made my head spin for a moment. "Let's have a look at you then," I thought, checking through his kit.

This guy was fully loaded, six spare magazines for his MP5K plus a couple of flash bangs. "This boy's either SAS or ex special forces," I thought. Mercenaries came to mind. That would match up with Weister's dirty tricks. "I must give him a call just to thank him."

"Do me a favour, Roxy, will you," I said. "Have a look in the kitchen for some keys to one of those Range Rovers. If you can't find any there, try next to the front and back doors."

She went off without saying a thing, which was okay with me, she had enough to take in for the moment.

I took his flash bangs and a small electronic compass, pulling his headset off, I checked to see if the channel was still open. As I did this, I heard a tiny voice in the ear piece. Quickly, I put it to my head to listen to what was being said.

"Conner to Price, come in."

"Conner to Price, come in."

Then "Price, if you can 'ear us we...he'din...in...yo' r 'dire..." the signal stopped.

I had no idea how far off they were or how many of them there was. Standing up, I noticed the state of the room. Smashed furniture lay strewn about the floor. Bullet holes made wavy lines right around the walls, cutting through paintings and fancy plasterwork. My eyes were sore from the beating, and rubbing them only made it worse. While I looked around, I saw the body of the old lady lying in the hallway. She must have taken the full force of the bullets because her cream blouse was in tatters covered in blood. Seeing her there, made me hate these murdering bastards. The effects of the drugs were kicking in nicely giving me more strength with every second that passed. I grabbed his spare mags and grenades and placed the MP5 next to the rucksack and went in search of Roxy.

I couldn't walk too fast from the pain in my side and had to make do with a kind of shuffling motion which seemed to take forever to get anywhere. I knew I had some strong painkillers somewhere in my rucksack, but to take more after a couple of syringe loads would be asking for it so I had a quick dig around and put six in my pockets for later. Using the doorway to have a rest, I looked round the kitchen. It was huge with a big old range under a large stone fireplace. In the centre of the room, there was a wooden table with six chairs dotted round it. Roxy sat on one of them looking at a small photo in her hand.

"What you got there, Rox?" I said, shuffling over to her.

"I found it in my pocket. It's a picture of two women. I feel I know them, but I just can't remember, Tom," she said staring at the small colour photo.

The anguish on her face made her frown. I could see her trying to bring back her memories. I tried to break the mood by asking if she'd had any luck in finding the car keys, but Roxy was miles away, searching her mind for some clue as to who she was.

Conner and Jones made their way through the wood at the bottom part of the hill. Now and again, they caught a glimpse of footprints. Each time this happened, Jones would squat down and check the pattern. This was easy in here because of the lack of snow fall.

"It's definitely Price," Jones said, getting to his feet. "You can work out the path he's taken. He'll head straight down the edge of this wood and then carry on down the next field following the line of the road," he said, pointing off into the distance.

Conner had no need to question Jones's methods. He knew Jones and Price had worked together in the past. The two men carried on until they came to the field.

Conner looked out across the open space. Everything was pure white. He cast his eyes towards the night sky saying, "Looks like the snow's easing off then."

"I'll try Price again," Jones said, leading the way down the field in the deep snow.

Conner followed in his footsteps. He didn't like crossing open ground when he knew one man was missing, and their target was an assassin who could quite easily be waiting for them somewhere up ahead.

"Jones to Price, come in."

"Jones to Price, come in, Price. Over."

"I missed the first message but caught the second 'Jones to Price.' That means there's at least two of them out there." Roxy was still looking at the photo when I had an idea. "Roxy, do you remember what you look like?" I asked more out of curiosity then anything. She looked up frowning and pushing the chair back when she stood up heading across the kitchen and out the door I had just come through. "Wait a minute, will you," I said, trying to keep up, but by the time I'd reached the doorway, she was heading out the one on the opposite side of the room. I leant against the doorframe resting my leg until I felt I could carry on.

Roxy stared at her reflection in the large mirror, as images flashed through her mind of yachts, sports cars, Stone, Tom Stone, something about that name, hotels and dead bodies, people screaming, a tall handsome man with black hair, and a younger man, and then the image of a blond woman came to the front of her mind. Quickly, she pulled the photo out, a smile came to her lips, and she mouthed the word Sasco.

Conner and Jones came to the far end of the field, Jones turned round and looked back the way they'd come, and then asked Conner what time he called Price when he'd said he was in the wood.

"How the fuck should I know?" was Connors reply.

"Because if you knew what time he was in the wood, we could work out how long it took him to get here, which might give us an idea as to how far he's gone," Jones said, trying to get through to Conner.

Conner looked around him and said, "We go that way up the field."

"Why?" Jones asked.

"Because if you think back to where those foot prints were..."

"Go on," Jones said.

"You went up then right. I went straight up. Price came down, and then he would have headed left up the field heading east to meet up with us."

"Sounds good to me," Jones said, indicating to Conner to lead the way.

"Roxy," I said out loud. Can you give me a hand? I'm having a hard time here." I used the sofa like a handrail and took a couple of unaided steps across to the wall, slowly ending up at the old lady lying on the floor in the doorway leading to the hall. Roxy came over to me smiling, "Tom, I've remembered my last name. It's Sasco."

I smiled at her saying "Well, it's nice to meet you, Roxy Sasco."

"And it's nice to meet you, to, Tom Stone," she replied. She turned away. Her smile slowly slipped from her face, more memories pushed their way back.

"The keys, Roxy, we must find those keys before his mates turn up."

Roxy lifted her closed hand in front of her out of Tom's view. The keys sat neatly in her palm. Why did she feel so much betrayal, so much deceit in her veins? Something was nagging at her subconscious trying to work its way through all the confusion.

She turned round holding them out in front of her. "I found them in the kitchen on the worktop," she said.

I took hold of them.

"You shouldn't be walking around, Tom. You're in no fit state," she said in a motherly voice, gently helping me to sit down. I knew something was bothering her, but I could only put it down to the smack on her head. I was actually feeling better than I looked, my body had taken a good kicking, and I had a nice fat lip and a swollen eye for my troubles. Adrenalin is a wonderful thing when you're in a bad way. It can keep you going for hours.

I was still trying to put some kind of plan together using what tools I had to hand like the Range Rover and weapons. There's always something that can be put to some use. I had started to wonder if Roxy had something to do with everything that had been going on. Okay, she had saved my life, but that didn't mean she was on my side. All I could do for now was play along and try to keep an overview of the situation. Paranoia can kick in so easily in my profession. It just creeps up on you like depression does. It's fair to say I had a lot going on in my head, but more pressing things needed to be dealt with for now. I wanted to get out of here, the sooner the better.

"Roxy, can you carry my rucksack and the handguns out to the Range Rover? I'll get the rifle and the MP5K."

"You're not carrying anything, Tom. Look at you. You can only just walk. Sit there while I put everything in the car," she said, picking the guns up.

I didn't want to start bossing her about, but I didn't like anyone touching my guns. It was like someone else driving your car when you're not in it. It just didn't feel right. She'd left the rifle for the next trip. I tried to bend down to pick it up. Bad idea. Pain shot through my stomach and sides where Roxy had bandaged my previous wounds that were now weeping from my beating.

She trudged through the deep snow across the front of the big house towards the cars, pressing the key fob as she approached them. The soft beep of the horn and flash of the indicators telling her the doors were now open. She felt around where she thought the door handle would be, pushing snow off the paintwork as she did. "Found it." Lifting it up, she pulled back opening the passenger door. Snow fell from above into the car's dark interior covering half the seat and part of the foot well. "Shit," she said, dropping one of the hand guns into the snow.

She took a step sideways to open the rear door, and her foot pushed snow over the fallen gun covering it. She pushed the overhanging snow off the doorframe not wanting the same thing to happen again. She opened it up leaving the guns on the back seat and headed back inside not realising she had dropped one of the guns in the snow.

Roxy came in from outside. "It's stopped snowing, Tom, but it's very deep out there. Are you sure you want to try driving in it?" she said. Her manner seemed a little more relaxed now she was keeping herself busy.

"We'll be fine" I said, pulling myself to my feet. She picked the rucksack up.

"Why don't you let me drive, Tom?" she said, helping me out into the hall.

"Are you a good driver then?" I asked, trying to walk a bit better now the painkillers were kicking in.

She kept looking forward guiding me along the hall towards the front door.

"There are three steps, Tom, and they're covered in snow so let's be…"

I cut her off mid sentence. "Roxy, I'm not a little boy I just need a bit of support. This was bloody frustrating. "ARRGH!" I shouted as the icy wind found my broken teeth, sending stabbing pains right up the front of my face.

She turned to me, asking, "What's wrong, Tom? Are you alright?"

"Oh shi, ma bloody teth," I said, rubbing my jaw with my hand. Together we shuffled through the snow heading for the Range Rover, Roxy giving me words of encouragement as we went.

She opened the driver's door all the way so it made it a bit easier for me, and then slowly she lifted one leg in and took my weight while I pulled myself in and onto the seat with a long painful groan.

Conner held his hand up. The signal told Jones to stand by. Slowly, Conner went down on one knee, holding his gun level with his shoulder ready to fire. Jones mirrored his actions. Conner pointed forward with one hand. Jones looked in the direction he was pointing. He saw the two people getting into a vehicle.

"What do you think?" Jones said.

"One male, one female, the male looks injured," Conner said.

"You okay, Tom," she said, frowning at me.

I nodded, as she closed the door. Before getting in, she cleared the front screen of snow and then the side windows.

I started the engine. Thankfully, it was an automatic. The sound it made was defiantly a V8, top of the range, probably less than a year old by the smell of new leather. I pressed a couple of buttons to adjust the seat to my liking. Roxy climbed in then got busy looking in the glove compartment, sifting through bits of paper. "All the documents are here, Tom. By the looks of it, they've only just taken delivery of this, because the registration document says 10/11/08."

"Do you want to take them?" Jones said.

Conner paused for a moment and said, "Take the shot, but for god's sake, don't kill him."

"That's easier said than done at this range," Jones said, getting into a comfortable firing position. "This is an assault gun not a sniper rifle."

"Stop fucking moaning and just take the shot," Conner said, getting ready to run at the target once Jones had done the business.

I sat in the driver's seat familiarising myself with the controls for a couple of seconds. For some reason, every car maker puts indicators or wiper blade controls and all the other stuff in different positions just to make it bloody awkward each time you get in a different kind of car. The petrol showed less than half full. "Bollocks," I thought, knowing how thirsty these things were.

"Where we headin Tom?" Roxy said.

"Well," was all I got chance to say when the driver's side window exploded into a thousand pieces next to my face. Instinctively, my body turned away from the glass because it blew inwards showering me with tiny shards. Roxy started screaming at the top of her voice. Yanking the gear knob back into the drive position, I hit the accelerator, but the car didn't move. Twang! Another bullet ricocheted off the body panel just below where the first bullet had shattered the window.

"Think, you fool," I said to myself, my mind went at two hundred miles an hour trying to figure out why the car wasn't moving. In the commotion, I'd totally forgotten about the bloody handbrake. I released it as the third bullet hit the door post not two inches from my head.

Conner was up and running at the target with his gun at his shoulder while Jones gave him cover. He dropped down onto one knee still keeping his gun aimed at the target. Then Jones got up and started running being only fifty metres from the car when they started to get incoming from the target.

I'd grabbed the MP5K off the back seat I'd taken off the other guy and gave them the good news. I had to keep them from getting any closer. My only hope was to keep firing short burst's because I didn't want to run out of ammunition, and it kept them pinned down. The Range Rover skidded about a bit, so I eased off the accelerator. The car started to move until the bastards shot the hell out of my tyres. Roxy was still screaming. I didn't know why until I looked at her holding her blood soaked hand. The first bullet must have hit it after passing through the window. Fighting the steering wheel, I tried to get the car to go in a straight line, but it wasn't having any of it. We were pushing snow into a pile in front of us now the tyres had gone.

"Get out, Roxy. Get out now," I shouted, coming level with the front door of the house. She looked at me in a daze, tears pouring from her eyes she held her hand close to her chest.

"Roxy, listen to me darling, you have to get out right now, or we're both going to die." She nodded slowly, pulling the handle back to open the door, I spun round firing again doing my best to stop their advance, but these guys knew what they were doing, while one fired at me the other came forward.

I had no choice. I had to get the rucksack from the back seat and my guns, if we were to stand any chance of escape. Kicking the driver's door open, I rolled out dropping down into the snow firing long continuous bursts from my gun. Both men dropped down into the snow taking cover.

Getting to my feet, I made my way as quickly as my injuries would allow round to the back of the Range Rover yanking the rear passenger door open, pulling the rucksack out. My eyes searched desperately for my guns, but I only saw one pistol and the rifle. Using the vehicle for cover, I grabbed my jacket which had the phones in I slung the rucksack over my shoulder. I didn't feel any pain now, my muscles filled with adrenalin. Roxy had disappeared through the front door of the house just before another hail of bullets came thundering towards us shattering all the glass in the Range Rover peppering the body work with holes. The noise was outrageous. "Bloody hell!" I shouted, grabbing the pistol.

I backed away from the vehicle heading for the open door of the house. Getting out one of the flash bangs I'd taken earlier pulling the pin, I lobbed it in the general direction of the gun fire, waited a couple of seconds and then ran for the door begging for it to go off. Gun fire exploded everywhere behind me making me instinctively dive for the house doorway, but something pushed me through it sending me sprawling onto the floor. Roxy slammed the big wooden door shut behind me, sliding the bolts across at the top and bottom, getting to my feet I grabbed her good hand dragging her along the hallway towards a door at the far end.

"Where are we going, Tom?" she said, half crying.

"I don't know yet, but we have to find another way out of here." I said dragging her along the hall towards another big door. I kicked the door open, dragged Roxy through and then closed it behind us. We were in a large dining room with wood panelling on the walls and a huge table in the centre easily big enough to seat twenty people.

"Come on," I said, as we made our way to the far corner of the room towards another doorway on the opposite side. When we approached it, we heard gun fire again.

Conner went forward because Jones was firing at the front door. Bits of wood flew off in all directions as the bullets impacted deep into the oak. Conner signalled him to go right so he could see round the front of the Range Rover. Jones did this, then Conner threw a flash bang into the car through the driver's side window. After a couple of seconds, it went off filling the car with smoke. Jones appeared from behind a small bush further along the front of the house, waving his hand to give the all clear sign to Conner. They both approached the solid oak door, Jones said in a whisper, "If he's waiting on the other side of this, he's in for a shock," he said, pulling a grenade out.

Conner reached into his belt kit to get one out, but his phone started to ring.

"Guess you'd better get that," Jones said, standing back from the door.

Conner pulled his gloves off and got the phone out. Pressing the button, he said "Sara" and waited for the reply.

"Why haven't you been in contact? It's been over two hours since your last call," Sara said.

"Look, Sara," Conner said in a rushed manner, "We're right on top of the target, so if you don't mind, I'll call you back when I have something to tell you." Conner turned his phone off looking over at Jones smiling.

Jones frowned at him, shaking his head. "You'll lose those balls of yours at this rate."

Each man placed a grenade next to the door pulling the pins at the same time and then ran for cover on the far side of the Range Rover.

Just sit there Rox I have to do something. "What, why?" she said. "Just stay there will you" I said. I went back through the dining room and placed a grenade in the door frame, these big old houses have deep casements. I used the surround to wedge the device between the frame and door.

Kneeling down I checked the grenade again pulling the pin, gently, "that should slow them up a little" I thought, heading back through the room I repeated the exact method on the second door, it's a fool proof set up, they can't see the grenade and they can't reach or see it. Roxy sat watching me still holding her hand, "You want them dead. Don't you" she said.

I'd have to sort it out, or she'd bleed to death in two or three hours, the smell of boot polish and leather filled the air. I flicked the light on hoping by being on the far side of the house our pursuers wouldn't see it. Thankfully, there didn't seem to be any windows, which made me feel a bit more secure for the moment. Looking around, the walls were full of pictures of race horses, rosettes, and photos of the old lady with a young girl that looked like her daughter, possibly in her late twenties early thirties. The room was painted in a light cream colour with terracotta tiles on the floor. The smell of leather seemed to be coming from all the riding boots and straps over on the far side. I sat Roxy down on a small stool and started searching for something to wrap around her hand to stem the blood. But first things first, "Tom, I've been shot." She said looking up at me. "I know you've been shot Rox, just try to suck it up" I said. "It really hurts Tom" she said, turning her hand around, looking at the wound.

"I know, Rox. Don't worry. I'm on the case," I said with my head in one of the cupboards. "Try to keep your hand up. I think it will help." I didn't know if it would, but that's what my dinner lady used to tell me when I was at school.

"Let's try this," I said gently placing a thick white dressing over the hole and then wrapping a length of bandage round her hand. The blood soaked through at first but slowed once I'd built a few layers up. I was kneeling in front of her tying the bandage off when a huge explosion shook the house. Roxy jumped "Wha...what was that, Tom?" she said, gripping me round the shoulders. I was more concerned about the grenade sitting in the door just a couple of feet away, especially when I didn't know a direct exit to belt out of.

Jones's head popped up from behind the Range Rover. He couldn't see a thing because of all the dust created by the explosion. Conner looked over at him and then gave a nod in the direction of the door. Jones brought his gun up ready to fire, Conner slowly went forward one step at a time. Once through the doorway, he waved Jones to follow him in.

The two men stood amongst the rubble and smashed wooden door, scanning their guns back and forth. The only person in view was an old lady lying on the floor about ten feet away. Conner looked at her, saying, "We didn't kill her. Whoever did that did it from inside that room over there." He pointed his gun in the direction of the body.

Jones went forward slowly taking a wide angle to get a better perspective of the doorway, using his night sights he checked out the room then gave the nod, whilst Conner moved along the wall leading up to the opening.

"Do you see anything," Conner said, pulling out another flash bang. Jones just shook his head, squatting down. Conner pulled the pin and threw it into the room and then stood back as the dull explosion went off.

Jones flew past Conner heading into the room, giving a few short bursts from his gun to give Conner some cover. Conner followed him in. After a few seconds, the smoke cleared to reveal Price's dead body lying in the corner.

"Well, that explains why we couldn't reach him," Conner said, walking over to the blood splattered body.

"Look here," Jones said picking up a plasti-cuff that had been cut in half. He looked around him at the state of the room, noticing the bullet holes and broken furniture. "Looks like Price came in through the window judging by the damp patches on the floor, and then he got jumped, a fight broke out. He won then, tied our man up using these," he said, holding the cuffs up, "And then someone shot him from behind by the looks of these wounds." Jones now squatted down next to Price's body.

Conner went back through to the hall, whilst Jones was checking the body out. "They went this way," he shouted, heading towards a door at the far end of the hall. Jones came running out from the lounge just as Conner was about to open the big old oak door.

"Don't fucking move" he shouted, Conner turned the handle. "Its not like he had any time to set traps, he's on the run and he's got baggage" he said, knowing exactly what Jones was on about. Slowly, Jones squatted down beside Conner's right leg next to the door frame. He had a quick delve in his pockets and pulled a trace wire out. Running it up the slit between the door and the framework up to the handle where the internal workings stopped the wire from going any further. "It's safe," Jones said, standing up.

"Keep an eye out for booby traps," Jones said. Turning away, he wanted to check Price out again, Conner looked at him, and opened the door, the sound of the grenade slowly rolling across the 200 year old wooden floor boards was barely audible above the bits of rubble and plaster falling from the ceiling, Jones saw it though, grabbing Conner's arms from behind he yanked the big Scot backwards, pulling him with all the strength he could muster.

Conner reacted in an instant, thinking the target had taken Jones out and was now trying to sort him out. He spun around pulling his hand gun out in the process, ready to give him the good news. The explosion blew Conner clean over Jones sending him flying back out through the front door along with dust and splinters of wood landing on the rubble and bits of wood that was left of the front entrance to the house.

After some sorting out and a lot of cursing he came back in to find Jones in the front room.

"He's taken Price's gun and grenades, so there's a good chance he's running out of ammunition," said Jones.

"What makes you think that? He's probably better armed than we are judging by the way he's taking people out left right and centre." Conner said, he went into the dinning room and walked around the large table in the middle of the room.

The door wasn't quite closed making Conner weary of what lay behind the solid oak door.

"Let's go," I said, getting to my feet, pulling her arms off me and after hearing the first grenade go off. "The adrenalin must be wearing off," I thought, because all my aches and pains were starting to come back.

"Check to see where that door goes, will you?" I was hoping it lead outside, judging by the gear in this room. She turned the big old key in the lock and pulled the door towards her letting a cold draft in.

"It's a porch," she said, wandering out through the doorway.

I found her trying to open a half glass panel door that looked like it hadn't been used since the house had been built.

"Let's have a go," I said, squeezing past her in the small dark porch, stumbling over shoes and wellies that were scattered around the floor. It didn't help with the rucksack being so bulbous. I gave it a pull and noticed the bolts top and bottom. As I pulled the top one back I heard faint voices heading our way. Quickly, I yanked the bottom one across but didn't get chance to stand up when the grenade went off behind us.

CHAPTER 16

Sara took a sip of her wine. She was concerned about the whereabouts of her sister. She should have been at the hotel by now. Malk could see the frustration in her face but didn't want to say anything in case he got a mouth full off her. He typed away at the laptop checking on the three men who he'd sent after Stone. The screen showed all three of them inside a large manor house. Two were moving one stood still. The image showed a detailed outline of the house in grey with a few outbuildings dotted around the main structure. Fine lines filled in with a different shade indicated where the roads were. The three pulsating red dots showed his men. When a blue one appeared, that gave the location of the target. But unfortunately, there wasn't any sign of it at the moment.

"Just type in Roxy's number Malk. Let's try to pick her signal up." Sara said from over near the bar.

Malk tried her number but to no avail. He rubbed his eyes, having not had any sleep for over 24 hours. It was starting to tell on him. Glancing at his watch, it read 3:45 a.m. He sighed, "There must be a way of locating her." He pulled up a route map on the laptop showing her last known location and then typed in Summerbridge which was where she said she was heading. He hit the enter key. The screen showed the most direct route from Knaresborough to Summerbridge. He then typed in places to stay overnight en route. A couple of seconds later, the screen showed a short list of hotels, public houses, and bed and breakfasts complete with phone numbers.

"Sara," Malk said, looking up from the screen, "Do want me to ring these places to see if anyone matching Roxy's description is staying there?"

"No," Sara said, walking towards him, "I'm going to call Dad and ask him to come over."

Malk's heart nearly stopped when he heard her say that. He didn't want Karl Sasco getting involved in this. Things had a bad habit of getting very bloody when he was around. "Though thinking on it, how it could get much worse?" he thought.

Karl walked slowly along the jetty in the bright midday sun towards his Bentley, his phone started chiming. The tone of the phone told him it was Sara calling.

"Hello, my darling, what's wrong?" he said in a soft voice.

"Dad, I'm worried about Roxy. She hasn't turned up yet."

Karl's mind started to race. He had received a text from her yesterday telling him she had been successful in getting the list from her contact at Interpol. And she had even sent the more important names over using her secure "text burst," the scrambler ensuring confidentiality from prying security services. "When did you hear from her last, Sara?"

"She rang me earlier on today saying she'd be with me within the next couple of hours, but I haven't heard anything since."

Karl knew Sara wouldn't have phoned him unless she was out of ideas. He stopped walking while he gathered his thoughts. The six bodyguards that were following him automatically took their positions around him, all facing out in different directions scanning the area behind their sunglasses.

"Sara," he said, "did Roxy tell you she had to change her car? That could have delayed her."

"Why? When?" came Sara's reply.

"She was in a place called Knaresborough when the police caught up with her, so she had to blow the car." Karl said, wondering why Roxy hadn't told Sara about it.

"What?" came Sara's voice over the phone. "I thought Roxy wasn't known to the police over here," she said, annoyed at the fact that her little sister had to use false IDs. Tears started to form in her eyes. "Dad, I think Tom Stone's got Roxy."

Karl's grip on the phone tightened as the veins on his temple swelled with rage. He spoke softly into the phone, "Don't worry, Sara. I'm coming. Everything will be fine. I will see you soon. Is Malk with you?" he asked.

"Do you want to speak to him?" she said.

"Yes, put him on."

"Malk, Karl wants to speak to you," she said, handing him the phone.

When he raised it to his ear, a cold sweat came over him. Not many people got to talk directly to Karl Sasco. Most went through Tony Weister, his right-hand man.

He held the phone to his ear, saying, "Malk here," and waited for the reply. It seemed to take forever, but in real time, it was only a fraction of a second.

"Malk," came the soft voice, "I want you to look after Sara. Don't ever leave her side. I'm putting a lot of trust in you, Malk, so don't let me down. Do we understand each other?"

"Yes, we understand each other, Mr. Sasco," Malk said, trying not to sound too scared.

"Good" came the reply. At that, the phone went dead.

Karl put the phone back into his trouser pocket. Taking his sunglasses off, he looked out over the bay at the palms blowing in the breeze. His pale blue eyes glistened in the sunlight.

"Are you alright, Mr. Sasco?" one of the bodyguards asked.

Karl turned his head to look at the man who had spoken to him, putting his sunglasses back on, but didn't answer.

He carried on towards the car, the driver got out to open the rear door for him. Karl knew that at least two of the men behind him would now have their guns out at the ready. He nodded at the driver then climbed into the cool leather interior. His men piled into two black Mercedes that were parked behind the Bentley. Then the three cars pulled away, one of the Mercedes passed Sasco's to give front and rear protection.

"Where to, sir?" asked the driver.

"My villa and call my pilot. Tell him to have the helicopter ready for my arrival." Sasco was quietly raging inside. He wanted this bastard Stone, and he wanted him alive. Looking out through the tinted glass as the three cars sped along the dry dusty road, "He's going to beg me to kill him" was all that was going through his mind.

Malk looked over at Sara. She'd fallen asleep in the chair just after finishing the call with Karl. The half empty glass of red wine she was holding had fallen to the carpet making a small stain. He decided to get a bit of shut eye while things were quiet. He set the laptop to alarm if any change occurred and got comfy in his chair. His eyes were so raw from being awake for so long he found it hard to relax from being over tired, but he was soon nodding.

He woke up with a start. "Too fast," he thought. Makes you feel all sick inside and upset. He rubbed his eyes trying to get the sleep out of them. It was then he noticed the small green dot flashing on the screen, and the annoying pinging sound coming from the laptop. A number was flashing alongside the dot, "(86043496rxy)." He looked at the number, and then it twigged "RXY" is Roxy.

"Sara," Malk said in a loud voice. She moved around trying to get comfy, making small murmurs as she did. "Sara," he said again. This time he added, "I've found Roxy."

She sat bolt upright straight away. "Where is she?"

"Being chased by our three men by the looks of it," he replied.

Conner looked at the big old door that led out to some other room. It looked safe, and he couldn't see any way of getting Jones fancy little wire thing down the edge of it, so he just pulled it open. Conner shouted, "Grenade!" diving to the ground to escape the blast. Jones turned on his toes diving sideways out of the way. He hadn't even landed when the explosion went off blowing bits of timber and plaster everywhere. Both windows in the room blew out sending shards of glass flying in all directions. Conner took some of the blast on his legs, sending him reeling across the floor. Luckily, he didn't sustain any real injuries, but he was quite shaken all the same. Jones looked over at where Conner had been. There wasn't anything left but bits of rubble and smashed timber. The dust cloud was like pea soup, so he didn't see any reason to move until it had cleared.

"Conner," he shouted. "Conner!" No answer. It didn't mean he was dead, more likely just shaken or deafened by the explosion. Just then a figure came crawling across the floor towards him kitten style, elbows and shins. Jones pulled out his 9 mm pointing it towards the ghostly figure, but it was Conner. He put the gun away.

When Conner reached him, he rolled over onto his back, saying "I'm gonna get that fucker, if it's the last thing I ever do."

"Fuck's sake!" I shouted, as the grenade went off at the far end of the other room. Roxy flew into me pushing us both through the doorway out into the snow covered courtyard rolling across the icy cobbles. Once I got my bearings, I looked over at Roxy, saying, "You okay?"

Getting to our feet, she nodded, saying, "Yes, I think so. What was it?"

"I put a booby trap on the other door in case our friends followed us, and it looks like they found it." I said, taking two more grenades from my pockets that I'd taken from Price. I pulled both pins and sent them bowling through the small utility room into the kitchenette room. Taking her hand helping her to her feet, I said, "Time to go." We looked around trying to see a way out of the courtyard. The tall buildings on either side of us blocked out most of the moonlight, that was now pushing its way through snow clouds as they dispersed. Seconds later, two massive explosions could be heard inside the house as a huge cloud of dust and debris blew out through the doorway we'd just come from.

"Holy fucking shit!" Jones shouted, as he saw the two small objects heading towards them, knowing they had less than ten seconds before they went off. He leapt over the huge oak table in a bid to put some kind of shield between him and the grenades. Conner was only a fraction of a second behind him but still got caught by the massive blast throwing him clean over Jones and into the chairs that surrounded the large table, ending up in the opposite corner of the large room.

This section of the house seemed to create most of the walled area, making it impossible to work out where we were in relation to the front, casting dark shadows across the snow covered cobbled surface sections that jutted out like outhouses. Most had windows in them with prison style bars running top to bottom at the first floor level and up, but none at our height. I could only think they were storage places or garages. “Come on,” I said, leading her across the open courtyard, hoping to find a way out. As we went around the corner of one of the walls, I noticed the actual shape of the area was like a large F. This wasn’t visible from where we had entered it. We carried on past the next building, me still partly dragging my bad leg while Roxy did her best in her cut off shoes.

Conner got to his feet shouting with rage, “That fucker dies, end of chat!” and he sprayed the far end of the room with gun fire, only stopping to reload. Jones joined in, taking turns to move forward. In a relentless torrent of bullets, they went forward into the next room, only to see two grenades come bouncing towards them. “RUN FOR FUCK’S SAKE RUN,” Conner shouted, turning on the spot, smacking straight into Jones. The force of the two grenades exploding blew the two men into the walls then bowling over each other across the dinning room floor, deafened from the sound of both explosions and covered in cuts and bruises. They lay there, moaning. His eyes obscured by debris, Jones spat out a mouthful of dust. Conner looked at him, “Come on,” he said, grabbing at his gun.

We heard gun fire from behind us. They must be entering the utility room. “At least they wouldn’t be able to see us from the doorway,” I thought. We rounded the corner that opened up into a covered car port, but it was a good sixty feet long by twenty feet wide. Being pitch black apart from the far end where the moonlight showed open ground, Roxy didn’t look too keen about going through it, so I just pulled her along with me.

“Tom, I don’t like it.”

“That’s because there’s nothing to like about it,” I said, as we made our through the darkness.

Jones stood back from the doorway, and Conner walked forward bringing his gun up into the firing position. "Ready," he said.

"Ready," Jones replied as he let loose a volley of bullets into the room past what was left of the doorway. When Jones did this, Conner went forward right up to the opening. As soon as Jones stopped firing, he started covering the other side of the dust filled room.

In this covered over area, the ground felt wet underfoot as we made our way through the darkness. The smell of straw and wet mud filled the air here. We kept stumbling over bits of what I thought were old machinery or fencing as we carried on through the inky blackness. I could only hope that our pursuers didn't round the corner behind us as we would be silhouetted against the far opening. We were halfway through when the muffled explosion went off somewhere behind us. I paused looking back the way we'd come and then set off again, only to trip over something laying in our path. We both went down legs and arms sprawling everywhere.

"That's just fucking wonderful," I rasped, now covered in what smelt like slurry.

Roxy started crying, saying she'd had enough. "I want to have a rest," she said.

"Get up. Get up now," I hissed at her. I had to be firm, or she'd just collapse in a heap. Pulling her to her feet, I carried on not wanting to get into an argument about how the guys chasing us were only seconds behind us. As we came out the far end, we were straight into the foot deep snow again everything looked so peaceful and still.

"Where do you think we are?" Roxy asked looking around.

"At a guess, I think we're round the side of the main building," I said, letting go of her hand, trying to get my bearings.

Roxy looked at me saying, "Why don't we take the other Range Rover?"

"Because we don't have the keys, Roxy," I answered, trying to make the rucksack a bit more comfortable.

"But the keys I gave you earlier had two sets on them."

I looked at her. "Come on then," I said, grabbing her hand again, heading left along what I thought to be the side of the house.

Jones threw the flash bang past Conner into the dust filled room and stood back. BOOM! The device went off, and both men rushed in firing low hoping to shoot their target in the legs. It would be his own bloody fault if he was lying on the ground and ended up dead. They waited until the smoke started to clear, Conner went through into the second part of the room. "It's clear," he shouted back to Jones who was now looking out through the back door at the courtyard. Conner came back through the room and into the porch.

Jones said, "Look here." He squatted down. "That's blood, and look at the way the snow has been dragged to one side in this set of tracks."

Conner looked over his shoulder at the pattern in the snow. "What you thinking?"

Jones stood up, saying, "We know one of them is injured, so that's got to slow them down a bit, but what we don't know is if they are waiting for us to walk into a trap." He stepped out into the courtyard, looking up at the high walls. The stars were out now, emphasising the shadows cast by the house and out buildings.

Conner came up beside him, saying, "If I were him, I'd keep running. Try to escape. They don't know how many men are chasing them."

"That's true," Jones said, slowly walking towards the opposite wall following the tracks. "But what we've got to consider is this guy's not your average Joe. He knows how to avoid detection. My guess is that we're only able to follow him because he's picked up a passenger on the way somewhere, which will alter his way of thinking, giving us the advantage of speed."

"If you say so," Conner said, not looking at all impressed by Jones's little speech.

"Right. You cover the corner while I go wide," Jones said, checking his gun.

Conner nodded as he went forward, readying himself for another trap.

As we made our way along the side of the house, my leg kept giving way under the strain. Roxy did her best to support me, but I still went down a couple of times. The snow had covered all the unevenness of the ground which didn't help our cause. As we rounded the corner, an old barn jutting out from the main house came into view. It was the one we had seen when we first came up the field from the crash site. It gave me renewed strength in my legs as we headed towards it. I asked Roxy to get my pistol out of the jacket pocket.

She rummaged about and said, "It's not there, Tom.

We didn't have time to stop. "I must have put it in the rucksack earlier. Don't worry about it," I said, as we eventually reached the barn. I looked back across to where we had come from. It was a good 100 yards. The barn was only the size of a double garage made of slatted timber with a curved corrugated roof like an old aircraft hangar. We made our way slowly along to the end, and then taking the rucksack off, I told Roxy to stay put while I had a quick look to see if anyone was out front guarding the house.

Jones lifted his hand signalling to Conner that the area in front looked clear. Conner moved round the side of the out building cautiously not wanting to make himself a target as Jones covered him from his position over near the opposite wall. Once round the corner, Conner squatted down keeping his gun at his shoulder so Jones could move forward. It was a slow process, but it meant they stood a good chance of surviving a bit longer than Price had.

Jones went forward slowly. He started to see the large covered area up front. He didn't like the look of it at all. "Easy ambush," he thought to himself, as he waved Conner forward.

I went down onto my belly and then slowly went forward looking round the corner of the barn. I could see the Range Rover closest to us covered in snow. Beyond it, the one we had used shot to bits halfway up the front steps. I got to my feet and made my way round the corner towards the first vehicle. I checked the door handles as I went past, but it was locked. I had to get those other keys one way or another, so I headed across the front of the house hoping like hell no one would pop up from behind a bush or come out the front door. I approached carefully. It had been blown to bits along with most of one side of the Range Rover. I took a quick look in the hall. No one about, and then pulled open the driver's side door. I yanked the keys out of the ignition and was just about to head back when I noticed my rifle on the back seat. I reached in to get it but noticed how bent the barrel was. "Shit," I thought, closing the door. Just then Roxy came running round the corner of the barn dragging the rucksack waving her hand in the air. I hobbled like a man possessed back across towards her.

"They're coming, Tom. They're coming." I pressed the key fob desperately wanting the doors to open. I reached the Range Rover pulling at the door handle. It opened. "Get in" I said, as I pulled a huge lump of snow off the screen. Roxy literally leapt inside pushing the rucksack in as she went. I rammed the key in the slot, but it was the wrong one and jammed. I wiggled back and forth cursing to myself, "Shitting bastard! Bloody twating thing!" After what seemed like forever, it came free. I gently pushed the other key into the slot and turned it. The engine roared into life.

Sara tried calling Conner's phone, but it was turned off. "That bastard's going to pay for ignoring my orders," she hissed, pressing the number for Price's phone. It started to ring.

Roxy heard the small buzzing sound first but couldn't work out where it was coming from. I was too busy trying to turn the Range Rover around with most of the windows covered in snow. I hit the house with my rear bumper with a thud and decided I had to risk getting out and clearing some snow off, it was then I thought about firing a few rounds off into the air just to deter our pursuers. If they were crossing the open ground heading towards the barn, there was no way they could know where the bullets had come from or where they were heading.

I ran back to the corner of the barn, squatted down and popped my head around the corner knowing the background would hide my shape. I saw the two men making their way across the open area, they stuck out like saw thumbs against the dark almost shear blackness of the covered area. I brought my gun up to aim and took a single shot at the one on the right hand side. He went down sideways, his partner letting a volley of fire straight at my position, sending chunks of brick and wood flying in all directions.

Jones dived to the ground at the same time as Conner trying to take cover from the gunshots. Only now Conner had a bad wound to his shoulder.

"He must be hiding somewhere near that barn," Conner shouted.

"Either that or he's behind us," Jones replied.

"Well, I ain't staying out here in the open." Conner said, rolling onto his back, sliding a new magazine into his gun. He had been shot so many times he'd lost count, it hurt like bloody hell and it would need sorting, but for now he would carry on.

"I'm with you on that one," Jones answered, doing the same.

"Head for that barn, and then we'll go from there." At that, Conner gave a few short bursts form his gun as Jones ran forward a good twenty yards and then dropped down firing so Conner could move forward.

I cleared the screen like a man possessed and ran round pulling great handfuls off the other windows. "The rest will fall off," I thought, jumping back into the driver's seat. I pulled the gear leaver back into the drive slot and gently set off along the snow covered drive. Thinking about the guy I had fired at, I was sure I had hit him, I wanted to injure him to slow them down. If he was dead his partner would just carry on.

Roxy was in the back seat now looking for the buzzing sound. "Is your phone switched on, Tom?" she asked from behind me. "Because I can hear it." I was about to answer when the back window exploded inwards as a hail of bullets thundered into it.

Conner reached the corner of the barn and then he heard the engine noise so carried on past the gable end towards the sound with Jones in hot pursuit. The two of them rounded the corner, seeing the Range Rover pulling away. Both men raised their guns firing at the same time, they kept running forward.

I pushed the accelerator down hard, hoping the vehicle wouldn't just start sliding around. It worked. We were making good progress across the snow covered ground towards the long avenue of fur trees that were now coming into view. One of the side windows blew in as the bullets peppered the vehicle's body panels. The noise inside the Range Rover was outrageous as the bullets hammered into the body work. "Keep down!" I tried shouting over the ear-splitting sound.

Up ahead, the branches of the trees had been weighed down by the weight of the snow. It's strange what your eyes notice when all hell is breaking loose around you. The rear side window shattered as more bullets rained in on us. Roxy screamed as she curled up in the rear foot well, holding her hands over her face, protecting her eyes from the glass as it flew in all directions, covering the interior with tiny shard-like diamonds. The trees lining either side of the drive gently curved round to the left taking us out of line of sight of our pursuers. The gunfire ceased. I didn't slow down though. I kept going at a steady thirty along this smooth flat surface.

"Are you alright?" I shouted back at Roxy, but all I could hear was crying. "At least if she's doing that, she's alive," I thought. The trees started to spread out until open fields were all that surrounded us, covered in a thick blanket of untouched snow. Ahead, I could see where the driveway met the road. Although the snow had made a good job of blending everything into one colour scheme of grey, white, and black, it wasn't too hard to work out the lay of the land. I could only hazard a guess at which way to go as I hadn't a clue where we were now. Slowly coming to a stop where the driveway met the road, I tried to think which way would be best, left or right? To the left, the road went up a slight hill towards a wooded area. Looking right, it seemed to head down hill. I scanned the horizon for anything that might be familiar, but nothing jumped out at me, saying, "It's this way, stupid!"

Roxy had stopped crying and was now in the rear seat brushing the bits of glass off her coat. She didn't look too pleased from what I could see in the rear view mirror"

"You okay, Rox?"

She didn't move her head from looking down at her hand but quietly said, "I don't want this to be happening, Tom. I hate it. I don't even know what I'm doing here." Then without any warning she began to panic. "Where is it? Oh no, where is it?" she screamed.

"What?" I said.

"Where's my black briefcase, Tom? I must have it," she shouted at me.

"I think it's back at the crash site, Roxy. I don't know," I said.

"Take me there now!" she shouted.

What could I do? I turned round in the seat, saying, "We're going to a friend of mine, Roxy. He'll look after us, and we'll be safe" I promise. "And if you just calm down a bit, we might be able to get your briefcase as well," I said, but to be honest, I didn't give a sod about it, but sometimes you have to play ball a bit to shut someone up.

She didn't look too convinced at what I'd said.

"Can you pass me my phone? It's in the left hand side of the rucksack."

She moved it from where it had fallen down into the foot well onto the seat.

"Which side did you say?" she said, sounding a bit pissed off.

"Left."

She unzipped the pocket and pulled out the phone passing it over to me. I took it off her, and she managed a smile, as I turned back to face the front. "I know you won't let those men hurt us, Tom, and I do trust you," she said, staring at the back of my head with eyes as cold as ice.

I took the phone off her. Pressing the power button, I opened the drivers' door and got out. I looked back up the drive. There wasn't any sign of movement or sound, which wasn't necessarily a good thing. Scrolling down, I found Ian's number. I pressed the call button knowing he probably wouldn't answer like before.

Malk nearly leapt out of his chair when the signal started to sound.

"Sara, he's transmitting again," he said in an excited voice.

She looked at him. "What fucking good is that when these idiots won't pickup?" she stormed.

Malk typed away at the laptop. "Look here," he said, sliding the screen round so Sara could get a better view. "Our guys are up at the house. He's at the end of the drive that leads back onto the main road. If he goes left, they will be able to cut him off at this point here." He pointed at the screen showing where the house stood in comparison to the layout of the road. He looked up saying, "Try Jones's phone. You never know. He might have his turned on."

Sara scrolled down until she found the number. Pressing call, she sat down opposite Malk crossing her legs. It only rang twice when Jones answered it.

"Sara," he said, as he'd been told to.

She smiled. She liked a man who did as he was told. She said, "I have you outside the front of the house standing next to that pig head Conner."

Jones looked over at him and smiled, answering with a simple, "Yes."

Conner mouthed, "Tell her to go fuck herself," then he walked over to the other Range Rover.

"Can you see the target from your position?"

"No."

She got up out of the chair and sat on the arm of Malk's chair so she could see the map of the area.

"Head across the front of the house, from your position in an easterly direction for 400 yards. There looks to be one wall in your path. Go now so you can cut him off before he gets onto the main road again." Jones listened intently as Sara gave the instructions out and said, "Call me if the situation changes, Sara."

She ended the call and slid off the arm of the chair onto Malk's lap. Lifting his head up with her hands, she kissed him slowly on the lips, pushing her tongue inside his mouth as she did. He held her tightly as she ran her fingers through his hair. Under his trousers, she could feel him getting aroused. Pulling back she smiled, saying, "Don't forget who's in charge around here." She stood up and went over to the bar.

Malk just sat there. He didn't know if to leap out of his chair and give her a good seeing to or get on with his work.

She poured two glasses of red and continued like nothing had happened.

Jones told Conner what Sara had said about the road. He

agreed it sounded like a good idea but said, "Wouldn't it be easier just to take this Range Rover and follow him.

Jones looked at what was left of the vehicle and then looked back at Conner, saying, "And you think we can chase someone in that pile of crap, do you?"

"Just cause the tyres are blown out doesn't make it a write off. Driving has to be a shit load quicker than walking in this snow" Conner went on. "I don't even know why we're debating this," he said, opening the driver's door and getting in. He pulled his knife out and started cutting away part of the dashboard while he spoke. Seconds later, he had a handful of wires in his hand, and after a bit of cursing, he looked up at Jones as the engine burst into life, "Are you coming or what?"

Jones walked over to the passenger side. It was totally shot to bits. All the glass that had been in the windows was now covering most of the interior of the car.

"You do know both tyres are flat on this side, don't you," he said, sticking his head through the passenger window.

Conner put the Range Rover into reverse and floored the accelerator just as Jones pulled his head back. The vehicle flew back at a tremendous pace throwing snow high into the air as the flat tyres dug into the soft surface.

Jones leapt backwards, shouting, "Jesus! Watch it, will ya?"

Conner pulled up beside him sticking his face out through the hole where the glass would have been saying, "Get in. You know it's our best chance of catching him."

Jones walked round the front of the vehicle. He said nothing as he climbed in, pulling the door closed behind him.

"You ready then?"

Jones looked at him and nodded as Conner hit the gas sending an explosion of snow out from under all four wheels.

I just wanted Ian to answer the phone this time, just this time.

"Ay up, you old fucker," came Ian's familiar broad Yorkshire tone.

"What's happening, mate?" he sounded like he was on steroids or something.

"Listen up, fella. I need a big favour." I talked fast and to the point, not wanting him to start telling me all about his latest business dealings.

"Go on then," he said. "I'm all ears."

Holding the phone close to my mouth so Roxy couldn't hear, I said, "I need to come and stay with you for a while. Something's come up, and I need to disappear. Also, I need you to get something for me.

"No problem, mate, when can I expect you and what do want me to get?" he said, making noise's like he was moving around.

I told him about the men chasing me but left out the details, the less he knew the better. I gave him a description of the briefcase making sure he wrote down the right size and colour.

"What's the case for?" he interrupted.

"I'll tell you when I get there." I ended by telling him not to tell anyone about our conversation and finished the call.

Roxy shouted through the open door at me, "They're coming, Tom. Look!"

I spun around looking back up towards the house to see the other Range Rover tearing through the snow towards us.

"Put your seat belt on!" I shouted as I leapt into the driver's seat yanking the gear leaver into drive. I decided to head left uphill. Don't ask me why. It just seemed right at the time.

Sara looked down at the screen watching the blue dot as it slowly headed away from the red one, and then the red one started to follow. Malk looked up at her saying, "They're giving chase, Sara."

She gave Malk her phone saying, "Explain to them idiots my sister is with that bastard, and if they harm a hair on her head, I will personally pull the bloody skin from there useless bodies." She walked off into her bedroom slamming the door behind her.

Malk called Jones's number. It rang once, and he heard Jones shout, "Sara, I can't talk now. We're just behind him!"

Malk could barely hear him because of all the wind and engine noise in the background. "Pull back!" he shouted into the phone. "Pull back now."

But Jones replied, shouting, "I can't hear you…all bk ter!"

It wasn't until I had turned onto the narrow lane that I noticed just how deep the snow had drifted across it. I could feel the tyres skidding as the weight of the thick snow piled up against the front of the Range Rover. Steering close into the opposite wall, I hoped the tyres might get a bit more grip as the snow didn't look as deep on the right hand side compared to the left. It worked. We slowly started to gain more speed, although not much. I glanced at the speedometer, 15 mph. The other car looked like a speedboat the way it was chucking snow up behind it. "He'll be on us in minutes at this rate," I thought. My mind kept running different scenarios to what would happen if we jumped out and tried to leg it across the deep snow, but each time we were cut down before we got a 100 yards. 20 mph. "Come on." I was actually leaning forward trying to go faster. 25 mph.

"Roxy, pass me my gun and pull a couple of extra mags out of the right-hand pocket of the rucksack, will you?" I tried to sound calm, but I was flapping now. These guys didn't mess around. I was out numbered and out gunned. Add Roxy into the equation, and you get total fuck up time. I kept leaning forward willing the Range Rover forward. 26 mph. "Please come on." Roxy was leaning over the seats, trying to reach the rucksack.

"Faster."

"You're going too bloody fast," Jones shouted. "For fuck's sake, slow down!"

Conner was fighting with the wheel doing his best just to keep it going in a straight line as they came to the junction. He yanked the gear lever back into second then first, but he was going way too fast. "Hold on to your balls," he shouted as the Range Rover lost what little grip it had and went sliding across the narrow lane straight through the snow drift and into the dry stone wall buried beneath it. The impact threw Jones out through what was left of the front screen and sliding down the bonnet then over the snow covered wall, landing with a thud on his back.

The only thing that stopped Conner from doing the same was the steering wheel. He shouted, "Jones, Jones, you all right?"

Jones got up from the deep snow that had cushioned his landing shouting, "You bastard, get out of that fucking driver's seat, you twat. I'm driving now!"

Conner smiled. "Okay," he said, climbing over to the

passenger side.

As Jones got back in, he looked over at Conner's big smiling face, saying, and "Don't say a fucking word." He held his finger up. "Not one," he repeated. Conner started to whistle taking the piss out of him.

The other vehicle had slowed down as it came to the T-junction, but he'd left it too late and went sliding across into the deep snow drift as we went on. I could hear the engine screaming as he tried to reverse out onto the lane. 25 mph.

"Did you say the left pocket?" came Roxy's voice from behind.

"No, the right one." 15 mph. Slowly, the other Range Rover edged back into the centre of the lane. 18 mph. I pulled the gear leaver back into second gear in the hope it would help get more power to the wheels.

Roxy slid her phone into her pocket from where I'd put it in the rucksack making sure I didn't see her.

She eased herself back into the seat holding a couple of mags. I took them off her putting them between my legs. 25 mph. I glanced in the rear-view mirror. Way back down the snow covered lane I could see the other Range Rover skidding around all over the place, but he was definitely making progress.

The closer we got to the wood, the less snow seemed to be on the road surface. I could only put it down to the tree's sheltering it from the storm earlier on. Either way, our speed increased up to 30 mph, which was plenty fast enough for these conditions. We started passing the trees as the road went round a gentle left hand bend. It seemed to level out a bit thankfully. I couldn't see our pursuers any more as they were a good 150 yards behind us, but I knew they were making good progress.

CHAPTER 17

Tony Weister stood in the arrivals lounge at Heathrow looking at the people rushing around. He was to meet Baldman, Karl Sasco's most trusted 'cleaner' and that didn't mean he did all the dusting. It basically meant he cleaned up after a killing had happened, or he dealt with unwanted people by making them disappear.

Couples dragged their children along by the arm with promises of sun, sand, and sea, but Tony looked gaunt. His whole world had come crashing down around him in the past 24 hours, and the worry of what Sasco would do to his wife and child if he didn't find and kill Tom Stone was too much to think of. Tom bloody Stone, the bastard, he'd been told was so good. "Good at fucking everything up," he thought, and how the hell was he supposed to know he'd given a false name. Searching deep in his pockets for his cigarettes, he let out a long slow sigh. He'd never felt this down before. He knew it was probably down to the jet lag, but it didn't make him feel any better. Looking around at the signs, he saw the one he wanted: Gents. Wasting no time, he headed towards the toilets hoping there wouldn't be a queue. He had never met Baldman in person, he had seen him fly in and out from the villa after a meeting with Karl. His guts had been rumbling for a good half hour now. It was the flight that had done it. Flying and Weister didn't get on at all. Possibly because of all the alcohol he put away during the flight trying to calm his nerves a bit.

Once he'd done his business, he washed his hands in one of the many sinks. He looked up. "I look a mess" he thought. His grey linen suit had more creases in it than a dried up elephant and his pale pink shirt didn't look any better. He noticed a missing button. "Fucking hell," he groaned. It only went to emphasise how much weight he'd piled on over the years. In his eyes, he still had a 38 inch waist, but in the real world, it was closer to 48 inches, which was okay if you're six foot six, but Tony Weister was only five foot six on a good day. The shadow of two day's growth covered his chin, and the lack of sleep showed in the redness of his eyes. He didn't' find it surprising that he'd lost most of his hair either. A few wisps on top covered what was once a full head of thick black hair. Working for Karl Sasco had caused him so much stress over the years he was thankful to be alive let alone bald. He couldn't even remember the last time he'd stood in front of a mirror and looked at himself. "My God, what happened to you," he said quietly. It was then his phone started chiming. He pulled it out of his inside pocket. The tiny screen read, "New call." Flipping it open he answered it. "Weister," he said in a monotone voice.

"Mr. Weister, I have been sent to collect you. Can you please make your way to the front of the building straight away?"

Weister tried placing the accent, Russian or Czech, something like that.

"How will I know you?" he replied.

"Do not worry, Mr. Weister. I know what you look like."

Weister was about to reply, but the call ended. Sliding the phone back into his pocket, he wondered what information Sasco had passed onto these people who he was about to meet. As he walked through the terminal, his phone started to ring again. Weister ignored it this time. It would be one of two people, Sasco or the weird sounding guy from before. He convinced himself it was a matter of principle not answering this time. Why the hell should he jump every time his phone rang! He wasn't going to be pushed around. He tried convincing himself, but in the back of his mind, he was shit scared of Karl Sasco, and that would undermine his confidence every time.

Weister looked out through the glass doors of the terminal building at the pouring rain. It was still dark outside, but the orange glow of the street lamps made the rain shimmer as it hit the surface of the road. Each time the doors slid open, a chilling wind swept through them taking Tony Weister's breath away. "Bloody hell," he thought. It must be near freezing out there. His phone started to ring again. This time he answered it.

"Weister," he said calmly.

"Mr. Weister." it was the strange voice again.

"Mr. Weister, please come out of the building and turn left. You will see a black Mercedes limousine waiting for you." Again, the phone went dead before he had a chance to reply.

This made Weister feel a whole lot better about the situation. If Sasco had arranged a limo for him, he must have told these people to look after his second in command. Weister checked his reflection in the glass and then walked out into the cold dark morning rain. Pulling his collar up as he headed towards the parked car, as he approached it, the passenger side rear door opened. A tall slim man got out wearing a long dark coat. His pale complexion and totally bald head made his skin appear orange under the street lamps shining down from above. The lightly tinted glasses reflected the buildings internal lighting. He held his hand out to shake Weister's as he approached him. Raising his in response, Weister said, "My name's Weister, expecting the man to reply with his name.

"I know," he replied. "We have no time for pleasantries, Mr. Weister. We are already behind schedule. Now please get into the car."

Weister didn't like being told what to do by anyone, but he had a feeling it wouldn't be in his best interests to start an argument in the pouring rain. When he climbed in, he found himself face to face with a very large bearded gentleman pointing a gun at him. The man smiled and moved over to the opposite side of the car onto another set of seats facing towards the rear ones. It was then Weister noticed the other man. He looked like a smaller version of the big guy. Both men had handguns with silencers on. The door closed leaving Weister and the two men alone in the car.

"Either of you got a cigarette?" Weister asked hopefully.

Neither man moved or said a word. Just then a voice came over the speaker system.

"I trust you enjoyed your flight, Tony." It was Sasco. "These men are here to make sure you reach Sara in time, if possible. She knows you're on your way and will be sending Malk to meet you once you arrive at your destination. I will speak with you later."

Weister was about to ask where they were heading when he felt a sharp pain in his chest. He looked down at the small dart hanging out of him with a tiny patch of blood gently growing around it. "What? Wha..." But his eyes blurred as he slumped to the floor of the car. He tried to move, but his limbs didn't want to play. Everything started spinning as he lost consciousness. The car door opened, but the tall dark figure didn't enter. He just stood there looking at Weister's slumped body. He took a long drag on his cigarette, held it for a second, and then he spoke. The words formed clouds of smoke that drifted into the car's interior.

"Good work, gentlemen. Get him to the helipad immediately. You will receive new instructions once you've loaded him on board." The tall slim man closed the door of the Mercedes and walked off into the night.

Karl Sasco was sat in his Bentley when the phone call came. "Your associate Mr. Weister is on his way and on time," Baldman said.

"Thank you for such a prompt service again" Karl said, ending the call.

CHAPTER 18

I checked the mirror again for the umpteenth time, knowing our pursuers couldn't be far behind us. The moon was throwing a strange blue grey light across the road, emphasising the inky blackness of the shadows.

Maybe I was thinking too hard or just being paranoid, but it seemed everyone was after us now. I flicked the lights on and tried accelerating a bit, but the wheels started spinning again making the Range Rover skew sideways, so I eased off.

"Driving like that won't help," Roxy said with a smile, as she went through the names and addresses on her phone.

"What you looking for?" I asked

"Oh, anything that looks familiar," she replied.

I decided to let her get on with it, partly because I wasn't really that interested and I knew she wasn't being totally straight with me, and I had enough on my mind as it was. I have a pretty good sense of direction, and by my reckoning, we were heading in the general direction of the crash site, which was okay, because it meant we should be approaching the main road soon. Five minutes later the small wood on our left hand side ended abruptly as did the narrow little lane we were travelling along. I brought the Range Rover to a stop and climbed out telling Roxy to stay where she was, knowing our pursuers weren't that far behind. I just needed to have a quick look to see if the road was clear without actually pulling out onto it and risking being caught out by any more of these blood thirsty bastards.

Ten yards in front of me, there was a T-junction. I knew if we went right, it would lead us back to Glasshouses and eventually up into the Dales. On a clear day in the middle of summer, that would've been my ideal exit route, but with the weather we were having, it just made no sense at all. That meant going past the crash site. I rubbed my chin in frustration. I still had to get the other cases from where I'd stashed them at the cottage. A thought sprang into my mind, "What if John had already told them about where I'd hidden them?" I doubted if he would have had time to pass the information on, even so I'd have to check just to make sure. I looked back down the way we'd come, still no sign of our pursuers.

I opened the rear door pulling my rucksack out. Quickly, I went through the pockets checking what ammunition I had left. Six mags for my hand gun, each one held twenty rounds, one hand grenade, and a couple of Mars bars. I kept glancing down the lane as I worked.

"What you looking for?" Roxy asked, turning around in her seat.

"I'm just checking we still have everything," I said, without looking up I pulled the brief case out, gave it a quick once over and slid it back in again, sliding a couple of mags down the side of it as I did. I put two in the pocket behind Roxy's seat, knowing it's easier to grab them if you're driving than trying to stretch behind yourself. The last two went in the front with me. As I climbed back in, I thought I heard a loud bang. I paused for a moment, but I didn't hear anything else. It was then that all the aches and pains started up again. It's strange how you forget about them when your mind is concentrating on something else. I turned the key in the ignition, starting the engine, letting it idle for a minute, while I made my mind up as to which way to go. "What the hell" I thought, turning left towards the crash site. I gently accelerated down the hill. Roxy didn't seem too interested in what was going on, but I felt I had to tell her that this was the place where the crash had occurred. It only took us five minutes to reach the burnt out wreck of my Subaru. "That was a fucking waste of money," I thought, as we slowly passed it. I brought the Range Rover to a stop next to what was left of her BMW.

"OH SHIT!" Jones shouted, just when the engine literally blew up in front of them, throwing bellows of steam and smoke in their faces. Both men dived out the doors landing in the soft snow on either side of the road. Conner was up on his feet in an instant running around what was left of the front of the vehicle to see where Jones was.

He was sitting in the snow, looking at the smoking wreck as Conner ran over to him. "You alright, mate?" he asked as he got closer.

Jones slowly got to his feet, saying, "Never really liked that model anyway." He smiled at Conner and without saying a word, he set off jogging along the snow covered lane in the direction of their target holding his MP5K across his front. As he did, he shouted back to Conner, "You coming or what?" Conner was a bit taken aback at the way Jones had just leapt to his feet. There was usually some big debate about the whys and wherefore's of the situation.

He didn't question Jones's determination though, he just ran after him saying, "It's not very likely we'll catch him on foot, you know."

Jones said nothing. He just kept on jogging.

"You gonna let me in on this plan then or not?" Conner said, getting a bit wound up at Jones' lack of replies.

After five minutes, Jones eventually said, "If my reckoning is right, our vehicle is only a couple of hundred yards over there." He pointed in a south-easterly direction, as he carried on jogging.

"Yeah, so what about it?" Conner replied.

"What do you mean, 'what about it'?" Jones spat back at him, as he stopped. "Where's your fucking brain, Conner?" he said angrily. "Think about it for once in your life. Once we get back to the Land Rover, we have transportation, and once we have transportation, we can catch them. It's not fucking rocket science."

Conner looked at him for a second and said, "Oh," shrugged

his shoulders, and then set off running again. It didn't take them long to reach the junction just up from the Land Rover. Conner looked at his watch. "That took us just under seven minutes."

"Good, let's not hang around then," Jones said, heading in the direction of the vehicle which was now only fifty yards off to their right. It had a thick layer of snow covering it, making it blend in perfectly with the background.

They both slowed down as they approached it, breathing heavily from the run. Conner was the first to see the other vehicle stopped part way down the hill just in front of the crash site. "THERE HE IS!" he shouted, running towards the driver's door.

As Jones ran around to the passenger side, he ran his arm across the windows clearing as much snow off as he could. Conner did the same on his side and then both of them took a swipe at the windscreen. Conner climbed in, starting the engine, shouting at Jones, "Move your arse, will you!"

"Go!" Jones shouted, as he leapt in the passenger seat.

The wheels spun frantically, trying to get a grip on the slippery surface throwing snow in all directions, until Conner eased off the accelerator letting the tyres get a grip.

Jones made himself busy reloading both guns. He pulled at the large black carry all on the rear seat.

"Get some fucking grenades out," Conner said in a raised voice.

"Way ahead of you, mate," Jones replied, pulling a belt out that had twelve attached to it. "How do you want to play this?" Jones said, now checking his sidearm.

"You get in the back, so when we get next to him, you can blow his tyres from behind me without taking my bloody nose off."

Jones laughed as he climbed over into the rear, knowing Conner was referring to the last job they'd done together. It was over two years ago now, but Conner would never let it drop. They'd been tailing a couple of drug runners in Turkey just outside Marmais when all hell had broken loose. The druggies had made off in a Toyota Land Cruiser all guns blazing. As usual, Conner had leapt into the driver's seat to give chase. The only problem was the car he leapt into was a taxi, the driver got booted out, and the chase began down a rough dirt track. Conner got level with them, shouted, "Take the shot for fuck's sake," which isn't a good idea at sixty miles an hour on rough ground. Hence he lost a quarter of an inch off the end of his nose.

"You can stop fucking laughing, twat," Conner snapped at Jones, as he accelerated hard down the snow covered road. The Land Rover didn't take long to get to 60 mph down the steep hill.

"Do you really think we need to be going quite so fast?" Jones said, leaning forward talking directly into Conner's ear.

"Yes, I do," he snapped back at Jones. "You just concentrate on hitting the target and let me do the driving,"

Jones pressed the button to lower his window. Once it was a good way down, he eased himself partly out securing one foot under Conner's seat. "Ready when you are!" he shouted, squinting his eyes from the freezing wind Jones made sure he had a good grip on his gun.

Roxy looked over at me. "This is where my briefcase is, isn't it?" she said.

I looked over at her and said, "This is where you had the crash, Roxy, and that's all that's left of your BMW, I'm afraid, now if you don't mind, I thing we ought to be going"

She leant forward to get a better look at the wreckage without saying anything. Her eyes just stared at the now burnt out shell of twisted metal. "How did you manage to pull me out of that, Tom?" she said in a quiet voice.

"I couldn't just leave you in there, Roxy," I said, starting to get agitated.

"You saved my life, Tom," she paused and then added, "One day, I'll repay you."

I heard what she was saying, but my eyes were scanning the crash site for the body that should have been lying in the road. I spoke, but it was more of an automatic response than a reply. "I'm quite sure you'd have done the same, if the circumstances had been turned around." I said.

It was then I had a strange feeling of being watched. It's that second sense that everyone has when you know something just isn't right. Slowly, the snow around us started to glow, long shadows streaked out in front of us giving the impression we were falling backwards. The hairs on the back of my neck stood on end as the realisation of what was about to happen exploded into my brain sending shockwaves through my body. It was one of those dreaded moments in time when you know you've left it to late. This would never have happened if Roxy hadn't been with me. She was a bloody liability and it was getting right on my nerves.

Adrenaline surged through my veins. In an instant, I spun around in my seat knowing already what my eyes would see, almost like looking down a tunnel, your eyes zoom in on the approaching danger. Nothing else mattered. They were only 100 yards away bearing down on us at a ferocious speed.

"Oh no," I mouthed silently. I could see the guy leaning out the rear window holding his gun up ready to fire. I saw the flashes from the end of his barrel when he fired on full automatic, but my ears didn't hear anything. I knew they had the advantage. They'd caught me off guard. 'FUCK' I also knew I didn't have time to make a getaway. I was thinking all this in a split second, but it seemed to take forever. My hand found the gun without thinking, I moved my body into a better firing position pulling the trigger three shots, slight pause, and then another three shots, my eyes followed the target along the diagonal line of its approach.

Roxy looked like she was frozen in time, but it was only because her mind couldn't make out what was going on. I heard bullets impacting on the rear panel the second he found his target, a couple whizzed past my head shattering the windscreen.

In the background, I heard Roxy screaming at me, but I took no notice until she pulled at my arm probably wanting me to get out and run. Around me bits of plastic and leather were flying in all directions. The sound of impacting bullets buzzed around me like heavy rain smacking into polycarbonate sheeting. One clipped my arm missing my skin by a fraction of a millimetre. 'Twenty yards'. The sound of gun fire increasing, the ear-splitting barrage would make most people curl up into a ball, I very much wanted too, but these bastards needed slotting. I kept on firing at the driver.

Ten yards. The guy firing at us stopped! Not because I'd hit him, but because he disappeared back inside the vehicle. I didn't give a shit. I just carried on firing. Only now, my target was the radiator. He was so close I could see his eyes glaring back at me. I shouted at Roxy to get down, but it was too late, I pulled my second gun out flicking it to automatic. I just let him have it straight through the windscreen, everything was going crazy, the snow illuminated yellow by the headlights, snow flakes frozen in time. Small impact craters sent plumes of dust and inner lining out when each and every bullet slammed into the Range Rovers' hand made leather interior. Windows exploded inwards from the storm of metallic missiles flying in all directions.

The Land Rover was about to hit us. I must have found my target. The driver seemed to yank the wheel to one side causing the vehicle to strike us down the passenger side, throwing me backwards in slow motion I collided onto the dashboard sending explosions of pain searing through my body as my bruised ribs clashed with the steering wheel. "Arrgh!" I screamed, with pain causing my hand to release its grip on the gun.

I couldn't believe how much pain I was in as my body was catapulted back onto the centre console where I had started off. I eased myself back into the driver's seat. I didn't care about the other vehicle. I knew it would take a good distance to stop on the slippery surface. Having time to think things through would have been a real comfort but that never seemed to happen, these boys were good and fast and didn't seem to bother about who they killed to get their target. I pulled the gear knob into reverse and tried heading back up the hill in the opposite direction. It was then my eyes made contact with the maniac who'd rammed us. They were parked sideways across the road about fifty yards away. Even from that distance, I made direct eye contact with the man dressed all in white army gear pointing the gun at me. He didn't move a muscle, his partner dressed the same way leant over the bonnet of Land Rover Discovery to steady the rifle he was aiming directly at me.

"Do you have him?" Conner asked over the head set.

"I have him," came the reply as Jones focused his sight on the driver of the Range Rover using the bonnet of the Land Rover to steady himself.

"Take the shot then," Conner said.

"Sara wants him alive not dead," Jones said.

"Take the fucking shot," Conner hissed.

"Get the briefcase first," Jones replied.

By the size of the sights, he couldn't really miss me from that position, and whoever was giving the orders must want me alive, because from this distance, he could have shot my eye out with a weapon like that. My mind was going at warp speed trying to work out how the hell we could get out of this one when the answer came from behind us. Sirens. I presumed police sirens. Not that it made any difference. What would the other two do?

"Roxy, are you ok?" I asked without taking my eyes off the men pointing their guns at us. There was no answer, "ROXY!" I said sharply. Slowly, I looked at her, but she was nowhere to be seen. Her door was closed, but she was gone. A movement, in the corner of my eye made me spin my head back towards the men. The one who had been standing nearest me had gone. Conner moved forward using the car wreck for cover. At the same time, he made sure he wasn't blocking Jones' line of sight. Once he'd made it to the wreckage, he waved Jones forward.

I could see where this was going and decided it was time to leave so I selected drive on the gear box. "Fuck this," I mouthed, and hit the accelerator whilst flattening my body down behind the dashboard. WHACK! WHACK! SMACK! The seat above me exploded, when the sniper guy unloaded a full magazine of bullets into the interior of the Range Rover. "Holy bloody shit!" I shouted. I had no idea which way I was going nor did I give a shit so long as it was away from them. As quickly as the gun fire had started, it stopped.

Jones yanked the empty magazine out. Spinning it round, he thrust the new one into position ready to shoot again until he saw what was coming down the hill.

I took my chance to grab a quick look at what was unfolding just in time to see Roxy running like a mad woman towards me screaming, "Tom, don't leave me!" Eyes wide with fear, her face was streaked with blood.

Conner saw her running, "Now that's an easy target" he said to himself, not realising Jones could hear him, "Don't do it" Jones said over the coms.

Conner raised his gun and fired a single shot, Roxy dropped like a stone, the bullet slammed into her ankle shattering the bone and joint in one. "ARRGH" she screamed splaying out across the snow covered road. I heard the shot and watched her drop out of sight. Conner smiled, "That's going to slow him right down" he said. Jones watched the young women drop and the small explosion of blood from the impact leaving a trail in the snow. He didn't like the way Conner did business, but he had to admit it would make their job a lot easier.

I looked past her then at the man still remaining. He'd lowered his gun. "Why aren't you still firing?" I said to myself. I couldn't look in the rear view mirror because it had been blown off just seconds earlier, and there was no way I could turn around in my seat due to the pain in my chest and stomach. I braked slowly so I wouldn't go into a skid, while Roxy crawled across the snow leaving a long trail of blood in the snow. She eventually reached the passenger door still holding a black briefcase. "Silly bloody bitch," I thought. I managed to push the door open the minute she was within reach. A second later blue flashes sped across the snow covered road from behind me. The lights raced other across the snow disappearing behind us then reappearing again "Oh, this just takes the piss," I thought hearing the sound of car doors slamming and the unique sound of safeties being flicked off.

In my mind I could see the special ops police moving in, they would have their guns up high dressed in black with Kevlar body amour covering most of the essential organs.

Then a voice shouted, "Stay where you are! Armed Police!" I took a guess they weren't that far behind me judging by how close the voice had sounded through the bullhorn.

Conner ran over to the snow covered dry stone wall making no sound when he scrambled over it and into the field beyond.

Jones dashed forward using the wreckage as cover while he made his way up towards the Range Rover where his target was.

"Jones to Conner Come in."

"Go ahead," Conner replied.

"I'm in position. Twenty feet from the front of the target. Out," said Jones.

Conner was making his way up behind the wall when up ahead he saw two figures dressed all in black leap over the wall not fifteen feet in front of him.

He went down in a split second at the same time drawing his knife out. He lay dead still, his whites making him virtually invisible. Conner watched the armed policemen come closer. He knew what to do and when to do it. His breathing slowed down, he readied himself for the attack. The two armed policemen weren't looking for anyone on this side, so they moved forward just wanting to get in position. His eyes locked on both men flicking from one to the other. "Just a bit closer," he said to himself. "Come on." The two armed officers moved fast through the deep snow, their concentration focused on the guy in the Range Rover.

As they went slowly past Conner, both men turned to look over the wall to check their position to the Range Rover.

Conner's grip on the knife tightened, he focused on his target while the adrenalin rushed through his veins he leapt up at a frightening speed ramming the nine inch blade deep into the closest man's head just below his ear in the thin gap between the helmet and the shoulder guards. The blade plunged in right up to the handle. He didn't bother pulling it out. He just left it in the officer's head. By the time the other man had realised what was going on, his partner was dead on his feet, and Conner was on him ramming a second knife deep into his neck. Conner's grip on him was vice-like in its intensity. There was no struggle from his prey. Now Conner turned the long blade sideways severing the man's jugular and most of the nerves that ran through his neck. He felt the life drain out of the body as he let it slip to the ground. Slowly, he pulled the long blade out wiping it on the man's black Kevlar vest. Reaching over, he retrieved the other knife from his first victim. Looking down at the two dead bodies, he whispered, "Train hard. Work easy." He stood up and grinned, patting the closest one's helmet. "Jones, you ready down there?" he said softly into his throat mike.

"Yep, just say when," came the reply.

"You in the vehicle, raise your hands above your head now!" I didn't move. I wanted to see how sparked up they were.

"YOU IN THE VEHICLE, raise your hands NOW!" By the way the second command had come I knew it was odds on that at least five guns were aimed at my head. In my mind, I was looking down on the crash site from above, watching the police taking up positions all around me to cut off any escape route. That or get a clear shot at me. I looked past the crash site to where the sniper guy had been. He had disappeared. I knew the police marksmen wouldn't piss around with second warnings, but I also knew that due to our wonderful government, none of them wanted to be first to pull the trigger. That would mean a full enquiry and shed loads of paperwork, so whatever I did now had to be quick and precise. No fuck ups. I only hoped Roxy had enough about her to figure out what was about to happen. Gently, I slid the gear knob into second knowing it would give me more grip on the snow covered surface.

"This is your last warning. You in the car, show your hands NOW!"

Jones was about to call Conner again when the target shouted, "I have a bomb!"

"What the fuck is he on about?" Jones said out loud to himself.

Conner heard him in his ear piece and replied, "Fucked if I know."

I shouted back at the person giving the orders, "Tell everyone to back off. I have a bomb!" I knew it was going to be a long shot, but they didn't know if I was lying or not. I heard movement from somewhere off to my left. No one said anything for a couple of seconds, and then the voice from before spoke. He must have been standing just out of my range of view, because he sounded very close, suddenly the figure in black appeared by the drivers door, he was a good two metres away holding a bullhorn in one hand and a pistol in the other. "Take it easy, I just want to help" he said, sliding his gun into its holster. "We can work this out, everything's going to be fine" he said. Sliding his right foot forward to try and close the distance between us. I raised my gun just over the top of the door panel pointing it at him. "Slide back or take a bullet" I said. He did like I said and returned to his original position.

"Can you tell me your name?" he said.

"Listen up, fella," I said "There's a couple of right nutters down there armed with MP5Ks and they're not afraid to use them. That's why my Range Rover is full of fucking holes, so you'll probably understand why I'm not too crazy about leaving my car."

The special ops commander looked at the state of the Range Rover noticing all the bullet holes and glanced back at the man sitting in the driver's seat.

"Listen to me," the special ops commander started saying, but he was cut off mid sentence by the deafening sound of automatic fire.

Time stopped, for a fraction of a second, the racing blue lights slowed into long blue streaks of light smearing across the white background, I watched the guy standing less then two metres away from me take at least a dozen hits in a fraction of a second, most of which hit the side of his head. The horrific explosion of blood that burst out from the other side of his head took my breath away. This was the kind of thing that that sticks in your memory for good.

It had been one of the men chasing us that had popped up from only twenty feet away. He obviously wanted the police out of the equation. Roxy screamed at me to drive. Not like I needed telling. I hadn't even seen her climb in. My foot was already welded to the floor in a desperate bid to get away. Seconds later his partner appeared on the other side of the road. My eyes zoomed in to his right arm. "Grenade," I mouthed in disbelief. I watched him throw the small black object not at us but in the direction of the police. "Roxy!" I shouted, "Find my gun! I dropped it in the foot well somewhere." She looked up at me. She had that crazy look in her eyes. I don't know where her mind was, but it didn't look too pleasant. I ducked just as a hail of bullets ran across the bonnet ricocheting through the passenger side window. Bits of glass rained down on both of us. My face stung from the tinny shards that had being blasted out from the windscreen, embedding themselves into my face. I had to take some kind of control of the situation. My whole body told me to stay down and keep safe. "Bollocks! We're getting out of here!" I screamed at myself. I sat bolt upright just in time to steer the Range Rover round the upturned wreck in the middle of the road. The side panel of the vehicle scraped down my rear wing with an unearthly sound as metal scrapped against metal. My confidence started to grow. We had a good chance of escape. All I needed to do was get clear of the immediate area, and then I could start to… My train of thought was interrupted by the sudden explosion of the upturned vehicle we'd only just passed. I instinctively ducked away from the bits of car parts and flames flying past us in all directions. The Range Rover heaved into the air from the force of the explosion lifting the rear a good four feet up from behind then ' BANG' the impact of it smacking back to earth gave all my cuts and bruises the chance to remind me they were still here.

My ears rang from the sound of the grenade. Everything looked like I was seeing it through a camera lens. Then real time came rushing back at me when a second explosion went off right in front of us throwing snow and dirt through the gap that had been the windscreen. I covered my face with my arm in a desperate hope of protecting myself. Our tyres were blown out from underneath us by a third explosion. The Range Rover nearly tipped over throwing Roxy clean out of her seat and onto the centre console. Her head smashed into my knee knocking her unconscious, sending bolts of pain through my entire leg. Overwhelming nausea ripped through my body to the point where I barely remained conscious. My eyes went all blurry, my mouth dried up. If it hadn't been for the fourth explosion, I probably would have fainted. It wasn't as close as the other three, but I got the gist of it. They wanted us dead or alive. I had no idea how far we'd gone down the hill, but I knew it wasn't far enough.

Roxy was out cold. Her head was bleeding from somewhere above her hair line. That's where I thought it was coming from. Even with the full moon outside, it was still virtually pitch black in the shadow of the interior of the car. Our speed had been severally reduced now, and I knew it wouldn't take long for our pursuers to catch us up.

I fought wildly with the steering wheel while the Range Rover skewed from side to side. Whatever I did seemed to make things worse, but slowly, I managed to gain some control over the vehicle as we made our way towards the bottom of the hill.

Sara stared at the laptop screen, the coloured dots merged and separated again. "What the hell are those idiots playing at?" she hissed out loud, she tried phoning them for the umpteenth time.

Malk just typed away updating the information as they both watched the screen. He was looking for places where he thought the target might head for and tagging them.

Conner jumped over the wall looking around him at the carnage. He counted twelve dead bodies he walked over to one of the cars, seeing a special ops man reaching for the door he pulled his gun and slotted him, not even stopping to check the dead man afterwards. He had no time for these jerks, he gave a big yawn and looked inside the car, but the grenade had totalled the V70.

Jones jogged over to him holding his gun at the ready. He had a quick look around and said, "Take one of their headsets just in case they have some back up on the way." He looked up into the night sky for a second and then added, "The only reason there isn't a chopper on us is because of the bad weather."

Conner yanked a headset off the nearest body, saying, "They won't get far. That last grenade took out most of their tyres." At that, both men made for their Land Rover at a fast jog.

I didn't want to ease off on the accelerator even when we rounded the bend at the bottom of the hill. I just kept going. In the distance, I could see the sun slowly starting to form over the hills. A soft red glow swept across the open fields bringing with it a slight change in temperature; not that I would feel it, my injuries were doing a fine job of keeping me warm. Time wasn't on my side. We had to go to ground just to take the heat off us for a while, and basically, so I could sort myself out. My eyes scanned the road for a sign of escape. Anything would do. All I needed was a farm track or even a main road crossing the one we were travelling on. After five minutes my hopes were starting to wear a bit thin when—bingo!—a T-junction. It might not sound like much, but any chance of losing them would do for me. I turned left still fighting with the wheel as the arse end slid way out into the middle of the road. I tried to turn into the skid, but the lack of tyres worked against me, we slid across the snow covered road and down into a small ditch opposite. I cursed when the front of the Range Rover nosedived into the snow filled ditch.

I looked over at Roxy, saying, "Looks like we're walking from here on." She just didn't get it she had only come around from being knocked out, so I imagined her sense of reality was a little blurry, but credit to her, she didn't start whining about it either. I took the opportunity to reload and sort my stuff out, ready for what ever came our way. I gave Roxy some painkillers from my kit and strapped a tight bandage around her ankle. "You're going to have to lean on me but we have to make tracks" I said.

Malk looked up from the laptop screen saying, "This may sound a bit daft, but have you tried phoning Roxy lately? She's transmitting, which as you know means her phone is switched on."

Sara looked at him and then at the laptop. She pulled her phone out and asked Malk if Roxy's signal was still overlapping with Tom Stone's.

"Yes, at this moment they are stationary next to a small T-junction three miles away from Conner and Jones' location."

"What are they doing?" she asked.

"They've just started to move again and by my reckoning should be with the target in approximately five minutes judging by the speed they seem to be doing."

Sara flicked her phone open and said Roxy into the mike, which dialled her number automatically.

I pulled the rucksack on while we made our way across the snow covered road, trying to think of what to do next when the answer came thundering towards us. At first, I couldn't figure out what it was as the ground beneath me started to vibrate then the noise grew louder and louder. Suddenly an orange light shot across the field followed by another. I drew my hand gun out ready to give whatever was coming the good news when the biggest snow plough I'd ever seen came around the corner pushing a wall of snow in front of it.

"This is our way out of here," I thought. Waiting until the driver had seen me, I started waving my hands above my head in a bid to stop him. He slowed right down, and then he brought the huge yellow vehicle to a standstill. He raised the massive plough section with a hiss of hydraulics. The long bar of flashing orange lights spinning made sure anyone coming along the road would see him, like you could miss the ten ton bright yellow truck blocking the whole width of the snow covered road. The driver climbed out of the cab and down over the wheel arch. He looked in his late fifties with a mass of white hair and he wore a thick blue lumber jacket. He looked over towards the Range Rover while he approached and then at Roxy who was now trying to stand just off to my left.

"Looks like you're in the shit," he said in a very strong Yorkshire accent.

"No, actually it looks like you're in the shit," I replied pointing the gun at him.

He looked at me saying, "You know what you can do with that, don't you?" He turned away and started walking back towards his truck. I couldn't believe the balls of this fella. He didn't even blink when he said it.

"Oy!" I shouted trying to get his attention, but he just shouted back at me without turning around:

"Fuck off!"

I fired a single shot into the ground in a bid to stop him, but he just carried on. He was about to climb back into the cab, so I decided to let him know I was serious. I took aim and shot him in the knee. I didn't want to, but the circumstances forced me to ignore my usual ethics, he fell backwards holding his leg shouting something about bastards and shit heads.

"Come on, Rox. It's time to go. It's time we weren't here," I said, grabbing her hand.

The old guy lay in the snow cursing at me as I helped Roxy into the cab.

I turned to look at him before closing the door, saying, "All you had to do was help us out, but you had to play the hard man, didn't you?" He was about to start gobbing off, so I closed the cab door, checked if Roxy was okay, and then had a good look at the controls. The driving stuff was pretty straight forward, but the rest was all bollocks to me. Nothing was labelled, and by the looks and smell of the cab, he must have lived in it. On the dash, a small Christmas tree wobbled around as it changed different colours. He even had Christmas cards hung on a string across the back of the cab. The gears were all over the place. I selected what I thought to be second crunching the cogs into position, the huge snow plough heaved and growled and then slowly started to move forward. Once we were going, it wasn't too bad, but the steering was a bit on the baggy side due to the sheer size of the wheel. It was two foot across!

I was so busy driving I hadn't noticed Roxy talking into her phone.

Sara waited with bated breath while the phone rang. It seemed to ring forever, until she heard the sound of her sister's voice on the other end.

Roxy looked at her phone as it chimed away. On the screen, it read, "Sara." She pressed answer as she brought the phone up to her ear.

"Sara," she said in a searching tone.

"Roxy, it's Sara your sister."

Roxy's mind raced trying to put all the images in her mind in the right order, but she felt so confused. "Things are so confusing, Sara. I don't know what's really going on. We had a car crash, and Tom saved me. I feel so lost," Roxy said, trying to place things in the right order in her mind.

"Listen to me, Roxy. You have to listen to me. It's Sara. Are you alright?"

While she spoke into the phone, Sara watched the signal as it moved along the road. She placed her hand over the phone telling Malk to get the other two on his phone. He tired calling them, but neither of them answered. He knew what it was like when you're chasing a target. In the real world, its sod the phone just try to stay alive, but he still kept trying.

Jones fastened his seat belt because Conner was going like an idiot down the hill not wanting the target to make any distance from them. Conner knew the odds were in his favour which made him even more eager to find his prey. Jones looked over at Conner who seemed to be in a world of his own. "Why don't you slow down a bit? You know he isn't going to get far, not in this weather."

Conner didn't even bother answering him. He just went faster. Jones could feel the Land Rover starting to slide around as it lost traction on the thick snow. Up ahead, he could see the bend in the road.

"Just fucking slow down NOW!" he shouted, not wanting to make it two crashes in one night.

Conner slammed the brakes on, deliberately making the Land Rover skew from side to side. Somehow he kept control as it slid down the road at a thunderous pace. Conner started shouting like a mad man, "You're a bloody wuss, Jones! No fucking balls! How the fuck you ever passed selection beats the crap out of me, you yellow bastard!"

Jones sat there not really listening to Conner's outburst. He was more concerned at the angle the Land Rover was now sliding at. A gentle pirouette would describe it. His side was leading the way pushing a plume of snow up in front of them as they went. Conner was still ranting on as the vehicle went backwards into the snow covered banking throwing it into a wild spin. Jones braced himself hard against the door pillar as the G-force pulled at him from all directions.

Eventually, the Land Rover came to a sudden stop facing the opposite bank.

Roxy listened to the soft voice on the other end of the phone talking to her. She spoke of her father and two brothers and the wonderful time they'd had last year skiing in the Alps. Roxy started to feel confused when all the memories came flooding back into her head: pictures of a huge motor yacht then a picture of a smiling man. She felt close to him, but she didn't know why. Then

Tom's face came to the front of her mind. It filled her with warmth, but she also felt hatred as well.

"Roxy is anyone with you?" Sara asked in a soft loving voice.

"Yes, why?" she replied.

"Can I talk to them, Roxy?" Sara asked, hoping she could somehow bring the whole situation to an end.

"Why do you want to talk to him?" Roxy asked looking over at Tom driving and doing something with his phone at the same time.

"It's not a prob…" The signal cut off in mid sentence leaving both Roxy and Sara wondering why the other had finished the call so abruptly.

"Oh for fuck's sake," I moaned, my phone went dead on me. The tiny screen flashed, "No signal." I placed it between my legs on the seat so I could try Ian again later.

We were making good progress now. It didn't seem to matter how deep the snow was. This big old snow plough just went through it like butter.

Jones looked over at Conner, saying, "Get Sara on the phone NOW! NO MORE BULLSHIT!

Conner made a gesture like a woman holding her handbag in front of her making a "Ooooooo!" sound in a high pitched voice.

Jones looked at him coldly. "Make the fucking call," he said slowly.

"Jesus," Conner replied, while he retrieved his mobile from deep inside his coat pocket. "You do know she'll go ape shit, don't you?" he muttered.

Malk was taking a piss when the phone started ringing. "No bloody calls. Then just when you want a piss," he ranted away out loud whilst walking through into the main room doing his fly up.

Sara answered the call, she looked over at Malk trying his best to sort himself out. Her eyes looked him up and down as he entered the room.

"Sara," she said in a cold tone.

"Sara, it's Conner. We have a big problem here."

"You'll have a bigger one, if you haven't got good news for me, Conner," she said flatly.

"You don't understand, Sara. The police are involved now. The job's been compromised." Conner was speaking fast with a no nonsense tone to his voice.

"You're the fool, Conner," Sara snapped back at him. "I've been trying to contact you for over an hour now. Why the hell did you turn your bloody phone off?" She paused to compose herself.

Malk could see how pissed off she was and wasn't about to step in. Holding her hand over the phone, she asked Malk to get her a drink.

"What's happening?" Jones asked.

"I think she's having a drink!" Conner replied, looking puzzled.

"Conner," she hissed down the phone, "IT WAS ME WHO ORDERED THE POLICE IN!"

"WHAT?" Conner said with disbelief.

Sara continued, "The armed police you met are on Sascorp's payroll. I told them to intercept you. Now get their Commanding Officer on the phone now!"

Conner looked over at Jones. His face said it all, and then he said, "You know those special ops back there?"

Jones gave a long sigh saying, "Go on."

Conner closed the phone cutting Sara off, "They were working for Sara."

"What do you mean, 'working for Sara'?" Jones said calmly.

"They were Sasco's men," Conner said, handing the phone to Jones when it started to ring.

He flipped it open. Holding it to his ear, he said, "Sara."

She knew Jones was the one with the brain, so she didn't insult his intelligence.

"Tell me what has happened since we last talked, Jones," she said calmly.

He told her everything that had occurred over the last hour, including the fact that Conner had taken three of the armed Police out before they had even said a word. He told her how in such volatile conditions many lives can be lost in a matter of seconds.

She said nothing. She just listened, and then once Jones had finished, she said, "I don't hold you responsible, Jones. It sounds like Conner gave you no option but to follow his lead. I have no time for mavericks in my business. He's a liability and a danger to the operation."

Jones could tell by the way the conversation was going what was coming next, but what Jones didn't know was Conner could hear every word through his head set that both men were still wearing.

Sara continued, "We have no option, Jones. Conner must be eliminated. Do you understand?" He paused, but only for a second, he knew if he didn't do this both of them would be dealt with, and as much as he liked Conner, he didn't like him that much.

"I understand perfectly, Sara. Consider it done."

She liked his reply, quick and to the point. "Jones, when you've completed this operation, I may have a job for you. Call me again once you've dealt with the immediate problem." She finished the call. Turning to Malk, she said, "Things may be looking up," then she took the drink out of his hand.

Conner looked at Jones like a dog looks at its owner wanting its dinner. "Well, what's she want then?" he said in a bored tone which was very unlike him.

"Don't worry about it, mate," Jones said calmly. "I smoothed it all out with her. It's not a problem."

"Nice one, fella," Conner said, now sounding more like himself. He added, "Fucking hag, thinks she knows it all."

"Yeah," Jones replied.

"Get that flask out the back, will ya?" Jones said, as he pulled his handgun out checking the chamber was full.

Conner climbed out, saying, "Lazy twat," He slowly walked around the back through the snow to open the rear door. Jones released the safety on his gun and turned around ready to give Conner it from where he was sitting. Conner opened the rear door bending down to open the carry all. Jones could hear him sifting through the bag.

"Come on," he said in a loud voice, knowing Conner was about to stand up holding the flask of gin, but Conner was no fool.

He might have only heard half of what Jones was talking to

Sara about, but he had got the gist of it and knew the only way he could beat Jones was to play along. Jones brought the gun up ready to fire. The deafening sound inside the Land Rover nearly blew the windows out as Conner fired the MP5K from behind the rear seat. The torrent of bullets ripped through the upholstery and into Jones's body making him dance around uncontrollably. Conner continued firing even when he stood upright. He only stopped when he ran out of bullets. Jones was in bits, literally, half his head had been blown clean off as had one arm. Conner walked calmly round to the driver's door sliding another magazine in. He opened the door looking at Jones body, pinning it up against the door shouting, "Not so fucking smart now, are we, ya wee fucking shite!" He glared at what was left of Jones's pulverized body. Placing the gun on his seat, he let what was left of him drop to the ground. The snow turned red instantly where Jones landed.

Conner stood over him, saying, "Not so fucking smart now, are we?" He lit a cigarette and then climbed back into the Land Rover, placing his gun next to him on the passenger seat. He smiled and started to laugh out loud then he set off down the snow covered road.

Sara was walking back and forth across the room, still holding the drink in her hand.

"You want another?" Malk asked, walking in with a fresh cup of coffee.

"He should have been in touch by now," she said quietly.

Malk took a sip from the cup, saying, "Who should have?"

"Jones. I asked him to deal with that pig Conner," she replied.

Placing the cup on the small table next to the laptop, Malk said, "Maybe he was just leading you on, Sara. You know how close these S.A.S. guys can be. By all accounts, those two have worked together for years. You can't just expect one of them to slot the other on the promise of a job."

Sara looked at him and then said, "One, they're ex SAS, two, they both know their lives wouldn't be worth living, if they ever crossed me, and three, everyone has his price. You of all people should know that, Malk."

"Ok, you got me there," he replied, sitting down in front of the laptop.

"See if you can pick up, Roxy," Sara added.

Malk typed away only stopping to take a sip from his coffee.

Sara's phone rang. She didn't wait to hear who was on the other end. She just presumed it would be Jones. "Have you dealt with him?" was all she said.

The answer she got sounded a little confused. "We will be with you within the hour, Sara," the voice said.

She didn't click at first, the voice seemed familiar, but it wasn't Jones's. Then she remembered about Tony Weister. Karl had said he was using the Baldman to ship Weister over to her.

"Good, I will send Malk to meet you. Thank you for your prompt service." She ended the call.

Malk looked up from his typing. "Who am I meeting, Sara?" he said.

"Tony Weister," she replied.

Malk was a bit taken aback. He'd only met Weister once before, and even then it had been very brief. Being Karl Sasco's number two, he carried a lot of weight behind him. By all accounts, he wasn't a man to be messed with.

"If you don't mind me asking, why is he coming here?" Malk asked, expecting a mouthful for questioning Tony Weister's movements.

Sara placed her glass on the table when she sat down opposite him.

"Weister thinks he's coming over here to help us catch Tom Stone," she said calmly. "What he doesn't know is when you meet him, instead of bringing him to me, you're going to take him to Jones where he will be killed."

Malk leant back in his chair and asked, "Why didn't Karl just kill him back in Puerto Rico to save him flying over here."

Sara looked at Malk like he was a small child saying, "because if he dies overseas, it can't be traced back to Karl, can it?"

Malk felt a right dickhead for asking such a bone question.

"So when am I meeting him then?" Malk said, getting up from the chair.

"You've got time to finish your coffee. He won't be here for twenty minutes yet," she said, checking her empty glass.

Keeping his cool, Malk took her glass to refill it. He didn't mind slotting most people, but this was a big player. Although he wasn't scared, he wasn't too happy about it either. It wasn't uncommon for people in his position to be used as tools in the game of elimination and then end up in a gutter somewhere with a bullet in the head.

He brought the drink back to Sara, she could see the look of concern on his face. "Malk," she said, "You're not going to get yourself in trouble over this hit. Karl has already dealt with Weister's family. It's just a matter of tying loose ends up. That's all!" She paused, giving him a slight smile and carried on. "Look, if it will put your mind at ease, give Karl a ring and ask him for yourself," knowing full well Malk wouldn't dare phone Karl. He wasn't that stupid.

CHAPTER 19

The sun started to rise slowly over the hills making me pull the visor down from the glare shining straight into my eyes. Half an hour had passed, and there was still no sign of our pursuers. It bothered me, because I knew we couldn't possibly outrun them in this thing. Up ahead, I saw a roundabout. It could only be the A69 from memory, as it ran roughly from north to south paralleling the A1M.

I took the first exit heading for Ripon, knowing that from there I could get onto the motorway and then head north to Scotch Corner and across to the Lake District where Ian now lived. I had no intention of driving this big numb twat all the way and someone was bound to report it missing at some point. I'd aim at ditching the plough in Ripon for a new car. Like all dealerships, it's usually all down to bullshit. They tell you what you want to hear just to get a sale. The youngest salesmen are usually the keenest to start chatting away and let you take the car out for a test drive. Then I just leave them in the middle of nowhere. I know it's cruel but so is being shot at.

Roxy seemed to be in a dream world by the look on her face. Sometimes she'd look over at me but didn't say anything. Whoever she had been talking to on her phone had caused this sudden change in character. She looked a bit lost, so I decided to let her get on with it.

Fifteen minutes later, we came to the outskirts of Ripon. There wasn't much traffic about, due to the amount of snow on the road, and the only ones who had tried to get to work had failed leaving there cars abandoned half on and half off the road. I saw a bunch of people standing at a bus stop stamping their feet trying to keep warm. It made me smile. "Like the buses are going to be running," I muttered to myself. Just past the next roundabout, a fuel station was lit up like a Christmas tree with different coloured lights that changed every few seconds. I'd totally forgotten it was so close to Christmas. McDonalds had a small queue of traffic waiting outside the drive in, which didn't surprise me as wherever I went around the world someone somewhere would always want a Big Mac. I decided we had time to make a pit stop as our pursuers hadn't shown up yet, and I doubted if they even knew where we were now.

"You want something to eat?" I said in a hope of breaking the silence.

"Okay," she said blankly, not even bothering to look at me.

I pulled the big old yellow snow plough onto the garage forecourt next to McDonalds blocking off part of the fuel pumps. The old girl inside the garage wiped the window trying to see what was going on but didn't seem too bothered and carried on reading whatever she had on her counter.

"Are you staying here while I get us some food or coming with me?" I said, hoping to get more than a grunt from her this time.

"Just get me something sweet and a cappuccino," she said, as she stared out through the side window.

I had no idea what was on her mind, and to be honest, I didn't really care. I climbed down from the cab taking my gun with me. Low cloud filled most of the winter sky making the whole place look totally miserable. The only good thing about it was the wind had dropped. The roads were still dead apart from the odd four wheel drive sliding their way around the roundabout in a bid to get to work. Everyone still had their lights on, even though it was getting light, to say it was dull would have being an understatement.

I ordered the food and went to look out the window while it was being cooked. Still no sign of anyone following us.

My phone started to buzz in my pocket. I pulled it out. "Ian calling," it read on the tiny screen.

"How's it going," I said.

"Everything's ready, Tom. Just call me an hour or so before you get here."

"Thanks again, mate. Got to go. Cheers." I said, closing the phone, seeing my order waiting for me at the counter.

Back in the cab Roxy listened to her sister talking bringing back all the memories about her brothers, the family, and all the good times they'd spent together. She felt like a huge weight had been lifted from her shoulders now she knew who she was and what she had to do.

"Listen," Sara said, "We are tracking you and will be at your location in less than an hour, so keep him there so we can bring an end to all this."

Roxy listened and then said, "Don't worry, Sara. He's going nowhere" Roxy Sasco said adding. "And Sara, I sent Dad the first stage of the list, but I still have the main part with me. Interpol has someone feeding them information on our dealings. You have to see the list and match it up with the one you have back at home." Roxy paused watching Stone through the part misted up windscreen, "Look if this all goes wrong, the disc is in my briefcase, I have placed it in the slot under the lib and sealed it in, see you soon" at that she finished the call.

Malk stood with his hands in his pockets trying to keep them warm while he watched the helicopter coming into land not fifty yards from where his car was parked.

He didn't like Tony Weister, not one bit, and the feeling was mutual from both sides, the only problem being Weister was above him in the pecking order. Once the down draft had eased off, Malk walked part way over to the helicopter and waited as two men climbed out. They looked around them to see if the coast was clear and then dragged the unconscious body that was Tony Weister out, dropping him onto the wet tarmac.

A tall man climbed out from the helicopter and followed the two men dragging the body bag. "This is for you," he said, holding a small black envelope out in front of him.

"And what am I supposed to do with him," Malk said, looking over at Weister's body.

"We will put him in your car, and then Sara will tell you what to do next."

"Who are you?" Malk asked.

The man looked at him, smiled, but said nothing. Once his men had loaded Weister into Malk's car, the helicopter left again.

Malk was about to call Sara when his phone started to buzz. It was Sara.

"Listen to me very carefully, Malk. Take Tony Weister to Tom Stone's cottage and stay there with him until I call you again. Use whatever methods you see fit to get as much information on how he contacted Stone for this job. We need to find if he has any family, Malk. We need a lever. Someone is trying to bring the family down, and we believe whoever Weister got Stone's number from is behind it. Do you understand?" she said. Malk listened to her and then asked, "Why take him to the cottage?"

"Because it is my belief that he will head back there soon, and you're the perfect person to meet him, and, Malk," she added, "When he does appear make sure he sees Weister first." She ended the call before he could say any more.

He had no idea what kind of mind games she was playing, but the one thing he was sure about it was going to get messy.

Something was going down. He just knew it. The Sasco family had been at the top of its league for over thirty years now. "Maybe cracks are starting to appear," he thought. Either that or Karl had got in with the wrong people which wasn't out of the question even with the reputation the Family Sasco had. There's always someone somewhere waiting to try and take their place.

He decided to head for Stone's cottage and see what if any information he could get from Weister before the target showed up.

I finished the last of the milkshake making a good old slurping sound, then Roxy said, "My sister wants to meet up with us to see that I'm okay. She wants to thank you for looking after me."

I sat for a moment watching people trudging through the snow while I put all the rubbish into the paper bag the food had come in. The heater was doing a good job, but the cab windows were still a bit steamed up.

"What did you say your sister's name was?" I asked.

"Sara, why?" she replied.

It was as if my mind had fallen into a pit of dark memories until names of past hits came rushing back at me.

That name "Sasco" and the mobile phone from back at the crash site. "Sara." I looked at Roxy, saying, "Your family name isn't very common, is it, but it is well known." As I spoke, I picked my gun up from where it was laying on the seat between us. I carried on.

"Your father's name used to be Karl, didn't it?"

She looked at me like a cat watching its prey. All the softness had gone.

"It's all over, Tom," she said.

It was one of those moments that freezes in time, when you just know you've fucked up good and proper. I raised my gun knowing in the back of my mind that she'd probably emptied it of bullets whilst I was getting the food, what she didn't know was that I had my gun under the bag pointing directly at her. I pulled the trigger on the one I had picked up off the seat, I pulled twice at the trigger aiming it at her head.

Click. Click.

She pulled a gun from somewhere. Pointing it at me, she said, "My sister will be here soon, and then she will take you to my father because he wants to meet the person responsible for killing his wife, newborn child, and two sons. That is the only reason you're not dead right now, Tom, if that is your real name."

I looked at her then out through the front windscreen, saying, "I don't know what you're talking about, Roxy. I think you're very confused and upset after the crash."

She pushed the gun into my side saying in a soft voice, "Please be quiet, or I will have to shoot you, Tom."

"I'm no good to you dead, Roxy," I said.

"We both know that shooting you through your groin won't kill you, so please don't insult my intelligence," she said, pressing the gun in harder.

"Ok, you got me there," I replied.

She was good, but her over confidence was going to be her downfall. She was too close to me, far too close. "How long until your sister gets here then?" I said.

"Oh there is one thing I want to know Roxy, when we kissed did you mean it or were you just bluffing?" I asked in a soft tone, she looked at me swapping hands on the gun, when she did this just for a moment the barrel was pointing away from me.

I fired two shots, they both went straight into her lower stomach.

Her hand went limp then she made a strange rasping noise. I picked her phone up while she held her hands close to her belly desperately trying to breathe. I found Sara on the list and pressed call. It only rang once.

"Is that Sara?" I said.

"Where's Roxy," she hissed.

"Listen, Sara, this is the sound of your sister taking her last breaths."

I held the phone to Roxy's mouth, she slowly slid sideways leaning against me as the last remains of her breath left her body.

"You're next, Sara, if you don't stop this," I said.

All I heard from the tiny speaker on the phone was a voice screaming, "ROXY!" I ended the call then pushed her lifeless body upright into a sitting position. The last remnants of mist cleared from the screen, I looked at her next to me. I had nothing to say. No one had ever showed me affection the way she had. I hated myself so much I punched the steering wheel. Why was it that everything I went near seemed to fall to pieces or turn against me? I couldn't help but question my own existence on this planet, to kill and keep on killing. I knew I couldn't blame anyone else for my choice in career, but everyone has a limit. I'd been taken in by her looks only to have it all turn to shit time and time again.

It's fair to say that I've never really believed in God, but sometimes, when all hell is kicking off and the bullets are flying around your arse and at times like this, it would be nice to think that someone somewhere up there is watching over me. I don't know. Maybe that's my cause on this world, to sort the bad guys out and send them on their way.

One day, I would sit down and think about that one, but for now, I had to sort myself out and put some distance between me and Roxy. "This one will take a long time to get over," I thought to myself as I closed the cab door behind me.

Sara had to get the briefcase at some point before any of the authorities got their hands on it. She knew the location would cause some kind of interest. This was annoying for her, because she usually had Malk to deal with these sort of things. She decided to use one of the car franchise companies they used to collect it.

After a short while on the laptop, she had a telephone number. "Can I speak to the manager, please?" she said.

"John Rogers speaking," he said.

"This is Sara Sasco. You will be aware that Sascorp is your main contractor," she said.

He quickly pulled her details up on his computer screen. "Yes, Miss Sasco, how can I be of assistance?" he said.

"I need you to go and collect a briefcase for me the second we finish this phone call," she said.

"We don't actually do that sort of thing, Miss Sasco. Can I…"

Sara interrupted him. "Listen to me, Mr. Rogers. Your job will be terminated, if you do not do exactly what I ask. The package I need collecting is a black briefcase" she said and then went on to give him all the details of its location and what to do with it once he had it back in his office.

He got the message loud and clear. Once he had finished talking to Sara, he had gone straight up to the petrol station where McDonald's restaurant is. He saw the big truck, the sight of Roxy's lifeless body bringing a rush of nausea, fear and hyperventilation. He took the case back down to his dealership and placed the black briefcase in the main office safe. Sara had promised him £30,000 for doing this, and that money was to buy his silence for life. She had explained to him what would happen to his wife and son, if he didn't comply with her wishes. She knew his prints would now be all over the truck's cab, so the minute she had finished talking with him, she ordered some of her men based in Leeds to go and deal with him and bring the case back to her complete with the list of Interpol and MI5 agents working on the field that would have great value to all of Karl's businesses.

CHAPTER 20

Conner sat at the junction in the road with the engine ticking over. He looked down at the tracking device in his hand thinking about what Sara had said about the briefcase. "Must be worth a lot to them," he thought. "More than they are paying me anyway."

He set off heading towards Ripon with the sole purpose of getting his hands on that case, no matter what.

Sara sat alone in the penthouse, tears running down her face. She looked down at the laptop screen. Roxy's ID marker sat motionless on a garage forecourt as the target moved slowly away along a road with a marker (A69) next to it.

"He's on foot," she mouthed, picking her phone up wiping the tears from her face as she did.

Karl Sasco had been in the air for just over three hours on his way to England on board one of his many private airliners when his phone started to ring.

"Sara calling."

He had a bad feeling about this call. He knew she wouldn't call him unless something was very wrong.

"Hello, my dear. What's troubling you?"

Sara wanted to sound strong for her father to make him proud of her, but she just fell to pieces when she heard his soft strong voice.

"He's killed Roxy. She's dead. That bastard Stone has taken my little sister from me." She broke down sobbing uncontrollably, as she fell to the floor crying for her sister. Karl could only listen to his daughter crying in the background. Then the strength went from his legs, he sank to his knees still holding the phone to his ear and then dropped it as his hands fell to his sides.

The bodyguards had never seen their boss like this. None of them said a word in fear of what he may do.

Karl Sasco one the most feared men alive actually had tears running down his face.

In the background, one of the men made a call on his mobile.

Thousands of miles away a phone rang in an office. The tall man sitting behind a huge handmade old oak desk answered the call. He listened to what his contact had to say then ended the call. He smiled and walked over to the window that overlooked the grounds to the huge manor house. "Sir, the helicopter will be here in ten minutes" his aid said. The tall figure turned to look at the young man standing in the doorway. "Excellent, thank you" he said.

Karl knelt there for nearly an hour before getting to his feet. He knew nothing could be done until he landed in England. Looking around him, all ten bodyguards stood patiently waiting for instructions.

"Get me Robinson," he said and then added, "Get him to the airport for when we land and fetch his family as well."

As he spoke, he pulled the gold plated hand gun out looking at the inscription on the side of it: "TO STEAL A SOUL AND KILL A MEMORY." So many of Karl's enemies had been silenced by this gun, and now he would use it again to reap revenge on Tom Stone. "This time, he will die," he said under his breath.

I walked at a steady pace along the snow covered pavement with my rucksack and waterproofs on. I didn't look out of place though as most people seemed to have the same sort of clothing on. It had taken a good twenty minutes to get to the centre of Ripon. I'd passed a garage on the way down but didn't fancy anything on the forecourt, just loads of small hatchbacks. I needed something like a four wheel drive in this weather if I was to stand any chance of getting to the Lakes.

More and more people had decided to brave the snow making the place seem a bit more welcoming as opposed to the empty streets when I'd set off.

The market square looked to have all the usual big high street names like Boots, Woollies, and Sainsburys, which is all well and good if you're out shopping for Christmas, but I needed a car. After a couple minutes of just checking the place out I spotted the taxi rank. If they didn't know where the main dealerships were, no one would.

Tapping on the driver's window of the first car, I waited while the bloke inside gave me a funny look and then lowered the window.

"Where you want to go, mate?" he said, as the smell of hot coffee drifted out from the interior of the car.

"Are there any decent four wheel drive centres around here?" I asked, rubbing my hands together.

"How do you mean 'four wheel drive'?" he replied, taking a slurp from the plastic cup.

"Is it me," I thought.

"A garage that sells Land Rovers and shit," I replied.

"Oh, yeh, get in. It's about two miles out of town." he said, starting the car's engine.

I threw the rucksack onto the back seat and climbed in the front. As he pressed the trip button on his rip-off-o-meter, I noticed it started at one pound ninety-five before we'd even set off.

We went around the market square then along past some shops and a Mitsubishi garage. I was about to say, "That'll do," but he decided we needed to get through the traffic lights up ahead, that and make his little journey worthwhile, a mere four pounds wasn't going to cover the cost of another cup of coffee. "Out of bounds," the cab driver said. I looked at him.

"What is?" I said.

"Well, that's what you've been doing, isn't it," he said.

Then I twigged. I know it sounds daft, but when all hell is breaking loose around you, your dress sense just doesn't come into it. I must have looked a total bag of shit. I could sort things out once I had got to Ian's.

"Not far now" he said. We went over a big old stone bridge with a river running under it.

A couple of minutes later we arrived at a very new looking Land Rover garage with every make and model parked around the huge building. A young lad had the job of trying to scrape the snow off the thirty plus vehicles that sat in front of the glass fronted showroom where three salesmen stood all with cups of coffee admiring what a splendid job the young lad was doing. They all had matching jackets, shirts, and ties. It was then I decided not to dump a sales guy on the test drive. I had my cards, and all being equal I would be able to drive out of here "clean."

I gave the taxi driver a tenner and climbed out saying, "keep the change."

As I approached the entrance, one of the salesmen walked over to open it for me.

"Thanks, mate," I said, wiping my feet on the large mat.

"My name's James Ingham, senior sales colleague. How can I help you?" he said in a very charming tone.

"I need a four wheel drive, and I need to take it straight away" I said with a smile.

He looked at me and crossed his arms, saying, "We can't really do that as most of these vehicles will need taxing and registering."

"Okay then," I said, "Let me put it another way. Do you have anything I can buy now?"

He looked at me and then asked, "Would you like a coffee while…"

I cut him off. "Listen up, fella. I'm not wanting finance or some special deal. Just show me what I can have right now."

The other two came over to see what was going on and more than likely try to get a sale themselves. I placed the rucksack on the floor and sat down in one of the comfy chairs looking at these three guys brainstorming about what they had to sell me. After ten minutes and a cup of coffee, the eldest of the three said, "I'll sell you my car, if you want."

The other two looked on knowing they couldn't help me and not quite believing what he had said.

I placed the coffee down next to me, saying, "What are you selling, my friend?"

"Follow me," he said, heading for the staff entrance next to the service area. We went along a short corridor and turned left into a large open plan servicing area with several makes of four wheel drive vehicles on ramps or sitting with their bonnets up.

"Where is everyone?" I asked.

"Some training issues on health and safety at work," he said.

"That's my car," he said, pointing at a very impressive black sport Range Rover.

"It's only a month old, top of the range, every conceivable extra, and if you want it, I'll take sixty grand for it."

"Ok," I said, "Let's do the paper work."

"What" he said, "aren't you going to make me an offer or something?"

"Look," I said, "If you want to start pissing around with the price that's up to you, but as far as I'm concerned, we have a deal. Now, let's get the bloody paper work done so I can be on my way, shall we."

Conner drove slowly through Ripon town centre following the flow of traffic. He kept looking down at the tracking device next to his gun on the passenger seat. "The target must be within three miles judging by the scale of the map," he thought. He'd tracked people many times before over the years, but this time he was in it for the money, enough to set himself up for life. Slowly, the cars started to thin out, he headed out of town in the direction of what looked like a trading estate. Up ahead, he saw a roundabout at the far end of an old stone bridge with open fields to either side. Over to his right he noticed a new bridge with what looked like a duel carriageway on it. He pulled over just after the roundabout to check his gun had plenty of rounds left in it. "Ah, fuck it," he said, sliding a new mag into the MP5K. He still had his whites on even though they had a fair splattering of blood on them from earlier on. He had a good look at the tracking device once more and then looked up ahead at the industrial estate. From where he was parked, there only seemed to be one way in and one way out. He sat for a couple of minutes just looking for any signs of movement. A set of recent tyre tracks had come and gone in the last hour he guessed by the lack of snow in left the tread marks. Selecting second gear, he set off towards the target again.

The helicopter that had dropped Tony Weister off came into land on the private grounds of Harewood House. Two men climbed out and waited until a large dark blue Lexus with blacked out windows arrived. Once the rotors had stopped and the air was still, a tall bald man appeared from the front passenger door then walked over to the two bodyguards.

"Is everything going according to plan?" he asked.

The taller of the two men spoke first, "The Sasco family is not aware of what is unfolding, sir, but we do have a problem," he said.

The second man carried on the report, "As you requested, we have been monitoring Sara Sasco's laptop and phones. She has sent her main bodyguard to Mr Stone's house with Tony Weister in order to retrieve as much information from him as possible and then to lay in wait until Mr Stone returns to that location. She has also given specific instructions that no harm is to come to Mr Stone until her father arrives," he said, passing a thin plastic folder containing all transcripts of the phone calls Sara Sasco had made since she had arrived in the country.

The Baldman quickly flicked through it, stopping only to check the odd detail.

"Good work," he said.

"You mentioned a problem," he said.

"Yes, as you know, Sara brought in some outside help to catch her target. Well, it appears that two of the three men hired are dead," he said.

"Stone," Baldman said.

"Yes," the second man replied.

“The problem is we have the third man within 400 metres of Mr Stone,” he said.

“Can we intercept?” Baldman asked.

“We have two cars on route, but they are at least ten minutes from the target.” he said.

“It was inevitable that we would possibly lose part control of this situation” Baldman said calmly. He paused and then said, “Call Mr Stone. Tell him he is in imminent danger and to use all means possible to get the device to a safe place, and don’t under any circumstances tell him who you are,” he said.

The taller of the two men pulled his phone out. He flicked the encryption button on then just said, “STONE,” into the mike.

CHAPTER 21

I pulled my phone out while we walked from the service area back to the showroom. Flipping it open, the screen said, "new caller." My mind raced for a moment as to who it could be.

"Hello," I said, not giving my name.

The voice on the other end sounded electronic in a strange way, almost non-human. The only thing I could think that would cause that effect would be if the user had a scrambler fitted. It wasn't uncommon for the people I dealt with to use such methods of contact, because keeping your identity secret was the name of the game in my profession.

"Mr Stone, please listen to what I have to say," the voice said.

That single sentence stopped me in my tracks.

"You are in danger, Mr Stone. You have to leave now. You have to make sure that the device is kept safe."

I kept listening, "One of the men tracking you is within 50 metres of your location. You must leave immediately, Mr Stone."

The phone went dead.

The old guy standing next to me asked, "Is everything alright, sir?"

"Yes," was all I could think of to say?

Suddenly, it dawned on me. I had left my rucksack in the showroom with my jacket next to one of the sales desks.

Instinctively, my hand felt my lower back hoping like hell my gun was still there.

"Oh shit," I said out loud, realising it was now in one of the side pockets of the rucksack from when I'd been in the taxi. I ran forward down the corridor everything seemingly in slow motion then real time burst through my veins with the violence of a hurricane, the showroom, my heart pounding in my chest bursting through the door in a bid to get to my stuff before the other guy entered the building. My eyes scanned the showroom. While I sprinted across towards the sales desk something moved in the corner of my eye. I lunged towards the sales desk, a figure standing outside. I turned my head just in time to see the flashes coming from the end of the gun he was holding at shoulder height. It felt like the air around me had turned solid taking my senses into overdrive. Everything seemed to freeze in time now the first of the bullets smashed into the wall of plate glass that made up most of the frontage of the showroom. The salesmen didn't even have time to react since they were between me and the man firing on full automatic. Each man seemed to jerk around as their bodies shook from the amount of bullets and glass entering them.

I hit the floor grabbing the rucksack and scrabbled along ending up behind the table and chairs where I had left my coffee only five minutes before. Ripping the Velcro pocket open, my hand found the gun in a matter of seconds. The table just off to my right exploded into a thousand pieces. Another torrent of bullets thundered in towards me.

I was pinned down good and proper this time, with no real way of knowing how far away from me he was. Sticking the gun over the edge of the upturned chair, I fired a few rounds off in the general direction I thought he was in with a hope that the guy would dive for cover, giving me a chance to pop up and slot him. The second I'd fired the rounds, I popped up ready to give him the good news only to get massive fist in the face.

It knocked me over backwards but not unconscious. I rolled over ending up on my feet with my gun aimed directly at his head with both hands.

"Drop it," he said,

“Not fucking likely,” I replied. He was a big man, well over six foot and built with it from what I could tell. His white coveralls were splattered with blood. His face looked hard, chiselled like stone but with a slight covering of stubble.

“Listen, my little friend,” he said, “I want that briefcase, and it doesn’t matter to me if you’re dead or alive. Now drop the fucking gun and move away” he said again.

The only big problem with the situation I was in was that I didn’t actually know if I had any bullets left in my gun. We both knew that once the gun was lowered he’d kill me where I stood, so I had no choice. I pulled the trigger.

“How far are you from Mr Stone’s location?” said Baldman into his phone.

“We’ve just arrived. We’re going in.”

A few seconds passed by, and then the voice continued, “We have a situation. Stand by.” A few more seconds passed.

A short volley of shots could be heard in the background as Baldman sat listening to what was going on.

“The device is safe. Repeat. The device is safe. The target is dead.”

“Well done, gentlemen. Make sure our friend understands what he must do now. Out.” He finished the call. Opening the folder on his lap with a photograph of Tom Stone on the front of it he smiled, “Soon this will all be over, my friend,” he said to himself.

He didn’t need telling that my gun was empty. I pulled the trigger once more just to make sure. I knew I’d fucked up.

A smile grew across his face as he raised the MP5K up to his shoulder saying, “You stup…”

The sound of gunfire exploded all around the showroom as the hail of bullets tore into the soft human tissue, sending small explosions of blood flying in all directions.

I dived to the floor not quite sure if I was dead or not. I know that sounds daft, but from where he was standing, there was no way he could have missed me.

The sound of footsteps crunching over broken glass that covered the floor broke the silence that seemed to encompass me laying on the hard tile surface.

"Mr Stone," said a voice.

"This is getting fucking weird," I thought.

"Mr Stone, are you alright?" said the voice again.

I looked up from my sprawled out position on the floor, hoping I wouldn't be looking down the barrel of another gun. A man was standing about ten feet away dressed in black coveralls holding some kind of fancy gun that I'd never seen before. It seemed to have the magazine running along the top of the gun with a laser sight on the lower section.

It was then I noticed the others. All dressed the same, all well armed. I got to my feet slowly not quite sure what was going down. I was unarmed and outnumbered. I felt strangely naked, no gun, nothing. "This must be what it feels like to be normal," I thought.

"So who are you then?" I asked.

"All you need to know, Mr Stone, is that if we hadn't been here you would now be dead and your briefcase would be in the hands of some rather unscrupulous characters," he said.

"So what happens now?" I asked, seeing the other men turn and walk out of the showroom through the gaping hole that used to be the plate glass frontage crunching over the thousands of shards of glass that now covered a good half of the tarmac out front. The man in front watched them leave and turned to face me. I tried to make his face out from behind the mirrored face shield, but it was impossible.

"You need to know that the Sasco family will stop at nothing to get their hands on that briefcase, Mr Stone. As we speak, one of their men is trying to extract information from a Mr. Weister." He paused and then added, "He's the one you believe you've been working for, but he is just a puppet," he said.

I looked at him and then down at the rucksack, saying, "I know you probably won't tell me, but how come you know all this?" I was about to carry on when he raised his hand in a gesture to stop me.

"Mr Stone, you have to understand that these people who are chasing you are very well connected. If you have any relations, they are in grave danger, Mr Stone. Do you understand?" he said.

"You're talking about my father, aren't you," I said.

"Goodbye, Mr Stone," he said and turned away, heading in the same direction the men had gone.

I knew it was pointless asking any more questions. He was obviously a messenger of sorts, but for whom. I reloaded my gun and checked the dead body for any clues as to who he was. He had nothing on him, which didn't surprise me. Even his gun was empty. "Bastard," I said, looking at him. His bluff had got me shitting myself. Credit to the twat though. I fell for it.

"Time to go," I said to myself and walked through to the service area to see if the sport Range Rover had the keys in it. They were. Complete with a small white tag with some numbers scribbled on in black felt tip. "Service number," I thought.

I climbed in placing the rucksack on the passenger seat next to me. I had no idea of what had just happened. The only thing I could be sure of was everything I thought I was in control of had just evaporated into nothing. I felt a strange sense of being used. "A puppet," the man had said, but who's pulling the strings and for whom. I turned the key in the ignition selected drive and set off again.

I hadn't seen my father in over ten years, and we never really got on, but that didn't mean I wanted him dead, or worse tortured. I pulled in at the entrance to the garage and pulled my phone out. Scrolling down the list of numbers until I found the one I was looking for. I pressed call and waited. After a couple of rings, a voice said, "This number is no longer available," and then a dead tone sounded. I tried once more just to make sure I hadn't misdialled and closed the phone placing it on the seat next to me. There wasn't anything else I could do for him. He could be living anywhere unless something had happened to him. He could be dead for all I knew. It sort of bothered me now I thought about it. "Should have kept in touch," I thought. "But it's too late now."

Sara watched the target move from the outline of the garage. Conner's signal stayed still. She found it almost unbelievable that the target was still alive, let alone heading off again with her briefcase. She picked her phone up saying, "Malk," into the tiny mike.

Malk had been in Tom Stone's cottage for just over an hour when his phone started to ring.

"Sara," Malk said.

"Has Weister told you anything yet?" she asked.

"No, but it won't take long," he said, looking over at Weister tied to the chair next to the kitchen table. Weister was looking at the body lying on the floor trying to work out who he was.

"Make him talk, Malk. We need a lever," she said and then ended the call, knowing Malk had a gift at getting people to talk.

He walked over to where Weister was, pulling a chair up opposite him.

Weister looked at him knowing if he didn't tell him everything Malk would put him in a place worse than hell. He'd seen him work, and even after all these years, he couldn't get the images out of his head.

"You know who that is?" Malk said, glancing at the dead stinking body sprawled across the floor.

"No," Weister replied.

"That, Tony, is John. You remember John, because he is the one who gave you Tom Stone's number."

Weister looked at Malk, saying, "He told me his name was Lee. I did all the usual checks and made the usual calls, and he checked out. You know I did. This isn't my fault."

"That's where you're wrong, Tony, because from what I've been told, you got one of the others to find someone for you while you were looking at property in New Zealand."

Weister looked at him saying, "How did…" He stopped. He realised the only person who could know about his plans was Karl Sasco, he had the ability to check the bank accounts of all his employees.

"Does Karl know about this?" he said, looking down at the dead body again.

"Oh, come on, Tony. You know Karl knows everything that's going on around him. That's why you're here to help us find Tom Stone. All I'm going to do is jog your memory, just in case you've forgotten any details we need," he said, pulling a set of small vice like devices from his jacket pocket.

"Don't do this, Malk. I've loads of money put away. You can have it all. There's at least a couple of million in my account. So, what do you say, Malk? Come on. You'll be a rich man," he said with tears in his eyes.

Malk pulled out a small deep blue velvet cloth about eight inches square from his jacket pocket placing it in front of him on the table. He then placed the set of small clamps on the cloth in a neat row. Each one had a screw handle with a small spike on the inside of the adjustable screw section. Each device was only a couple of inches in length but could be unscrewed up to three inches if needed.

"So, how are we going to play at this, Tony?" Malk said, folding his arms in front of him.

Weister looked at him and then at the set of clamps on the table. He knew what was coming, if he didn't tell Malk everything he knew. He looked at the clamps again the sweat started to run down his face. He felt ill. His temples felt swollen and throbbed away like a jackhammer inside his head.

"Please" he said. "Please don't do this."

Malk looked at him. He knew he couldn't take any kind of pain. In fact, he looked positively ill. His skin had gone very pale, and his eyes seemed to be glazed over in a lost in space kind of way.

"TONY," he said in a loud voice, trying to get his attention.

But Tony Weister was in a bad way. His heart was beating irregularly while his chest muscles tightened. Each breath took forever to reach his lungs, stars exploded in his eyes making him feel dizzy.

Malk sat back with a worried expression on his face. "Oh, fuck," he said, standing up, kicking the chair away.

"TONY!" he shouted again, but it was too late to do anything. He placed his fingers on Weister's throat to see if there was a pulse. Nothing.

"Ah, bollocks," he said, looking at the dead body.

He pulled his phone to call Sara just as it started to ring.

CHAPTER 22

Karl Sasco walked slowly down the steps from his plane and onto the tarmac of the hangar where the huge jet had come to a standstill. The two bodyguards that had exited first stood either side of the steps. Over to his left, three other guards held Martin Robinson and his wife next to the two Mercedes that had brought them to the airport. On his right, two more Mercedes were parked. Both had four men in each. He stopped halfway down the steps casting his eyes over the scene in front of him. He pulled his phone out saying, "Malk," into the tiny mike.

Almost instantly, it was answered, "Karl," Malk said, almost shocked that Karl Sasco had called him directly.

"Malk, how is Tony doing?" he asked.

What could he say? He knew Weister had been sent over here to be killed, so he told him. "He's dead," he said.

"Excellent work, Malk. Meet me at Sara's hotel so we can talk some more," he said, finishing the call.

Malk couldn't quite believe it. Karl Sasco was actually in the country and wanted to meet him. This was unheard of, but it still left a problem. Sara would want some kind of information from Weister.

"Shit," he said to himself, he called Sara's number, knowing he was in for a good bollocking.

Her phone rang engaged. That only meant one thing. She was talking to Karl. "This might work in my favour," he thought. He kept trying until he got through.

"Malk," she said, "I hear Tony is no longer with us. Tell me, did you manage to get anything out of him before he died?" she said.

"Sorry, Sara, he had a heart attack on me," he replied.

"Well done, Malk. That's a first for you, isn't it. Head back to the hotel once you're done there. We need to talk," she said, ending the call.

Malk had a real bad feeling about things. He took his things from the table and made his way out through the rear door and along the back of the cottage. As he rounded the gable end something caught his eye, a movement off to his right behind the hedge. He pulled his gun out just in case Stone had doubled back on them. He stood still just watching the hedge for a good five minutes, but nothing moved. Making his way along the gable of the house, he took a quick look around the end to make sure all was clear.

His car was still where he had left it, but something just wasn't right. He called Sara again.

"Yes, Malk, what's wrong," she said flatly.

"Do you still have Stone on your screen?" he said.

"Yes, he looks to be heading up the A1M. He's not hanging around either. The read out states his speed at 105 mph. Why," she said.

"I don't know," he said, "but something's very wrong here. If you don't hear from me in the next ten minutes, then presume the worst," he said, closing the phone.

He walked slowly over to his car checking behind himself as he went. Once he was next to the BMW, he walked around it checking the film of mist that had settled on the bodywork. Next, he squatted down to check under the body. Nothing.

As he started to stand, he looked at the gravel, and then at the car again. His eyes followed the slight difference in colour on the surface. It looked as if someone had recently walked over it towards the field or from the field over to his car.

"This one's good, and he's switched on. It would be a benefit to have him working for us," said the first man.

"Make the call," the second man said.

Sixty miles away the helicopter made a steep banking to head towards the location of the two men that were hidden from Malk's view.

"How long until he gets here?" said one of the men, watching from his view point in the barn.

The other glanced at his watch, saying, "less than seven minutes." He studied the man with his high power binoculars and then added, "What if he just pulls a gun and kills the boss?"

"He won't," said the first man, as the sound of the helicopter started to fill the air.

Up above, Baldman looked down on the approaching cottage with the tiny figure of a man standing out front next to a car.

"Land over there next to his car, if you can," he said, closing the file on his lap with a picture of Malk on the front of it.

Malk watched as the helicopter circled once and started to come in for a landing not fifty feet from where he was standing. "Must be Karl," he said to himself, wondering why his boss had decided to meet here instead of the hotel.

The black and red helicopter touched down as Malk held his hand up in front of him to protect his face from the down draft. After a couple of minutes, the rotors stopped turning, and the silence of the winter countryside filled the air again. Malk watched as the side door opened. He straightened his jacket and walked towards the aircraft. As he approached it, a tall man climbed out. He was wearing a long dark blue winter coat that looked like cashmere. His black highly polished shoes crunched on the gravel surface as he walked towards him, but the thing that Malk couldn't really miss was the blue tinted glasses on the bald head. His skin looked very pale like someone who never came out in the sun. Malk guessed his age at mid thirties, but it was hard to tell as he seemed to have no hair whatsoever. He raised his hand to shake Malk's as he drew closer.

Malk responded out of politeness and curiosity. "Must be a

new addition to the Sasco organisation," he thought.

"It's a pleasure to meet you, Malk," he said, adding, "I have an offer for you. Obviously, I don't expect an answer straight away, but it will certainly change your lifestyle for the better." Both men walked along the track that led away from the cottage. Malk listened to what Baldman had to say.

Once he'd finished, he stopped and looked at Malk but said nothing. He just smiled and then placed his hand on Malk's shoulder. Two hundred yards away, the two snipers both had their lasers aimed at the rear of Malk's head. They knew if the boss adjusted his glasses, it was "goodbye Malk."

Malk looked at the man in front of him, thinking, "Whoever you are, you've got balls and money," and then he thought about the deaths of Karl's sons and daughter.

"Are you working for Tom Stone," he said.

Baldman smiled, shaking his head, "Oh, Malk, you're so wrong. There are things going on that you couldn't even start to imagine. I am not your enemy, Malk. Although we have many things in common, we are simply at opposite ends of the same road.

"You still haven't answered my question," Malk said, taking a step backwards as his arm muscles flexed in readiness to pull his gun.

"Be careful my friend. This is simply an offer of employment" he said raising his hand towards his glasses.

Malk knew a signal when he saw one. He also knew it was very possible that at least one sniper would be tensing his trigger finger as he spoke.

"You have to understand that if I accept your offer the family Sasco will be on my back in a matter of days, so you better be ready for a war, because Karl won't let it rest. That I can promise you," Malk said, looking straight into the bald man's eyes.

"Karl Sasco has outgrown his usefulness. The family is at its weakest now. There are only two of them left now, and they are chasing false hopes, my friend. Everything that has happened over the past six months has been controlled by me." He paused and added, "Nothing is what it seems."

At that, he turned away from Malk and started to walk slowly back towards the cottage, leaving Malk standing in the middle of the track.

He shouted, "What's your name," as he followed Baldman down the track.

He turned around and looked at Malk and at the snow covered fields that surrounded them.

"I love this time of year. Everything is so sharp. You see. There's nowhere to hide. Even the trees have no cover. It's the quiet before the storm, Malk. This is when it starts in the cold, cold depths of winter. You want to know my name? You are indeed a brave man" Baldman said, "but time may not be on your side. You need to be careful of who you tell this to," he said looking back at Malk.

Then said, "My name's Alexander Meakes."

"Come on. Walk with me, Malk. We have much to discuss."

Malk walked by his side as the two men talked about what kind of work he would be doing for him, if he decided to join Meakes. In the background, the sound of the rotors turning seemed to fill the air all around them. Seconds later, the engine fired up giving the helicopter the power it required to take off.

Meakes looked at him, saying, "You know there's nothing wrong with change, my friend. It's part of life. No one will blame you for wanting to stay with the Sasco family, but heed my warning, Malk. As sure as the sun rises, it also sets, my friend." He paused and then added, "And the clock is ticking."

Malk watched as the helicopter lifted off and then sped away over the fields and into the distance. He decided to keep this little discussion to himself for the moment, as he wasn't sure if it was a set up by Karl to see how loyal he was. He'd seen it before. In fact, he'd set a few colleagues up in the past using a double bluff to see if they would bite. Worked every time as well.

He got in his car still thinking about the meeting and then turned the key and set off heading for the hotel.

CHAPTER 23

Karl walked over to where Robinson was standing next to his wife. He looked at Robinson and then at his wife. She was in her late forties, medium build with long straight brown hair. The look on her face said it all. Her eyes looked nervous, she had no idea what was going on or why she was here.

"My name's Karl Sasco. I don't believe we have met."

She put her hand forward to shake his. Karl grabbed it tightly and then in one smooth movement pushed her hand back over on its self instantly breaking her wrist. She screamed in agony as she tried to pull her arm back, but Karl held on tightly. He looked at Robinson and over at his daughter. In a split second, he spun around lifting her clean off the ground bending her arm back at a ferocious speed snapping the elbow joint in the process. This time, he let her drop to the floor, part sobbing, part whispering to herself. Karl squatted down in front of her saying, "Your husband hasn't been totally honest with you over the years. You see, he has a thing for little boys and a big thing for gambling. Did you know the deeds to your house are in my name?" He looked up at Robinson and added, "He's been sleeping with pretty much anyone who'll have him."

"No, no," she murmured. "It's not true."

Karl stood up, saying, "Martin, any pain that happens today

is by your doing. You see, those men you sent me were less than useless. In fact, they caused more damage than Tom Stone has."

Robinson's face flinched.

Karl saw it. He leant close to him saying, "What do you know about Stone? Tell me now or your wife will suffer."

"All we know is that he's a world class assassin. He used to live in Harrogate but moved down to London to work for a local debt collector."

"Go on," Karl hissed.

"We don't know what happened, but he just disappeared one day. Then we started getting reports about a crack shot assassin who always hit his target. 'The left eye' He never missed," he said.

"Who was he working for," Karl said, now looking over at Robinson's wife.

"It was the Chow family at first, and then he moved on to..."

Karl interrupted him, saying, "Johnny Meakes."

Robinson said, "How did you know that?

"Because that bastard tried to have me killed. He sent Stone to kill me, but he fucked up. He killed my wife and child. That's how I ended up owning the casino you're so fond of. You see, it was me who wiped out his family."

Robinson looked at him and said, "You didn't kill them all."

Karl almost froze in mid sentence. "What?" He lunged forward pushing the gold barrel of the gun hard against Robinson's temple.

"The boy was in private school when you burnt his family alive, so you see, he's the rightful owner of the casinos."

"Tell me his name or your daughter will take a long, long time to die."

"Alex, his name is Alexander Meakes," he said.

"And where will I find him?" Karl asked slowly.

"No one knows. He disappeared not long after his family was murdered. Some say he killed himself, others that he just went travelling. I'm telling you the truth, Karl. He..."

The single shot exploded through his brain exiting straight into his wife who was still rocking back and forth on the floor cradling her broken arm until the bullet tore through her upper chest killing her instantly.

Karl flipped his phone open, saying, "Baldman," into the mike.

Seconds later, a man's voice answered.

"What can I do for you, Karl?" Baldman said.

"I need you to find someone for me," Karl said.

"What name and which country?" Baldman asked.

"The name's Alexander Meakes, and he is believed to be living in England," Karl said.

"We will be in touch," the call ended.

Karl smiled at the thought of catching up with the one that got away. "No one ever gets away from me," he said to himself as he walked towards the young girl who was crying uncontrollably.

"Put her in my plane and look after her until I return," he said, climbing inside the waiting Mercedes. The driver closed the door as the others climbed into the other cars. "Take me to Sara," he told his driver, and the convoy pulled out from the aircraft hangar into the cold winter's evening.

A smile grew across Alexander Meakes's face. Karl Sasco had no idea what was unfolding right in front of his nose. Sasco thought Baldman was a specialist at getting rid of unwanted people. The Sasco family trusted him without question. They didn't even realise that the international cartel that Sascorp had bought the device from was owned by a sub-company of Alexander Meakes's trading as LEXAN, plc. Meakes laughed out loud.

"Is everything alright, sir?" his assistant asked.

"Oh, yes, my friend, everything is just fine," he said, looking out the side window of the helicopter. A thousand feet below the Sport Range Rover was entering the Lake District with the device on board.

I punched Ian's number into the built in phone as I drove along the duel carriageway that would eventually lead me to his farm house on the outskirts of Windermere.

"Take the next turning on your left," said the soft female voice from the Sat Nav.

He'd told me that once I left the main road it would only take me twenty minutes to reach his farm. The long drive had been a blessing in some ways. My body had relaxed from all the shit it had taken over the last few days, and I had had time to work a few things out in my mind.

The Sasco family obviously had plenty of pulling power on both sides of the pond, and as yet, I didn't know how many actual family members were running the firm. My guess was that it would be like most family run firms or organised crime cartels. The father would pull the strings with his siblings doing the dirty work with whatever manpower they had to hand. I knew from what had passed that whoever was left of the family would be after me for killing Dean Sasco on the plane and Roxy a few hours ago. It's one thing having the police after you, because they have to follow the rules. It's easy to lose them, but the sort of people I dealt with played by a totally different set of rules, i.e. shoot first, shoot some more, and then ask questions later. If you're not dead, that is.

Just then my phone started to ring. I pulled over onto a grassy verge.

"Hello," I said in my usual tone.

"Mr Stone, I have a job for you," the voice said.

"It was the same monotone voice from before."

"Go on," I said.

"From what we hear, Mr Stone, you're the best in your particular line of work, and if you're interested, we would like to offer you a job," he said.

"What's the target, and when do you require it to be dealt with?" I asked.

"The name is not important. The fact that it needs to be dealt with urgently is." the voice said.

"Seeing that you know my name and what I do, you will also be aware of how much the job will cost," I said.

"Yes, Mr Stone, we know, but Mr Stone, you need to understand that this particular contract will be your last. Do you understand?" the voice said.

I pressed end call, placing the phone on the seat next to me. I didn't like being told what to do with my life. Doing a contract killing is one thing but being told to retire by someone, well, that's just bollocks. Flicking the indicator on, I pulled out again and carried on.

Sara watched the target move towards a place called Windermere. She called her driver from the penthouse telling him to bring the car around to the front of the hotel, and then she called Malk telling him to head for Leeds Bradford airport where he was to meet her at the helipad. Then she called Karl. She told him what she was going to do. He agreed instructing his driver to head for the nearest helipad. An hour later, Sara and Malk where flying high over the Yorkshire moors heading toward the Lakes in the private helicopter she had chartered. While Karl boarded his, he flipped his phone open saying, "Vladimir." It only rang once.

"Yes, Mr. Sasco," said the broken English voice of the Russian.

"Are you in position yet, my friend?" Karl said.

"The problem will be—as you say—taken care of soon," he said.

"Good. You will be well rewarded, Vladimir. Call me when you have the target in sight," Karl said, ending the call.

I drove up the dirt track that led up towards the farmhouse. I have to admit I felt a bit envious of the size of place Ian had got. In my mind, I'd seen him living in a rundown old house with tatty windows and an overgrown lawn, but that couldn't have been further from the truth. I followed the drive lights that led up to the very grand looking double fronted house. I had to smile. Sitting in front of the double garage was a very nice new Aston Martin Vanquish. "Bloody hell," I thought. The old bugger has actually made something of his life.

I pulled up next to the car, taking care not to ding it when I opened my door. I pulled the rucksack out and then walked over to the front door, pressing the bell a couple of times just for good measure.

Nothing happened, so I tried it again. Still no answer. Just then a voice from behind me said, "Hello, Tom."

I spun around expecting to see Ian, but instead, I was staring at a tall bald man in a long winter coat. He held his black leather-gloved hand out to shake mine, saying, "You have no idea how long I've been looking forward to meeting you, Tom."

I shook his hand and pulled my gun out, saying, "It's nice to meet you. Now who the fuck are you?" I hissed twisting his arm around until he fell to the ground, "Tell me now, or you'll never be able to use this arm again." I said placing more pressure on the tendons.

"Tom," he said in quite a calm voice under the circumstances, "we met many years ago when you used to work for Dave Meakes."

I eased off slightly, saying, "How do you know I worked for Mr Meakes?"

"Because he was my father," he replied.

I released my grip, letting him stand upright.

He looked at me brushing the dirt from his clothes.

"Tom, many years ago my father sent you over to Puerto Rico to kill a man, but the job went wrong. I don't blame you for what happened, because back then everything was crazy. People were getting killed all over the place. No one had any honour or respect for each other. The man you were sent to kill was Karl Sasco. Back then he was all mouth and very wild, but his reputation for torturing his enemies was well known. He killed women and children, anyone who stood in his way. He wiped out one firm in London just for taking back their own territory. That's when my father stepped in. He sent you over to Puerto Rico to blow the mad bastard up. My father thought all had gone according to plan. Everything went quiet, no more killings, no more torturing. You were made part of the Meakes firm," he said.

"I remember," I said, putting the gun away.

"Trouble is you killed his wife and son. Karl Sasco lived. He waited until my father thought everything was okay, and then he struck. He burnt my family alive, Tom, and killed all the people who worked for him. He thought he'd killed you, but you were out of the country, weren't you. Then you went underground for a couple of years and remerged, no name, no ID. You just vanished off the system, it was then I started to hear of this assassin, used many names, many faces. You see, Tom, for the last two years you've been working for me," he said.

"What?" I replied.

"Here's the times and dates of all your jobs over that period," he said.

Handing me a blue folder with my photo on the front, I had to hand it to him. He'd done his homework. Flicking through the pages and pages of meetings, flights, car hire and hotels made me wonder if there was anything this guy couldn't find. If he put his mind to it.

"So, what happens now?" I asked, only just realising how dark it had got, as the drive lights flickered on automatically.

He held his hand to his ear for a couple of seconds as if listening to a tiny speaker.

"His sniper is in position, sir," the voice said into his earpiece.

Meakes looked around the drive area like something had bothered him.

"What's wrong," I said.

"It appears the Sasco family are on their way," he said.

Just then a set of headlights came up the driveway towards us.

Vladimir's eye stared into the sights on the high-powered rifle. He watched Stone like a cat studying its prey. His breaths became shallow, as his heartbeat slowed in readiness to pull the trigger. He spoke softly into his throat mike.

"Target acquired. Do you want me to take the shot?"

Karl listened to Vladimir's soft Russian accent over the speakers in the helicopter. He tried to imagine what he could see, watching the micro thin cross of the sights hovering over Tom Stone's head.

"Take the shot, my friend. I will be with you in twenty minutes," he said, pulling a Cuban cigar from the holder in the armrest. He rolled it back and forth in his fingers. He knew by the time he took the first drag on his cigar Stone would be dead.

Sara asked the pilot again how long it would take to reach the target. Malk just sat opposite her after being picked up from the side of the road. Sara had had the pilot fly in on his signal to save time. The first he had known about it was when Sara had told him to pull over.

The helicopter flew over the fields and roads below at a tremendous pace. It was dusk outside giving the fields below a soft tinge of orange as the sun started to go down on the horizon. He looked at her, thinking if what Meakes had said was true. He couldn't imagine the world without Karl Sasco. He'd worked for him for so long. Sara looked confident, and then again she always did. He wondered if that would be their downfall, overconfidence.

"You're very quiet," she said, looking over at him.

He looked back at her. "You know what, Sara," he said without even taking his eyes off the view outside.

"No, but carry on," she said.

Malk looked at her, he leant forward resting his elbows on his knees.

"Why are we chasing this?"

The pilot interrupted saying, "Mr. Sasco has just called. Tom Stone is dead."

Sara nearly leapt from her seat. She pulled her phone out just as the pilot said, "We're coming into land, Sara. You see those lights over there?" He pointed with one hand. "That's where it is," he said.

Sara and Malk both looked out the windows towards a large farmhouse that had lights leading up the driveway towards it. From where they were landing, it looked to be about a hundred yards off.

CHAPTER 24

The headlights approached us and stopped just behind the Range Rover. There was some movement from inside the vehicle, and then a man got out holding a silver briefcase. I smiled as I recognised Ian's face. He took a couple of steps towards us, and then without warning the right hand side of his skull literally exploded as the high velocity bullet that had impacted through his left temple a fraction of a second before exited taking his life with it.

Vladimir smiled when he saw the target's head explode. "Stone is dead," he said into his throat mike. He slowly packed his gun away into its neat black briefcase style box and walked up the hill towards his car like nothing had happened.

I was about to run forward when Alexander placed his hand on my chest, saying in a quiet voice, "Stay where you are, Tom. Vladimir is a very good shot, but he will undoubtedly be in constant contact with Karl Sasco."

"I've seen his work," I said, checking my gun had a round in the barrel. "He's good but not as good as me. He still works for the Russian mafia, doesn't he," I said, looking at Ian's body sprawled across the mono block driveway, his hand still clutching the briefcase I'd asked him to get me.

Just then the sound of a helicopter started to fill the air as the aircraft appeared from nowhere. It must have flown up the valley and then over the house from behind, it started to land somewhere in the field next to the farmhouse.

"Inside quickly," said Alexander, pulling me through the open doorway of the house, closing it behind us.

"Listen, Tom. In a minute, Karl and Sara Sasco will be here. They want that briefcase, and I'm going to let them have it," he said placing his hand on the rucksack.

"You're fucking not," I said blankly.

"Let me show you something, Tom," he said, opening the rucksack, pulling the briefcase out.

"I'll kill you where you stand, if you try giving that to them," I said, pointing the gun at his head.

"All is not what it seems, Tom," he said, opening the small flap on top of the case. Pressing his thumb against the small screen, then a second flap opened, it had being perfectly hidden with no trace of any outline, "What the hell" I said. Alex turned the case to show me what lay beneath, a small vial, made from glass with steel caps to both ends. Alex pulled the vial from its foam surround holding it close to his eye. A tiny red laser beam shot out from the end making a micro bright red line between its lens and his retina. "Perfect" he whispered, placing it in his pocket.

I watched him slide the octagonal glass inside his right jacket pocket, making a mental note for later just in case things got a bit sticky.

"I presume asking what that thing is would be a waste of time" I said still watching him work. "You're a bright person Tom, to know when to stop" he said.

Typing a set of numbers in, a gentle hiss came from the case as its seal released its grip.

"You see these containers, Tom." He pointed towards the coloured liquids. "They are a blend of every kind of deadly toxin know to mankind. There never was any bomb in here," he said.

"Why," I said, looking down at the open case.

"You're telling me everything that has happened to me over the last few days has been a load of bollocks?" I said.

"No, far from it, Tom. Everything you have been through has

been leading to this moment in time." He stood up. Meakes didn't want to lose Tom now. It had taken so many years to track him down. After hundreds of close calls, he had eventually managed to take control of where and when he was, and who he was killing.

Stone was clever and Meakes knew if he smelt a rat he would have just gone to ground. So he had used false names and spent hundreds of thousands of pounds to ensure every detail had been checked to be just perfect when the "set up" hits had taken place. Alexander Meakes had created so many false IDs and adverse situations in order to find Stone he had made himself a target for just about every crime lord on the planet. The sole reason he wasn't dead, was because nobody knew what he looked like. Many times crime bosses had bragged about slotting him only to find out later it had been the wrong man. And now Alex had connections all over the world using his pseudonym Baldman. They all trusted him and respected this ruthless killer.

I looked at Meakes knowing he had an ulterior motive. I didn't know what it was although I had a good idea it would involve putting me through some kind of crap. Meakes didn't come across like a killer, but he was wealthy and obviously had plenty of fire power at his disposal.

"You owe me, Stone," he said, closing the briefcase, "You owe me a lifetime of loss. Years ago my father sent you to do a job, to kill a man, but you failed, and because of that failure you now owe me." We both stood up, Meakes straightening his jacket in the process. Some people just look smart no matter what situation they are in, and Meakes was one of those people.

"You know the type of business your father was in Alex, and if you did your sums you would know that when he sent me to kill Sasco, I was only 19 years old."

"Old stories of what my father did have a place and a time Tom, and if you think by reminiscing about old times is going to get you out of this, you're wrong. Time is not on our side, once we have resolved this matter, our differences can be dealt with, until then I suggest you do as I say."

Alex had a point, but if he thought for one second I was going to fall for all the crap he was coming out with, he was wrong. The sound of footsteps broke the silence between us.

I turned around, standing in the doorway was a tall blond women. Her hair pulled back into a ponytail. She walked over to where we were standing. Sara looked at the two men as she drew closer. Concealed in her flowing top she had a long twin bladed knife, in a sheath attached to her forearm.

"Hello, gentlemen," she said.

All I could think was this must be Sara Sasco. She was stunningly beautiful and built like an athlete. In the background I could hear someone moving about outside.

"Sara, I've found Stone and the briefcase, but Stone won't be telling us the code. He's had half his head blown off," Alex said. She walked around us like a cat circling its prey, she stopped in front of Alex, "So you're the great Baldman, my father speaks very highly of you" she said. I looked at him then back at Sara, "I have seen you at the villa but never had the time to stop and meet you, it truly is a pleasure" Alex said kissing her hand. She smiled, pulling a 15inch blade out from nowhere, resting it on my shoulder, for a second before lowering it.

"And you would be?" she said, turning to face me. She blinked slowly keeping her stare pinpointed straight into my eyes. "This is my acquaintance" Alex said, not giving me a chance to make a complete balls up of the situation.

Then the penny dropped. Meakes had held me back because he had to make sure Ian would be coming up the drive. Somehow he must have known about the briefcase I had asked Ian to fetch for me and about the sniper up on the hill somewhere.

The Sascos didn't actually know what I looked like so they just presumed this Baldman who worked for them slotted me and retrieved their precious briefcase. Now he stood there taking all the bloody credit for something that never really took place. I had to hand it to Alex, he knew his stuff.

"So Baldman?" Sara said, looking him in the eye, "You seem to have tied all the ends up, Karl will be very pleased" she added.

Just then a figure appeared at the door. He looked at Sara and then at me. His eyes locked with mine for a second and he looked at Baldman, saying, "What the hell is he doing here?"

"What do you mean?" Sara asked, raising the long blade towards me but still looking at him.

The silhouetted figure raised his hand pointing at me saying, "THAT'S T..."

"Enough of all these mind games" I pulled my guns and firing two shots within a fraction of an inch of Meakes's head at the person standing in the doorway. He flew backwards out onto the drive his arms raising upwards involuntary from the force of impact, with a neat pair of holes in the centre of his forehead.

A second later my gun was aiming directly at Sara's head, this all happened in less than a second in real time. "One move, pretty, and you're going the same way your friend did," I said calmly.

Alexander Meakes looked at me then walked over to the doorway, he paused for a moment, his slim figure silhouetted against the moonlight outside, looking out at the body lying on the drive face down. He walked out into the freezing night air, squatting down by the body he rolled it over. Passing his hand slowly over its eyes to close them

"Our debt is settled. You've just killed Karl Sasco. Come, my friend. We need to go. I am quite sure that back up will be on its way," he said, heading out across the driveway.

"What about this one?" I shouted from the hall. Still holding the gun to her head.

"Kill her. She's too dangerous to be left alive," Alex said.

I lowered the gun from her temple saying, "Do you know who I am?"

She looked straight at me. She wasn't even scared. Her flawless complexion looked so soft under the dim lighting. "All I know is you're with Baldman, and that makes you a dead man," she said without skipping a beat.

Firing a round just millimetres from her temple. She flinched at the sound of the gun exploding next to her ear. I cracked her on the side of her head with the butt of the gun knocking her out cold. I saw no reason to kill her. For all she knew I was dead, and as for Karl Sasco, I'd never met him until a couple of minutes ago, and now he was dead. I guess he was out of the equation also. I turned and walked away from her unconscious body out into the cold night air.

Alexander smiled to himself as the sound of the gunshot echoed around the driveway. He was standing next to a black Mercedes when I appeared from the darkness of the hall. I walked towards him and stopped by Ian's dead body. So many people had died because of this man, and for what I wondered. He probably thought he had me now. I could just see his mind working overtime. His life wasn't going to be to long though.

"Come on, Tom. We have much to talk about," he said. I turned around at the sound of a helicopter coming in low across the open fields. "Back up" I thought.

"I don't know about the talking. I'm ready for some sleep," I replied. I decided to do him once we were inside the car and then get the driver to take me where I wanted to go and sort him out after.

I climbed into the rear of the Mercedes, and Alex got in the other side. Then the doors closed.

"Tom," he said, taking his blue tinted glasses off.

"Don't take this personally."

"That depends on what it..." I felt a sharp pain in my thigh when the dart hit me. In an instant the car started to spin as my body started to lose its strength, I yanked the small dart out. While my other hand fumbled around trying to find the gun.

"Why have yoo..." Just then, Alexander Meakes phone started to vibrate making a gentle soft sound like a breeze sweeping through a wind chime. It seemed to fill my head making me feel numb.

"I trust the package is safe" Karl asked, while his helicopter swept over the large farmhouse.

"Yes, Karl, the package is safe like we agreed," Alexander said, sitting back in the white leather seats of the black Mercedes. It pulled away and vanished into the cold winter night.

Alex looked down at Tom's unconscious body. "Now you're mine," he said.

END